MURDER AFTER THE MATINEE

MURDER AFTER THE MATINEE

Lorna Snowden

Matador
9 Priory Business Park,
Wistow Road, Kibworth Beauchamp,
Leicestershire. LE8 0RX
Tel: 0116 279 2299
Email: books@troubador.co.uk
Web: www.troubador.co.uk/matador
Twitter: @matadorbooks

ISBN 978 1800461 888

British Library Cataloguing in Publication Data.
A catalogue record for this book is available from the British Library.

Printed and bound in the UK by TJ Books LTD, Padstow, Cornwall
Typeset in 11pt Minion Pro by Troubador Publishing Ltd, Leicester, UK

Matador is an imprint of Troubador Publishing Ltd

Thank you to:

Peter Snowden (husband)
for providing support
(and advice – which I mostly took!)

Vicki Slater (younger daughter)
for reading the whole thing
(and apparently enjoyed it although she doesn't read books!)

Louise Abbott (best friend)
for reading the whole thing
(and enjoyed it - yes, she does read books!)

Fiona Snowden (elder daughter)
for not reading any of it
(but promises faithfully that she will – and review it!)

1

Lydia Buckley

Lydia Buckley was hurled through the door of Lewis Marshall estate agents by the gale-force wind. As she pushed against the door to close it, the wind obligingly dropped and it slammed shut with a loud crash. The venetian blind on the inside of the door slapped noisily against the glass and one or two brochures slid from their rack onto the floor. Lydia spun round and glanced at the woman behind the desk who wore a slight frown at the intrusion.

'Sorry,' Lydia gasped, 'it's just so…' she tailed off as the woman, who was on the phone gave a tight smile, picked up a pen and began to write something down. She reminded Lydia of her old headmistress, brown hair flecked with grey pulled back in a severe bun, a slim figure in a black suit with a cream blouse which fastened at the neck with a large, tied bow. A bit 'no-nonsense', actually, a lot 'no-nonsense' Lydia decided as she picked up the brochures and replaced them in the rack. She straightened up, noticing a beautiful oak chest of drawers, on top of which was an elegant vase filled with what looked like white roses on lush, thorn-free green stems. Behind the receptionist's desk were two, partitioned offices, one with solid walls and an opaque glass door, the other had clear glass and was currently vacant. It housed a photocopier, a range of filing cabinets and a small desk with a computer screen, a telephone and stationery odds and ends. Lydia ran her fingers through her chocolatey hair in a fruitless effort to tame the wild curls. The warmth of the office had made her too hot, so she opened her coat, removed her scarf, and made her way to the Perspex display stands holding details of properties for sale.

Lydia scanned the properties looking for those in her price bracket, and her eyes were quickly drawn to a rather lovely cottage with two bedrooms. It had a neat garden, roses round the door and a picket fence: Lilac Cottage, although Lydia could not see any lilac trees. *I could always plant some lilac… but I don't have any gardening equipment… or knowledge – actually, do I even want a garden at all?*

Vinnie had always tended their garden in Oxford – Lydia had just enjoyed the outside space, and she doubted that Vinnie's new wife, Vivienne, would risk damaging her false nails doing any gardening.

She sighed and moved on to a fairly modern townhouse, 22 Larch Gardens. This had an open plan lounge/diner/kitchen with stairs from the lounge up to two double bedrooms and a decent-sized bathroom. The outside had a patio and pebbles but no lawn or garden at all. *More practical, but I'm not sure about pebbles.* She moved on passing larger properties, properties for renovation, terraced houses, and on to apartments.

'Oh my, that's gorgeous!' she exclaimed aloud. Number three Meadow Croft was an ultramodern, newly built apartment with a balcony, patio doors, picture windows with views over the dales, a fabulously appointed kitchen and an en suite master bedroom with dressing area. The apartment was part of the conversion of a beautiful manor house which sat within its own grounds.

'Would you like any help?' said a rather imperious voice. Lydia turned to find the woman had silently risen from behind the desk and was standing next to her.

'Um, well I'm interested in purchasing a property here in Ashdale, but I'm not sure I know quite what I want. I need at least two bedrooms, but I don't know whether I want a modern apartment, a practical townhouse or a cute cottage,' Lydia finished rather lamely, waving a hand in the vague direction of the property details.

The woman smiled. 'Is the property just for yourself?'

'On the whole, yes,' replied Lydia. 'My son is at university so he'll be home in the holidays, but it will just be me in term time.'

'Do you have a mortgage arranged or a property to sell?'

Lydia shook her head. 'No, I've nothing to sell and I'm a cash buyer. I'm living with my sister at the moment, as I've been waiting for some funds to come through – which they now have, so I'm in a position to purchase immediately.'

The receptionist smiled even more pleasantly. 'What a good position to be in. Do you have a car?'

'Yes, but I'll only need one parking space – Matt doesn't have a car, he borrows mine when he's home.'

'I see, and do you particularly want somewhere here in Ashdale or would you consider Harrogate?'

'Well, as much as I like Harrogate, I would prefer Ashdale. I mean it's only five miles from Harrogate, but I do like the market-town atmosphere and I've made friends here.'

'Well in that case, may I suggest you view all three types of property to see which one feels right?'

'That would be marvellous. Actually, I quite like the look of these three.'

'That's a very good start,' replied the woman, whisking a brochure of each from their respective holders. 'I could probably arrange all the viewings on one day, if that would be helpful? The cottage and the apartment are currently empty and the owners of Larch Gardens both work, so perhaps a daytime viewing? Do come over to the desk and we'll look at the diary.'

Lydia followed the receptionist to her desk where a small sign told her that Ms Felicity Reid was the office manager. On gazing around the office, the flowers on the oak chest caught Lydia's eye once more. 'What are those beautiful flowers? They look a bit like roses.'

Ms Reid tapped her short but manicured nails on the keyboard. 'They're ranunculus,' she replied, 'they're perfect for a vase display and—' Suddenly the door crashed open and a blast of wind swirled around the office blowing the brochures to the floor once more, as the inner office doors behind the reception desk rattled. Felicity sighed and raised her eyes heavenwards. The outer door was slammed noisily shut against the wind and a man wearing an orange hi-vis jacket and a bag over one shoulder approached the desk.

'Morning Felicity,' he said cheerfully, it's a bit breezy out there.' He slapped a pile of brown and white envelopes on the desk, carefully placing a neon-pink envelope on the top. 'Looks like a Valentine card to me, does that.' He winked at Felicity, who blushed. 'It's for the boss though,' he added.

Felicity frowned.

The postman chuckled. 'However…' he paused dramatically and lowered his voice 'I wouldn't have thought it was from Mrs M.'

'I think it's highly unlikely to be a Valentine card for Councillor Marshall,' Felicity said haughtily, returning to her screen.

The postman shrugged and winked again. As he turned towards the door, his large postbag caught the edge of the pile of letters on the desk and they all fell to the floor at Lydia's feet.

'Oh goodness!' exclaimed Felicity, standing up to look over her desk.

'It's ok, I'll get them.' Lydia bent down to retrieve the letters, and as the postman opened the door again on his way out, the wind blew the whole stand over which sent all the brochures sliding across the floor. The neon-pink envelope skittered away from the pack of post. Lydia quickly followed it and managed to retrieve it before it disappeared under the heavy chest of drawers.

The postman had to use both hands to pull the door closed as he fought against the wind. He did this with such force that the blind flapped against the glass and promptly fell to the floor in a heap.

The inner office door was suddenly wrenched open. 'What on earth is going on out here?'

Lydia jumped up with the neon-pink envelope in her hands and came face to face with a rather portly man wearing round spectacles. She suppressed a giggle, as Billy Bunter came to mind, although she quickly realised that the clearly expensive, dark grey suit, with light grey shirt and a silver-grey tie, was no school uniform.

Ms Reid, looking horrified, turned to face him. 'Oh! I'm so sorry Councillor Marshall, but every time someone comes in or out, the wind makes it very difficult to shut the door.'

Councillor Marshall surveyed his estate agency, taking in the brochures and the blind on the floor, and Lydia. His gaze fixed on the envelope as Lydia walked to the desk.

'What's that?' he asked warily.

'It's for you,' answered Lydia, placing the envelope on the desk.

Councillor Marshall took a step backwards and stared at the envelope as though it might suddenly explode. 'What is it?'

'Um... a card, I guess,' answered Lydia, refraining from adding '*obviously!*' to her answer.

'Where did you get it? What are *you* doing with it? Are you a new postman? Err... postlady?'

'No, no...' stammered Lydia.

'This lady is a client, Councillor Marshall,' explained Felicity. 'The wind blew all the post onto the floor and she very kindly picked it up.' As Felicity spoke, Lydia bent down and gathered up the rest of the envelopes and placed them on the desk.

Cllr Marshall smiled uncertainly.

'Oh, well... Um, splendid, splendid, err – thank you very much,' he mumbled and quickly scooped up the letters. He cleared his throat in an effort to regain his equilibrium. 'Now, I do hope we can help you. Are you buying or selling?' he asked Lydia as he mustered his best client smile.

'Buying,' Felicity answered quickly, 'I'm just about to book some viewings, hopefully for Monday.'

'I shall look forward to it, I think I'm free on Monday... Felicity?' Councillor Marshall looked Lydia up and down and smiled lasciviously.

Lydia immediately pulled her coat closed around her.

'Well, I shall have to ask the Baxters at Larch Gardens if it's convenient,' said Felicity '...and I rather think you've an appointment at 10.00 a.m. on Monday, so perhaps Mr Craven —?'

'Nonsense, I shall take this lady, Ms... err ... Mrs?' fished Councillor Marshall.

'Ms Buckley, Lydia Buckley,' answered Lydia. 'But please, don't rearrange your schedule on my account, I'm quite flexible on timings.'

'Absolutely no problem. Felicity here will organise it, won't you Felicity?' he smiled broadly at his office manager who pursed her lips disapprovingly. 'Good, well I'll see you on Monday morning then.' And with that, he turned, walked back into his office and closed the door.

Felicity looked at Lydia, 'Is Monday morning convenient?' she asked shortly.

Lydia nodded, 'Yes, I can be here for 10 o'clock, although I'm happy to see Mr Craven – I know his brother you see.'

'Councillor Marshall is the senior person and he'll be able to offer his extensive knowledge and experience. Mr Craven will take Councillor Marshall's current appointments.' The no-nonsense headmistress was back and Lydia simply smiled in agreement.

'Right, well I'll make the necessary arrangements. Would you give me your mobile number and if it proves difficult to organise, I'll call you.' Felicity tapped Lydia's details into the computer.

'Perhaps you might also like to take the property details with you,' she suggested and slid the brochures across the desk.

Numbers thus exchanged, Lydia fastened her coat and wrapped her scarf around her neck again. She tucked the property details, one for each of her forthcoming viewings, safely into her bag and walked over to the door. She carefully picked up the blind and laid it on the chest of drawers, then taking a deep breath, she opened the door, stepped outside and quickly closed it before the wind could wrench it out of her grasp. Hoisting her bag onto her shoulder, Lydia braced herself for the walk up across the Market Place to the post office.

One gust of wind was so strong, it stopped her in her tracks and caused her to stumble awkwardly, into a lamp post behind her. At the same moment, a man walking towards her was pushed forward quicker than was comfortable and he grabbed at railings on the edge of the footpath to maintain his balance. His trilby hat, however, carried on its forward momentum until it hit Lydia squarely on her chest. She caught the hat and held on to it tightly until the gust of wind died down.

The man approached her and held out his hand for his hat. 'Jolly windy today.' He was probably in his early sixties, blue eyes twinkling with amusement. Blond but greying hair and a small, neat moustache completed the look; he spoke with a cut glass accent.

'It certainly is,' replied Lydia handing over his hat.

'Thank you very much for catching my hat, it is rather one of my favourites.'

'I think your hat rather caught *me*,' Lydia laughed.

'Then my hat has exceedingly good taste. Good day to you, Madam.' And with that, he placed his hat on his head, nodded his head respectfully, and walked on.

Lydia watched him walk away – he reminded her of a famous actor… what was his name? The name annoyingly eluded her as she crossed the road, but she could hear him saying, 'I say!' and another catchphrase, 'Ding dong!' What on earth was his name?

Lydia bought a few bit and pieces in the post office and then decided that she would treat herself to lunch at the Forget-Me-Not Café, which was owned by her sister, Kate. She settled at a table, removed her coat and scarf and retrieved the property details from her bag. Looking at the brochures, Lydia smiled contentedly to herself. It was hard to believe how her life had changed in less than a year. It was only last May when she had left Vinnie and their lovely house on the outskirts of Oxford to move into a bedsit. When Kate had invited her to spend a fortnight at their home here in Ashdale in the summer, she could not have imagined the enormous impact that the visit would have on her life.

At the end of the six-month lease on her bedsit, Kate had persuaded Lydia to leave Oxford altogether and move lock, stock and barrel to Ashdale. So, in December she had moved in as Kate and Ben's lodger and joined their circle of friends which included Amy and Tom Craven. It was at a Christmas party that she had met Tom's brother Greg, there was an instant attraction and they'd been dating for the last two months.

With hindsight, Lydia had come to realise that her marriage had been over for a long time, but that she had just clung on to it. When they'd made those marriage vows, Lydia had sincerely meant *till death us do part* and had looked forward to marital life with this good looking and confident man. But Vinnie had simply carried on as before, charming everyone and flirting unashamedly with most of the women he came into contact with.

There were business meetings that went on late into the evening and conferences that seemed to last a week, in distant hotels. There was no doubting that Vinnie was very good at his job, they had a lovely house and the bills were paid on time and he was genuinely delighted when their son, Matt, came along, but then Lydia found herself at home alone night after night with a young child.

About a year ago, fate had stepped in when Vinnie was involved in a minor car accident in a place he wasn't supposed to be, with a woman who was most definitely not one of his golf buddies. It was then that Lydia realised that Vinnie was a serial cheater. Matters had come to a head one warm evening last May, when Vinnie had been faffing around in his shed and, as she walked past the shed, she heard him say, 'Pregnant?'

It was after that bombshell that Lydia moved out of their house and Vivienne had moved in. Of course, Vinnie had tried to persuade her not to leave and said that he wouldn't see Vivienne again, that *they* could make changes and save their marriage. But, as Lydia pointed out, there was a baby on the way and Vivienne would therefore always be a part of their lives.

Vivienne moved in cosily with Vinnie; she gave up her pole dancing career and had been living with him for about a month when he came home from work one Friday evening and she had supposedly lost the baby that afternoon. Vinnie did ask if Lydia would reconsider, now the baby wasn't going to happen, but she had made her mind up that enough was just enough.

Since then, she had happily made a life for herself in Ashdale by joining the local amateur dramatic group, the Ashdale Players, where she was the prompt for their forthcoming production of *Aladdin*. Thinking of actors brought to mind the man with the hat she had met briefly in the Market Place. Lydia frowned: *I wish I could remember the name of that actor though, it's driving me nuts. Kenneth Williams? No, he was too nasal, and it wasn't Terry Scott…* Lydia shook her head in frustration, and decided that it would come to her eventually.

Vinnie Buckley

In Oxford, Vinnie Buckley checked his depleted bank account. 'Christ, Lyds,' he muttered, 'you've just cost me ten thousand pounds for each of our twenty-five marital years, I hope I don't regret letting you go.

'Vinnie, are you ready? The taxi's here?' Vinnie winced at the shrill voice. Funny that, Vivienne's voice had never bothered him when they'd met on secret assignations at various hotels, but then they'd not done much talking. If only things had been different with Lydia – it wasn't his fault that women found him attractive. Still, she was someone he always trusted, she had always been there for him to talk to and he'd loved her, he really had, but he so enjoyed women's company, the flirting and chasing (and the conquests if he was being completely honest). If only Lydia had been more *fun,* yes that was it, more fun.

'Vinnie!' the voice was sharper now.

'Yes, Viv just coming,' he called back.

'It's Vivienne, sweetheart,' came the reply from the doorway. 'You know I don't like to be called "Viv".' Vinnie glanced up at the young woman in her designer outfit, with matching designer shoes and handbag, hair professionally bleached and highlighted at a trendy and expensive hair salon, recently manicured and pedicured nails, spray-tanned and ready for the pricey cruise she had booked as a 'Valentine surprise' on *his* credit card. Vinnie quickly logged out of the bank on his laptop and shut it down.

'Let's go then.' He crossed the room and taking her by the elbow, gently guided her in the direction of the front door. The divorce from Lydia was final, she was paid off and he was now married to Vivienne. That *was* what he had wanted, wasn't it?

The taxi driver had filled the boot with suitcases. 'Vivienne, you'll be over twenty-five kilos with that lot!' Vinnie was shocked at the amount of luggage. 'Do you really need *all* of it?'

'I *do* need it all and, as we are flying premium class, we are allowed two bags each, so I've just used one of your suitcases.'

Vinnie opened his mouth but before he could speak, Vivienne put her hand gently on his cheek.

'Darling, wait until you see the lovely new things I've bought,' she stage-whispered suggestively and just loud enough for the taxi driver to hear. 'You're really gonna enjoy them.' She kissed him lightly and fluttered her eyelashes before sliding onto the back seat of the taxi. The driver watched appreciatively as her skirt slid up her shapely legs, then he shrugged at Vinnie and gave him a 'what can you do' look, and slammed the boot lid closed.

Vinnie stared out of the car window as they sped towards the airport. Holidays with Lydia had never been this expensive although they hadn't gone for the cheapest option either. He would have to speak to Vivienne when they got back about reining in the spending, especially now that he had bought Lydia's share of the house and increased the mortgage. Perhaps he might suggest that Vivienne got a job, after all she was only thirty-four – but maybe not pole dancing again he decided. Vinnie sighed. If he was honest though, he thought it highly unlikely that Vivienne would agree to going back to work at all. Perhaps they should try for another baby. He glanced at Vivienne who licked her lips suggestively and squeezed his hand. Vinnie felt a stirring in his groin; damn she was sexy, maybe a baby wasn't a good idea, she might go all mumsy like Lydia had. Vivienne had not mentioned babies since her miscarriage and she had coped with it bravely, even without any medical attention, but he guessed that the incident had put her off further pregnancies, at least for now.

The taxi pulled up to the departures drop-off area and Vivienne eagerly got out of the car. The taxi driver unloaded the boot with Vivienne's three cases and Vinnie's one.

'Enjoy yer 'oliday, mate,' he quipped and winked as Vinnie handed over the fare.

'Thanks,' muttered Vinnie as he looked for a luggage trolley. They checked in without a hitch and headed up to the VIP lounge for pre-flight drinks and snacks.

Once settled with a gin and tonic, Vivienne struck up a conversation with a woman on the next table and Vinnie checked his phone for emails. One email was from his bank confirming the transfer of two hundred and fifty thousand pounds to Lydia. He wondered what Lydia would do with the money, and decided that she would probably buy a place of her own. He hoped she was happy, but he had no idea what she was doing or even if she was seeing someone else, as Matt was deliberately tight-lipped about his mother. Vinnie decided there and then to send Lydia a text, just to confirm he had sent the money and wish her well. *That's all it is,* he convinced himself, tapping out a message, but before he could press Send, he became aware that Vivienne's conversation with the woman on the next table had stopped. He glanced up and realised that Vivienne was staring at the screen on his phone.

'Why are you texting *her*?' she demanded.

'I'm just making sure that the money has transferred successfully and asking her to confirm it, Viv, that's all,' replied Vinnie.

'Then why have you put a kiss at the end? And how many more times do I need to say that it's Vivienne – not Viv?'

Vinnie looked back at the screen and deleted the 'x. 'Sorry, it's just habit, that's all.'

'Well how many times do you text her?'

'I don't text Lydia at all,' Vinnie explained, 'I meant it's just a habit to put a cross at the end of my texts.'

'What? To everybody?'

'No, not everybody, but you know what I mean.' Vinnie was becoming exasperated at the nagging. 'Come on, Vivienne, how about we go look in duty-free?' He stood up and held out his hand. Vivienne pouted and tossed her head before taking it.

'Ok, let's go shopping.' She marched towards the door of the lounge. Vinnie sighed; this was getting to be hard work. Vivienne was great in bed and fabulous arm candy but, if he was being totally, totally honest, she was a pain in the butt to live with.

Lydia Buckley

Lydia exhaled and sat back in her chair. The jacket potato with coronation chicken and salad had been lovely and she had read through her property sales brochures; it was time to make her way home. Tonight, she was going the Valentine Ball at Ashdale Hall with Greg, her sister Kate and her husband Ben, along with their group of friends. She was really looking forward to it. Lydia stood up to put on her coat and scarf and as she made her way to the door, she stopped to make way for an elderly lady struggling to walk with a stick.

'Miss Phillips! Miss Phillips!' a voice called from behind. The elderly lady stopped suddenly and turned around. Lydia also stopped and then it came to her: *Phillips! Leslie Phillips! That's the name of the actor*. She smiled to herself and turned to see who had called out.

'You've left your shopping.' Kate came up behind Lydia with an old-fashioned string bag containing one misshapen paper bag.

'Oh my!' exclaimed the elderly lady. Lydia took the bag from Kate and passed it to Miss Phillips.

'Thank you, dear,' said Miss Phillips taking the bag, 'that's my great-granddaughter's birthday present.' She smiled and turned away as her attention was caught elsewhere.

Lydia smiled and turned to Kate. 'Leslie Phillips!' she announced.

'Is she?' Kate said and glanced at the elderly lady who was now sat chatting happily to her friend.

'No, not *her*. Leslie Phillips, the actor.'

'Where?' frowned Kate, glancing out of the window.

'Not here,' laughed Lydia. 'That actor whose name I couldn't remember – Leslie Phillips. You know, said things like "Good Lord" and "Ding Dong!"'

'Oh right,' replied Kate, completely mystified. 'See you at home later tonight then, with glad rags on.'

'Ok, bye for now.'

As Lydia headed for the door, a buzzing sound came from her bag and she immediately rummaged for her phone. The café door suddenly opened and the wind gusted in and as Lydia turned her back against the draught she was immediately pushed slightly forward as someone cannoned into her.

'I say! I'm awfully sorry, it's this wind.'

Lydia recognised the voice and turned around.

'Well, hello again,' the smooth and cultured, chocolatey voice said. Lydia smiled as she saw the 'man with the hat' or Leslie Phillips, as she had re-christened him,

'Hello,' she said, 'what a coincidence.'

The man closed the café door. 'It seems that we are destined to bump into one another. I do hope I haven't hurt you.'

'Not at all, please don't worry.' Lydia smiled as she looked at the twinkling blue eyes.

'Were you just leaving?' he asked.

'Actually, yes.'

'In that case, let me open the door for you.' He stepped back to the door and grasping it firmly, gallantly wrenched it open. 'Pleased to have met you, again,' he said as he lifted his hat with his other hand and smiled politely.

'Likewise, and thank you very much.' Lydia dipped her head in acknowledgement and walked out into the street. How wonderfully gallant the man was, a real dapper gentleman.

Lydia glanced at her phone, a text from Vinnie:

Transfer completed.

Yes, she knew – she had already checked her bank account.

Lydia smiled, life was definitely on the up.

2

Councillor Hugo Marshall

Hugo Marshall recognised the envelope straight away and had put it in his desk drawer. It was addressed in the same style as the previous two – *Mr Hugo Marshall* and marked *Private & Confidential* across the top. The contents were probably the same. He didn't think the author had changed his or her mind, though why the bright-pink envelopes he couldn't imagine, they simply drew attention. He supposed that was what the author wanted, to embarrass him, to make him nervous – well they had damned well succeeded!

After lunch, he sat in the leather executive chair behind his large oak desk, took the envelope out of the drawer and placed it on his desk. It didn't disappear in a puff of smoke no matter how many times he wished it would. The loud pink colour made him wince, it clashed with the bland colours of his office, with the neat lever-arch files on shelves to his left and the bookcase to his right; all this was at risk. Reluctantly, he slit the envelope with the silver opener his wife had bought him on his recent birthday and slowly, his pudgy fingers extracted the folded paper.

He read the few words and closed his eyes. He would have to speak to Simon, put a stop to the partnership and call it a day. There was too much at stake here – his reputation and his business, for a start, not to mention his appointment as mayor in a couple of months. If anything were to come out to ruin his political and social life, Celia wouldn't be understanding.

He knew that Celia enjoyed her status as the wife of the owner of the town's oldest and most respected estate agency. She was on various charitable committees and attended endless functions – her photograph, which regularly appeared in the local paper, depicted a woman of generous proportions suitably attired with matching hat, handbag and shoes, and always with a string of real pearls around her neck. Celia was already preparing her wardrobe for her role as lady mayoress, and Hugo knew that she was already visualising herself in the mayoral limousine, wearing the chains of office.

Hugo and Celia lived in a detached house with a large garden on the edge of Ashdale, on an executive housing development known locally as 'the posh houses', where Celia planned to hold 'at homes' and summer afternoon teas for her charities. Then there was her brother, Charles Lewis, Hugo's absent and lazy business partner – heaven forbid he found out. Although it would serve Charles right if the agency folded.

Any scandal or change in financial circumstances regarding the agency would certainly have an impact on Charles and his affluent lifestyle, including the impending golf club captaincy, the private box at the racecourse and his beloved classic car. But to be hauled into court, possibly in front of Charles's magistrate-wife, Beatrice, was the most unbearable thought of all. No, thought Hugo, this would never do, this business with Simon had run its course, and he reached for the telephone.

As his fingers reached the handset, the phone rang and made him jump. He took a deep breath to steady himself, cleared his throat and picked up the receiver. 'Marshall,' he said curtly in his best professional voice.

'Hello, Hugo,' a smooth silky male voice answered him.

'Simon, the very person…' Hugo began.

'I don't have time to talk now, I just wanted to confirm our meeting for Monday morning at ten thirty.'

'Actually, I've a client to see, so can we reschedule?' asked Hugo hopefully.

'No, I'm afraid not. Your secretary has just called mine to ask that, but it's not possible to change my plans, so you'll have to reorganise your meeting.'

'I'll see what I can do.' Hugo tried to sound important.

'You don't have a choice though Hugo, do you? I'll see you on Monday.' And with that, the line was abruptly silenced. Hugo chewed his lip thoughtfully and then put his head in his hands – how on earth was he going to resolve this?

A soft tap on his office door made him sit up and quickly stuff the pink envelope and its contents into the top drawer of his desk. He plastered a smile on his face.

Felicity appeared. 'I've spoken to Mr Saxby-Jones's secretary, but unfortunately the Monday meeting cannot be rearranged, so would you like me to reschedule the viewings with Ms Buckley, or ask Mr Craven to do them?'

'You'd better ask Mr Craven to look after Ms Buckley. No point in moving everyone around,' replied Hugo with a sigh.

'Very well, Councillor Marshall.' Felicity left the office, closing the door behind her.

Hugo exhaled, sat back in his chair and closed his eyes, sure that he had the beginnings of a headache. The telephone rang again; he sighed and snatched up the receiver. 'Marshall!' he growled.

'Hugo dear, I just thought I would give you a quick call to remind you to go to the bank for some cash for this evening, I'm not sure we can use cards.'

Hugo closed his eyes as his head began to pound. 'I was just on my way to the bank, Celia, no need to worry.'

'Have you booked the taxi for six forty-five? We don't want to be late – you know I'm on the welcoming committee.'

Hugo wondered, not for the first time, why Celia couldn't do these things herself.

'Yes, all sorted dear.' Hugo picked up a pencil and wrote *taxi – 6.45* on his blotter.

'And don't forget we're picking up the Smythes on our way, so we'll need a decent-sized vehicle. I don't want to be squashed in the back of mini.'

Hugo added *for 4* to his blotter note. 'I don't think they use minis for taxis,' he muttered, too audibly.

'Don't be silly dear, of course they don't, but you know what I mean, and don't be late home from work.'

'No dear, must go, bye,' Hugo replaced the receiver without waiting for Celia to respond. He stood up, put on his overcoat and walked out to the main office.

'Felicity, I wonder if you could organise a taxi for this evening to take four people to Ashdale Hall for six forty-five. We are collecting the Smythes on the way, they live on Marlborough Drive,' he said as he headed to the main door. 'And we need someone to replace this.' He glared at the blind which was still sitting in a heap on the oak chest.

'I've already spoken to Sid about the blind and he'll be along to fix it on Monday morning,' replied Felicity.

'Thank you. I'm just popping out to the bank and to do some errands, I'll be about an hour or so.' Hugo pulled on the door and was surprised when it opened with more force than he anticipated, allowing a gust of wind to swirl around the office, once more scattering brochures and property details across the floor. He pulled the door closed with difficulty and stomped off down the street.

Maggie Clark

Maggie had reached the end of a busy morning at WOW! As she walked into the staff room, she saw that Zoe had already switched the kettle on, and was checking her hair in the mirror. Her highlighted hair was still sleek and kink-free thanks to the hair straighteners she used every morning to keep the graduated chin-length bob in the style she had chosen rather the mess her naturally curly hair preferred.

'Phew! What a morning, thank goodness the kettle is on,' Maggie said.

'Do you want your usual coffee?' Zoe organised two mugs, put a spoonful of coffee into one and waited for Maggie's reply.

'Yes, please,' answered Maggie as she opened the fridge to extract milk and her lunchtime sandwiches. 'Are these fancy prawn sandwiches yours?'

'Yep,' chuckled Zoe as she put the drinks on the table and sat down, 'and they're not that fancy.' She took a sip of coffee, closing her eyes to savour it.

'Nearly all my clients are having their hair done for the Valentine Ball tonight. I almost wish I was going,' Maggie said wistfully.

'It's the same with my beauty clients. We've spent the last few days waxing, doing spray tans and nails.'

'It's no wonder Bella is so excited about going to the ball with Simon tonight, she's positively sparkling,' said Maggie referring to their bubbly young blonde receptionist.

'Mmmm,' replied Zoe thoughtfully as she ate her sandwich.

Maggie frowned. 'What's the matter, is something wrong?'

'I can't believe he's actually taking her,' answered Zoe, not quite meeting Maggie's eyes.

'Oh Zoe,' Maggie tutted, 'why wouldn't he take her?'

'I can't help feeling that something isn't right. How long has Bella been dating Simon?'

'Um, just over a year, I think.'

'And yet he still lives with his wife!'

'Well, when you say "lives with", but it's not in the marital sense is it? I mean they just share the house,' Maggie pointed out.

'Oh, I know what he *says*,' retorted Zoe, 'but they seem in no hurry to divorce. They continue to live in the same house in supposedly separate rooms and they both have new partners, but you've got to admit that it's weird. When most couples break up, they live apart. I couldn't wait to get rid of my ex.'

'Well, not everybody has an ex as greedy as yours. And as Simon says, they can't sell the house.'

'Is it even on the market? Zoe took another bite of her sandwich before continuing. Then there was last Easter and Christmas, Bella didn't see Simon at all then …'

'Simon explained all that, he went off down south somewhere at Easter to see his sister and spent Christmas with his father… something along those lines,' said Maggie with a vague wave of her hand.

'I suppose,' replied Zoe thoughtfully, 'but what about the time it was Bella's birthday? Simon was away on a course.'

'But these things happen, he didn't choose to be away,'

'It was over a weekend. Courses don't take place over a weekend.'

Maggie looked sternly at Zoe. 'Are you sure you're not just a teeny bit jealous?'

Zoe sighed and crumpled up her empty sandwich bag. 'No, I'm definitely not jealous! Just very suspicious.'

'Really?' Maggie replied with a hint of sarcasm and raised her eyebrows.

'Ok, there was a time when I first met Simon and we got on so well that I thought he might ask me on a date, and yes, I was surprised when he hooked up with Bella, but…' Zoe hesitated before continuing briskly, '…anyway that was a long time ago. I'm over it and have nothing to be jealous about. We're just good friends now, that's all.'

'Then why aren't you happy for Bella? Everyone else is.'

'Because the relationship between Simon and Bella has not moved on – he's met her parents, they think he's the best thing since sliced bread and he knows all Bella's friends, but the problem is that it's all one-sided – Bella has never met any of *his* friends or family.' Zoe stood up and walked over to the sink with her empty mug.

'Have you talked about any of this to Bella?'

Zoe sighed and turned around to face Maggie. 'I once asked her why she hadn't met Simon's father and she told me that he would be really upset if he knew Simon and his wife were splitting up. Simon thought it would be easier to tell him once they'd gone their separate ways.'

'Well there you are then, it'll sort itself out. Anyway, doesn't Simon's wife... Annabelle, isn't it? Doesn't she have a boyfriend herself now?'

'Apparently.' Zoe shrugged her shoulders.

Maggie looked steadily at Zoe. 'You need to get over this. Bella will be upset if she thinks you still harbour feelings for Simon,' she said.

'I don't "harbour feelings for Simon", protested Zoe, doing air quotes with her fingers. 'And another thing... I also think the age gap of about twenty years is too big,' she added.

'Some couples cope with that,' answered Maggie.

'Well it didn't do Charles and Di any good, did it?' Zoe snapped. She sighed impatiently. 'Maggie, I'm not jealous! Ok? Look, can we just leave this? I'm finished with lunch and I need to take over reception whilst Bella takes her lunch break.'

Zoe almost threw her mug in the sink and left the staff room.

Maggie sighed. *Well you sound jealous to me, lady.*

She stood up and cleared away Zoe's empty sandwich bag along with her own and washed both mugs.

Maggie had been good friends and a business colleague with Zoe for many years. They'd worked at the same salon in Harrogate, and when Zoe had opened WOW*!* Maggie had not hesitated to leave the Harrogate salon to join her in Ashdale.

Zoe had set up her business some eight years ago following a very acrimonious divorce. The building itself had once been two cottages and was owned by a large property development company. They'd done a marvellous conversion on the properties and Zoe told Maggie, that the minute she saw it, she knew it was just perfect for her business. The original front doors had been knocked together to form one impressive entrance, and inside, where the original lounge and dining room had been was the reception area with the hair salon behind it. On the right-hand side, was the Relaxation Room where clients could wait for appointments or friends in comfort. A hallway led to the treatment rooms and kitchens had become the staff room and Zoe's office. A staircase led up from the staff room to Zoe's first-floor flat.

Maggie was becoming increasingly concerned that Zoe seemed to be so at odds with the relationship between Bella and Simon. Yes, there was twenty years difference, but you only had to look at them together to see that Simon really cared for Bella.

Maggie thought back to when Simon had joined the Ashdale Players some eighteen months before, at the start of rehearsals for *Babes in the Wood.* He was charming, witty and intelligent – a surveyor or architect or something, and so good looking with amazing blue eyes. His enthusiasm and good sense of humour had been a breath of fresh air for the Players and everyone liked him. He had joined Maggie and Zoe's circle of friends and it had seemed that he and Zoe would get together. But then Simon had suddenly asked Bella out on a date and they'd been a couple ever since.

Maggie sighed and shook her head. She checked her choppy black hair in the mirror, fluffing out the layers and turning her head so the light caught the recent red highlights. Yes, she still liked the effect and would keep the colour, at least for the next six weeks.

Later that afternoon, as Maggie was helping a client on with her coat, she became aware that not all was well at the reception desk. Zoe was talking to a frowning young woman with long brown hair caught up in a high ponytail.

'So, you won't let me speak to her then?' the brunette snapped.

'I'm so pleased you like your hair, Mrs Armitage,' Maggie said to her client, a little louder than was necessary.

'I'm afraid not. This is neither the time nor the place,' Maggie heard Zoe reply tersely.

Maggie cleared her throat and smiling brightly at her client led her to the desk. 'Would you like to make another appointment, Mrs Armitage?' The older woman was rummaging around in her handbag, clearly oblivious to the tense atmosphere at her side.

'I don't have my hair done very often dear, but I'll come back again,' replied Elsa Armitage. 'Now where *is* my purse?' Maggie kept the smile on her face, but her eyes strayed to the brunette woman glaring at Zoe.

'There really is no more to say then, is there?' the young woman snapped.

'No, not at the moment,' replied Zoe calmly. The brunette turned and marched out of the salon. Elsa finally found her purse and Maggie took the payment, wishing her a wonderful evening at the ball, and yes, she probably would see her at the rehearsal tomorrow. As the door closed behind Elsa, Maggie turned to Zoe who was very busy with bits of paper. The diary wasn't laying open in its usual spot on the reception desk, but Maggie could see it poking out from underneath some papers that Zoe was shuffling around. She sighed and picked up the diary to see who her next client was.

'Is everything all right?' she asked.

Zoe turned and smiled over brightly. 'Yes, no problem,' she replied. 'By the way, your next appointment, Mrs Halford, is here already.'

'She's a bit early and what with Mrs Armitage not taking as long, I'm getting ahead of myself,' Maggie said happily – but

Zoe seemed miles away and did not reply. Maggie shrugged and collected her client from the Relaxation Room.

As Mrs Halford was being shampooed by one of the juniors, Maggie glanced at Zoe who was staring thoughtfully at the poster of the forthcoming panto, *Aladdin,* in which Simon was playing Abanazza. Although he was the panto 'baddie', there was no mistake that his handsome face had an enigmatic smile. Bella was also a member of the Ashdale Players and had the minor role of Char Sue, handmaiden to the Emperor's daughter. Maggie was wardrobe mistress (being quite handy with a sewing machine) and Zoe was in charge of make-up. The panto's opening night was in four days and excitement was building. Most of the residents of Ashdale attended the annual panto at some point and the production was known (and now expected) to be full of double meanings, possibly a little risqué in places, with humorous references to topical or local issues

When Bella returned from lunch with Simon, she was positively glowing and not just from the gusting wind. 'Look what he's bought me,' she said gaily and pulled a box from a small carrier bag with a jeweller's name on the side.

Maggie wandered over to the reception desk and noticed that Zoe had managed to smile. She was quietly relieved that the box was too big for a ring. Bella opened the box to reveal a silver necklace set with a beautiful blue topaz stone surrounded by clear diamante crystals and a pair of earrings to match. Maggie assumed it wasn't white gold and diamonds with the topaz.

'It's lovely, absolutely gorgeous,' she told Bella. 'Will you wear it tonight?'

'Oh yes,' breathed Bella, 'I simply can't wait.' she put the jewellery away and hurried to the staffroom to put the gift in her locker and hang up her coat.

Maggie leant against the desk and folded her arms. 'What was all that about earlier? With that brunette woman?' she asked.

'Oh, nothing much,' answered Zoe with a vague wave of her hand, but Maggie wasn't convinced.

'Hmm, well it wasn't a happy conversation,' she said and narrowed her eyes at Zoe. However, at that moment the door opened.

'Oh, here's my next client,' said Zoe breezily. 'Good afternoon, Sandra, how are you?'

The woman smiled at Zoe. 'I'm afraid I'm a little early,' she said as she unbuttoned her coat.

'It's absolutely fine, the room is ready for you. I was just waiting for Bella to return. Ah, here she is,' Zoe replied as the receptionist reappeared. Zoe hopped off the chair and escorted her client down the hallway to her treatment room. Maggie watched her go, thoughtfully. *Something's going on!*

An hour or so later, as Zoe said goodbye to Sandra, Maggie overheard Bella tell her that a Verity Kent had phoned and could Zoe call back? Zoe frowned and nodded tightly before slipping back to her office to make the call. When she returned, Maggie noticed that Zoe seemed flustered.

Towards the end of the afternoon, as Maggie was glancing through the appointments diary, the door to the Relaxation Room opened and a forty-something woman stepped into the reception area.

'Do you think Zoe will be much longer? I've only just over an hour left on my parking ticket,' she said to Bella.

'I'm sure she won't be long, Mrs Allen,' replied Bella, 'she must have got waylaid by another client.'

'I'll just go and see what's happening,' Maggie told the client with a smile. 'Please just take your seat again.' Mrs Allen withdrew back into the Relaxation Room and Maggie looked enquiringly at Bella

'Zoe went to answer her mobile and hasn't returned,' Bella explained, 'that was about ten minutes ago.'

Maggie frowned as she slipped down the hallway and into the staffroom, Zoe rarely returned or accepted personal calls during the work hours.

The door to Zoe's office was open ever so slightly so Maggie couldn't help but overhear what Zoe was saying. 'I don't know what to think Simon, to be honest.' There was a pause as Zoe was evidently listening to someone on the other end. Eventually she replied, 'We've got to talk about this, I don't like being deceitful.'

Maggie tapped on the door and pushed it further open.

Zoe glanced up suddenly, looking somewhat flustered. 'I've a client waiting Simon, I shall have to go, bye,' she said into the phone and immediately disconnected the call. 'Hi Maggie, just coming,' she said brightly.

'Are you sure everything is all right, Zoe?' Maggie asked with concern. 'It seems as though you've had a bit of a traumatic day?'

Zoe smiled. 'No, everything is fine, Maggie, so don't worry.' And closing the office door behind her she walked to reception.

Not for the first time that day, Maggie watched Zoe walk away from her and felt that something was very wrong. She sighed. Well whatever it was that was bothering Zoe, it was something she didn't want to talk about.

The afternoon drew to a close and the rest of the staff had finally left leaving just Maggie, Bella and Zoe. Maggie closed and locked the door.

'Yay!' Bella shouted excitedly, 'Time to par-tay!' Maggie smiled and looked at Zoe who immediately lowered her eyes and made a big deal of using a calculator.

'Now you have a great time tonight. Wear that beautiful jewellery and we'll see you at rehearsal tomorrow,' Maggie told her.

'Yeah, I hope you enjoy yourself tonight, Bella,' added Zoe flatly.

Maggie scowled and looked at Zoe who kept her head down as she cashed up at the till. A mobile phone chirped and Bella dug in her pocket and her face crumpled as she read the message,

'Oh no!' she wailed and tears formed in her eyes.

'Whatever's the matter?' asked Maggie. Even Zoe looked up from what she was doing.

'Simon's cancelled tonight. He says his father has been rushed to hospital and he's on his way there now.'

'Oh good grief!' murmured Zoe, not very sympathetically.

Maggie glared at her, but fortunately Bella hadn't noticed.

'I do hope it's not serious,' exclaimed Maggie. She put her arm around Bella. 'That's really unfortunate, pet. I know you were so looking forward to going to the ball… but there will be other times, you know.'

'But this was so special, being Valentine's Day and everything.' Bella sniffed as she held back tears.

'I know, but Simon can't abandon his father. Maybe you can speak to him later,' Maggie suggested.

Bella shook her head. 'No, he says that he'll just see me tomorrow at rehearsal.'

'Well…'

Maggie was cut short by an insistent buzzing from a phone set to vibrate-only, Zoe immediately pulled out her phone and pressed the answer key. 'Hi,' she said quickly, then there was a pause as she listened to the caller. 'Nothing, why?' she asked and frowned. As she listened, Zoe suddenly glanced up at Maggie and Bella, then averted her eyes and turned away from them. 'I'm not sure that would be a good idea. Just hang on a minute, let me go to the office.' Zoe quickly dumped the paperwork and her phone on top of the till drawer, picked the whole thing up and walked away down the hallway.

Maggie sighed and turned back to Bella. 'Come on, your father will be waiting.' Maggie took Bella's arm and gently steered her towards the staff room.

'You don't think that's just an excuse and that Simon is trying to dump me, do you?' asked Bella tearfully.

'No, of course not, don't be silly. He wouldn't make up

something like that. Look at that lovely jewellery set he's just bought you – it's not the sort of thing a man does when he's about to say goodbye, is it?' Maggie handed Bella her coat and the bag containing the new jewellery.

'No, I suppose not.'

'Come on, Bella, this is just very unfortunate, but I'm sure that Simon will make it up to you.' Maggie held open the door. 'There's your father, look.' Maggie waved vaguely at the car idling in the car park.

'Ok, see you tomorrow then,' Bella said as she stepped outside.

'Bye,' called Maggie.

'Bye.' Came a voice from the office. Maggie closed the door and turned back into the staff room to change her shoes and put on her coat, however she could not help but overhear Zoe's conversation in the ensuing silence.

'Sorry, that was just Maggie and Bella leaving. Are you sure it will be all right? I don't want to upset Bella anymore.' There was a pause as the caller spoke, before Zoe replied, 'but Simon…' Zoe was interrupted as the caller spoke again. Eventually she sighed and continued, 'Fine, I'll come, but I'll have to get on and get ready. What time will you pick me up? Crikey, that's only an hour away. Ok, let me go now. See you soon. Bye.'

Maggie, realising that Zoe thought she was alone, toyed with the idea of staying right where she was so Zoe would see her when she came out of the office, but instead decided to make a sharp exit. She grabbed her coat and bag and silently let herself out through the door. Once in her car, she took a deep breath.

Should she have stayed? Maggie was a strong, independent woman who normally wasn't afraid to speak her mind, but she knew she had been known to put her foot in it many times before. She and Zoe did not socialise a great deal outside work and panto commitments, but they were very good business colleagues and trusted each other implicitly, so Maggie knew there was something that Zoe wasn't talking about. She decided to bide her time and not rush to confront Zoe until she could find out more.

Maggie looked back at the salon, and saw that the lights were on upstairs in Zoe's flat – no doubt she was rushing around getting ready for wherever she was going tonight. As Maggie started the car engine, a thought occurred to her. *Is Zoe going out with Simon tonight? What if Zoe is secretly seeing Simon?*

Given the last couple of conversations that Maggie had overheard, it seemed a distinct possibility. Maggie wondered if she should have stayed and talked to Zoe, after all, but the timing was wrong for a heart-to-heart, and Maggie had a feeling that any such conversation might end up as a confrontation. She shook her head and let in the clutch. The panto opened next week and it wouldn't do to have issues and an unpleasant atmosphere. Whatever was going on would have to wait until after it was over, but she was in no doubt about one thing – that this would all end in tears.

3

Elsa Armitage

Elsa looked up at the imposing façade of Ashdale Hall admiring the stately pillars supporting the portico entrance.

'Oh Brian,' she sighed, 'isn't it magnificent? I do hope we meet some lovely people and make new friends.'

Brian Armitage paid the taxi driver and stuffed his wallet back into his trouser pocket.

'What do you mean "new friends"? We've already got friends… like Barb and Col.'

'Oh yes, I know but they're not very adventurous, are they? I mean every week we do the same thing… go for a drink, and then either back to theirs or ours for supper. We always go on holiday to the same hotel in Bournemouth, same time of the year… last week in July, first week in August. And we can't go abroad because Barb won't fly… she says it's dangerous … but it's no worse than driving all the way to Bournemouth. That chap who has the allotment next to yours, Alf, he goes with his wife to Spain for three months every winter… it must be so nice not to be cold …'

Brian sighed. 'Well, let's make sure we enjoy it then and get inside out of the cold,' he said, taking his wife's arm. 'You're right, it's quite some place this.'

Elsa relaxed at Brian's more positive tone. She saw this evening as a rare chance to widen their social circle as she felt they had got into a bit of a rut since Brian's retirement.

'Now remember,' Elsa began as they walked under the portico entrance, 'mind your manners tonight and no drinking pints of beer – it's wine with dinner, and liqueurs after.'

'But I don't like wine and liqueurs,' protested Brian. 'I bet they have beer.'

'You do like wine – you've drunk it before, and this isn't the sort of place to knock back a few pints, Brian.'

'It's gonna cost a pretty penny, this. You might have won the tickets, but they don't include taxis and drinks *and* we don't know anybody—' Brian broke off suddenly as Elsa stopped and pulled him to one side,

'Now, look here,' she said quietly, 'we're going to enjoy this evening… *you're* going to enjoy this evening. We rarely get dressed up and go somewhere special and I've been looking forward to this for a long time, so please, put a smile on your face and stop moaning. Now, I'm just going to powder my nose, so will you take our coats to the cloakroom and then just wait here… please?'

Ashdale Hall was a privately-owned luxury hotel set in acres of landscaped gardens and woodland on the outskirts of Ashdale itself. It was the ancestral home of the Worthington family and the current incumbent was Sir James Worthington, who upon the demise of his father, had set about turning the beautiful residence into a profitable business. The Valentine Ball had been organised by his wife, Lady Victoria, and her committee ladies, in support of the current mayor's charities with a view to it becoming an annual event. Millions had been spent on bringing the house up to a five-star standard and as Elsa entered the powder room, she marvelled at the opulent décor and fittings. Around a dozen ladies, dressed in fabulous evening gowns chatted, powdered noses, applied lipstick and fluffed hair.

The fierce wind from earlier in the day had died down, but Elsa wanted to check that her new hairstyle was still looking neat. Another, younger woman, stepped up to the mirror; she wore a black, lacy, corseted dress with ruffles that were mid-thigh length at the front and dipped to floor-length at the back. Elsa considered that it was more of a wild-west saloon girl costume than black-tie evening dress. She stared as the young woman ran her fingers through her long loose brunette tresses and tossed her head and then, catching her eye, glared at her. Elsa quickly looked away, embarrassed.

When Elsa was satisfied with her appearance, she went to find Brian. 'The loos are incredible,' she told him, 'absolutely gorgeous.'

Brian tugged at his shirt collar in a vain effort to loosen it.

'Leave your collar alone,' whispered Elsa, 'you'll make it dirty. Have you got our tickets handy?'

They joined a small queue of people waiting to enter a large reception room regally named *The Kensington Suite*. When they reached the doors, Brian handed over their tickets and Elsa's heart sank as she saw him immediately scan the room for a bar and spot it in the far corner.

'Half a cider as usual?' he asked Elsa under his breath and headed off towards it without waiting for a reply. Elsa was taken aback for a moment until a hovering waiter holding a tray of drinks approached.

'Would Madam like a glass of champagne?'

Elsa gratefully took a glass.

'… And perhaps one for sir?' the waiter added.

Elsa hung her evening bag over her arm and took another glass. 'Thank you,' she said and hurried after Brian before he could order half a cider. Elsa caught up with her husband halfway across the huge room, 'Brian, hold on!' she hissed, 'I don't want cider.'

Brian turned around. 'Oh?' he frowned.

'They're giving away champagne, look I've got you a glass.'

'I don't want one of those love, you have them both.'

'I can't stand here with two glasses, it doesn't look right. No one else has two glasses,' her eyes darted left then right.

Brian smiled. 'Well in that case, why don't you go over to the window and put one on the windowsill whilst you hold the other? I'll just get a beer and come and join you.' He put his hand gently under her elbow and turned his wife in the direction of the windows.

Elsa sighed and walked as quickly as she could without seeming to hurry. She put both glasses on the windowsill and squinted out into the night, but she could only make out a terrace with a stone baluster looming out of the darkness, so she turned around to face into the room. Another waiter had appeared, as if by magic, with a tray of full champagne glasses.

'Would Madam like some champagne?' he asked politely and held the tray out towards Elsa.

'Well… thank you.' Elsa took another glass of the fizz. The waiter moved away and Elsa took a sip – it was cold and delicious. She could get used to this!

The room was filling up now and Elsa could no longer see the bar; she hoped Brian would be able to make his way through the crowd to find her. Most of the guests seemed to be in groups as they laughed and chatted – and as the noise level increased it was almost impossible to make out any conversation. The group in front of her parted to make way for Brian as he carefully held his pint of beer and another glass of champagne.

'Phew!' he exclaimed, 'that was tricky, but I did manage to get you another glass of champers – I thought it would save having to buy you another drink later on.' He reached behind Elsa to put the glass on the windowsill and noticed the two glasses already there. 'Flippin' 'eck love, you're gonna be three sheets to the wind at this rate and I can't carry you with my back!'

'Shush Brian! It's not often I have a few glasses of champagne.'

The group directly in front of them were twenty-somethings; the girls stood giggling with their backs to Brian and Elsa as they posed to take selfies on their mobile phones. Elsa was decidedly unimpressed with their evening wear.

'The youngsters of today have no idea how to dress,' she told Brian. 'There was a young woman in the powder room who was dressed like a wild-west saloon girl complete with lacy black Victorian boots! Those girls aren't adhering to the black-tie dress code either… I mean, look, two of them have short dresses on… and just look at that girl with the long red hair – her dress (if you can call it that) is barely there… it's no more than a see-through long coat over a band of fabric about two feet wide… it'll ride up when she sits down and be quite indecent! The only one appropriately attired – in a long dress, is the girl with short spiky hair!'

Brian obligingly looked at the girls. At that moment, the girls turned around to take another selfie to include the grand décor of the room, and Elsa gasped in horror. 'Good grief!! Brian, just look at that! That long dress is split down to her navel and up to her…. in fact, no Brian, turn away!' Elsa suddenly noticed Brian's appreciative grin and she pulled him round so his back was to the group.

'Elsa…' he began in a mild protest.

'No sense of shame… I do hope they're not on our table, otherwise it will quite spoil the dinner.'

'Well, at least they'll be sitting down,' reasoned Brian. Just then, there was the sound of a gong and the chatter immediately died away.

'Ladies and Gentlemen, dinner is served. Would you all please make your way through to the ballroom.'

The group of young people in front of Brian and Elsa eventually began to put down their empty glasses and move forwards.

'Right,' said Brian decisively, 'drink up the one in your hand and take the other two with you. Go and find the seating plan then make your way to our table. I'll just finish this beer and get a refill and see you at the table in a couple of minutes.'

'But—' began Elsa.

'Go on, I'll be right there,' Brian nodded in the direction of the door. Elsa sighed, finished her second glass of bubbly, picked up her drinks from the windowsill and made her way to a large easel which held the seating plan.

It took a little while to find their names and discover that they were placed on table forty-seven. Elsa followed the crowd into the magnificent *Buckingham Ballroom* and marvelled at the crystal chandeliers and ornate plasterwork picked out in gold paint on the ceiling. There were fifty round tables, each with a snowy white cloth, ten red napkins and a tall lily vase filled with red water beads topped with a beautiful display of red roses and ostrich feathers as a centrepiece.

It was quite easy for Elsa to spot table forty-seven and she made her way there, carefully threading her way between people and chairs. The other eight dinner guests were already seated at the table, chattering in their couples when Elsa put down her two glasses of bubbly. She smiled and looked at each couple in turn, ready to acknowledge and say good evening, but nobody looked in her direction, so she simply sat down to wait for Brian.

'Here we are, luv,' Brian made his way carefully to Elsa's side and put down another glass of champagne. Elsa glanced up at her husband and then at the (now) three glasses of bubbly in front of her.

'Brian, really – another one?'

'The waiter saw me with my pint an' he had some spare champers on his tray so he suggested I take one for my missus.' Brian winked and Elsa felt herself blushing. 'Anyhow, it'll save me having to buy you drinks won't it?'

Councillor Hugo Marshall

As coffee was served on the top table, Hugo was aware of Celia talking non-stop to Sir James Worthington about the forthcoming mayoral year and all the fundraising events she was planning. Sir

James's eyes had glazed over and he had obviously zoned out of the conversation, Hugo imagined he was probably wondering if he could find an excuse to leave the table.

'So, Sir James,' Celia drew breath, 'what do you think?' she asked intensely and put her left hand on the host's arm. Sir James abruptly came back into the moment and realised an answer was expected from him although he had no idea of the question.

'Well, I'm sure we can consider the possibility,' he replied tentatively, hoping for an appropriately neutral answer. Celia's grip on his arm tightened in excitement.

'Oh! Sir James, how wonderful, we are so appreciative... aren't we Hugo?' She grabbed his arm, forcing him into the conversation.

'Hugo! Sir James has agreed to support all the fundraising events during our mayoral year.' Hugo raised his eyebrows in surprise and glanced at Sir James who looked slightly shocked and alarmed.

'Sir James ...' Hugo began, but Celia still had a grip on an arm of each man, and, with each syllable she banged their arms on the table as if she were holding a gavel in each hand.

'This is absolutely marvellous,' she chanted. Her hands lay still but she gripped their arms as she continued, 'our mayoral term will be recognised as one of the most memorable for years to come I'm sure.'

'I'm sure it will,' said Sir James dryly as he gently removed Celia's hand from his arm. 'You should perhaps also speak with Carlton Banks of Aztec Developments, he's the sponsor of this event and he's most influential in this area.'

Hugo recognised the deflecting tactics with wry humour.

'He's on the table behind you – the chap with the maroon bow tie, sitting next to the lady in the gold dress.'

Hugo and Celia turned, and as Hugo's glance swept around the table behind them, he caught the eye of Simon Saxby-Jones, who smiled and raised his glass in acknowledgement.

'Hugo, do you know that man? Who is he?' Celia asked impatiently.

'I've met him before, probably at one of those network lunches,' replied Hugo vaguely.

'Well, he clearly remembers you *and* he knows Carlton Banks. Go and talk to him, and get him to introduce you,' urged Celia. 'At least smile back Hugo, and stop staring,' she added.

Hugo smiled weakly back at Simon, who stood up and made his way over to the top table. Celia beamed at his approach, and Hugo just felt a bit sick.

'Hugo, how delightful to see you again.'

Hugo held out his hand in response to Simon's proffered handshake and winced slightly as Simon squeezed his fingers rather more determinedly than was absolutely necessary. Simon, aware of Hugo's discomfiture, looked him straight in the eyes, rather like an alligator viewing its victim, before dropping Hugo's hand and turning to Celia. 'And you must be the delightful Mrs Marshall, Mayoress-Elect.'

Celia suddenly came over all girlish and for some reason blushed as the incredibly blue eyes turned to her.

'Oh, please call me Celia,' she simpered and lowered her eyes coyly. Hugo cleared his throat

'I wonder if we… er, I mean if you…' he began uncertainly.

'Of course, of course, but some other time perhaps, eh?' interrupted Simon smoothly. 'I've just come to borrow Sir James and Lady Victoria. If I may, sir?' Simon turned to Sir James who seemed absorbed in folding his napkin. He looked up brightly. 'Absolutely Simon, be right with you.' He gently tapped his wife's arm; 'I'm so sorry to interrupt, Victoria, but I'm afraid we're needed elsewhere.'

Lady Victoria looked at her husband with gratitude whilst Charles Lewis sniffed and pursed his lips.

'You'll consider my proposal though won't you, Lady Victoria?' he asked pompously.

‘I’ll discuss it with my husband. James, Charles was suggesting renaming The Ashdale Mile as The Lewis Marshall Mile. We can certainly put it to the Racecourse Committee,’ she replied non-committally.

‘Good! I’m chairman of that committee,’ said Charles smugly. Sir James and Lady Victoria exchanged glances and stood up to go with Simon. Following the departure of the Worthingtons, Hugo turned his attention back to the couple on his right – local celebrity Fiona Cavendish and her husband Bruce Harvey. Fiona was an actress in a very popular soap opera which was filmed in the district and as the funds raised this evening were to go to a charity she supported, she had graciously agreed to attend the ball to meet, greet and provide photo opportunities for those who asked.

Simon returned to the table almost immediately and whisked Fiona away to prepare her for the next part of the evening which left Hugo with Bruce. Hugo was interested to learn that Bruce Harvey, also an estate agent, specialised in Spanish property. He explained to Hugo that he was looking for an agent in the UK through which to market his company, Spanish Sun.

‘You know, I may be interested in that, myself,’ Hugo ventured.

‘Really?’ exclaimed Bruce, ‘Should we go somewhere a little quieter and discuss it further? Or perhaps, even better, arrange a meeting for another day; although I’m only in the UK until the end of next week,’ he added. Hugo glanced at Celia who, deprived of her aristocratic and celebrity guests had moved to the other side of the table to join the Smythes and her brother and sister-in-law. She was deep in conversation.

Hugo made up his mind.

This was something he like the sound of and to heck with what Charles might think.

‘Now is absolutely fine, let’s go elsewhere and talk,’ said Hugo decisively.

Celia looked up as the two men left the table and seemed about to say something but then changed her mind – Hugo knew what she was thinking; that befriending a celebrity's husband might be fortuitous for their mayoral year.

Lydia Buckley

On table twenty-eight, Lydia was enjoying herself with Greg and her friends. They were a group of ten, made up of Lydia and Greg, Tom Craven and his wife, Amy; Tom and Greg's sister, Chloe Appleton, with her husband Will; Kate and Ben, and finally friends Louise and Jake Robson. They'd finished the coffee and the men had gone to the bar to buy liqueurs.

'So how are you getting on as prompt for the panto, Lydia?' asked Louise, a striking blonde with amazing eyelashes courtesy of her salon, Lush Lashes.

'I'm really enjoying it,' replied Lydia, 'everyone has been so nice and I've asked them if I can be in it next year.'

'How are the ticket sales going?' asked Amy, idly stirring the bowl of brown sugar with her coffee spoon.

'I think Saturday evening is sold out, so it's just as well that you've all bought your tickets, and the matinée is looking pretty full too. I can't believe the show opens on Wednesday, though. On one hand, time seems to have flown by, but on the other, I seem to have been immersed in *Aladdin* for months.'

'We always have a great time,' said Amy, 'and the Saturday-night final performance has been known to go a little… off-piste, shall we say?'

'Well if they go too far off the script, I shall despair,' said Lydia firmly. 'Doing two performances in one day is bad enough without the cast making up their own lines!'

'Don't forget that my café is open exclusively for the Players between the shows next Saturday. Everyone usually comes over for something to eat,' said Kate twiddling a permed ringlet around her finger.

'Oh, I hadn't realised that; how lovely of you,' replied Lydia.

'I do simple home-cooked meals and desserts and it seems to

go down well – it also means that people don't have to go home between performances or take off make-up. It's something I've done for several years and it's a great atmosphere, complete with a lot of teasing about blunders and bloopers – a chance for everyone to chill before the next show.'

'Don't mention blunders and bloopers, I'm hoping that the next three rehearsals will iron those out! It's a great script – Desmond is a very talented producer and director, and I still laugh at some scenes even though I've watched them many times. You're all in for a great evening's entertainment.'

'Who knows, Lydia, you might decide to write the next panto yourself,' suggested Louise.

'Oh no, definitely not.' Lydia shook her head. 'I shall leave that to the brilliant Desmond. He's got the right sense of humour, whereas I don't. I'll just try another novel, I think.'

'How has the first one taken off?' asked Amy as she picked up another spoon and pushed it into the sugar.

'Absolutely brilliantly. I'm rather astounded, to be honest,' answered Lydia. 'Of course it helps that Louise here is so understanding and lets me do lashes on an ad hoc basis, so I've plenty of time to write.'

Lush Lashes, was Louise's lash and nail bar in Harrogate, and Lydia supplemented her income by working a few hours each week.

'So, are you going to write another novel?' Kate asked her sister.

'Yes, I think so. Now that I've done one, I feel more confident about how I write,' replied Lydia.

'There are a couple of chocolates left, does anyone want another?' said Louise, picking up a plate.

Amy looked up from the sugar bowl. 'Oh, yes please!' She reached out towards the proffered plate and caught the coffee spoons with her arm. They flipped and catapulted sugar through the air and peppered a young woman who was trying to squeeze around the chairs behind them.

Amy jumped up in alarm. 'God!! I'm so sorry,' she exclaimed as the young woman in a black lacy dress stared angrily at Amy.

'What on earth were you doing?' she retorted.

'I'm sorry,' said Amy again, 'it was an accident.'

The woman dusted brown sugar granules off her ample cleavage,

'It's gone everywhere,' she complained. Amy brushed a few granules off the woman's shoulder, but she recoiled from Amy's touch and slapped her hand away.

'Get off me!' she snarled and stalked away.

Amy turned to her friends. 'Oh dear, I think I've just upset someone.'

'Crikey! It was only a bit of sugar,' remarked Louise.

'Actually, it was quite funny to watch, how you aimed that sugar so accurately at her cleavage whilst making it look like a simple accident.' Lydia put her hand over her mouth to contain her giggles.

'It *was* an accident…' began Amy but then saw the mirth in their eyes and started to smile. Kate and Louise also began to giggle as Amy swept up the sugar that had landed on the tablecloth.

'Perhaps you could use the sugar incident in your next book!' suggested Chloe with a chuckle.

'I might do just that!' replied Lydia. 'It's never a dull moment in Ashdale.'

'Have you decided to settle here now?' Chloe asked seriously.

Lydia looked at her friends and smiled. 'Yes, I think so. My settlement from Vinnie came through only today and I've arranged some property viewings for Monday.'

The men arrived at the table with the liqueurs and Tom had caught Lydia's last remark.

'Oh, that reminds me,' he said, 'I'll be doing your viewings on Monday as Hugo was unable to rearrange his meeting.'

'Oh, that's much better, I would much rather be shown around by you than that Councillor Marshall – he kept giving me strange looks, I felt quite uncomfortable.'

'Oh, he's harmless enough. He just sees himself as a bit of a ladies' man although it comes across as a little bit inappropriate at times. He's probably still somewhere in the eighties in the days of the "little girls in the office who do a bit of typing" and giving them an odd slap on the bum.'

'I bet he doesn't slap Miss Reid's bum though!' giggled Lydia.

'Good God no!' replied Tom. 'He just sees her as a very efficient secretary who will never let him down. She's utterly devoted to him but he doesn't realise it. He relies on her to buy birthday and Christmas presents for his wife, brother and sister-in-law, all wrapped and ready to give, along with reservations for his wedding-anniversary dinner complete with suitable card and gift.'

'Really? There are there still men like that?' Lydia was astounded. 'Does he remember her birthday or buy her something at Christmas?'

'Not until I joined the firm. I found out about her birthday quite by chance and now *I* make sure he gives her a little something, and the same at Christmas.'

'That's really thoughtful, Tom. I'm sure she's very appreciative.'

'The first time he gave her a birthday present, she blushed so much and was almost overcome with delight.'

'Well I think it's very sweet of you to remind him,' Lydia declared.

'That's my Tom,' interjected Amy, 'a real sweetheart.'

Greg cleared his throat.

'Being a sweetheart clearly runs in the family,' Lydia said softly to him.

Greg smiled at her, then picked up a spoon and gently tapped his glass to get his friends' attention.

'Here's a toast to all of us,' he announced raising his glass. 'Happy Valentine's Day.' They all picked up their glasses and repeated the toast, clinking the glasses together in the middle of the table.

Elsa Armitage

Following the superb dinner was the ubiquitous auction. Brian had gone off to the bar for another pint and Elsa was sitting alone. She sighed and then made up her mind to go and have a look around the gorgeous venue.

Elsa made her way back to the foyer and crossed the bottom of the staircase to the other wing, past the *Balmoral Bar* where some of the guests had sought refuge from the auction. Around the corner from the bar were two interconnecting rooms, *The Sandringham* and *Windsor Suites.* Through the open doors Elsa could see (and hear) a wedding party raucously enjoying their evening reception. As Elsa walked away from the noise of the wedding party, the hallway grew quieter and she came upon *The Frogmore Library.*

Elsa turned the doorknob and found to her surprise that the door wasn't locked; she slipped quietly inside, breathing in the rich smell of old leather. She took in the parquet flooring, oak panelling, wing chairs and tiffany lamps. Rows and rows of old, leather-bound volumes with faded gilt lettering were safely tucked behind glass-fronted doors. It was a place of calm and serenity and Elsa felt a million miles away from the noise and razzmatazz of the ball.

Having revelled in the silence and calm for a few minutes, Elsa let herself quietly out of the library and walked down the hallway to a room at the end, regally called *The Osborne Suite.* One of the double doors was open and Elsa could see that the room was already set up for the following morning's breakfast for the hotel guests. She could hear voices and, not wanting to disturb people, she simply peeped around the door, and was completely taken aback to see the suave and handsome Simon Saxby-Jones. With his back to her, his hands were on the shoulders of a woman with highlighted brown hair whom Elsa couldn't quite see, but who was wearing a striking turquoise gown.

'You do trust me, Zoe, don't you?' Simon said quietly, bending his head towards the woman's upturned face.

Zoe? Elsa immediately looked away feeling somewhat embarrassed at witnessing this private moment. She stepped back behind the door and took a deep breath, then realising she ran the risk of being discovered if she stayed there, headed back down the hall towards *The Balmoral Bar.*

Elsa and her friend Barb helped with refreshments each year at the panto performances and knew all the cast members. Elsa had been surprised to discover a year or so ago that the dashing Simon Saxby-Jones had started dating that young, naïve Bella, rather than, as she expected, the attractive and vibrant Zoe. However, seeing him now, with Zoe, made Elsa smile somewhat smugly, knowing that she had been right all along about Zoe being the right person for Simon. Did anyone else know? Had she unwittingly stumbled on a secret?

Wait until Barb hears about this!

Lydia Buckley

'How much longer does this damned auction go on for?' grumbled Louise.

Lydia looked at the programme. 'Five items to go, and then the dancing starts.'

'Thank God for that, I hate auctions at dos like this.'

'It's the best way for them to make oodles of money,' said Greg.

'Well, there are certainly a lot of people here with plenty of money to bid on things they don't really want, or could quite easily just buy on a whim,' observed Tom.

'Like item number fifteen – a year's supply of firewood,' laughed Amy, pointing to the auction list.

'Right, well I'm just going to pop to the Ladies before the music starts,' announced Lydia. 'I shan't be long,' and she made her way out of the ballroom to the powder room. When she had finished and reapplied her lipstick, Lydia pulled open the powder room door and recognised a man hurrying past and disappearing into the ballroom.

Simon Saxby-Jones! I bet you wouldn't bid for anything rash, like a year's supply of firewood!

She chuckled to herself.

4

Isabella Sturdy

Bella kept her phone in her pocket all morning, checking every so often to see if she had received a message. Her mother served up their Sunday lunch and as Bella glanced at her phone for the umpteenth time – there was still no message from Simon.

Claire Sturdy looked at her daughter. 'Darling, looking at your phone every five minutes isn't going to help. Simon said he'd text when he could so you'll just have to be patient. Now, eat your lunch before it gets cold.'

Bella pushed a piece of beef listlessly around her plate. She just had no appetite, and was still upset about not going to the eagerly anticipated ball. It would have been the first time that Simon had taken her out with his friends and she had bought a new dress and shoes, especially. Her mother had been sympathetic last night as Bella had shed a few tears, but had reminded her that Simon's first priority was his father and that Bella should be thinking about poor Simon rather than feeling sorry for herself. That there would be other balls and occasions, and to appreciate the beautiful gift she had as a Valentine's present.

Bella knew all this of course, but it wasn't the first time that plans had had to be cancelled at the last minute and, somehow, it made her feel nervous. She had picked up glances and eye rolls from Zoe each time there was an 'arrangement deviation' as Zoe called them – and, at one point, Zoe had even had the nerve to suggest that these last-minute cancellations were perhaps excuses. Had this been an excuse not to take her to the ball? And if so, why? Simon had told her umpteen times that he loved her – it just didn't make sense.

Not for the first time, Bella wondered if Zoe mightn't be a teeny bit jealous. Admittedly, everyone had been surprised that she and Simon had become a couple, in fact it had amazed even Bella herself.

Well to heck with them! We are a couple whether they like it or not! But what if…?

Suddenly her phone tinkled as a message was delivered and Bella saw immediately that it was from Simon. She grabbed the phone and read the text. Her mother looked at her questioningly and gave her an 'I-told-you-so' look when Bella smiled.

'His father will be ok. He just needs to rest; apparently it was a mild heart attack.'

'Now what did I tell you? You really should have more faith in Simon and not be so clingy. You don't want to frighten him away.'

'You're right, Mum, but sometimes I just can't believe he's fallen for little old me.'

'Darling, you're a lovely, attractive, well brought-up young lady. Any man would be proud to have you on his arm, isn't that right Jonathan?' Claire turned to her husband who was busy on his phone. 'Jonathan! Not at the table please.'

Jonathan Sturdy, a man in his fifties with thinning grey hair, looked up sharply.

'What?' he said vaguely. Then, noticing his wife's raised eyebrow and her glance at his phone, he pushed the device away. 'Oh, right…, what were you saying dear?' he finished lamely.

Claire sighed and turned back to Bella. 'Is Simon able to attend rehearsal this afternoon?' she asked.

Bella nodded. 'Yes, he says he'll see me there.'

'Well why don't you wear a nice dress – the navy blue one is very pretty.'

'Mum, it's a rehearsal, not afternoon tea, jeans will be fine.'

'Well I always think a woman should look attractive to her man, you wear your jeans all the time...'

'So does everyone. Jeans will be fine.'

'Well at least put some make-up on... what do you say Jonathan?'

Jonathan jerked his hand away from his phone, which he had secretly returned to under the table, and smiled at his wife. 'Probably, dear.'

Bella pushed away from the table and stood up. 'I'm going to take a quick shower before I go,' she said rushing out of the room and upstairs.

Technically, the Sturdys lived at Harefield House Farm, but as the farm was no longer an agricultural business, the family had dropped 'Farm' from their address. When Bella's father had originally inherited the farm, he developed two redundant barns into rather nice four-bedroomed properties which he had then sold for a healthy profit. This had been ploughed back into a new business venture: Harefield Park, whereby the farmland was converted into a holiday park for campers and touring caravans.

The park included high-quality facilities, with bathrooms and a laundry area, picnic tables, country walks and trails, and the holiday park also offered discounts for local attractions. The business had flourished and was on the brink of expansion. Jonathan had offered his daughter an administrative job in the office, but Bella wasn't interested in office work, or working with her father and had declined the offer. Fortunately, her younger brother, Joe, was finishing his business-management degree and couldn't wait to get involved in Harefield Park.

Harefield House was situated down a country lane off the main Ashdale-to-Harrogate road. The drive into the small town took Bella past a tree-lined former railway line now used as a cycle and public path on her left, and some of her father's land on her right. Next was what had been her great-uncle's property – Thornberry Farm; the brown and green fields separated by lines of dry-stone walling so typical of the Yorkshire Dales.

On this rather damp and grey Sunday afternoon as she drove to Ashdale, her mother's words stuck in her mind: *Don't be so clingy, Bella.* She tried to be cool and sophisticated around Simon, but whether she tried to reply with a witty remark, or say very little and appear nonchalant, she felt that everything she said and did came across as naff and immature. In reality, she was terrified he would leave her for someone more sophisticated and glamorous, like the women who came to the salon for treatments. Maybe she ought to take advantage of the staff discounts and have her nails done and a spray tan. But Bella, at twenty-four, wasn't a high maintenance girl, she didn't have expensive tastes or wear designer clothing, she walked dogs and rode horses in her spare time. Her long blonde hair was usually in a ponytail at weekends or in a neat bun high on the top of her head for work. She had no desire to become a high-flyer and she loved her simple reception job at WOW!

Her mother thought Simon was a gentleman and eminently suitable as a prospective son-in-law, although at first, both her parents had been sceptical about the age difference of about sixteen years. Her father said very little about Simon, but she was sure that he had come to like him as they were now working on a project together.

Bella drove into the Jubilee Hall car park and pulled up beside a red Astra with an open tailgate. She got out and noticed with disappointment, that Simon's Porsche wasn't there.

Brian Armitage was moving items around inside the Astra.

'Hello Brian,' she called.

'Now then, young Bella,' he replied as he pulled a crate of beer towards him. The Astra was full of boxes and bottles of wine, cardboard trays of plastic-wrapped juice drinks, cartons of crisps and bags of popcorn.

'Can I take something in with me?'

'Aye, thanks love, anything you can carry. It all has to go in.'

'Excuse me, are you Brian Armitage?' Bella and Brian turned around at the sound of an unfamiliar voice behind them. A tall, muscular young man stood in front of them, and Bella was immediately drawn to his startling blue eyes.

'I am, lad,' replied Brian standing up straight. The young man held out his hand in a proffered handshake.

'I'm Nick Bradley, I'm here to help backstage. I understand your usual chap isn't available and I've been asked to give you a hand to bring stuff in.'

Brian shook Nick's hand. 'That'd be grand. It all has to come in, ta.' Brian grasped the crate of beer, heaved it out of the car and steadily made his way to the hall.

Nick turned to the car and glanced at Bella.

'Hello Nick,' she said warmly, 'I'm Bella Sturdy, welcome to the Ashdale Players.'

Nick grinned. 'Thanks,' he replied, 'nice to meet you.' Then, grasping hold of two bottle bags of wine in each hand, he followed Brian into the hall.

What a nice guy, Bella thought as she picked up a large box of assorted crisps, and what amazing blue eyes!

The Jubilee Hall, built to commemorate the diamond jubilee of Queen Victoria in 1897, was a hive of activity as cast and crew made final preparations for the panto. The original building had been a large oblong shape with a good-sized stage at one end and the kitchen and main entrance at the other. Between the kitchen and main entrance was a door which led to a small hallway and the toilets. More recently, an extension had been built on the other long side of the building opposite the main entrance, known as The Annexe, which effectively doubled the overall square footage of the building. The cast and crew of the Ashdale Players used the key-coded back door, and made full use of the annexe area, which was split into three rooms for the Green Room and dressing rooms for the cast. Simon, however, insisted on using the Parish Clerk's office as his own private dressing room, given that the Parish Clerk always went skiing during the week of the panto.

In the kitchen, Elsa was in charge of issuing instructions and directions as to what went where, as she chatted about holidays to her friend. 'So, what I was thinking Barb… given you don't want to fly, was to go on one of them cruises. Brian, could you take the raffle prizes through to the Green Room please after you've put those crates next to the fridge… Barb, could you put the urn on? It'll take about three-quarters of an hour to boil and, if you…' she pointed at Nick, 'could put the wine on the worktop, please… Wasn't that right Brian? Cruising.'

'Aah, yes love – this is Nick, he's helping Graham backstage this week but he's giving me a hand just now,' explained Brian.

'Oh, well, pleased to meet you,' replied Elsa giving Nick a cursory nod before turning to Bella. 'The crisps can go on that shelf down there, please… Anyhow, as I was saying… cruising, Barb, that's what we should do. There's no flying involved and there'll be lots to do… a new place every day, just imagine it… it'll be a far cry from Bournemouth!'

Bella put down her carton of crisps and went into the Green Room to find Zoe laying out make-up and brushes, whilst Maggie was heaving a sewing machine onto a large table. Lydia was also there taking costumes out of a large box and arranging them on hangers on two rails.

'Hello Bella, you ok? Have you heard from Simon yet?' Maggie came over and put her arm around Bella's shoulders.

‘Yes,’ replied Bella, ‘apparently his father had a suspected heart attack but he’s going to be all right. He just needs lots of rest. I haven’t actually spoken to Simon, it was just a text this morning, but he’s coming to rehearsal today.’

‘Well that’s good news.’ Maggie squeezed Bella’s shoulders reassuringly. ‘It’s a shame that you both missed the ball last night, but I’m sure Simon will make it up to you.’

‘I guess so,’ sighed Bella. She thoughtfully watched Maggie walk away and then caught Lydia’s eye. Lydia looked straight at Bella and then started to say something, but then apparently changed her mind and closed her mouth firmly. Bella frowned slightly, then shrugged her shoulders. Meanwhile, Zoe was seemingly engrossed in sorting out cosmetics and brushes, setting up mirrors and generally trying very hard to look busy. Bella half thought that Zoe might have had a comment to make and was sure that she was deliberately keeping her eyes averted.

Maggie broke the awkward silence. ‘Right! Well, let’s get these costumes to the dressing rooms,’ she said a little too brightly and just as she grasped a rail, the doors to the serving hatch between the Green Room and the kitchen suddenly opened.

‘Bella, love,’ called Elsa, ‘Desmond is asking for all the cast to go into the hall.’

‘Be right there, thanks Elsa,’ replied Bella, and, with another glance at Zoe and Lydia who were both heads down and very busy rummaging in boxes, she walked out of the Green Room.

Desmond Carmichael was tall with an athletic build and close-cropped black hair. He had been active in amateur dramatics for most of his life and more recently had ventured into script-writing for the Ashdale Players. He tended to gesticulate over-dramatically with his hands in conversation, and as he spoke there was a slight emphasis on the letter ‘s’ which came across as almost a slight lisp. Bella’s eyes scanned the hall as she walked to the stage to join the rest of the cast gathered in front of

Desmond, but she was disappointed to realise that Simon had still not arrived.

Desmond clapped his hands to gain the cast's attention: 'Well people, we are almost at show-time once again,' he began, expansively gesturing with his hands. 'We'll begin today with the musical numbers as Kevin…' and he threw his right arm out to the side in the general direction of the sound and light desk '…is set up and raring to go.'

Kevin popped up from behind his two laptops, positioned on top of a control desk full of knobs, switches and slider controls. He pushed his glasses up his nose and grinned at the cast.

Desmond carried on: 'We've got Graham, as usual, backstage, but we've a new side-kick for him, please welcome – Nick!' Desmond gestured theatrically towards stage left, and Nick was shoved out of the wings onto the stage. Nick smiled and held up his hand in acknowledgement then disappeared back again.

'So, can you all take your places please for the opening song? Oh! Where's Simon? Bella darling – what *have* you done with him? Is he coming today?'

Bella simply nodded.

'Good, good. Come on now, quickly please.'

The cast took up their positions and Nick closed the curtains; then, on Graham's command, he opened the curtains as the music began.

Bella could see Maggie and Zoe seated in the audience watching the song, and they applauded enthusiastically at the end. Desmond then called for the song and dance routine which ended the first act. This was an energetic number and the choreography had been a challenge for everyone. Now, for the first time, Bella felt as if she was getting the hang of the moves, and at the end of the number, the cast congratulated themselves for getting through it without any glaring errors.

Bella noticed Maggie go up to Desmond and say something to him; Desmond nodded and turned to the stage. 'Bella darling,

Maggie would like to borrow you to check on your costume. The rest of you, again from the top.' Bella hopped down from the stage and followed Maggie to the changing room.

'I hadn't realised what was involved in that dance routine and I think your costume may be too restrictive,' said Maggie, 'so could you slip into it and come into the Green Room?' Bella nodded and a few minutes later, she was in her costume and going through the dance moves. Maggie observed with an expert eye.

'Yep, I'm going to have to make that slit down the side a bit higher. Just hold still while I get my seam ripper.'

Bella obediently stood still while Maggie picked at the stitches.

The hatch to the kitchen was still wide open and in the silence Bella and Maggie couldn't help but overhear Elsa chatting to Barb. 'Ashdale Hall is a gorgeous place and I've never seen so many posh people… everyone was dressed up – well apart from one woman who looked like a wild-west saloon girl. There was so much glitzy jewellery and fabulous dresses… and I had real champagne – four glasses, *four!* But you'll never guess who else I saw…' there was a pause, during which Barb presumably feigned ignorance, 'Simon Saxby-Jones… with Zoe! I didn't know they were together!'

'Really? But are you sure they were together? I thought Simon and Bella were a couple? I mean, maybe Simon and Zoe were both there, but with different people,' Barb suggested cautiously.

'I don't know if they arrived together, but when I saw them, they were alone in a room down a corridor so maybe it's not common knowledge but I saw him kiss her.'

Bella felt the air leave her lungs as she heard Elsa's words and froze.

Maggie stopped ripping stitches, stood up and strode across to the open hatch.

'Elsa!' she cried, 'Bella has just heard all of that!'

Elsa and Barb turned around guiltily, and Lydia looked up from making coffee.

An all-consuming anger replaced the shock, and Bella, clenching her fists, marched out of the Green Room allowing the door to slam behind her. She walked straight into the hall where the cast were just coming off the stage. Zoe was threading her way along one of the rows where she had been sitting, and Bella stopped right in front of her.

'Were you at the ball with Simon last night?' she demanded loudly.

The chatter in the hall died away.

'What?' said Zoe, alarmed. She took a step backwards, 'No, I did not go to the ball with Simon!' she said carefully

'You're lying!' spat Bella.

'Bella, Bella, what is all this?' A silky voice broke in as Simon made his way through the cast.

Bella spun round to face him. 'Were you with *her* last night?' Bella pointed a shaking finger at Zoe.

Simon calmly placed his hands on Bella's shoulders and looked directly into her eyes.

'You know perfectly well I was at the hospital. Now who has been telling you otherwise?' he said smoothly.

'Elsa said she saw you with Zoe at the ball last night.'

Everybody turned to stare at Elsa who, with Maggie and Lydia, had followed Bella into the hall.

Elsa turned pink with embarrassment. 'Well it was definitely Zoe – and a man who looked like you from the back… of course it might not have been you… on second thoughts, I think I may have been mistaken. After all, I had drunk a bit of champagne and…' Elsa blustered, backtracking hastily.

Simon smiled patronisingly at Elsa, who caught the look and frowned.

Bella felt the anger disappear as rapidly as it had arrived. She began to feel the beginnings of the usual embarrassment and humiliation that always seemed to appear when she was with Simon, only this time it was staged, for all to see.

'Well, there we are,' Simon said magnanimously. 'I'm sure there must be a lot of men who have brown hair, and as it was a black-tie event he would be wearing a black jacket – isn't that right, Zoe?'

Simon looked steadily at Zoe who held Simon's gaze for about three seconds before turning her eyes to Bella.

'It… it wasn't Simon,' Zoe said quietly.

There was an audible exhalation of breath as the cast, who had been listening in stunned silence, relaxed. Zoe's words had taken the heat out of the situation.

'Come on, everyone – get your drinks organised,' Desmond announced. 'Fifteen minutes until we start again and I want to begin with Act One, Scene Four. Graham, Nick – can you set the stage please?'

The cast gratefully dispersed to the kitchen's serving window, the drama over.

Lydia Buckley

As Simon pulled Bella to his chest in a reassuring hug, Lydia noticed he looked at Zoe over Bella's shoulder with one eyebrow slightly raised and an imperceptible but triumphant grin.

Very smug. Smug with a capital 'S'.

Zoe returned his stare with narrowed eyes and tight lips.

Now that, is one furious lady!

Lydia returned to the kitchen to get her coffee, where Elsa and Barb were busy making drinks for the cast and crew, so she stood out of the way by the hatch into the Green Room. Zoe was putting on her coat and Lydia saw Maggie grab Zoe's arm.

'Zoe? Are you leaving?'

'I'm done here, everything is ready for the dress rehearsal tomorrow night and I think it's best that I go now.' From Zoe's curt reply, it was clear that she was still angry.

'For God's sake, Zoe – Elsa made a mistake that's all. I didn't know you were going to the ball, you certainly kept that quiet.

Who's the mystery man, anyhow?' she smiled mischievously.

Zoe didn't return the smile. 'It's nobody else's business whether I was at the damn ball or not, never mind who I was with!' she snapped, shaking off Maggie's hand.

'Sorry, I just thought…' Maggie was taken aback.

'Well if people just stopped thinking and assuming, there wouldn't be a problem. Look, Elsa's all embarrassed, Simon will be all over Bella like a rash and I don't need to sit here amid sniggers and finger-pointing so I'll see you and Bella at work tomorrow – ok?' Zoe fastened her coat and picked up her bag.

'Ok, I see your point. I'll have a word with Bella before we leave here and make sure that everything is ok. You're right; we don't want an atmosphere at the salon tomorrow.'

'Thank you. That would be appreciated!' And with that Zoe marched out of the Green Room.

Lydia took her coffee back into the hall and settled down to concentrate on the script. Desmond took the cast through two or three scenes and then went back to work on the musical numbers, focusing on the final song and walk-down.

Lydia, being relieved of prompt duties for a while picked up her mug, and collected half a dozen other discarded mugs that were lying around the hall, and took them into the kitchen, placing them on the worktop near the sink. Barb immediately began to wash them up as Elsa was dejectedly drying previously washed crockery, and she looked so despondent that Lydia felt sorry for her.

'You ok, Elsa?' she asked gently.

Elsa shook her head. 'I never meant to upset young Bella like that, I didn't know she'd overheard… but I honestly thought that it *was* Simon and that he and Zoe had got together. You see, I knew that he took up with Bella after they were together during the last panto, but I always thought that he should have been with Zoe… I mean… when he first joined the Players, he seemed very smitten with her… and after all, Zoe is very attractive and they're of an age… but he suddenly started going out with Bella. Well, Bella could almost be his daughter when all's said and done and I always thought he'd made a mistake. So, I wasn't surprised to see him and Zoe together, so I thought… I assumed he and Bella had broken up,'

Elsa began drying the mugs that Barb had just washed and carried on talking. 'You see, me and Barb do the refreshments every year, but we only turn up the weekend before the show starts, so we've to catch up on all the news and gossip then. Last year, there was a bit of a to-do between Graham and John – that's the chap who helped backstage then, well by the time we came to the show they wasn't speaking… but during the matinée, you could hear them bickering. It was all anyone could do to get them to carry on and do the final show together on the Saturday night. Well me and Barb hadn't a clue what was going on. Isn't that right Barb?'

Barb opened her mouth to speak but never got a chance to even draw breath as Elsa swept on. 'It were just the same last summer with Sheila Houseman… she runs the bakery in the Market Place. I just asked how her son and daughter-in-law were getting on – they'd been only married six months, and Sheila bit my head off. Well, how was I to know that the young bride had left Sheila's lad and run off with someone else? Me and Brian had been on holiday and missed all the hoo-hah. Took over all huffy did Sheila, thought I was being untactful like and I was just being friendly.' Elsa paused for breath and Lydia took the opportunity to bring the conversation back to that afternoon.

'Of course, you didn't mean to upset Bella, it must have been a case of mistaken identity.'

'I was so sure it was Simon though.' Elsa put a mug down on the counter-top a little too firmly.

'What *did* you see, exactly?' Lydia asked.

Elsa nodded and put down the tea cloth, obviously glad to tell her story again, in spite of everything. She recalled how she had been fed up on her own, and gone for a bit of a nosey round the hotel. How she'd come across the open door of the room set up for breakfast and overheard Simon and Zoe.

'But what made you think it was Simon?' Lydia asked.

'Well I only saw him from the back as I said, but you can recognise someone from the back, can't you? I remember looking for my Brian in a supermarket once when we had got separated and I clocked him straight away standing in a queue. I know he's my husband, and of course, I should be able to pick him out... but it was the way he was standing and the style of his hair – what there's left of it. Now, maybe I don't know Simon that well, but his voice was like Simon's... some men have distinctive voices, don't they? ... like that Graham Norton who always does the Eurovision Song Contest, and although you don't see him, I can always tell when it's his voice... well, the chap with Zoe *sounded* like Simon.'

'I can see what you mean,' agreed Lydia understandingly. She toyed briefly with the idea of telling Elsa that she had also seen Simon, but decided to keep it to herself for now.

'Unfortunately, Simon says he wasn't even at the ball, apparently he was at the hospital as I believe his father had a mild heart attack on Saturday afternoon.'

Elsa sighed and shrugged her shoulders. 'Must have been his twin then,' she muttered.

'Don't worry Elsa. Look...' Lydia nodded her head in the direction of the stage, where the cast had finished the rehearsal and were busy packing up. Elsa glanced through the serving window into the hall and saw Simon stood talking to Desmond, his arm casually draped around Bella's shoulders. '...Bella and Simon are as happy as ever, so no harm done and I'm sure Zoe will calm down.'

Elsa smiled. 'I suppose so,' she conceded.

Lydia left the village hall and drove the short distance to Buttercup Crescent where she lodged with Kate and Ben and their daughter, Olivia. The Simpsons lived in a large four-bedroomed detached house on the relatively new Meadows development on the northern outskirts of Ashdale. The top floor had a big double bedroom with an en suite which they'd let out temporarily to Lydia.

As she freshened up, Lydia couldn't take her mind off the afternoon's incident. She too, had seen Simon at the ball and it definitely *had* been Simon, no mistake about it; but why had he denied being there? Had he been with Zoe? If so, why were they in a room down a corridor away from everyone? She also wrestled with her decision not to back up Elsa and speak up about seeing Simon as well. But she felt that, as someone relatively new to Ashdale, it was prudent to keep quiet until she was more familiar with the dynamic of the people she spent time with, and not make the mistake that Elsa had. It was abundantly clear to her that Zoe knew more than she was letting on and it bothered her that poor Bella might be in for a nasty shock after the panto.

It suddenly struck Lydia that there *was* a way to find out if Simon was telling the truth and it could be done quietly without anyone knowing – ring the hospital. Brilliant idea though it was, she told herself, it was poking her nose into something that did not concern her.

But a little impish voice pushed its way into her head. *It's just a phone call and then you'll know.*

She put down her hairbrush. *Don't get involved.*

Just make the call, it'll only take five minutes.

It's none of your business.

'For goodness sake!' she said aloud, exasperated by the arguing voices in her head.

She picked up her phone and Googled the hospital number.

'Hello? Yes, I'm enquiring about a patient by the name of Mr Saxby-Jones – he came in yesterday evening with a suspected heart attack... you may have him under "S" for Saxby or "J" for Jones... oh, right. I may have the wrong hospital of course, but thank you for your help.'

Now you know Simon was lying.

Not necessarily, he could have been admitted to another hospital.

Lydia sat down on her bed. What did she know for sure? Simon had definitely been at the ball and had lied to Bella.

She sighed. It was probably better to leave well alone, at least until after the panto. It wouldn't do to have tensions and upset during the coming week.

Her phone chirped, with a text message from Greg:

Are you on your way? Dinner almost ready.

Lydia texted back:

Just leaving xx

She dropped her phone into her bag, picked up her coat, and shouted a goodbye to Kate and Ben.

Greg lived a short walk from the Simpson's, his 'executive' apartment being located on Clover Rise in a block of six two-bedroomed units. It was minimalistic in style, predominantly in white with lots of chrome and glass and an occasional splash of emerald green for contrast. Lydia let herself in when Greg pressed the entry button and took the lift to the top floor. He met her at the door and briefly kissed her cheek as she entered the apartment. Greg was a tall and broad-shouldered, with thinning light brown hair and hazel eyes. He was a journalist for the borough newspaper, The *Harrogate Herald* and had never married, although there had been a couple of serious relationships. When any kind of serious commitment had loomed, however, things had rapidly gone downhill. Lydia wasn't put off by this revelation as she was enjoying her new independence, but equally happy to have an intelligent and caring man in her life.

'Dinner's ready and the wine is poured, Madam.' He grinned and made a mock bow.

Lydia laughed. 'Fool,' she teased him.

'It's only salad, lasagne and garlic bread but it's all home-made,' he said as he began to open the oven and don a pair of oven gloves.

'Perfect!' replied Lydia. Greg was an excellent cook and Lydia had enjoyed many meals of his 'home-made' variety. They settled at the glass-topped dining table which was protected with a padded cover and a white tablecloth, and Greg raised his glass. 'Cheers,' he said and Lydia clinked her glass with his.

'Cheers,' she replied.

'I thought Saturday night at the ball was great fun. Did you enjoy it?' Greg asked as he served up the lasagne.

'Yes, I did, and thank you for my ticket. Ashdale Hall is a beautiful hotel isn't it?'

'It certainly is; I remember interviewing Sir James Worthington at his launch party after all the renovations to turn the place into the hotel. We had a grand tour. Did you know there's a fabulous spa in the south wing?'

'I saw it mentioned in the literature in the entrance hall, I wish now that I had gone for a bit of a wander.'

'Oh God! I'm so sorry, I never thought to ask you on Saturday night if you would like me to show you around. Tell you what – I'll treat you to a spa day as a sort of belated Valentine's gift – seeing as how I forgot to buy you a card.' He looked at Lydia sheepishly.

Lydia was taken aback. 'You don't need to do that!'

'No, I know I don't, but I would like to.'

'Well, thank you very much, that would be lovely. I'll ask Amy if she'd like to come too.' Lydia smiled at Greg who simply passed her the garlic bread.

'You get on well with Amy, don't you?' he asked.

'Yes, we really hit it off from the first time we met, although I must say that everyone has been so welcoming, I'm so glad that I decided to move to Ashdale.'

Greg poured more wine into their glasses. 'How are you getting on with the panto folk?' he asked.

'Oh, they're very friendly too. Of course, I'm only the prompt as all the parts were cast by the time I moved here, but I'm hoping to be a cast member next year. There was a little drama this afternoon though, over a misunderstanding about a relationship.'

'Oh? Do tell – I like a bit of gossip,' Greg nudged Lydia and waggled his eyebrows.

'It was about Simon Saxby-Jones, do you know him?'

'I've met him at a couple of functions and to be honest I found him pompous and self-obsessed. He's an architect with Aztec Developments – married the boss's daughter. He's tipped to take over when father-in-law retires later this year. Why what has he done?' Greg took a drink from his glass and smiled appreciatively.

'Well, his marriage must have broken down because he's now dating Bella Sturdy. However, Elsa, who does refreshments at the panto, happened to be at the ball last night and she saw a man who looked like Simon supposedly kissing Zoe, who is our make-up lady.'

'Good grief!' Greg put down his fork in surprise, 'I haven't heard anything on the grapevine about his marriage breaking down and I don't think Carlton Banks would be very pleased about it. He wouldn't want to hand over the firm to an *ex* son-in-law.'

'Well apparently Simon hasn't actually left his wife, they still share a house, but not in the marital sense,' explained Lydia.

'So, you're saying that Simon still lives in the same house as his wife, but he's dating Bella and has been seen with Zoe? Well, isn't he a busy man!' remarked Greg and picked up his fork again. 'There could be a story brewing there.'

'The point is,' continued Lydia, 'that Simon denied being at the ball at all – he said he was at the hospital with his poorly father.'

'So, he wasn't with Zoe then and Elsa just made a mistake?'

'I don't know about being with Zoe, but *I* saw him… for definite, just after the auction when I went to the Ladies.'

'Why did he deny being at the ball at all, then?' Greg frowned as he struggled with the concept.

'I don't know, he was supposed to take Bella, but he cancelled at the last minute. Then Elsa says she saw him with Zoe. So, I thought that perhaps he *had* gone with Zoe, told a lie about his father to Bella and that he and Zoe are having a secret affair.'

'O-k, but perhaps his father was ill and therefore he cancelled going with Bella, but then his father recovered in time for him to go to the ball at the last minute?' suggested Greg as he selected a piece of garlic bread.

'No, his father was never admitted to hospital.'

'How do you know that?'

'I rang the hospital to ask about a Mr Saxby-Jones, they'd not got a patient of that name,' Lydia said a bit sheepishly.

'You did what? I thought I was the investigative journalist here.' Greg looked at Lydia with surprise.

'I just made the call on the spur of the moment.'

'But hang on, if you saw Simon at the ball, why didn't you say so this afternoon? I have to say…' Greg took another drink of wine, '…this wine from MegaMart is quite good.'

'I was going to, but Elsa then assumed she had made a mistake and I decided to let it go rather than interfere and cause a bigger upset. Once the panto is over, I'm sure they'll all sort themselves out.'

'He's a good old-fashioned cad. What do these women see in him? I always had a feeling that he only married Carlton's daughter to get his hands on the company.'

'Have you met Simon's wife? What's she like?'

'She's quiet and mousey, but very polite. Not a stunner, in fact, you might say rather plain or "low maintenance"; she's a stay-at-home wife.'

'Rumour has it that she has a boyfriend.'

'Really?' Greg shook his head, 'I would be very surprised, although they do say that the quiet ones are the worst.'

'It sounds like a real-life soap opera,' giggled Lydia. 'I'll keep you up to date as the week progresses. That lasagne was amazing!' She put down her knife and fork and grinned at Greg.

'Oh, I'm quite a dab hand in the kitchen, I once thought of going on that TV programme where you've strangers round for dinner and then go to theirs – *Come Dine With Me* – but I didn't get round to applying.' Greg picked up their plates and cutlery, rinsed them under the tap and placed them in the dishwasher. 'Now, tell me about your viewings tomorrow with Tom. Where are you going?'

Lydia told Greg how she couldn't make up her mind about the type of property she wanted and that Miss Reid had suggested she view each of the properties, Lilac Cottage, Meadow Croft and Larch Gardens.

Greg scratched his chin. 'Hmmm, Larch Gardens is on the Treesdale estate, which was once Manor Farm owned by old Alf Treesdale. His only child, a daughter called Irene, married Carlton Banks and they eventually had Annabelle, who as you know went on to marry Simon Saxby-Jones. Irene died when Annabelle was a little girl and when Alf died, Carlton developed the housing estate on the farmland and called it Treesdale. Carlton kept the farmhouse, had it extended and upgraded and added a large landscaped garden. It's known now as The Manor.'

'I've seen the entrance to that, it looks lovely.'

Greg began to dish up his signature chocolate mousse. 'Carlton still lives there, but Simon and Annabelle live in Harrogate. No doubt Simon will inherit The Manor someday as well.' He placed two bowls and spoons on the table.

'So you see, all very different properties to view – I'm so looking forward to it. This looks delicious, by the way.'

'I'm glad that you're going with Tom rather than that Billy Bunter-lookalike, Councillor Hugo Marshall. Tom will look after you and give you sound advice.'

'Yes, I'm glad that I'm going with Tom as well, Hugo Marshall gave me goose bumps.'

'I shall look forward to hearing all about the properties, but don't do anything rash whilst I'm away on this blasted conference in Birmingham.'

‘Oh, I won’t, I want you to come and look at my shortlist before I decide.’

‘By the way, I can confirm that Robbie Parker will come to your opening night to review the panto. He works for our sister paper in Leeds, but he’s agreed to come over to Ashdale as apparently he knows the area and actually volunteered to do the job.’

‘That’s good news, I’ll mention it to Desmond when I see him tomorrow. What’s Robbie Parker like?’

‘He’s really nice, sense of humour, chatty so he should be ok. In fact, he’s working on a new story and has asked me to help with some research, so I thought I could do that in the evenings next week seeing as you’re tied up with the panto.’

‘I shall miss you next week.’

‘I’ll miss you too, how about we have a romantic evening tonight to see us through until I come back next weekend?’ Greg waggled his eyebrows suggestively and Lydia laughed.

5

Lydia Buckley

On Monday morning, Lydia arrived at Lewis Marshall in plenty of time for her ten o'clock appointment and was relieved to be able to open the door easily this time. The blind still lay in a heap on the chest of drawers, but a wiry man in overalls was rolling up his sleeves and glaring at it purposefully, an open toolbox on the floor at his feet.

'Good morning.' Felicity welcomed Lydia with just a hint of a smile. 'I'll let Mr Craven know you're here.' But in the office behind her Tom was already on his feet, raising his hand in acknowledgement. Lydia was once again struck by his resemblance to Greg; Tom shared the same hazel eyes as his older brother, and sported trendy designer stubble.

'Morning Lydia, I'll just get my briefcase and we'll be off,' he said.

Five minutes later they were settled in Tom's car and heading out of the village. The weather was cold and the sky was dull grey with a thick blanket of cloud.

'I thought we would start with the furthest away and work our way back,' he said. 'Do you have the brochures? If not, I've spare ones.'

'Yes, I've brought them, but I'm still not sure which I prefer so I'm quite happy to take your advice.'

'We'll go to Lilac Cottage first.'

Lydia retrieved the details from her bag and glanced at the photograph of the pretty cottage, feeling her excitement mount as Tom drove northwards through Ashdale and out into the countryside.

The cottage was situated down a small un-made lane off the main road to Ripon, and Tom carefully manoeuvred the car around bumps and potholes.

'Hmm, I'm not sure I like this approach road,' mused Lydia.

'All part of the rural charm,' replied Tom with a grin as he pulled up at the side of a stone cottage next to a peeling white picket fence which was missing several planks. They got out of the car and walked round to the front gate. Lydia stared in dismay at the tangle of weeds, grasses and brambles.

'*At the front of the property is a natural cottage garden filled with a variety of old-fashioned country plants and flowers*,' Tom read aloud from the description.

'Well it's certainly "natural".' Lydia did quote marks with her fingers.

'I believe the photographs were taken last year or thereabouts and no one has bothered with the garden since. Do you like gardening?' he asked brightly.

Lydia shook her head. 'Never really done any gardening… Oh well. Point number one: will require a gardener,' and she mimed writing a list.

'Well, once the weeds and stuff are cleared, it shouldn't be too bad,' Tom replied cheerfully, 'let's go on.'

The small gate was a wooden affair clinging haphazardly to a rotting gatepost. Although Tom carefully used both his hands to lift the gate on its hinges to open it, as he swung the gate gently the gatepost gave way and collapsed onto the garden path leaving Tom holding the gate.

'Oh hell,' he muttered. Lydia clasped her hand over her mouth and muffled a giggle. Tom laid the gate on the weed-covered flower bed next to the path, gathered up the bits of gatepost and placed them with the gate.

'Point number two:' said Lydia adding to her imaginary list, 'New gate and post.'

Tom glanced at her, cleared his throat, and switched into professional mode. 'Shall we go inside?'

The old wooden door was poorly fitted; it looked as if six or seven planks of peeling varnished wood had been hastily fixed together and fastened onto the door frame by two large rusty, but oddly ornate hinges. The trellis supporting the climbing roses was broken and long thorny branches stretched across the door in wild abandon.

'This door would be better as a gate,' Lydia commented.

'It's vintage,' said Tom enthusiastically. 'You know… retro.'

'It wants replacing. Point number three: needs a new front door and trellis.'

Tom pushed the mortice key into the lock and was surprised to find some resistance, as the key stopped part of the way in. He bent down and peered into the keyhole. 'It looks as if something has been stuffed into the keyhole from the inside. We'll have to go in through the back.'

They followed a path around the side of the cottage.

'Point number four: needs new fence,' muttered Lydia as she followed Tom around to the back.

'I think a new back door would also be a good idea,' Tom suggested, eyeing the wooden door with peeling paint and rusted ironwork.

'Tom …' began Lydia, 'I think I can confidently say that this cottage isn't for me. It's too dilapidated and nothing like the brochure.'

Tom was apologetic. 'Lydia, I'm so sorry, I've not done any viewings on this property for months and I had no idea it was in this state. If you like it, however, you could put in a low offer and maybe…?'

'It doesn't matter, it's not practical for me. I don't think I want to be quite so isolated. It just appealed in a rosy-coloured-spectacles kind of way. Let's go to the next place.'

The grey sky had grown lighter and a weak winter sun was trying to break through the cloud, although it was still cold. They settled themselves back into Tom's car and he manoeuvred back down the lane to the road before turning back towards Ashdale.

'There's no street lighting at all around here, is there?' asked Lydia.

No, that's the joy of living in the country,' Tom quipped.

'Where to next then?' asked Lydia as they approached the town.

'Larch Gardens,' he replied, 'although I'm not sure you'll like where it is.'

'Why not?'

'Let's just say it's not the prettiest street in the town. Now I'll say no more as I don't want to cloud your judgement.'

Tom refused to be drawn any further on the merits or otherwise of Larch Gardens and Lydia had to be content with checking out the area from the car.

Tom turned off the main road onto the Treesdale housing estate, and after a few minutes turned left into Larch Gardens. There were about half a dozen semi-detached houses on each side of the road before approaching the townhouses. Lydia eagerly looked out of the window to spot the For Sale sign.

'There it is,' she said and pointed out the sign which appeared to have fallen over, 'it's blown down.'

Tom stopped the car a little further along on the left.

'Actually, this is the house here, number twenty-two. Someone's moved the sign.'

'Why?'

Tom sighed. 'Because they can.'

Lydia looked apprehensively at Tom as she got out of the car and walked towards the houses. Number twenty-two was the middle house of a block of five, each had a small front garden with fences separating the properties.

As Lydia and Tom walked past number twenty, a snarling wolf-like animal leapt at the fence baring white fangs dripping with saliva. The large dog barked ferociously as its huge paws clawed at the not terribly substantial fence. Lydia screamed and jumped away from the lap fence panels as they bent under the dog's weight.

'Satan!' screeched a woman's voice from inside the house. 'Down!'

The front window was flung open and a large woman wearing a T-shirt stretched to its limit over her ample bosom leaned out. 'S' all right, love,' she shouted at Lydia with a little less volume, ''e won't 'urt ya, an' he's chained up.' She turned back to the dog, 'Down!' she yelled again, then with a nod at Tom and Lydia, slammed the window shut.

Lydia was clutching Tom's arm in fear as Satan gave one last snarl before slinking off into a kennel near his owner's front door.

'Oh my God!' she whispered, Tom opened his mouth to say something but before he could speak, the door at number twenty-four opened and a young woman pushing a pram appeared. Her lank hair was pulled back into a severe ponytail and she wore a padded coat with a torn pocket; a toddler followed her with a slightly older boy trailing behind. The older child pushed and poked the toddler, who immediately burst into tears.

'Terry-Jason…' the young woman grabbed hold of the boy's arm and wagged her finger at him, '… if I've told you once I've told you a thousand times – leave your sister alone!' He instantly started to wail even louder than his sister, '…and Carrie-Louise…' she continued, turning to the toddler, '…stop being a baby, he didn't hardly touch you.'

Both children were now bawling at full volume as the young mum walked down her garden path. 'Morning,' she called chirpily to Tom and Lydia, 'getting out nice I see.' She waved her hand vaguely at the sky and without waiting for any response, turned and walked down the road away from them. Lydia watched the little family then she turned to Tom who took one look at her face,

'It's a "No" isn't it?' he asked gently. Lydia nodded and without another word, they made their way back to the car giving the fence at number twenty a wide berth. As they buckled up their seat belts, Tom's mobile rang.

The call was brief and when he disconnected, he turned to Lydia: 'That was Felicity, the owners of the apartment at Meadow Croft have just accepted a cash offer on the understanding that there are no more viewings, I'm afraid.'

'Oh no.' Lydia was disappointed. 'I was so looking forward to seeing that one.'

'Look, let's head back to the office and talk more about what you're looking for.'

'The problem is that I really don't know what I'm looking for. I just want my own place.'

'Ok, well instead of rushing into a purchase, why don't you consider renting for a while?'

'Renting? Wouldn't that be just throwing money away?'

'Not necessarily; consider the pros and cons of renting versus buying.' Tom pulled away from the kerb and spoke as he drove, 'Number one, renting allows you the flexibility to move when you want to, once you're past the initial six-month period and move on to a month by month basis. Number two, moving costs are much more economical as you don't need a solicitor or necessarily even an estate agent. Number three, repairs to the property through wear and tear are usually the landlord's responsibility.'

'I agree with all of that, but I would be paying rent on top of the usual monthly bills, whereas if I buy, my outgoings would be less as I wouldn't have a mortgage – plus my money would be invested in the property which presumably would increase in value over the years,' Lydia pointed out.

'In the first place, you're not sure of what type of property you want to buy, whether it's a house or a flat. You've just received your settlement and are looking forward to your own space but…' Tom paused as he stopped at a junction and looked both ways before he pulled out and continued talking, 'you could rush into buying a property that isn't right for you which could be an expensive mistake.'

'Ok, I see what you mean, renting in the short term might be a good idea until I really know what I want to buy.'

'Absolutely. The other thing to consider is buying an investment property with your settlement money – either a house or a flat, which you then rent out. The income from that would then pay your rent on the property you live in.'

'Good heavens, I hadn't thought of becoming a landlord, but it's an interesting idea. Do you have any properties to rent on your books?'

'Yes we do, actually it's an area of the agency that I'm trying to expand. I don't think Hugo is very excited about it – he's very old school. But as property prices rise, I think more people will consider renting.' Tom slowed to carefully overtake a tractor and continued towards the town centre. 'Hugo is going to hand me the reins of the agency whilst he's the mayor and I want to take the business forward. I'm hoping that at the end of his mayoral year, he decides to retire and gives me the first refusal to buy the agency.'

'Oh Tom, that would be marvellous,' enthused Lydia, 'Let's hope he makes that decision, he is retirement age after all.'

'He may well be retirement age, but there's life in the old dog yet. I think he's got a secret lady friend,' Tom chuckled.

'What! Councillor Marshall having an affair? What makes you say that? You don't mean with Felicity Reid, do you?'

'I don't think its Felicity, but he's been rather secretive – furtive phone calls, that sort of thing – and lately, he's been receiving pink envelopes,' Tom winked meaningfully.

'He got a pink envelope on Saturday morning. I was there when the postman delivered it actually. In fact, it fell onto the floor, I picked it up and gave it to him – he did look red-faced and flustered, to be honest,' Lydia replied.

'The Mayoress-Elect had better not find out or she'll have his guts for garters,' Tom laughed. 'Think of the scandal, it will ruin her mayoral year and her position in the borough. Hugo would have to leave town.' They arrived back at Lewis Marshall and Tom asked if Lydia wanted to come in and look at rental properties.

'I've a client to see at Lush Lashes in Harrogate, so I don't have time at the moment, Tom. But I'll look online and if there's anything that takes my fancy I'll let you know. You've given me food for thought though regarding buy-to-let so I'll consider that idea.'

They said their goodbyes and parted company. Lydia found she was excited at the prospect of buying a property to rent out and decided she would talk it over with Greg when he returned from his conference.

Councillor Hugo Marshall

Hugo pulled into a bay in front of a parade of shops before the entrance to the industrial park. He drummed his fingers on the steering wheel thoughtfully, unsure how he was going to broach the subject of his intention to resign from the Planet Properties partnership. It had all started so well, the idea of a simple partnership buying properties to let out, but Simon had employed some underhand tactics involving bogus buyers and false offers which had led to purchasing properties for less than market value. Hugo hadn't realised at first that the bogus buyers were dubious associates of Freddie's, and by the time he became fully aware of what was happening, the property portfolio of Planet Properties was quite substantial.

Hugo thought about Freddie Flannigan, the a small-boned Irishman who wouldn't have looked out of place on a racehorse, although he'd once told Hugo that he hated 'the beggars' and had never backed a horse in his life, let alone ridden one. Hugo had never trusted Freddie for some reason – he thought he looked shifty with his hooked nose and beady eyes which were usually narrowed, and never missed a trick. His hair was thin, wispy and grey and too long over his ears. He reminded Hugo of Scrooge, a skinflint by nature who wore only second-hand clothes because, as Freddie had pointed out, new clothes were second-hand the minute they'd been worn once so there was no point in paying a fortune first time round. Hugo had to admit, though, that Freddie's one redeeming factor was that he was something of a mathematical genius and was a fully qualified accountant who had then moved on to become a mortgage advisor which brought in lucrative commissions while still providing opportunities to 'do the books' for selective clients such as Simon Saxby-Jones.

Hugo remembered when Simon had first approached Freddie it was on the understanding that Freddie would be paid a generous fee to prepare accounts for a new company that he and Simon were setting up. However, when Simon had explained more about the dealings of the new company, Freddie had seen an opportunity to enhance his personal finances and had thus insisted on becoming a partner in Planet Properties.

Things had been fine until Simon had pushed a new project through their company – Woodside Farm, a run-down smallholding just outside the borough. The retired couple who had owned it had been shown plans for two executive-type houses on their land, each with a large garden. As the couple lived in an adjoining bungalow, they were content with this. However, as soon as Planet Properties had completed the purchase, Simon had submitted an amended application for ten houses, and then sold the development on to a national housebuilder for a very healthy profit. The elderly couple now found themselves next to a family housing estate.

Although none of the dealings involving Planet Properties was illegal or tax evasive, Hugo was increasingly uncomfortable with the methods used to purchase the properties. His (and Simon's) association with the company was unknown to anyone outside Freddie's office, but Hugo felt they were pushing their luck and that a time would come when his business dealings with the company would come to light.

They had done two more projects like Woodside, but although they had been out of the Harrogate district, his position as a local councillor and the impending mayoralty had made him even more anxious, and he had decided to cut and run. Hugo took a deep breath, and pulling himself together, got out of his silver Mercedes and entered the One-Stop shop. A national coffee chain had installed a self-service hot drinks dispenser and Hugo selected a mocha coffee, deciding that he needed a chocolate fix this morning – having seen the state of Freddie's kitchen and toilet, he had vowed never to risk any contact with either facility.

As Hugo parked, discreetly out of sight, at the rear of Freddie's grimy office, next to Simon's Porsche with its pretentious number plate *SSJ 1*, he felt a wave of disgust at the sleaziness of it all. His resolve to resign strengthened; he steeled himself with a sip of coffee and strode purposefully into the meeting.

Simon, wearing an expensive navy suit and a rather smug expression had already made himself at home; relaxed with one knee over the other, his laptop was already open on Freddie's desk which indicated that this may not be just a catch-up meeting.

Freddie sauntered in from his kitchen and placed a none-too-clean mug filled with a muddy coloured liquid, which Hugo assumed was tea, on his desk and sat down.

Hugo took a deep breath, puffed out his chest and spoke determinedly before his nerves got the better of him.

'Morning chaps. Look here – I want to be upfront about this and say that as we've finished our latest project and have reached a sort of quiet spot, I'm looking to leave the partnership. As you know, I'm to be the next mayor and I'm tidying things up a bit and… well, to be frank, I would rather not be involved in the sort of thing we've been doing. Not that its illegal or anything, just… you know a bit underhand… no, not underhand… just… well anyway, I want to resign really, that's all.' Hugo stopped pacing backwards and forwards, put his coffee down on Freddie's desk and sat down.

Freddie took a slow intake of breath and looked at Simon,

'I see, well I'm sorry old man, no can do,' Simon said calmly and raised his cup to his lips.

'What do you mean?' gasped Hugo.

Simon finished his coffee before turning to Hugo's stricken face. 'I've another project for Planet Properties, one that will give us around three million pounds each and we need you on board with us,' he said smoothly.

Freddie's eyes opened wide, 'Holy Moley! T'ree million you say? Tell me more.'

'Th-Th-Three million?' stammered Hugo faintly. 'Oh God, what does that entail?'

'I've a client who has just had plans passed to convert his redundant buildings into four executive homes,' Simon told them. 'I'll recommend that he approaches Lewis Marshall as an agent on the basis that they have small developers already on their books—'

'But I don't have any small developers,' interrupted Hugo.

'You do, you have Planet Properties and there will be others, courtesy of Freddie's acquaintances, all of whom will submit bids. You, of course, will recommend Planet and our bid will be the best, so my client will choose us. Once we buy the land and buildings with the current planning for say, two million, we'll re-submit revised plans for at least eighty houses, then sell to Aztec Developments for twelve million. So allowing one million for costs, we make a substantial net profit.'

Hugo was unable to speak. This was not going to be as easy as he'd planned – he realised with a surge of panic that he'd been naïve to think they'd just let him walk away.

'Ah to be sure, if that comes off then I'm off as well,' said Freddie. 'I'll not be working any more, I'll take me little pot o' gold an' bugger off, so I will,' and he rubbed his hands together with glee.

'We can dissolve the partnership at that point and take our three million each plus our individual share in the partnership's surplus after tax, etcetera,' said Simon. 'This will be our last project.'

Hugo looked uncertainly from Simon to Freddie. 'I'm really not happy about this. Where is this client and his land, Simon?'

'Ah, well he's actually on the outskirts of Ashdale.'

'What?' spluttered Hugo, 'On our doorstep? Are you mad?'

'No one need know about us individually – people don't usually look into property transactions, and anyway it would be Aztec who builds the houses, Planet is just the middle agent,' Simon explained patiently.

'But Planet will be named on the planning submission…' Hugo pointed out.

'Of course, however, no one connects you or me with Planet, just Freddie, and of course, and his lips are sealed through client confidentiality,' Simon smiled conspiratorially at Freddie and flicked an imaginary speck of dust off his trousers.

'And you don't think your client will have anything to say? He thinks he's getting four executive homes, but he ends up with a housing estate of eighty on his doorstep. It will be Woodside all over again, but ten times worse.' Hugo could feel the flush rising over his face. 'No, sorry but no, I can't agree to this, I've my mayoralty to consider.' He sat back, folded his arms across his ample chest and blinked through his round spectacles.

'Well now, that there's a problem you see,' Freddie said in his soft lilting Irish accent. 'I'm all for it, as is Mr Saxby-Jones, so democratically I'm not sure you've a choice, Councillor Marshall.'

'The thing is Hugo, old chap…' Simon steepled his fingers and looked at the ceiling, 'Freddie is absolutely correct, you and your mayoralty are in the minority, so I'm afraid you're outvoted.'

'Well I won't be a part of it – you can do it without me,' Hugo snapped.

''Fraid not old boy, I'm going to need your agency to push the fake bids through and recommend Planet Properties in the first place, and before you say any more, you should consider the implications …'

'Implications? What implications?' spluttered Hugo as he uncrossed his arms.

'If your fellow councillors got wind of the… deals, shall we say? … that you've already been involved with and how you made your secret stash of money from those. I think the word you used was "underhand". They may change their mind about the mayor-elect…' Simon looked at Hugo pointedly.

'Are you attempting to blackmail me?' Hugo asked pompously.

Simon laughed. 'Of course not Hugo, I'm merely pointing out that sometimes people find things out quite by accident and I, we …' he waved a hand in Freddie's direction 'wouldn't want your mayoralty to be jeopardised.' Simon leaned back in his chair and looked straight at Hugo meaningfully.

Hugo glanced at Freddie, who grinned back at him, feeling like a rabbit in a burrow cornered by a weasel. He opened his mouth, but no words came out, knowing that Simon meant every word. He mentally reviewed his options, (a) agree to this project, or (b) risk his reputation. A vision floated before his eyes, several money bags came with option (a) and a furious Celia with option (b). He thought quickly and realised that he had no choice but to go along with this outrageous final project. Hugo closed his mouth, cleared his throat and took a mouthful of his mocha. The sugary, chocolatey coffee tasted like nectar and, as the sweetness hit his palate he knew what he had to do.

'Fine, fine, as it will be our last project, I'm on board. In fact, I may take a leaf out of Freddie's book and bugger off after this!' He smiled weakly at Simon who simply raised an eyebrow. 'So where exactly on the outskirts of Ashdale is this property?'

'It's a place called Thornberry Farm, previously owned by a Joshua Clegg,' replied Simon.

Hugo frowned thoughtfully. 'Now where have I heard that name before?' he muttered.

'He came to see you about a year or so ago, about retiring and buying somewhere smaller.'

'That's right, now I remember, but how do you know him, Simon?'

'When I heard he might be selling Thornberry Farm, I went to see him and offered him a fair price, but he turned me down.'

'You probably didn't offer him enough,' said Freddie with a grin. 'He's as tight as a leprechaun's pocket, that one.'

'How do you know Joshua Clegg, Freddie?' asked Hugo with surprise.

'Oh, I don't! But I did enjoy a pint or two with his shepherd, so I did. Never bought anyt'ing new didn't Josh, always second-hand. A typical Yorkshireman!' Freddie chuckled.

'Well he's all but given the farm away now, to his nephew who happens to be my client, Jonathan Sturdy,' Simon said seriously.

Freddie roared with laughter. 'Would ya believe it!' he cried. 'Turned you down, Mr Saxby-Jones! That'll be because he wouldna' want to pay the income tax!' Hugo and Simon failed to see the humour and looked stony-faced at Freddie until he pulled himself together.

'That's as may be,' began Simon, 'but we've an opportunity to make some serious money if we work *together*.' He looked pointedly at Hugo.

'Just one small issue though…' Hugo reached into the inside pocket of his jacket and withdrew three bright-pink envelopes, 'I've received another letter and, to be honest, they make me nervous – one of the reasons I wanted to leave the partnership.'

Simon sighed. 'I thought we had decided that they were meaningless and sent to you by an anti-establishment individual, someone against the mayoralty,' he said.

'What are these?' asked Freddie, reaching out for the envelopes.

'They're anonymous letters that I've been receiving since Christmas.'

Hugo passed them to him and Freddie opened the top envelope and read the enclosed letter out loud:

Are you being entirely honest?

He glanced at Hugo and read the second letter:

Are your business dealings totally transparent?

'The third one I only received the day before yesterday, I think somebody knows what we're doing,' Hugo said drumming his fingers nervously on his knee.

Freddie frowned and opened the last envelope, reading aloud:

What if your fellow councillors found out?

'Ah to be sure, they're meant to scare you that's all, and they've used words cut out from newspaper and magazine pages – very amateur. I would just throw them away, so I would.' He put the letters back into the envelopes and passed them back to Hugo.

'That's exactly what I said,' Simon smiled patronisingly at Hugo. 'They don't say anything specific, they're just clutching at straws. This is the work of someone just trying to put the wind up you before you become mayor. Ignore them, that's my advice.'

'Do you think we should still go ahead with this new project then?' asked Hugo half-heartedly, his hopes of a change of mind dissolving rapidly.

'Absolutely! I'm not running away from this opportunity because of a couple of ridiculous letters. I bet most of your councillor colleagues get stuff like this and never say a word. Hand them over and I'll dispose of them.' Simon held out his hand,

'No, no, I'll do it, then I know for definite that they're gone.

I'll burn them.' Hugo stuffed the envelopes back into his jacket pocket.

'Right, down to business then. Here are the approved plans for Thornberry Farm and the buildings.' Simon opened his briefcase and withdrew large sheets of paper, which he spread out on Freddie's desk.

'My client, Mr Jonathan Sturdy, will come to you Hugo and you'll offer to market the development for a 1% commission of the sale price. That's a better percentage than the Harrogate agents will offer on a deal like this and your agency will get twenty thousand pounds for the privilege. You'll contact your developers and confirm a closing date for offers, say after one month. By then you'll have received four or five sealed bids to discuss with Mr Sturdy. You'll recommend Planet and we'll purchase the property.' Simon glanced up at both Freddie and Hugo to make sure they were following him.

'Now, the executive houses on the current plans, if built, would sell for a total of around six million, but with the purchase price and build cost totalling four million, our profit would be just two million. But that gives the plan credibility as far as Mr Sturdy is concerned and, actually, once we purchase the property, we can do what we like with it.'

Simon went on to brief Freddie and Hugo on his discussion with the bank and how the finances would work. Freddie talked about the tax payable and how the partnership would eventually cease and how they would receive the profits of the business.

Once the meeting was over and they'd parted company, Hugo headed back to his agency and disappeared into his office with instructions that he wasn't to be disturbed.

He felt that he was at a crossroads and was being railroaded down a road he did not want to take. He acknowledged that, theoretically, Simon's plan should work and it wasn't strictly illegal, although the business of making up sealed bids and not passing on authentic ones was doubtful. He also realised that *he* personally would be in the firing line because of the issue with the bids. But if he did not do as Simon asked, he was sure that Freddie's acquaintances would be asked to spread rumours of the unsavoury goings-on at Lewis Marshall which would inevitably lead to an investigation into his conduct, resulting in total embarrassment for which Celia would never forgive him.

On the other hand, if the project was brought to a successful completion and he received three million pounds along with the proceeds of the dissolved partnership, well, he could 'bugger off' with or without Celia. Hugo chuckled, he was sure that Celia would follow the three million pounds wherever it went, and as for the agency, he suspected that Tom would be interested in buying it, or at least his share – Charles and Beatrice could please themselves.

Hugo stretched back in his chair and thought more about the three million pounds, then recalling he had three pink envelopes in his pocket, he frowned and reached inside his jacket to withdraw them. He thought about burning them, but where? He did not smoke so matches and lighter were not to hand. They had central heating at home so no real fire and there were smoke detectors at the office. Hugo still felt uneasy about the letters – he couldn't shake the feeling that they were written by someone who knew what was going on and that he was being played. It could only be Simon or Freddie.

Suddenly an idea struck him: could Simon and Freddie be in cahoots? Were they trying to frighten him into being a passive partner in Planet, a partner too scared to ask questions, but a partner who would take all the flack in the event they were rumbled? The more Hugo thought about it, the more he became convinced that Freddie was behind the letters, at Simon's behest.

Hugo needed a backstop plan, his eyes fell on a business card given to him by Bruce Harvey at the ball and an idea began to take shape. He reached for the telephone and dialled.

Lydia Buckley

That evening, when Lydia returned home from rehearsal, she phoned Greg at his conference hotel and had a long chat with him. She told him about Tom's idea of buying a rental property for additional income and to rent a property herself. Greg was initially sceptical, but knowing that Tom wouldn't have given her bad advice, suggested that she kept her options open and look at all types of property. Lydia also told Greg about Tom's plans and hopes for the agency and Greg laughed about the possibility of Hugo Marshall having an affair. They chatted about the hotel and Greg's colleagues at the conference, and he mentioned that one of the guys had a birthday tomorrow so they were all going out. They agreed to have a chat on Wednesday evening when Lydia came home after opening night and she could tell him how she had got on with Robbie Parker.

As Lydia settled into bed and decided to read for a while, she saw that a message had come through on her phone and picking it up she was surprised to see that it was from Vinnie:

Hi Babe, not had confirmation from you that you've received all that money? Hope you're ok. Vinnie xx.

Vinnie was thinking about her at eleven o'clock at night? More like thinking about the money! Lydia sighed and quickly typed a reply:

Settlement received, thank you.

Vinnie texted back almost immediately:

Sorry, just realised that it's 11 with you, I'm in Antigua so only 7 xx.

Lydia laughed to herself. Antigua? Vivienne was still in spending mode then.

Good luck with that, Vinnie.

6

Maggie Clark

The following day, Maggie walked into the staff room at WOW! to find Zoe folding freshly laundered towels.

'Morning Zoe,' she said and smiled.

'Morning Maggie. You're early, it's only half past eight.'

'I wanted a chat before the others arrive. Coffee?' Maggie flicked the switch on the kettle.

'No thanks, I've already had one. A chat about what?' Zoe put down the towels and looked questioningly at Maggie.

'About you and Simon.' Maggie looked straight at Zoe, who looked away and picked up the last towel to fold.

'There is no "me and Simon" so there's nothing to say.' Zoe picked up the pile of towels and headed for the door into the salon.

'Wait a minute, Zoe, please – I'm your friend, you can be honest with me.'

Zoe turned around and plonked the towels on the table between them as Maggie continued: 'Elsa was right, wasn't she? You did go to the ball with Simon.'

Maggie moved around the table and caught Zoe's arm. 'These things happen, you're not entirely to blame, but if you're having an affair with Simon, just think of poor Bella.'

Zoe snatched her arm away from Maggie. 'I am being honest with you. In the first place, I did *not* go to the ball with Simon, and secondly, I'm *not* having an affair with him. That's all I'm prepared to say, so just drop it, ok?'

'But Elsa said…'

'I know what Elsa said and she was mistaken.' Zoe picked up the towels and marched out of the staffroom.

The door swung shut behind her with a bang and Maggie winced.

God! What a mess!

There had been real tension between Zoe and Bella since Sunday afternoon and they were barely talking to one another; the other staff members were picking up on it and muttering between themselves. Maggie sighed – well there wasn't anything she could do if that was all Zoe was prepared to say.

The back door opened and Bella entered the staffroom.

'Hello love,' Maggie smiled warmly as she spoke, but her smile faded as she took in Bella's sullen expression. 'You ok?' she asked.

Bella shook her head. 'I haven't slept well since Sunday and I know that Zoe is avoiding me, I just don't know what is going on.' Bella took off her coat and hung it up.

'Have you spoken to Simon about this?'

'No, not really. He won't talk to me whilst he's at work and with the rehearsal last night and another tonight, and the panto opening tomorrow night, there isn't really a chance.' Bella rummaged in her handbag for something.

'I'm sure everything is ok. Elsa was mistaken that's all,' Maggie said kindly.

Bella found what she was looking for and turned to the mirror. As she put in a pair of neat gold earrings, she looked at Maggie through the polished glass. 'Then why is Zoe being… well… weird?'

'I think she feels awkward about what Elsa said and a bit embarrassed at the public revelation of her new man,' Maggie replied. 'The kettle's just boiled, would you like a coffee?'

'Yes, please. So, you don't think she was with Simon then?' Maggie saw the hope in Bella's eyes and turned to make the coffees.

'Zoe said she wasn't there with Simon and he told you that he didn't go at all. We've got to accept what they say, and we've no reason to believe they're lying.' Maggie stirred the coffee and passed a mug to Bella. 'Just put it behind you, Bella, and don't lose any more sleep over it or allow it to spoil your relationship with either Simon or Zoe.'

'Thank you, Maggie. I never thought that Zoe may be feeling awkward or embarrassed, but I guess that might explain why she's a bit off.'

'I'm sure that's all it is. Anyway, let's crack on with the day.' Maggie smiled as Bella's mood visibly lifted and she looked more like her usual, bubbly self.

Maggie picked up her mug and headed towards the salon, mentally praying she was right.

Jonathan Sturdy

Jonathan Sturdy took a deep breath and stretched his back. He had been sitting at his desk for the past two hours going over the estimates and costings for the expansion of his business. When Simon had phoned to confirm that the council had passed both sets of planning permission, Jonathan had been quietly relieved. He had come a long way since his father had died prematurely of a heart attack some ten years ago and left him the family farm. Jonathan had always known that he did not want to be a farmer, out in all weathers for twelve months of the year, so he had gone down a different path with the establishment of Harefield Park. It had been incredibly successful and Jonathan wanted to build more facilities for his guests, to include an indoor/outdoor swimming pool and a clubhouse restaurant with entertainment space.

When Uncle Joshua had decided to retire, he had simply sold the neighbouring Thornberry Farm to Jonathan for one hundred thousand pounds. Uncle Joshua and his late wife had not been blessed with children and now as a widower in his late sixties, he had decided that his nephew and family could have their inheritance early. Uncle Joshua had bought a small retirement home in Ashdale and intended to enjoy his twilight years without worrying about sheep.

Jonathan had recently applied to the council to create both a static caravan park and log cabin lodges on some of the Thornberry land, which would also have access to the new swimming pool and clubhouse. Simon had offered to draw up and submit plans to convert the Thornberry farmhouse and buildings into a small development of four executive homes with large gardens including a pony paddock. Simon estimated that the buildings would then sell to a small developer for around two million pounds, although Jonathan had thought he may develop them himself, as he had done with his own farm buildings.

Jonathon frowned when he thought of Simon. He was very appreciative of Simon's expertise as an architect – he was very good. When Bella had introduced Simon as the man in her life, initially Jonathan had been worried about the large age gap, but he had eventually relaxed and even become friends with him as they discussed the proposed development plans. As time had gone on, however, Jonathan had become uneasy about the issue of the estranged wife with whom Simon still shared a house and for which, apparently, he couldn't find a buyer. There was always a plausible explanation for why the house had not sold: they were stuck in a chain, or the buyers had changed their mind and so on, and all of this was accepted without question by Claire and Bella. Jonathan however, was becoming doubtful and although he could not put his finger on exactly why, he just felt, well uneasy. He kept his thoughts to himself as he knew perfectly well that to cast doubt on Simon's credibility to his daughter and wife would simply cause an upset. But they'd been dating for over a year now and still there was no sign of the impending Saxby-Jones divorce.

There was also another factor – if he was completely honest, he could not understand what Simon saw in Bella. He loved his daughter naturally, but she was a fresh-faced country girl who was perhaps slightly immature, and certainly not the glamorous false-nailed, Botoxed, hair-extensioned executive wife/hostess type of woman he imagined Simon would go for – and that bothered him. Perhaps he was wrong, and for once he hoped he was, because if Simon was taking advantage of his daughter… well, he had better watch out.

Claire seemed to hang on Simon's every word, and Jonathan was unhappy with the somewhat flirty banter between them – he thought it was inappropriate. Claire was clearly flattered and was an attractive woman not so many years older than Simon himself, and Jonathan couldn't help thinking that Simon was using his relationship with Claire as a way of ingratiating himself with the Sturdy family. He had tentatively suggested to Claire on one occasion that he thought Simon should tone things down, but Claire had brushed him aside, telling him not to be so boring and that Simon was just being friendly.

Jonathan had let the matter drop but part of him hoped that the Saxby-Jones house did not sell, that Simon managed to reconcile with his wife and simply buggered off out of their lives, letting Bella down gently. Now that the planning permissions had been granted and Jonathan did not need the architect's expertise any longer, he had no desire to spend any more time than necessary in Simon's company.

Jonathan heard the sound of an approaching car and glanced through the window to see Simon's car turning into their entrance. He saved the programme on his laptop and tidied away some of the papers before standing up, sighing. Hopefully, this would be the last meeting now the plans had been passed.

Jonathan opened his study door and walked silently down the stone-flagged hall in his slippers and could not help but overhear the conversation in the kitchen.

'Good afternoon Claire, how are you? You look lovely today, is that a new dress?' Jonathan rolled his eyes at Simon's words. *Here we go again.*

'Oh, hello, Simon, yes it's a new dress, how clever of you to notice.'

'I thought I hadn't seen it before.'

'Do you always remember what I wear?'

'Actually, I do, I always think you look stunning.'

There was the sound of girlish laughter. 'Oh, Simon really, you haven't seen me first thing in the morning in my pyjamas.'

There was a slight pause before Simon spoke with a meaningful tone. 'No, I haven't, have I?'

Jonathan frowned and strode into the kitchen. 'Oh, there you are darling,' Claire said lightly. 'I'm just making some tea, or would you prefer coffee, Simon? I've a lovely Victoria sponge cake as well, would you like a slice?'

'Coffee for me please and a slice of cake would be lovely Claire, thank you,' Simon replied smoothly.

'Good afternoon, Simon,' Jonathan said purposefully and held out his hand. Simon responded and shook it in a manly greeting.

'Jonathan, good news about the planning, eh?'

'Tea for you, Jonathan?' asked Claire as she busied herself with cups, saucers and plates.

'Yes, tea, please. Very good news indeed, it means that—'

'Slice of cake, Jonathan?' Claire poured boiling water firstly into a warmed teapot and then into a small cafetière before noisily putting the kettle back onto the Aga. Jonathan waited until Claire walked to the other side of the kitchen and opened the fridge door.

'Go on through to the office, Simon, we'll talk in there.'

Simon nodded, left the kitchen and headed down the hallway.

Claire returned with a bottle of milk. 'Did you want some cake Jonathan?' she said a little more firmly as she filled a milk jug.

'Claire, we are not having a nice little afternoon tea-party, Simon is here on business… and I do wish you wouldn't encourage him to flirt with you, it's quite shameless.'

'Don't be silly darling, I don't flirt with him, he's almost a son-in-law and we get along really well. Now do you want a slice of cake or not?' Claire picked up a cake knife and began to cut her Victoria sponge into neat slices. 'I'm afraid I can't join you as I've arranged to go into Harrogate – I'm taking Marjorie and we're meeting Celia Marshall at the Palm Court Café. Poor Marjorie has found herself on Celia Marshall's new committee and has begged me to join them.'

'Why "poor Marjorie"?'

'Well Celia Marshall and her husband Hugo are to be the next mayor and lady mayoress and Celia is already setting up her fundraising committee, but Marjorie didn't want to be a part of it.'

'Well, couldn't she just have said no?'

'She did, more or less – actually she said she didn't think she would have the time, but Celia simply said, "Nonsense, you'll enjoy it so I'll include you and see you on Tuesday at three!"'

'So how does that involve you?'

'Marjorie wants me there to support her – she couldn't cope with Celia otherwise.' Claire finished preparing the tray. 'Darling, I've asked three times now if you would like a slice of cake.'

Jonathan sighed. 'No thank you to cake, just a cup of tea… and mugs would have been fine.' He looked at the tea tray of matching china complete with silver cake forks and napkins.

'Nonsense, mugs are only for us in the mornings, you can't expect guests to drink tea out of mugs in the afternoon.' She shook her head in horror at the thought.

'I'll take it through,' said Jonathan firmly. 'You get off to Harrogate.'

'Thank you, darling,' Claire smiled winningly at her husband and hurried into the hallway. Jonathan followed her with her handbag which she had left in the kitchen. She buttoned up a beautifully cut camel coat and teamed it with a cream and black silk scarf, slipped into a pair of black court shoes and took her handbag from Jonathan before heading out of the door. 'Say goodbye to Simon for me,' she called.

Jonathan went back to the kitchen and ignoring the prepared tea tray, poured a mug of coffee for Simon and a mug of tea for himself and took them both to his study.

'How is your father doing?' Jonathan asked as he placed the mugs carefully on his desk.

'Very well, much improved and thank you for asking,' Simon replied. He had taken off his overcoat and was sitting down.

'I want to thank you for all your work in preparing and submitting the plans for the Thornberry house and buildings, I'm extremely grateful. Was it a difficult decision for the planning committee?' began Jonathan as he passed a mug of tea to Simon, who looked slightly surprised at the change of crockery and lack of cake.

Simon talked in more detail about how the planning meeting had evolved, the points raised by the committee and the final decision to approve the plans. When he had finished talking, he put down his mug, cleared his throat and slightly changed the subject, 'I wondered if I may be of assistance with the next step.' Simon sat back and crossed one leg over the other. 'I would like to suggest Lewis Marshall as your agent for selling the Thornberry project. They're a local firm with good contacts for small developers and I believe they would take a smaller commission than the agents in Harrogate.'

'Well, to be honest, Simon, I hadn't thought of selling the Thornberry project at this stage,' Jonathan replied.

'What?' Simon sat up, then relaxed and smiled as he noticed Jonathan's surprise at his reaction. 'How do you mean, not selling?'

'I intend to employ the same builders who renovated my barns, then sell the houses one by one.'

'Really Jonathan? I'm surprised, as I thought you would have wanted to get on with your static caravan park, pool and clubhouse.'

'Oh, I do, but that will be done by different builders.'

'But they're both huge projects, how will you manage them both at the same time?'

'My son Joe, will be home by the summer and he'll come on board with me; he can take on the clubhouse etc. and I can oversee the house renovations,' Jonathan said easily.

'Might I make a suggestion?'

When Jonathan nodded, Simon carried on speaking: 'Why not sell Thornbury as it is to a small developer now? You would probably get in the region of about two million by the middle to end of April.'

'So soon?' Jonathan was surprised at the timing.

'Yes, usually developers have to submit bids by a certain date, then with the help of your agent, you then decide which one you want.'

'It all sounds very simple.'

'It is very simple, and you would then have the capital and time to invest in the expansion of Harefield and you'd be able to open the new site and amenities quicker.'

'I see...'

'Whereas if you borrow to build Thornberry, you would be waiting for around twelve months before you could market the houses and then you've all the hassle of buyers with mortgages, etcetera.'

'That's true, but I would make more profit by doing Thornberry myself.'

'Ahh, but would you? Although you could expect around six million in final sales, the project would cost two million or so to build *and* you would be paying for the loan in the meantime, which would eat into your profit. Selling Thornberry now makes more financial sense.' Simon smiled pleasantly.

Jonathan stood up and walked to the window, he looked out over green fields and pondered Simon's words. He knew perfectly well that selling Thornberry as a development project now was the best option, but for some very strange and perverted reason, he did not want to agree with Simon immediately. 'Hmmm, I do see your point, but I'll think it over and discuss it with Joe and see what his opinion is.'

'Come on Jonathan, it makes business sense to sell now, whatever Joe says. After all, he's only a kid straight out of uni.'

Jonathan bristled at Simon's words, his son may be only 'straight out of uni' but he was an intelligent young man and fully invested in the Harefield Park business. Jonathan was looking forward to having him full-time in the business.

'Joe will be a full partner in the business and this expansion was mostly his idea, Simon, I value his opinion.' Jonathan was quite firm.

'Quite, and I'm sure he'll see that selling Thornberry now makes the most sense.' Simon smiled and stood up. 'Let me know if you want to discuss anything more.'

'Actually, there is one more thing.' Jonathan had suddenly made up his mind and turned to face Simon. 'What are your intentions regarding Bella?'

'I beg your pardon?' Simon's smile faded immediately.

'What are your intentions regarding Bella?' repeated Jonathan.

'I'm not sure I follow you? What do you mean "What are my intentions?" Isn't that a somewhat old-fashioned question?' Simon asked lightly, as though unsure as to where this conversation was heading.

'My daughter appears to be in love with you, but you're still a married man with no sign of becoming unmarried. I'm concerned for her, naturally,' Jonathan spoke quite pleasantly with no aggression and Simon visibly relaxed.

'There's absolutely no need to worry, Jonathan, my intentions are quite honourable. Once my house has sold, the divorce will be settled and finalised. I can then explain everything to my father; I don't want to upset the old man before then, especially now that he's had this heart attack. I'll be able to spend more time with Bella after it's all sorted.' Simon spoke whilst he put on his overcoat and found his leather driving gloves in the pockets.

Jonathan had the distinct impression that Simon was avoiding looking at him. Although, once he had picked up his briefcase and found his car keys, he looked at Jonathan and smiled:

'Anyway, I'm pleased that I was able to help you with the plans and we got the right result. I must go now as I've another appointment to get to.' He held out his hand to shake Jonathan's. 'No need to see me out, I know the way.' Simon turned and left the office.

Jonathan listened to his footsteps echoing down the hall and into the kitchen; he heard the outside door open and close, and only then did he realise that he was holding his breath.

He waited by the window and watched Simon drive away.

Why do I feel there's something dishonest about you?

Councillor Hugo Marshall

Hugo was restless; he'd been unsettled since yesterday's meeting with Simon and Freddie. He hadn't slept well either and Celia had banished him to the guest room, which if he was honest, had been better for thinking.

He paced back and forth across the front of his desk. To say he was disappointed that Simon was opposed to dissolving the partnership was an understatement – he was gutted. Hugo had thought that by cutting his ties with Planet Properties, he would be free to enjoy his mayoral year without worrying. But now, his worst dreams had been realised; Simon's latest project wasn't only ridiculously ambitious, but it was on the outskirts of Ashdale itself, and the very nature of the size of the proposed development would undoubtedly attract unwelcome attention.

Their previous ventures had attracted a few grumbles locally but because they were outside the borough, nobody on the local council had even known about them. Simon was pushing things too far this time and Hugo knew he had to stop it somehow. He reviewed his options again: (a) dissolve the partnership at Planet Properties – well that was clearly not going to happen; (b) find and speak to Simon's client at Thornberry Farm and warn him – which would inevitably cause a massive fallout with Simon (and probably Freddie) resulting in the spread of malicious rumours about the mayor-elect's business conduct; (c) cross his fingers and hope the revised planning application for the eighty or so dwellings would be refused – that was far too hazardous and unlikely, as the council were under pressure to provide more housing; which left (d) leave or sell the estate agency.

Hugo had considered option (d) late into the night and the more he thought about it, the more he liked it. He just wasn't sure how Charles would feel, but if he picked up the phone and made the call, he might find out. He made a decision, and picking up his phone he called Charles's mobile. He looked at this watch, two-thirty – he was probably at the golf club.

'Charles! Hugo here, I need a bit of a word, is now a good time?'

'I suppose so, will it take long?' was Charles' gruff reply.

'It depends really; look you know my stint as mayor is coming up, well I've had a meeting at the council offices recently and it transpires that I shall be busier with engagements than I had originally anticipated, which means that I'll not be able to spend much time here at the agency…' Hugo picked up a pen and idly began to doodle on his blotter.

'I thought we'd agreed that young Tom would handle things.'

'Yes, we did, but the thing is, Charles, that I really want to retire altogether, sell the agency – take a leaf out of your book, that sort of thing…' Hugo held his breath for the reply.

'Really? Good grief! That's a bit drastic, isn't it? Don't know about selling up, Hugo, we get quite a tidy income from it.'

'Yes, you do Charles, for very little effort as well, if I may say. Look, I'm not getting any younger and I think Tom might buy it. He's a damn fine agent, and, if I'm not mistaken, he's been offered other positions from our rivals. We wouldn't want to lose him.' Hugo continued doodling.

'Well quite, but selling up?'

'I think we should approach Tom and see what he says. After all, I'll still be around to hand over and so on, but I'm quite serious Charles,' Hugo chewed the end of the pen.

'Yes, I can see that. Well, I'll tell you what, let me think it over and we can get together after Beatrice and I come back from our cruise at the end of March, eh?'

'But that's six weeks away, anything can happen in six weeks!' The pen clattered onto the desk.

'Hugo, it's not the sort of thing one can rush into, there are lots of things to consider.'

'No, not really Charles, you'll get a lump sum from the business and the property, which you can invest elsewhere and get an income from, that's all there's to it as far as you're concerned.'

'Well, I don't know about that Hugo.'

'Charles, when was the last time you even came to the agency, let alone saw a client?' Hugo gabbled.

'I've been very busy with other projects actually.'

'Exactly! And now, I would like other projects of my own.' Hugo was aware that he was sweating and that the hand holding his phone was shaking.

'What does my sister have to say about this?'

'I haven't spoken to Celia about it. I don't believe it concerns her particularly.'

'It's all a bit sudden this – are you in some sort of trouble Hugo?'

'Don't be ridiculous, I've given the matter a great deal of thought actually and my mind is made up. I'm going to retire so you either buy me out or I sell my share to someone else!' Hugo tapped his finger firmly on the desk and caught the tip of the pen, which shot off the desk onto the floor.

'I don't want to work with someone else. Look at least give me a few days to think this over, Hugo, to look at all the alternatives.'

'There *are* no alternatives Charles, I want to sell and that's that!' Hugo picked up a pencil.

'I can't talk further about it here, we need to at least get the business appraised. Look, make an appointment with our accountant to get his viewpoint on the way forward. Let's at least get some sound financial advice.'

'Thank you, Charles, I'll do that but please, consider what I've said.'

Hugo let out a long breath, it wasn't quite the conversation he had envisaged but at least Charles had agreed to a meeting with the accountant.

Charles Lewis

Charles ended the call abruptly and turned to his companion. 'He wants to sell the agency, damn fool!'

Carlton Banks sighed. 'Is that so bad?' he asked.

'It's a good business and a good return. Why on earth would we want to sell it?'

'Do you know, it might be of interest to me.' Carlton steepled his fingers.

'Whatever for, Carlton? Aztec is a development company.'

'Yes, but we build houses, don't we?' Carlton winked. 'It could provide another way to keep more of what we make. I'll talk it over with my son-in-law, Simon, see what he has to say.'

'Do you discuss everything with Simon?'

'Most of the business ideas, yes. I'm expecting him to take over in a year or so when I finally retire, and an estate agency could be a new division within Aztec.'

Charles shrugged,

'Let me know what he says, it will be interesting to hear his views.'

Councillor Hugo Marshall

Hugo felt that, overall, the conversation hadn't been too bad – more positive than not and a request to see the accountant was a good sign. He just needed to hurry things along so that the deal could be done before Simon started on the revised plans for Thornberry Farm. He made a call to the accountants and confirmed an appointment for himself and Charles for Friday afternoon.

Hugo then sat back in his chair and realised he was quite breathless and his heart was beating fairly quickly. He took a few moments to calm down and then thought about his meeting planned for this afternoon with Bruce Harvey. The idea of a small but lucrative Spanish property consultancy appealed to Hugo, he would be able to use the current office for a reasonable rent from Tom along with advertising in the windows to lure… no encourage, folk to buy Spanish property. A lot of people talked about retiring to Spain and the property market there was very stable now and as far as Hugo knew, no other local agency had Spanish property on their books.

Hugo had money tucked away and he fancied the idea of buying a place and renting it out as a holiday let when he wasn't using it himself. Celia would know nothing – it would be his secret little nest egg. This was definitely the way forward – sell the agency to Tom, which would prevent Planet Properties from buying Thornberry Farm and therefore put an end to Simon's project, resulting ultimately in the dissolution of the Planet Properties partnership. Hugo felt positively perky as he told Felicity he had a client to see and would be gone for the rest of the afternoon.

Nick Bradley

Nick Bradley put down the plastic crate he was carrying and studied the list of props required for Act One. He was surprised how much he was enjoying the role of assistant stage manager given that he had not taken it on through a desire to be part of an amateur dramatic group. When Graham had asked if he would be his assistant, he had seen it as an opportunity to be closer to someone he was interested in.

The Ashdale Players had made him feel very welcome and included him in the general banter, and he particularly liked Lydia, the prompt. She was a new recruit as well, so they chatted together during tea breaks and swapped titbits of gossip.

As Nick carefully put the last item into the crate, he heard angry voices outside the prop-room door:

'My relationship with Bella is at rock bottom, thanks to you, Simon – and it's created an atmosphere in my salon.'

'I'm not concerned about your salon or your relationship with Bella, as I told you on Saturday night, nothing will change in the immediate future.'

Nick froze, he was trapped in the awful situation of either eavesdropping on a private conversation or making a noise to alert them that someone was in the prop room.

'Well that's just where you're wrong, Simon. I'll keep silent until after the panto, and then I expect you to come clean and speak to Bella on Sunday, because if you don't, then I'll tell her everything on Monday.'

'Now, just you listen to me Zoe, you'll say nothing at all… to anyone… at any time, do you understand?'

'I understand perfectly, but I'll tell Bella on Monday if you haven't spoken to her on Sunday – do *you* understand?'

'If you breathe one word of this, I'll not hesitate to do what I said. Do you really want to take that risk?'

'I don't believe you would or could do it, so don't threaten me.'

'Listen, you silly bitch …'

'Let go of my arm!'

Nick reached for the door handle in alarm and then stopped as he heard Maggie's voice.

'Zoe? Are you there? Oh, hi, Simon… Desmond wants everyone in the hall now before we start.'

Zoe and Simon said no more and Nick heard their footsteps receding. He quickly followed to join the others in the hall.

Desmond stood at the front of the stage, his cast and crew before him. 'Lovely people,' he began, 'I just wanted to thank you all for the hard work each and every one of you has put in to bring this panto alive. Tonight, we'll run through Act One without stopping as though it were a live performance; we've wardrobe, make-up, scenery and other front-of-house in the audience so you'll have some authentic reactions to enhance your performance. We'll have an interval so you can have a drink and I'll give you some feedback. Tomorrow, opening night – can you believe it – we'll have a reporter in the audience to give a review of the panto for Friday's edition of the local paper, so let's make our first show an especially good one. Finally, Kate Simpson has agreed, once again, to put on a tea for cast and crew after the Saturday matinée in her café. Ok – let's do it. Places everyone!' There were a few whoops and cheers as the cast and crew took up their places. Lydia settled herself in the prompt's chair and as Nick passed by, he put his hand on her shoulder:

'See you for a coffee in the interval?' he asked her quietly.

Lydia nodded and smiled.

Act One went without a hitch and when the curtains closed, Nick and Graham swiftly changed the scenery before heading out front for a drink. Lydia was in the front row talking to Simon and, as Nick approached, she indicated a mug of coffee on the chair next to her. As Nick sat down, Simon smiled and acknowledged him:

'Hi Nick, I was just asking Lydia how she came to join the Players, what about you?' Nick took a mouthful of coffee and looked at the panto baddie, Abanazzar. The friendly and cultured voice he now spoke with was very different to the villainous voice he used on stage. Nick would have put it down to great acting skills had he not heard that same Abanazzar voice used in anger with Zoe earlier.

'Actually, I was persuaded by Graham,' Nick replied, nodding in the direction of the Stage Manager, 'we work in the same office at MegaMart.'

'Oh really? What do you do at MegaMart?' Simon asked politely as he glanced distractedly around the room.

'I'm a graduate trainee. Megamart have a very good programme for graduates, starting at smaller branches, progressing to larger stores and, hopefully, up the ranks,' Nick told the back of Simon's head.

'I didn't know that. Where did you graduate?' Simon became a little more interested.

'Derby, I did a degree in business management.'

'You don't say! I went to Derby too, although I studied architectural design with business management. I wonder if the place has changed much. I remember one of my professors, Butterworth – we called him "Bumbly Butterworth" – don't suppose he's still there...' Simon thought for a moment, 'no, he must be dead by now, he was getting on a bit even back then.'

'I expect there have been many changes over the years, the uni itself is much larger now.'

'Yes, when I was there, studies aside, there was an incredible social scene – wild parties until dawn some weekends, and so many friends – male and female, especially female... if you get my drift.' Simon raised an eyebrow meaningfully and Lydia looked a little uncomfortable.

'I had some great friends too, but I seem to have lost touch with most of my them as some of the students went on to gap years and travelled, or even got married, but I needed to find work straight away,' Nick said a little sadly.

'Oh, I didn't keep in touch with anyone after I left Derby.' Simon waved his hand dismissively.

'There was a relationship I almost committed to, but it turned out we wanted different things, so I said goodbye, although I sometimes wonder if that was the right decision.' Nick stared into his coffee mug.

'Well, I would say you made the right decision to move on, hopefully to a promising career,' said Simon brightly. 'I made the decision not to keep in touch as I didn't want to be tied down. Too many of my fellow students got themselves entangled in relationships. Love 'em and leave 'em, sow your wild oats, etcetera, that's my advice.' Simon clapped Nick on the shoulder in a manly gesture.

Nick tried hard not to wince. 'My mother also went to Derby, she must have been there around the same time as you, maybe you remember her.'

'Good grief, Nick, there were hundreds of girls there, I doubt I would remember her.' Simon looked up and smiled as Bella appeared. 'Hi Bella. Nice chatting with you, Nick. Must go, I need a word with Dessie-boy.' Simon stood up, took Bella's arm and steered her away towards Desmond.

Nick looked at Lydia. 'He didn't even ask my mother's name. He's just not interested in anyone but himself,' he said as he watched Simon and Bella walk away.

'Did your mother ever mention Simon? I mean, is it likely that they met?' replied Lydia.

Nick didn't answer immediately, he just stared after Simon. Lydia followed his stare and saw Simon turn slightly and glance in their direction before turning back to listen to what Desmond was saying.

'I don't like that man, he can be a nasty piece of work,' Nick muttered as he turned back to Lydia.

'How do you mean?'

'Earlier this evening, I heard Simon and Zoe arguing. He wanted Zoe to keep quiet about something and she wanted him to come clean – it was about Bella.' Nick repeated what he had heard whilst in the prop room. 'Anyway it ended with him grabbing hold of her arm and calling her "a silly bitch". I was just about to intervene when someone, I think it was Maggie, called them back into the hall.'

'Do you think it had anything to do with that upset on Sunday, you know, when Elsa dropped her bombshell?' asked Lydia.

'Possibly, I really don't know, but there's definitely an unpleasant undercurrent involving Simon, Zoe and Bella.'

Lydia quietly agreed but suggested they keep it to themselves until after Saturday.

Nick glanced at his watch: 'I've to go and get ready to start again. Thanks for the coffee.' He stood up and disappeared behind the closed curtains.

Lydia sighed. It would seem that Zoe *had* seen Simon at the ball and that was the likely cause of their argument.

'Ok, panto people, let's crack on with Act Two.' Desmond's voice broke into her thoughts and she carried their mugs back to the kitchen before taking her place behind the prompter's screen.

7

Annabelle Saxby-Jones

Annabelle Saxby-Jones pressed the power button on her laptop, and picking up her coffee mug wandered over to the huge bi fold doors that separated the kitchen diner from the garden. Looking out into the misty dampness of the morning, she could not even see the end of their garden. Annabelle and Simon lived in a large four-bedroomed detached house in Harrogate on an 'executive' development. The house was too large for just the two of them, but Annabelle desperately hoped that soon Simon would agree to start a family; she was thirty-five and her biological clock was ticking. All their friends had children or careers and Annabelle had neither. If she was honest, she was just *bore*d – her only friends were wives of Simon's friends and whilst she didn't mind meeting for lunches or dinner parties, they just talked about their jobs or their children.

However, things were about to change and it was all because of the recent Valentine Ball. Simon had been so busy looking after the soap celebrity – Fiona Whatshername – that he had hardly spoken to Annabelle, so when Lady Worthington came over to talk to her she had been quite relieved. Lady Worthington was very elegant, her dark hair expertly fixed in a soft up-do, her make-up subtle and her skin quite youthful. She must have been in her fifties, as her eldest son was around Annabelle's age, but she could still easily pass for forty-five. They'd spoken about the fundraising events that Lady Worthington organised with her committee and Annabelle had been quietly envious, so when she'd been asked if she would be interested in joining the committee, Annabelle had jumped at the opportunity. Elegant, ladylike and glamorous was just the look that Annabelle desired and she resolved there and then, if having a family wasn't on the cards, she would reinvent herself.

Talking to Verity later in the evening, when Annabelle mentioned how youthful Lady Worthington looked, Verity had laughed and replied that it was all fake – false eyelashes, hair extensions, Botox, etcetera, and Annabelle had been shocked. Reflecting on the conversation on Sunday however, Annabelle had decided that she would give herself a makeover starting with eyelashes. She Googled lash extensions and was delighted to find that Lush Lashes in Harrogate was highly recommended, so on Monday she had called in for a patch test and was now on standby for a cancellation appointment.

On Monday evening, Annabelle had attended her first meeting with Lady Worthington's committee and yesterday an email from Lady Worthington had arrived asking her to prepare quotes from the suggestions she had made for the summer garden party. Annabelle was so excited and Simon had been pleased for her as well, he had even kissed her goodbye this morning and hugged her.

She glanced at the laptop expecting a bright screen, but it was black. 'Damn', she muttered and putting the mug onto the kitchen island, she made her way through the large polished marble-tiled hall to Simon's study. The lead for the laptop lay on the desk and as she picked it up she noticed the message light on the telephone flashing. Annabelle pressed the Play button and heard a man's voice: 'Hello Simon, Hugo here – well I expect you're probably on your way to work now so I'll call you on your mobile.'

Annabelle pressed Delete and returned to the kitchen where she plugged in the laptop and watched as it booted up. Sighing, she picked up the abandoned coffee mug and glanced at the clock on her way to the kitchen sink. Tasheka was late this morning.

Tasheka Dixon was the most dazzling cleaner Annabelle had ever come across. She usually wore black jeans in winter or black shorts in summer, always teamed with a brightly coloured, oversized T-shirt and either a black cardigan, jacket or raincoat, depending on the weather. Tasheka loved bright colours and her long nails usually matched her T-shirt, a combination which contrasted with her chocolate-coloured skin. Originally from Leeds, Tasheka had married a local man, settled down in Ashdale and had formed The Clean Team – Housekeeping and Domestic Assistance, with her equally colourful sister, Louella. Annabelle looked forward to Tasheka's visits, she loved her animated personality and attitude with a capital 'A'.

As she rinsed her coffee cup under the tap, there was a crunch of tyres on the gravel and a lime green hatchback ground to a halt. Even from her kitchen, Annabelle could the steady *thud, thud, thud*, emanating from the in-car stereo. The beat stopped abruptly and Annabelle watched the curvaceous woman slide out of the car, open the passenger door behind the driver's seat and pull out a bulky shopping bag. Tasheka clutched her raincoat together with her spare hand and used her ample hips to slam the car door closed before tottering across the gravel in black high-heeled boots. Annabelle smiled; Tasheka looked stylish and well-groomed and today she wore a hot-pink T-shirt with tight black jeans which looked fabulous against her dark skin – she certainly did not look like a cleaner. Annabelle returned to the breakfast bar where her laptop had just finished booting up as the back door opened and then closed with a bang.

‘Morning Mrs S-J, how are you today?’

Annabelle opened her mouth to reply but did not get an opportunity to speak as Tasheka carried on talking: ‘I’m sorry I’m late but I’ve had a situation this morning.’

‘A situation?’ Annabelle looked up from her laptop and waited as Tasheka removed her coat and boots before sliding her feet into a pair of pink, sparkly pumps.

‘Mmm-hmm, let me tell you!’ Tasheka pursed her mouth with attitude and pointed with her right index finger in emphasis, ‘It was a slow drive this morning outta Ashdale on account of the driver at the front was in no hurry.’ The finger wagged rapidly left and right as Tasheka got into her stride. ‘There was a small truck between me an’ this slow car, an’ as we got up close to that T-junction where you can turn right to Harrogate or left to Stonebridge, this car had no clue as to where he was goin’ an’ he kinda stopped and then started.’ Tasheka paused to take a breath, ‘Well, the truck must’ve nudged the car, ’cos the next thing I see, is an older guy gettin’ outta the car and a young guy gettin’ outta the truck and they start waving their arms about and having a hoohah.’ Taskeka waved her arms to graphically demonstrate her story as Annabelle’s eyes opened wide.

‘So, what did you do?’ she asked, knowing that Tasheka *had* done something.

‘Well, I gets outta my car and walked right up to these two guys who were cussing an’ carrying on an’ I said: ‘Can I stop you both right there’? Tasheka’s black ringlets shook as her head moved from side to side with each syllable, her hands were on her hips, ‘I spoke to the old guy first an’ I was real polite when I tells him, ‘Sir, you need to consult your map or sat-nav before you start drivin’ so’s you know which direction you need to go in.’ Then I says to the young guy from the truck, ‘An’ you need to be respectful of seniors an’ cut them some slack. Didn’t your momma teach you no manners?’

Annabelle let out her breath. ‘You said that?’ she gasped.

'I sure did, an' then I told them that if they wanted to carry on with their discussion, maybe they wanted to take it over to the layby across the road so's the rest of us can get on with our day.'

'What happened then?'

'Well we all jus' got back in our vehicles, the old guy turned left an' the rest of us just turned right, an' here I'm.' Tasheka was slightly breathless and her ample bosom quivered under the T-shirt.

Annabelle burst out laughing. 'Oh Tasheka, only you could get away with saying all that.'

'Well, it's just as well I did, or we would've been sat there all day. Now I gotta get on with my work as I'm already behind.' Tasheka pulled the vacuum out of the cupboard in the utility room and took it upstairs.

Ten minutes later, Annabelle sat at her laptop as Tasheka hoovered upstairs, the ideas for the garden party flowing as she Googled Punch and Judy entertainers, cheerleaders, fairground rides, health and safety requirements, licences, and marquees. After an hour or so, she stretched and stood up. She could hear Tasheka singing upstairs obviously plugged into her phone, the hoovering finished. Annabelle wished she could have witnessed the 'situation' at the junction this morning and smiled at the thought of the two men being confronted by a sassy and forthright woman. If only she had some of Tasheka's attitude and confidence, maybe Simon would take more notice of her.

Things had not been great between her and Simon for some time now; she understood that rehearsals were taking up a lot of his time, but she hardly saw him. Tonight was opening night so perhaps when the pantomime was over they could take a holiday somewhere warm and have some special time together. Suddenly the Spice Girls rendition of *Who Do You Think You Are?* interrupted her thoughts as her phone burst into life, the caller identity telling her it was Lush Lashes.

'Hello?'

'Hello, is that Mrs Saxby-Jones?'

'Yes, speaking.'

'Oh good, this is Caroline from Lush Lashes and I know this is very short notice, but I wondered if you would be free at 12.30 today, as we've just had a cancellation?'

'Oh, yes, that would be perfect I'll be there then, thank you.' Annabelle ended the call and smiled.

The transformation had begun.

The singing from upstairs suddenly stopped and Annabelle switched on the kettle; it was time for a coffee break.

Tasheka sat opposite Annabelle at the table,

'I meant to ask how the ball went, did you have a great time?' she asked.

'It was ok, they raised a lot of money,' Annabelle answered and shrugged her shoulders.

'What do you mean – "ok"? Didn't you have a real nice evening? Did you and Mr S-J have some quality time?'

Annabelle shook her head. 'No, not really, I didn't see much of Simon as he was so busy with VIPs.'

'But I hope you got some smoochin' time,' Tasheka persisted.

'No, Simon's not really into dancing – the evening was pretty much a business thing for him.'

Tasheka frowned. 'I s'pose you wore that lovely blue dress hangin' upstairs?'

'I did, it's my favourite evening dress.'

'I bet you look *real* nice in that dress.' Tasheka clicked her fingers, the hot-pink nails catching Annabelle's eye.

'Yes, that's the problem, I just look nice,' muttered Annabelle.

'An' what's wrong with looking nice?' Tasheka put down her mug.

'I don't want to just look "nice" I want Simon to notice me,' Annabelle blurted out. 'I haven't seen much of him over the last few months – he's so busy with clients, and then, of course there's the panto, so we don't get too much quality time.' Suddenly she felt her eyes watering and tears threatened to spill. 'I'm not even sure he still loves me,' she whispered before a tear escaped to roll down her cheek.

'What? Now why would you think that?' Tasheka frowned.

'Because we're not close. I feel like a housekeeper. There's no romance. I'm just too nice and I'm scared he might find someone else…' Annabelle sniffed and realised she was whining as she pulled a tissue from her sleeve. 'Sorry, I didn't mean to get all tearful, just ignore me.' She took a deep breath and tried to pull herself together.

'So if you don't wanna look all nice, I guess you wanna look all hot an' sexy.' Tasheka shook her shoulders seductively and her breasts jiggled under her pink T-shirt.

'Oh no, no!' Annabelle was horrified at the thought. 'I want to look glamorous. Simon doesn't like hot and sexy.'

Taskeka laughed. 'Listen honey, *all* men like hot an' sexy, but you gotta know how to push their buttons, you know what I'm, sayin'?'

'I'm going to change. I'm having Russian lashes done today and I'm volunteering with Lady Worthington. Simon was so pleased about that,' Annabelle gabbled and then stopped suddenly as Tasheka's eyebrows shot up.

'Russian lashes and volunteering with Lady W ain't gonna inject no romance Mrs S-J. Come on now, surely things ain't that bad. Simon married you, didn't he? Of course he still loves you, it's about bein' together and sharin' life. Me an' my Mikey jus' enjoy the times we get together, you know? When our little Shanice is in bed, that's when we talk 'n' stuff.'

'We– he, I mean it's rare that we – you know… get intimate, and I don't think he… well… fancies me anymore,' Annabelle stammered.

Tasheka jerked back in surprise. 'You mean you don' get all hot 'n' sweaty twice a week?'

Annabelle shook her head.

The pink-nailed forefinger appeared again as Tasheka pursed her lips and sighed: 'Mrs S-J, may I speak frankly wit' you?'

Annabelle nodded her head tentatively, wondering what was coming next.

Tasheka stood up. 'Now see here,' she began, 'we are both women, but very diff'rent women. I'm a voluptuous black woman with *curves* an' a booty that my Mikey appreciates, you know what I'm sayin'?' Annabelle started to shake her head negatively then, as Tasheka effected a twerk movement, the penny dropped and Annabelle vigorously nodded. 'He tells me I'm juno ... err... something.' Tasheka paused and frowned as she struggled to recall the word.

'Junoesque?' suggested Annabelle, 'it means a shapely figure, like the Goddess Juno.'

'A goddess eh? Yeah well, I guess that's what he does mean. Anyways, so men like my Mikey wants dark and juno... esk, but your man, Mr S-J he like jus' the opposite. He wants tall, blonde and... well, I guess you would say model-esk, you get my meanin'?'

Annabelle nodded, 'I mean Mr S-J obviously likes English rose and ladylike, but...' Tasheka paused for dramatic effect, 'when you get into the bedroom, men want hot, hot, hot – every time. You need to be like a ho!'

Annabelle blinked, 'A hoe? You mean stiff, like a garden rake?' She said incredulously.

'A rake? What the heck you talkin' about?' Tasheka's ringlets shook as her head moved with every syllable 'I meant a "ho", you know, an escort like my cousin Karenna, she makes a good livin' outta escortin'.'

Annabelle's mouth dropped open as she blushed. 'Your cousin is a...?' She began.

'She sure is and she's real good,' Tasheka confirmed. 'So my advice to you is to make sure that Mr S-J looks forward to comin' home every night on account of you don' want him gettin' his delights someplace else.'

Annabelle nodded, then frowned and shook her head. 'But… well… err…'

'Now if Mr S-J is being a little backward in coming forward, if you know what I mean, then you need to help him out an' make sure you're giving off the right signals.'

'You mean I should initiate things?' Annabelle said carefully.

'Oh no, no, no honey.' the finger wagged again. 'I mean you just gotta look the part – you gotta be a ho in private and he'll take it from there.'

'Look the part? A whore?'

'You need to visit, Lovely Lingerie, my friend's shop in Leeds. You tell Orlena that I sent you and she'll know that you mean business an' you ain't jus' lookin', you know what I'm sayin'? You gotta learn to make the most of what your mama gave you.'

Annabelle nodded and closed her mouth, which had fallen open. 'I think I know what you're saying, thanks, Tasheka,' she said carefully.

'Now, I gotta get back to work.' Tasheka drained her coffee mug, put it beside the sink and disappeared back to her cleaning.

Annabelle Googled the shop in Leeds – the pictures of red silk and black lace wispy pieces were, indeed, just what she needed, but some of the other items would definitely be staying on the shelves.

Lydia Buckley

Lydia carried her bottle of water to one of the treatment rooms. She enjoyed her few hours a week at Lush Lashes – Louise was a great person to work for and the reputation of the business was second to none. Lydia was appreciative of the work, and the flexibility of hours suited them both along with the fact that Lydia could be available at short notice. Lydia, in turn, enjoyed chatting to the clients, or rather listening to them; she found a wealth of gossip and characters, most of which she could use in her next novel. However, her next client might prove more interesting than most; it was Annabelle Saxby-Jones. When Caroline said that she had managed to fill the vacancy left by the cancellation, Lydia had been pleased, but, having learned it was Mrs Saxby-Jones, she felt somewhat apprehensive.

Annabelle didn't know that Lydia knew about Simon and Bella and there was no reason for her to find out. Lydia decided that she would just be professional, as usual, and listen to her client. Whatever the situation between Simon, Annabelle and Bella, it was none of her business, and after the panto, she likely wouldn't see them until later in the year at the read-through for the next production.

Lydia walked through to the reception area which was decorated in hues of grey, mocha and cream and looked at the blonde woman sitting there. She looked familiar, but Lydia couldn't think where she had seen her. She took her client to the treatment room and settled her on the couch. Soon, the eye pads were in place, and when Annabelle was comfortable with them with her eyes shut, Lydia began.

'Are you wanting long lashes for a special occasion or a more practical application that you would return for infills on a regular basis?'

'Oh, I would probably return for infills, I want them to be permanent.'

'That's absolutely fine.' Lydia began to make marks on the eye pads. 'What made you decide to have them now?'

'Well, I was at a ball last Saturday and I noticed how all the ladies looked so glamorous and I felt rather plain, to be honest.'

'Was it the Valentine Ball at Ashdale Hall?'

'Yes, it was.'

'I was there and I think we met.'

'Do you know, I thought you looked familiar. It was in the ladies' cloakroom wasn't it?'

'Yes, I remember you were looking for your friend but had just missed her?'

'Oh, that would be Verity, with the black lace dress and ankle boots.' Annabelle giggled.

'Yes, I remember her quite well,' said Lydia ironically.

'Everyone remembers Verity; she tends to stand out in a crowd. Did you enjoy the evening?' Annabelle asked.

'I did, well we all did. I was with a group of friends. How about you?' Lydia began to apply the lashes and she sensed that Annabelle had relaxed.

'It was a pleasant enough evening I suppose.'

'Pleasant enough? You don't sound as if you really enjoyed it though. Didn't you have a good table?'

'We had booked a table with a group too, but I didn't see much of my husband as he was busy with VIPs and so on. Daddy and Eleanor, that's Daddy's lady friend only talked to the couple they'd come with and I don't know them very well. Verity talked all the time to her friend, Diana – I just sat and listened.'

'That's a shame, but how come your husband Simon was busy with VIPs?'

'Well, Daddy's company, Aztec Developments, sponsors the ball each year so Simon sort of organises it and generally makes sure that event runs smoothly.'

'So, it's an annual event?'

'Yes, have you not been before?'

'No, I'm new to the area, I moved up from Oxfordshire a few months ago. It's very good of your husband to help out with the organisation.' Lydia was aware that she was effectively pumping Annabelle for information and she felt a little guilty.

'He works at Aztec and will take over as chairman when Daddy retires.'

'Really? Your father must trust him and hold him in great regard. How marvellous for you. Have you been together for a long time?' Lydia felt quite sorry for Annabelle as she listened to her talk about her husband, and thought what a rat Simon was!

'Simon joined Aztec about four years ago. I was engaged to someone else at that time, but then I found out that my fiancé had been unfaithful. I was absolutely devastated, but Simon was my knight in shining armour, he was so kind and understanding. We fell in love and were married within six months.'

'Wow! That was quick.'

'Well, we just… connected, you know? We had oodles of chemistry and I had been so upset.'

'I can imagine. It's not nice to find out your partner has cheated on you.' Lydia winced at her own words, not only because she was speaking from experience, but realising that of course, Annabelle would be finding out about Simon in due course.

'My fiancé had gone out on a stag night with his work colleagues and a couple of days later, I received photographs in the post showing him with this other woman draped all over him.'

'Really? Who sent the photographs? Oh, I'm so sorry I shouldn't be prying into your personal life, forget I asked that.' Lydia suddenly realised that she may be overstepping the mark, but Annabelle waved her hand vaguely in the air,

'Don't worry, it was four years ago and I don't mind talking about it,' she said airily. 'I've no idea who sent the photographs, they arrived anonymously in a plain brown envelope – proper photographs.'

'That sounds a bit strange, why would someone do that? Was there someone who wanted you to break off your engagement?'

'No one that I was aware of and I was so heartbroken, I just didn't want to see him again.'

'I guess you felt betrayed.' Lydia felt she was entering dangerous territory here, it was almost as if they were discussing what was to come.

'It was Simon who encouraged and persuaded me to break off my engagement because, as he said, a leopard never changes his spots, and once an adulterer, always an adulterer.'

Lydia's eyes popped wide open at this blatant piece of hypocrisy from Simon and she was thankful that Annabelle's eyes were shut. 'My fiancé always denied it of course and said he had been set up, but then he would say that.'

'Well as long as you and Simon have been happy, then perhaps it was meant to be.'

'We're hoping to start a family soon which will be just wonderful, although Simon isn't too keen, to be honest. I'm sure he'll be thrilled when the time comes, though.'

'Well, you know him best,' was all Lydia could think to say as she desperately tried to find a way to change the subject.

'However, in the meantime, I want to be more like the other wives – to be attractive and fabulous. I've been invited to work alongside Lady Worthington on her fundraising committee and she always looks amazing. I rarely wear make-up so I thought I would start with lashes. Simon isn't keen on women with lots of make-up, but I think that these lashes will look very natural.'

'Oh, they will, and I'm sure he'll approve.'

'Now,' began Annabelle, 'if you're new-ish to Harrogate, you may want to know the best places to eat and drink. Whereabouts do you live?'

'I'm living with my sister at the moment in Ashdale. I'm looking for a home of my own, though I'm not sure about what I want yet.' Lydia was grateful for the different topic of conversation and happily listened as Annabelle talked about the various small towns and villages of the surrounding area and filled Lydia in on the parts of the Harrogate district that she felt were the best places to live.

Eventually, Lydia switched off the angled lamp trained on Annabelle's lashes and straightened her back.

'Just stay still whilst I remove the eye pads and keep your eyes closed for a couple of minutes.' Lydia gently pulled the eye pads away and tidied up her kit and tweezers. Then she said: 'Now, slowly open your eyes, get used to the light and then when you're ready, sit up.' When Annabelle was sitting upright, Lydia handed her a mirror.

'They're gorgeous! Oh, my goodness, my eyes look so different, they're lovely. Thank you so very much.' Annabelle was clearly delighted with her new lashes.

'I've mixed up black and brown lashes as yours were quite blonde, and I thought a more natural look would be better for you.'

'I'm absolutely thrilled – they're perfect.'

Lydia gave her some lash maintenance advice and then took her happy client back through to the reception.

'I'd like to make another appointment with Lydia, if I may,' Annabelle said as she paid her bill.

Lydia smiled at her. 'Thank you, I'll look forward to seeing you again in about three weeks. Bye for now.'

'Bye, Lydia, and thank you,' Annabelle said gratefully.

Lydia smiled and returned to the treatment room to set up for her next client. She had mixed feelings about Anabelle's next visit, and could only hope that things would have been somehow sorted by then.

That evening was the opening night of the panto and Desmond had asked Lydia to look after the reporter. Desmond himself was just 'too excitable', busily flouncing around the dressing rooms and giving last-minute advice to his cast. Lydia nervously clutched a programme as she waited by the entrance for Robbie Parker. She had no idea what he looked like, but assumed that he would announce himself. She looked at her watch for the umpteenth time and noted that it was almost twenty-five past seven – Robbie was cutting it a bit fine, and soon she would have to take her place behind the prompter's screen.

Just as she was about to go back into the hall, a voice made her turn around. 'I'm the reporter writing the review this evening.' Lydia looked at the attractive, bearded man.

'Hi, I'm Lydia.'

The reporter smiled and Lydia was quite taken with his dark brown eyes and red-gold hair. 'I'm Robbie Parker, I'm sorry that I'm later than anticipated, I didn't leave enough time for the roadworks on the main road from Leeds.'

'Don't worry, you're here now. Would you like a drink?' Lydia asked and indicated that he should follow her to the refreshments window. 'There's beer, wine, soft drinks, tea or coffee.'

'Actually, I'd love a mug of coffee please.'

Lydia smiled. 'Elsa, could you get a mug of coffee for Mr Parker, please?'

Elsa nodded and quickly produced a steaming mug.

'There you go, lovey,' she said as she pushed the drink across the counter. 'Shall I get you another ready at the interval?'

Robbie grasped the mug and thought for a moment. 'That's very kind of you, but I think one mug of coffee is quite enough for me this evening, although I might be tempted by a glass of wine later.'

'That's no problem, I'll have a nice chilled glass waiting for you,' she replied with a smile.

Robbie turned towards the stage. 'I'm looking forward to seeing this panto.'

'Good, because I've reserved a seat on the front row for you, right where Widow Twanky can keep an eye on you!' Lydia smiled mischievously at Robbie as she led him to the front.

'Linda! How could you?' Robbie retorted with a grin

'Because it's the best seat… and my name is actually Lydia.' She indicated the empty seat with a Reserved sign on it.

'Oh God! I'm so sorry, I just misheard you.' Robbie was clearly mortified.

Lydia chuckled. 'It happens more often than you imagine, but just so you're clear on who is who, I've got a complimentary programme for you. Now I'd better go and take my place – it's show-time!' Lydia handed the programme to Robbie. 'I'll come back here with your wine during the interval when I can answer any questions. See you later.'

Act One went without a hitch and the audience joined in with the traditional 'Oh no it isn't' banter, laughing at Widow Twanky and booing Abanazzar. No one forgot their lines and as they launched into the song which closed Act One, Lydia left her seat and headed to the kitchen.

'It's going well,' remarked Elsa. 'Can I get you a drink as well?'

'Yes please, a coffee would be lovely. Having the audience makes so much difference to the cast, their reactions are more authentic and the atmosphere's brilliant,' replied Lydia.

Elsa produced a mug of coffee and poured a glass of white wine and, as she passed them to Lydia, the song ended and the audience erupted with cheers and loud applause. The house lights went up and everyone surged towards the bar. Lydia carefully manoeuvred through the crowd with her mug in one hand and the glass of wine in the other. At last, she safely reached the front row where Robbie stood looking out for her.

'A glass of chilled wine, lovely,' he said and gratefully took the glass, moving to sit next to her on the edge of the stage.

'What do you think of it so far?' she inquired.

'Rubbish!' Robbie quipped and grinned. 'Actually, it's very funny and I'm really enjoying it.'

'The cast will be delighted when I tell them that later – I can tell them, can't I?'

'Yes, you can definitely say that, although my review will have more detail. Can I just ask you something? I see that Simon Saxby-Jones is in the cast. I think I've come across him before, but I just can't think where. What business is he in?' Robbie sipped his wine,

'Simon is a director at Aztec Developments,' replied Lydia blowing on her hot coffee.

'Isn't Carlton Banks the big wig there?' Robbie wondered

'Yes, I believe so.'

'I thought as much, he has a daughter, doesn't he?'

'Carlton does, yes – Simon is married to her.'

Robbie suddenly choked on his wine causing him to cough and splutter. Lydia hastily took his glass and slapped him on the back. When he recovered, she handed back his wine.

'Sorry, went down the wrong way,' he croaked. 'I'm ok now though, what were you saying?'

'I just said that Simon had married Carlton Banks's daughter. Her name is Annabelle – do you know her?'

Robbie shook his head. 'I know *of* her. Apparently she keeps a low profile and is quite shy. Simon is just the opposite, I'm not surprised he's a main role in the panto – and the villain to boot!' The last five words were said quite sharply and Lydia frowned.

'You don't like Simon?' she asked

'No, not really, something happened a few years ago which I believe he had a hand in ...' Robbie zoned out and stared into the distance, and then suddenly snapped back into the present. 'Anyway, that's all history. I shall give an honest review of the panto and encourage folk to buy the last tickets.'

Lydia smiled. 'Thank you, Robbie, I'd better go. I should mention that I'll struggle to get out quickly at the end of the show to say goodbye.'

'Oh, don't worry I'll get off straight away back to Leeds. I'll be speaking to Greg sometime soon as he's doing some research for me on a new investigation.'

'Yes, he mentioned it. Well, it was lovely to meet you Robbie. Safe journey home,' Lydia held out her hand, Robbie shook it.

'Likewise. Greg is a lucky man.'

Lydia hurried back to the door to the dressing rooms where Desmond was hovering anxiously: 'Well darling, what did he say?' He chewed his lip nervously.

'He's loving it and will give us a great review,' Lydia replied. Desmond flung his arms around her and hugged her tightly.

'Oh, how marvellous,' then he turned to the cast and in a louder voice announced, 'it's good news, now go and break a leg!'

After the final curtain, the cast was excitable, and the atmosphere in the dressing rooms was buzzing. As Lydia made her way down the corridor, she heard snatches of conversation as the cast recalled moments of the show.

'I thought you had gone off-script when you walked away from me... The audience was great for the first night... What a fantastic atmosphere... They even got that joke, you know where you say...'

In the Green Room, Desmond positively beamed as the thespians shook his hand, slapped him on the back, hugged him and generally thanked him for producing and directing a successful pantomime.

At last, he held up his hands for quiet. 'Lovely people,' he began, 'I want to thank you for all the hard work, line learning and time you've put into bringing my creation to life. The audience *loved* you and you were all brilliant – just do the same for the next four shows!' Everyone laughed and cheered before drifting away to remove make-up and change. Lydia heard her name being called,

'Lydia! Have you got a minute?' Zoe waved a hand to attract her attention, Lydia nodded and made her way over.

'How can I help?' she asked.

'I wanted to ask if you were an employee or a freelance lash technician.'

'I'm freelance, but I also have clients at Lush Lashes in Harrogate,' replied Lydia as she watched Zoe tidy away make-up pallets and brushes.

'Well, I'm putting together some wedding packages and I wondered if you and I could come to an arrangement whereby you did lashes – you could come to my salon to do them.'

'I think that's a great idea, yes I would definitely be interested in discussing it further.' Lydia smiled happily.

'Can you come to the salon tomorrow afternoon, say around four o'clock?' Zoe zipped up her make-up bag and turned to Lydia, 'I'm not free until then,' she added.

'Four o'clock is fine with me, I'll look forward to it.'

'Great, I'll see you then. Bye for now.' Zoe picked up her coat and bag and disappeared into the corridor.

Lydia checked her watch – ten o'clock, was it too late to ring Greg? Probably not and they had agreed to talk this evening. Happily, she collected her things from the ladies dressing room and let herself out of the back door of the hall.

Twenty minutes later, Lydia sat in her pyjamas with a mug of hot chocolate and called Greg.

'Hi there,' he said as he answered. 'How was the first night?'

'It was brilliant. The cast performed really well, and the audience was responsive – the atmosphere was electric, a great start to show week.'

'How was Robbie?'

'He was very nice, chatty, sense of humour – just like you said and he thoroughly enjoyed the panto and will give great reviews.' Lydia tucked her feet under her as she snuggled into her chair. 'But you'll never guess who I had for a client this morning,' she added teasingly.

'Well it wouldn't be Simon Saxby-Jones,' Greg chuckled. 'How about the Mayoress-Elect, Mrs Celia Marshall?'

Lydia laughed. 'No, neither of those – it was Annabelle Saxby-Jones!'

'No… Really?' Greg sounded surprised.

'Yes, really and we had a lovely chat. She's actually quite sweet and definitely does not have a boyfriend! She told me that she and Simon may well start a family as she wants to have a baby. Honestly, Greg, I felt awful. The poor woman has no idea that Simon is seeing someone else.'

'Did you enlighten her?' asked Greg salaciously.

'No, I did not!' answered Lydia forcefully and then she softened, 'I just couldn't do it and it's none of my business.'

'I'm not sure I agree with you there. You know Simon is cheating. Wouldn't it have been kinder to tell her? The wife always being the last to know, etcetera.'

'Possibly, but she told me that she was engaged to someone before Simon, who had not been faithful. Her fiancé had been photographed with another woman and Annabelle was sent the pictures. I just didn't think it was the right time to say anything. Then she just chatted away about other stuff and the moment passed,' Lydia explained.

'She was sent photos of her fiancé with another woman? By whom?' Greg wanted to know.

'She doesn't know, they came in a plain envelope. She was devastated but Simon helped her through it, and then they got married – this would be about four years ago. Anyway, she's now decided to be a bit more glamorous, but subtle with it, hence the lashes. Funnily enough, we met in the Ladies at the ball last week, although of course, I didn't know who she was then – but it does confirm the fact that Simon did not take Zoe to the ball.'

'But what *is* baffling then, is why Simon told his young girlfriend he was taking *her,* if he knew all along he was going with his wife,' Greg pointed out.

Lydia finished her hot chocolate. 'The whole thing is baffling, but I'm sure it will all come out in the end, and both Annabelle and Bella are going to be very upset.'

'Not to mention Carlton Banks, this could be a scandal in the making …'

'Greg!' scolded Lydia.

'What? If I don't write it someone else will.'

'Please don't say anything – at least until after the panto… and don't involve me.'

'I'm not going to say anything, for now. It would require further investigation, and I would never involve you,' Greg reassured her.

Lydia yawned. 'I'm quite tired now, it's been a long day, so I think I'll say goodnight.'

Greg chuckled. 'Ok, sweetheart, I'm pretty bushed too. This conference is quite full on and I'm researching something for Robbie which I'll tell you about when I get home – it's quite interesting.'

'Do you know what time you're likely to be home on Friday?'

'Probably at the same time as you're leaving for the panto, so I'll see you when you get home. Sleep well, goodnight.'

'Goodnight, take care,' Lydia disconnected and smiled. She was very fond of Greg and hoped they would be a couple for a long time.

8

Annabelle Saxby-Jones

The following morning, Annabelle decided to take Tasheka's advice and paid a visit to Lovely Lingerie. She found the shop without a problem and slipped nervously inside. Touching the soft lingerie and marvelling over the intricate details of some of the camisoles, teddies, French knickers and negligees, Annabelle knew this was a whole lot different to her sensible M&S full briefs – just feeling the gorgeous fabrics made her feel sensuous; but what to buy? As much as she appreciated Tasheka's advice about being a bit of a good-time girl in the bedroom, she was envisaging a romantic seduction rather than fireworks. A woman with chocolate-coloured skin, short, spiky ruby red hair and the most amazing cheekbones approached her,

'Do you need any kinda help or are you jus' lookin'?' The woman sounded a little hostile and her face was stern. Annabelle felt immediately guilty of some misdemeanour and snatched her hand away from the silky teddy she had been touching.

'Er … both really,' she replied uncertainly. 'I was told to ask for Orlena?'

'You must be Mrs S-J. Tasheka said you might be stoppin' by.' Orlena visibly relaxed and smiled widely. 'She said you might need some advice, well I can tell you that you've come to the right place.' She waved a well-toned arm around and a dozen gold-coloured bangles on her wrists jangled.

'Yes, well… I think I quite like these negligees actually.' Annabelle tried not to stare at the long and very false eyelashes that Orlena wore.

'Well now, they're usually bought for honeymoons and are designed to only be worn the once.' Orlena winked at Annabelle, exposing glittery pink eyeshadow above the line of her eyelashes. 'If you're looking for…' she paused and raised a perfectly plucked and pencilled eyebrow, '…let's say excitement, then you need to look over here.' she extended the arm vaguely in the direction of the rear of the store and the bangles jangled again. She beckoned Annabelle to follow her with a wave of her hand; each finger was adorned with a ring and tipped with the longest crimson nails Annabelle had ever seen. 'I call it my special stock.'

'Special stock?' Annabelle trotted obediently after her.

'Hmm-hmm, it's what my girls buy when they have special clients.' Orlena had stopped in front of a garment rail of the flimsiest items.

'Special clients?' Annabelle stared at the rail, determinedly not looking at the shelves behind which displayed all manner of rubber and plastic objects.

'The school of sex has its own uniform and Tasheka told me that you needed something from my special stock.'

Annabelle swallowed and wondered what on earth Tasheka had told her.

Orlena pointed a crimson nail toward the changing cubicles. 'You get ready in there, and I'll pass you some things I think will do the trick.'

'But I just thought…'

'Don't worry, I won't be long.' Orlena disappeared while Annabelle stepped inside the cubicle and removed her jeans and sweatshirt.

In no time Orlena was back and passing a few items through the curtain. 'There you go. My personal favourite would be the red set.'

Annabelle looked at the garments – they were made of silk and looked feminine. There was a black fishnet piece which even had slits where nipples would protrude, Annabelle rejected that immediately. Then she picked up an ivory lace corset, which she would struggle to lace up, so that joined the reject pile. However, the red silk chiffon chemise and G-string set with a matching robe was beautiful and sexy – Annabelle knew that was the one.

'What do you think?' Orlena spoke from outside the cubicle, 'shall I take a look and give you my opinion?'

Annabelle clutched the silk robe around her in alarm in case Orlena might suddenly fling back the cubicle curtain. 'No, no, it's fine, and you were right, it's the red set.'

'You see, you need to make the most of what you've got, which is why I gave you the corset. I'm guessing that you want be ready for your man when he comes home so I *knew* that red set would look good on you.'

'Er… yes… thank you,' Annabelle pulled up her jeans.

'Just pass it out here to me – I'll go wrap it while you get dressed.'

Annabelle heard voices, as more women entered the shop. She could feel herself breaking into a sweat. What if someone she knew was out there? Her anxiety subsided as she heard Orlena talking to them:

'Morning girls, how are you today?'

'Fine thanks Orlena, I just want something special for this weekend.'

'Well you girls go ahead and have a look while I wrap this.'

As Annabelle finished getting dressed, she could not help but overhear the conversation from the cubicle next door:

'So, it's Paris for you this weekend?'

'It sure is and I'll get two grand for it.'

Annabelle's eyebrows shot up, *two thousand?* Maybe it was a modelling assignment.

'I'll have to work my butt off for it though – literally. This guy is an animal, he wants it in every room.' Annabelle gulped, but couldn't help eavesdropping further:

'Two thousand is a lot of money and presumably he'll wine and dine you as well.' There was a giggle. 'It sounds a bit like *Pretty Woman,* maybe he'll take you shopping and everything.'

'Kitty, I can assure you that he isn't any Richard Gere. He's obese with a face like a bulldog.'

Annabelle grimaced at the thought as she drew back her curtain and stepped out of the cubicle. She smiled nervously at the young, slender girl standing outside the next-door cubicle. She looked Annabelle up and down, but did not smile back. Feeling embarrassed, she hurried to the front of the store where Orlena was talking on her mobile; the red silk set lay unwrapped on the counter.

'Wha' d'ya mean you're not going to be home 'til ten o'clock? Well, I don't recall you mentioning anything about this at breakfast this morning. Now you just listen to me, Sandrine, you be home at six o'clock – do you hear me? Six o'clock. I'll not have you *not* coming home, do you hear me? An' another thing, I hope you're not going out with that waste-of-space young man, Conroy. He isn't good for you, in fact, he isn't good for anythin'. I don't care that he says he loves you, they all say that – my girls hear that all the time. Are you listening to me Sandrine?'

Annabelle turned away from the counter and looked around the store trying very hard not to appear to be listening to the conversation. As she waited, the two girls left the cubicle and came up to the counter. Kitty, who had been waiting outside the cubicle, rolled her eyes when she saw Orlena on the phone.

'We could be here a while,' she commented to her friend before turning to Annabelle. 'Who is she talking to?'

'Someone called Sandrine,' replied Annabelle, 'though I wasn't really listening.'

'You can't help but listen if she's talking to Sandrine. That's her daughter who is sixteen and thinks she can take care of herself, a bit like you were Coco.' Kitty nudged her friend.

'Yep, I thought I could take care of myself and I *did* take care of myself, so why did we all end up in this line of work, huh?' Coco joked, including Annabelle in the 'we'. 'You new around here, babe? I've not seen you before.' Both girls looked her up and down and Annabelle felt herself blushing. Behind the false eyelashes, nail extensions and fake tans these girls looked very young, and she wondered if they did what she thought they did in their 'line of work'.

'I'm not from around here, I've come from Harrogate,' she told them.

'Ooooh, from Harrow-gate,' mocked Kitty in a fake posh voice, 'I bet you get plenty of Richard Gere types there with loadsa money.'

'What is the going rate in Harrogate then, babe?' asked Coco, 'I bet you can charge up to two hundred an hour. I thought of going to Harrogate to work actually, so can you tell me which is the best hotel to use.'

'Well ... I ... um ... there are quite a few hotels, so it depends on the facilities you want really,' stammered Annabelle.

'Oh, I see, playing your cards close to your chest, huh? Don't want us from Leeds treading on your toes, hmm?' sneered Kitty.

'I'm not sure—' Annabelle tried to explain, but she was cut off by Orlena who had finished her phone call.

'Now listen here you two,' she said to Kitty and Coco with hand on hips, 'this lady isn't a working girl, she's a customer, so don't you girls go disrespecting her now.'

Coco gasped and immediately took Annabelle's hand. 'God! I'm so sorry, please don't take offence, it's not that you look like a working girl or anything.'

'It's fine… no problem, really.' Annabelle was relieved to have got all that straightened out. Whatever would Simon have thought if he knew she had been mistaken for a working girl, although the thought made her suddenly want to giggle.

'Now Coco, what have you decided on for your special weekend?'

Coco held up what looked to be three pieces of lace, two vertical and one horizontal, and as Annabelle gasped, Coco grinned at her.

'I know, not much to it, is there?' she said, 'but I feel as I ought to make an effort seeing as how he's paying for it.'

'I don't know how you do it,' Annabelle muttered.

'Are you being patronising, lady?' Kitty said crossly with her hands on her hips.

'No, no, not at all. I meant… aren't you scared? I mean, aren't these men strangers to you?' Annabelle explained hastily.

'Scared? Hah! No point in being scared in this line of work,' retorted Kitty.

'The problem is, that once you're earning, the money is so good, you just can't stop.' Coco told her. 'Sure, working in retail might be safer, but I wouldn't be able to afford my car and my holidays on a shop wage.'

Meanwhile, Orlena had wrapped both items in tissue paper and popped them into discreet, white carrier bags. Coco stepped forward and handed a card to Orlena so she could process the payment.

'I've a lovely apartment,' Kitty said firmly, 'which I pay for. I don't rely on no man to provide for *me*.' Kitty glanced at Annabelle's diamond-studded wedding ring, with barely concealed disdain. However, Annabelle thought about the irony of this statement because, in reality, it was men who provided Kitty with the funds for her lifestyle.

'It isn't always about sex,' Coco frowned at her friend and spoke more kindly to Annabelle, 'sometimes they just want a girlfriend. And on the odd occasion, we get to party with a few nice guys on a stag night, which again, doesn't necessarily involve sex.'

'Why would you go on a stag night, I thought that was men only?' Annabelle asked.

'Well, guys like female company, they like us to flirt and make them feel attractive and special. Sometimes the groom is set up with one of us, just for a laugh.' Coco took back her card and tucked it away in her bag.

'Couldn't that be misinterpreted though? If the bride found out, for example?' Annabelle was shocked at this revelation.

'Possibly, but we never find out about that as once the night is over, we go home – there are no repercussions for us. Are you ready Kitty?'

'Yes, let's go before you recruit Miss Harrogate here,' snapped Kitty.

Orlena glanced inside the bags before handing one over to Coco. 'See you around girls. Enjoy Paris, Coco.'

The two girls left the store and Annabelle handed over her bank card.

'I hope they didn't upset you. Tasheka will be mighty cross with me if they have spoiled your visit,' Orlena said as she processed the transaction.

'Not at all, I can understand that they may be wary of a non-working girl.'

'Well, that Kitty has a sharp tongue in her head. I think she's got issues about Coco's wealthy client and the trip to Paris, just 'cos she's not going,' commented Orlena as she dropped a receipt into Annabelle's white bag. 'Here's your card back and I hope you have a great time with your man. Tasheka says he's handsome but needs some help appreciating his wife. I bet you get some appreciation in that little red number!' Orlena raised her eyebrows knowingly, and Annabelle giggled with embarrassment as she picked up her little white bag and left the store.

As she drove home, Annabelle reflected on the conversation with Coco and wondered if her ex-fiancé, might have been right about being set up with a girl. Of course, she had not believed him at the time, who would? But now, after this morning's revelation, maybe he hadn't been lying to her. She sighed, it was all too late now anyway as she was happily married to Simon; so whether Robert had or had not been set up was irrelevant. The one thing that had always puzzled her though, was the photographs – who had taken them? Who had sent them to her, and why? She pulled up at a set of traffic lights and glanced at the white bag; it mattered not a jot about photographs she told herself, tonight she was going to make Simon love her – and who knows, they might make a baby.

Lydia Buckley

That afternoon, as Lydia arrived at WOW! she was immediately impressed with the stylish and professional atmosphere. Maggie waved a greeting from the hair salon, and at reception, Bella smiled to welcome her.

'Welcome to WOW!'

'Hi Bella. What a beautiful salon,' Lydia replied looking around.

'Zoe won't be long, she's just finished with a client and is tidying her room. Have you been to WOW! before?'

Lydia was pleasantly surprised by Bella's professionalism and the smart classical look of her blouse and skirt with her hair in a high bun. It was a far cry from the almost immature girl who attended rehearsals in jeans, sweatshirt with hair swept into an untidy ponytail.

'No, I haven't been here before. It looks amazing. Perhaps I should take a look at the treatments on offer.'

'Please, take a price list and have a look at your leisure.' Bella handed a booklet to Lydia, 'If there's anything of interest or you would like to know more about a particular treatment, just ask. Oh, here's Zoe for you.' Bella's smile vanished, and she turned away as Zoe approached the reception desk, busying herself with the diary.

Lydia picked up on the underlying tension between the two women, but only because she knew the cause. Zoe, looking immaculate as ever, had her best client welcome smile in place.

'Lydia, I'm so pleased to see you, I'm looking forward to working something out. Come with me, we can use my room.' Lydia followed Zoe down a corridor past treatment rooms on either side until they reach the last door on the right.

Zoe indicated the door on the left: 'That's the customer toilets, and that…' she pointed to the door straight ahead 'is the staff room and our facilities. This, is my room.' Zoe opened the door on the right and gestured for Lydia to enter. The room was decorated in very delicate shades of duck-egg blue and white, the window blind, towels and a throw were a rich shade of turquoise. It was spotlessly clean and there was a subtle scent of essential oils.

'Oh, this is gorgeous,' exclaimed Lydia.

Zoe smiled appreciatively. 'Thank you, that's exactly the reaction I hope to get from my clients. Please sit down, Lydia, and let us see if we can work something out to our mutual advantage.'

Lydia sat down on a white wicker sofa covered with the turquoise throw and pulled out a note pad from her handbag.

'Now…' began Zoe, 'I've designed some wedding packages to include the treatments we offer, and, as I suggested, I would like to add a lash application to some of them. We don't have any supplies or experience in lashes so I would expect you to provide your own equipment, is that ok?'

Lydia nodded. 'Yes, that's fine, I've all my own stuff.'

'In that case, I would suggest that WOW! include your charges for lashes in our packages and you and I come to a private arrangement on what is reimbursed back to you; it would probably be along the lines of a small percentage for us, just to cover the use of the treatment room. How does that sound?'

'That sounds fine, it's what I had in mind,' replied Lydia. She decided that she liked Zoe's straightforward no-nonsense approach and that to come and do some extra work in this lovely salon would be a welcome addition to her income. They continued to discuss their business arrangement until finally, they shook hands.

'Of course, it may mean that, although you're not technically an employee, you'll be expected to join us for the odd girls' night out, birthday celebrations, Christmas party, or indeed anything we can think of,' Zoe said mock seriously.

Lydia laughed. 'I think I can handle that.' She then thought for about two seconds before making what she hoped wasn't a rash decision: 'Zoe, there's one other thing I need to talk about.'

Zoe noticed the change in mood and frowned slightly, 'Go on.'

Lydia took a deep breath. 'I was at the Valentine Ball last Saturday and I saw Simon Saxby-Jones there. I didn't see you – just him.' Lydia held Zoe's gaze until the salon owner looked away, there was a long silence and Lydia could see Zoe struggling to decide what to say. 'Why didn't say anything to back Elsa up, last Sunday at rehearsal?' Zoe eventually asked.

'Because I've not been in Ashdale very long, and I'm still learning who is connected to who, and I didn't want to create further upset. But I do know *now* that Simon is lying to Bella and that he *was* at the ball, not with you – but with his wife.' Lydia watched as Zoe exhaled and visibly deflated. 'I should also mention that, only yesterday, Annabelle Saxby-Jones was a client of mine at Lush Lashes. She's very nice, totally in love with Simon and hoping to start a family in the not too distant future.'

Zoe's eyes widened in horror. 'Oh God! Did you tell her about Bella?'

'No, I didn't,' Lydia spoke steadily, 'but now I'm in a difficult position because I know Simon is cheating on both women and the longer I keep it to myself, the more awkward it becomes. Zoe, what is going on?'

Zoe chewed her lip, then stood up suddenly and walked to the window; she stared out for a few minutes as she made a decision, then she turned back to Lydia.

'It's a difficult situation and I can explain it to you, but you've to promise not to say anything to anyone else, at least for now.'

'Until the panto is over?'

Zoe nodded. 'Yes. This all started last Saturday, here at the salon. Bella had gone for lunch to meet Simon and I covered reception as I sometimes do. A woman with came in, she was quite full of herself, very confident, and asked about spray tans. As we were talking, she noticed the panto poster with Simon's picture on it and told me that she knew him as she was a friend of Bella's. I said that she had just missed her as she had gone for lunch with Simon and would be back in around forty-five minutes. She then asked why Bella would come back and I said because she worked until five-thirty. She was surprised because she thought that Bella didn't work.'

Lydia guessed where this was going. 'She wasn't talking about Bella, was she? Did she have long brunette hair by any chance?'

Zoe nodded.

'This was Verity and she was talking about Annabelle.'

Zoe walked back from the window and leaned against the treatment couch. 'How do you know Verity?'

'Oh, I met her in the Ladies at Ashdale Hall, but that was before I knew who she was,' Lydia waved her hand dismissively. 'What happened next? How come Verity hasn't told Annabelle?'

'She agreed to let me speak to Simon first to give him an opportunity to break it off gently with Bella.'

'Presumably you've spoken to Simon?'

'Yes.' Zoe pushed away from the couch and walked around to the other side.

Lydia watched her carefully; was she going to tell the truth or not?

There was a pause as Zoe seemed to be debating with herself about what to say. At last she lifted her head and looked Lydia straight in the eye. 'He was very non-committal, he said that he would deal with the situation and make the necessary arrangements in his own time. He also told me not to speak to anyone about it, because if I did, when my lease on this building comes up for review next month, he would use his influence to ensure that it wasn't renewed.'

Lydia was shocked and several questions sprang to mind. 'When was this?'

'At the ball last Saturday. To be honest, I was surprised to see him there given what he had told Bella about his father, but then again it was typical of him to let her down. Anyway, we happened to make eye contact and he motioned me to follow him. We went down a hallway into a room which, I guess, is where Elsa saw us. He put his hands on my shoulders and bent down to talk quietly into my ear, certainly not to kiss me – that's when he made the threat to close my salon.' Having got all that off her chest, Zoe sat down abruptly on a stool that had been under the treatment couch and put her head in her hands.

Lydia thought for a moment and then asked, 'Can Simon exert that kind of pressure on your landlord? Who is it?'

'I wasn't sure at first, as all my dealings have been with the estate agent, Lewis Marshall on the other side of the Market Square, and we usually just automatically renew the lease each year.' Zoe lifted her head. 'But I've read the lease again and the landlord is Aztec Developments. Simon is a director of the company so I guess he could throw me out. But Lydia, if I lose these premises, I'll lose everything, even my home – I live in the flat upstairs.' Zoe stood up and walked to the window again.

'They must need a reason to not renew the lease, presumably you've been a good tenant?'

'I've been a good tenant, but I'm scared he'll destroy my business whether I keep this secret or not, just because he can.' Zoe turned from the window and looked steadily at Lydia, 'He isn't as nice as he appears, you know.'

'So, what are you going to do?'

Zoe looked determined; she spoke quietly and firmly: 'I've told Simon that he must tell Bella the truth on Sunday, because if he doesn't, then I'll tell her on Monday.'

Lydia's eyes opened in surprise. 'And do you mean that?'

Zoe sighed heavily. 'Probably, I can't keep this secret much longer – I feel wretched as it is, and of course I can't predict what Verity will do. She phoned me earlier this afternoon and is pushing for me to tell Bella. I told her that I'll wait until Monday. The thing is, you also know now, so this situation has to be resolved as soon as possible before anybody else finds out.'

'I should tell you that Nick overheard you and Simon arguing outside the prop room on Tuesday evening. He heard Simon threaten to close your business if you disclose something about Bella, but he doesn't know the whole story.' Lydia felt it only fair to let Zoe know what Nick had told her.

'Oh God! I damn well *told* Simon that this would get out eventually!' Zoe flung her hands up. 'Well, I can't be responsible for anything that either Verity or Nick says, so it's almost out of my hands. We can only hope that we get through all the performances before the cat is totally out of the bag.'

'I agree, but what bothers me is why Simon is deceiving Bella? Usually "the other woman" knows she's just that, but in this case, he's practically living a double life,' remarked Lydia.

'I suppose Bella wouldn't have agreed to an affair as such. She thinks she's got a future with Simon, poor girl,' Zoe leaned against the window and crossed her arms.

'This will cause a great deal of unhappiness for a few people I should imagine; Bella's parents won't be impressed, nor will Simon's father-in-law.'

Lydia stood up. 'I've got to go, and so do you – we've both got a show tonight.'

Zoe paused by door. 'Lydia, thank you for this, it has been a great relief to talk to you. I'll let you know if anything changes.' She looked for much-needed reassurance.

Lydia smiled. 'Yes, of course. I'll do whatever I can to support you. Simon is a bully and should not be allowed to continue with this deceit.'

Annabelle Saxby-Jones

Annabelle stretched out in the warm water and breathed in the sweet aroma of her bath oil. She felt both apprehensive and excited at the same time. She had never been as daring as this; she hoped Simon's performance in the panto had gone well and that he would come home tonight in the same exhilarated mood as last night. He would see a new Annabelle, a sexy woman and not a quiet mouse. She would show him that she *was* ready to start a family, that she *was* mature enough for that responsibility.

At last, she stood up and stepped out of the bath, and grabbing a large, soft, towel, wrapped it around herself and walked into their bedroom. Having dried herself and moisturised her skin, she took the new red purchase out of the white bag and stepped into the tiny G-string – it barely covered her private place. She slipped the red silk chiffon chemise over her head and revelled as the soft fabric caressed her lithe young figure. She turned this way and that in front of the full-length mirror, liking what she saw although she thought that her hair could do with being longer – perhaps she should grow it or have extensions, like Verity. She felt her body tingle with anticipation – Simon would be home within the next thirty minutes, so leaving the matching red robe to one side, she slipped into her black satin pyjamas and robe to go and wait for him in the sitting room.

As soon as she heard the key in the lock, her heart began to pound – she listened as Simon removed his coat and shoes. He popped his head around the sitting-room door,

'Hi, sweetheart.'

'Hi there, how was tonight's show?' Annabelle mentally crossed her fingers.

'Very good. Not as great as last night, but no mishaps.' Simon stood by the door. Annabelle smiled in what she hoped was a sexy manner,

'Do you want a drink or anything to eat?'

Simon shook his head. 'No thanks, actually I'm going to go straight up and take a shower and then probably go straight to bed.'

Annabelle immediately stood up. 'I'll come up too then, I might read for a while.'

As Simon showered and prepared for bed, Annabelle removed her black robe and pyjama set, slipped on the red silk one and sat on top of the duvet nervously waiting for him to see her. Eventually, Simon snapped off the light in the bathroom and looked at his wife,

'Good God!' he exclaimed, 'What the hell have you got on?' Annabelle's eyes widened in shock. This wasn't the reaction she'd expected, but she carried on.

'I thought I would surprise you.' Annabelle pouted and moved slightly in what she hoped was a suggestive way. The robe slid off one shoulder seductively to reveal the almost transparent chiffon negligee beneath. Simon swallowed and appeared to struggle to find more words. 'Don't you like it?' she whispered, excited that Simon was speechless; and then, buoyed on by her growing confidence, she gazed at her husband coyly and playfully fluttered her eyelashes. 'I'm a woman with *needs* and *desires* and I thought I would spice things up a bit for you.'

Simon recoiled in shock. 'Spice things up?' he snapped, 'I was under the impression that I was already able to fulfil your 'needs and desires'. Are you saying that I disappoint you?' Simon was distinctly frosty now and Annabelle felt the situation getting out of hand. This wasn't supposed to be about whether Simon was a good lover or not – it was about passion and romance. Simon frowned as he waited for her reply. 'Annabelle?'

Annabelle was suddenly aware that she might have made a grave mistake,

'No!' she cried, 'of course you don't disappoint me! It's just that—'

'And why do your eyes look different?' He squinted at her.

'I've had lash extensions.'

'Lash extensions? Erotic underwear? Bloody hell Annabelle, I don't want a Barbie doll for a wife I want you – as you are… were.' Simon sounded quite cross now.

Annabelle looked away, this was going all wrong. Simon was supposed to be overcome with lust and desire for her, not making her feel stupid.

She took a deep breath. 'So, you don't like it then!' This was said more as a statement than a question.

Simon appeared to pull himself together. He frowned slightly, then his face softened and he smiled: 'Not on you, you're my wife, my princess…'

'I'm not a princess!' Annabelle retorted.

'Well, you are to me. You're my sweet little Annabelle, certainly not a tart from Leeds. Sweetheart…' he held his arms out towards her, 'what is this all about? Why are you wearing this?' he reached the bed and gently pulled one of the delicate shoulder straps.'

Annabelle flinched; she was way out of her comfort zone now and Simon seemed to be making fun of her.

'I wanted to be more like Verity and the other wives – they wear make-up and have hair extensions; they look glamorous. I wanted you to be proud of me, to *want* me, to be a mother to your children.' Annabelle spoke calmly although she was knotted up inside.

'But I don't want you to be like Verity and the others, I want you to be the sweet girl I married, not some wanton hussy. To be honest, Annabelle, I'm shocked. I didn't realise you had these… *desires*.' He said the words 'desires' with disgust.

Annabelle grabbed his arm. 'But Simon.—'

'I'm sorry, Annabelle, but you're not the woman I thought you were if you can be so easily influenced by other men's wives. I was so delighted when Lady Worthington asked you to be on her committee, she clearly recognised your potential as someone she would be pleased to be seen with, but now…' he trailed off, apparently lost for words. He shook her hand off his arm.

'But Simon…'

Simon stood up and walked towards the bedroom door. 'And I'm not sure about being a mother to my children.'

Annabelle gasped at his cruel words.

'I don't want a trophy wife – someone filled with Botox and plastered with make-up. I'm seriously disappointed in you, Annabelle, in fact, I'm going to sleep in the guest room tonight as I just need some space *and* I'm tired. I suggest you think about what you've done and hopefully, you'll see your error.'

Annabelle watched in horror as Simon left their bedroom. She heard the door to the guest room open and close, then there was silence. Slowly she stood up, peeled off the offending red chiffon set and put on her pyjamas. She got into bed and turned out the light, Simon had never slept in the guest room before. How could she have got all this so wrong? Why had she listened to Tasheka? She went over the conversation in her mind, Simon had been horrified and she felt completely humiliated.

As the minutes ticked by, Annabelle found she couldn't sleep. Simon's horrified face kept popping up in her mind and she wondered if he would still be upset in the morning.

Annabelle felt torn – if she was honest, there was relief at not having to go through with the sex act as she wasn't keen on whole huffing, puffing and sweaty business. But she knew that it was the way to make a baby and unless they did 'it' more often, she was unlikely to get pregnant. Recently she had thought herself to be undesirable to Simon; they rarely made love and when they did, Simon always initiated it. Annabelle found no pleasure in the act but felt it was her duty to pretend she did.

She reflected on her past relationship with her ex-fiancé – she had not thought about him since she married Simon, but she remembered how *he* had made her feel in their passionate moments – no pretence required there. However, Simon was her husband and if all she had to do was lie back and sort of enjoy the intimacy with him, then that was fine with her. She would simply revert to her natural self tomorrow and make things right with him.

However, Annabelle decided that she liked her lash extensions and she would keep her appointment with Lydia in three weeks to have them infilled whether Simon approved or not. The red chiffon set, however, was no longer required and would be relegated to the back of a drawer.

Vinnie Buckley

Thousands of miles away, on a cruise ship somewhere in the Caribbean, Vinnie sat thoughtfully on his cabin's balcony sipping a gin and tonic. It wasn't that he was unhappy or not enjoying his cruise – he loved the Caribbean and life on board the ship, he just wished he wasn't with Vivienne! There! He'd admitted it, it was Vivienne who made him feel negative and Vinnie wasn't normally a negative person. Vinnie loved people… wealthy people… wealthy women and they all seemed to like him. He was a successful advertising and marketing executive who played an acceptable game of golf, who held his head up on corporate race days and was a sought-after dinner guest. That was the solo Vinnie, the immaculately-dressed, self-assured Vinnie; but the Vinnie sitting on this balcony was apprehensive and not at all looking forward to the black-tie dinner that lay ahead.

Considering the mountains of luggage that Vivienne had brought with her on holiday, her evening outfits were less than substantial. Her daywear wasn't great either, but passable, as most of the fellow passengers wore swimsuits, shorts and T-shirts. Although he had noticed a few raised eyebrows at the *tiny* bits of fabric held together with string pretending to be a bikini that Vivienne flaunted. However, most of the time she lay flat out on a sunbed and only caused near heart failure with the senior cruisers when she moved to take a dip in the pool. He had banned one bikini though, as when wet, the white fabric had become transparent, which had nearly given Vinnie heart failure.

The evenings were another matter, if they'd gone to a resort full of young people then Vivienne would have blended in and Vinnie could have sat back and enjoyed the view. But the cruise was largely made up of older passengers enjoying some winter sunshine and the evening dinners, although not all black-tie, required a certain dress code. To be fair, the daily bulletin left in their cabin by the steward did provide guidelines on the evening's expected style, but only a vague description such as 'casual wear' or 'smart wear' or, as for this evening, 'formal wear'. So far, Vivienne had worn acid or fluorescent colours, tops that were slashed to the waist, skirts that were almost indecently short and one dress in a slinky fabric that had clung embarrassingly (for Vinnie) to her braless nipples. Now Vinnie wasn't a prude, far from it, after all, he had met Vivienne at a pole-dancing club and admired her moves, but now they were married, he felt that there was no merit in continuing to dress in the same provocative way outside of their bedroom.

Taking all that into account, Vinnie had cast his eye over her clothes whilst she had showered this evening and selected two dresses he thought would pass as 'formal'. He was also aware that having done that, Vivienne was likely to dismiss his selection on purpose and choose something different – possibly inappropriate, as she loved the attention and misguidedly believed it to be admiring. He had therefore taken the expensive step of purchasing a pink-diamond necklace and earring set to be worn only with one of the two selected gowns. Vivienne had been delighted and let him know how appreciative she was with an energetic love-making session when he had returned to the cabin with the gift a couple of hours ago. He thanked his lucky stars that there was only one black-tie night on this cruise and made a mental note to himself to go shopping with Vivienne beforehand should they go on a second cruise.

9

Annabelle Saxby-Jones

Annabelle awoke to the sound of rain on the bedroom window; she turned over and the cold, empty half of the bed reminded her that Simon was in the guest room. She thought back to the disaster that was last night and the things that Simon had said. On reflection, she decided that he had been upset because he had misunderstood her reasons for wearing the provocative red outfit – he'd obviously believed that she wanted more from him sexually than he was able to give. Annabelle surmised now that Simon wasn't the red-blooded demanding alpha-male type of man that other women seemed to assume he was.

Simon was a confident man, Anabelle told herself, who didn't need to prove himself in the bedroom department. All she needed to do was to reassure him that she was more than happy with how things were. The fact that they were not intimate very often was probably because Simon worked so hard; after all, he was soon to take over from her father which would mean more responsibility. She understood now why he was encouraging her to work with Lady Worthington – he could see that it would give her an interest and that she would meet the right sort of people. As for children, well Simon hadn't ruled it out entirely – it just wasn't the right time; she could see that now.

Feeling much more positive, Annabelle got out of bed, slipped on her satin robe and headed downstairs to make a start on breakfast. When Simon entered the kitchen, his usual fresh coffee, orange juice and warm croissants were waiting for him, along with a smiling Annabelle.

'Morning,' she chirped as she poured some coffee. 'Do you want some jam with your croissants?' Simon looked a little uncertainly at his wife, it was as if last night had never happened. Annabelle saw his apprehension, so she crossed the kitchen and wrapped her arms around him. 'I'm sorry for upsetting you last night, I thought that was what you wanted. I realise now that you love me as I am.' she looked into his eyes and was relieved to see him relax.

'I must say, you gave me quite a shock, Belle.' Annabelle tried not to wince at the abbreviation of her name. Simon would insist on calling her Belle sometimes, he said it was an endearment, but she didn't like it, and what's more Verity had started using it too.

'I thought about what you said and I want to be the kind of woman you can be proud of, so I'm going to throw myself into volunteering with Lady Worthington because I think I'll enjoy it.' Annabelle looked hopefully for reassurance from her husband and she was rewarded by Simon's huge grin,

'Now *that's* the Annabelle I know,' he told her. 'This is who you are. You don't need to role-play and pretend to be someone else. I love you just the way you are.'

Annabelle's heart soared. 'I also realise that as you're going to take over from Daddy, you've a lot on your plate,' she began, 'but I would like to think that you've not ruled out us having a baby at some point.' She felt Simon tense.

'We can plan for a baby someday, but I really want your father to know that I'm on the ball and not distracted by having a baby in the house, which would be a major disruption.' Simon sat down at the table and took a drink from his orange juice,

'Can we just forget last night ever happened?' she asked.

Simon poured himself a cup of coffee. 'Of course, we can.' He added milk to his cup and checked his phone. Annabelle, feeling very relieved, sat down opposite Simon,

'I'm looking forward to seeing the panto tomorrow. Verity is coming for coffee this morning and we're going to make plans. I think she and Harry will pick me up and then I can come home with you.' She broke into her croissant and buttered it.

'Oh sweetheart, I shan't be coming home until quite late because I'm staying for the after-show party. You should go home with Harry and Verity.' Simon finished his orange juice.

'Could I not go to the party with you?' Annabelle popped the prepared croissant piece into her mouth and revelled in its deliciousness.

'You wouldn't enjoy it, Belle, you don't know anyone and it's just a self-congratulatory pat on the back type of thing – you know, a bit luvvie.'

Annabelle frowned and glanced at Simon, but he simply tucked into his croissant,

'I might want to join the Ashdale Players for the next show, I quite like the idea of being on stage.'

Simon roared with laughter. 'You wouldn't remember your lines. Sweetheart, it's not your thing, and you would be too nervous.'

Annabelle opened her mouth to reply but Simon's mobile rang and cut her off. Simon glanced at the display, 'Sorry, must take this…' he got up and headed for his office.

Once again, Annabelle would never have admitted to eavesdropping, but it was impossible not to hear Simon's conversations when he was in his office and she was in the hall. So, this morning, when Simon was taking the call, Annabelle found it necessary to go and add more water to the vase of flowers on the hall table.

'Freddie, is everything all right? … No, I haven't spoken to Hugo since Monday, but I do know that he isn't on board with our latest project – at the moment. He told Charles that he wanted to sell the agency when Charles happened to be with Carlton, who in turn discussed it with me. I've recommended that Charles does not sell the agency – yet … Yes, I think Charles will take my advice and not sell. Don't worry about Hugo, he'll have to work with us on this, his reputation is at stake. Look let's talk next week…'

Annabelle finished adding the water to the vase and quickly tiptoed back to the kitchen. When Simon returned, there was no indication that she had ever moved.

'Everything ok?' she asked nonchalantly.

'Yes, just work. I'll have to go, and remember that tonight I've a client meeting, so I'll grab something to eat with him and not bother coming home before the panto. I'll see you when I get home around ten thirty. Have a good day, sweetheart.' Simon picked up his phone and left Annabelle at the table.

'Good luck for tonight, darling,' she called after him. The front door opened then closed and he was gone. Annabelle hummed to herself as she tidied away the breakfast things and returned upstairs to shower and dress. When she came back down, as it was only nine-fifteen, she decided to do some more work on Lady Worthington's garden party until Verity arrived.

When Verity rang the doorbell at eleven o'clock, Annabelle was engrossed in her project; she quickly saved her work and shut the laptop before going to let her friend in. As soon as the door was open, Verity marched in waving a bottle of champagne. She looked her usual well-groomed self in skinny, ripped designer jeans, a cream blouse which was trendily half-tucked into the jeans and a cropped, leather jacket. Her hair was in a high ponytail and swung from side to side behind her as she walked. She air-kissed each side of Annabelle's astonished face and headed to the kitchen, 'We need glasses Belle, I've news.'

Annabelle hurried after Verity. 'Isn't it a little early for champagne?'

'It's never too early for champagne, darling.' Verity removed the foil wrapping and deftly untwisted the wire cap.

Annabelle shrugged and placed two champagne flutes on the table. 'What are we celebrating?' There was a pop as the cork was pushed out of the bottle and Verity filled the flutes.

'Well, Harry has just agreed that I can have a party to celebrate my fortieth, oh…' she paused and frowned, 'is "celebrate" the right word to use for one's fortieth? Anyway, it's going to be huge and I want you to help me organise it. Cheers.' Verity handed a flute to Annabelle and clinked them gently.

'Me?' Annabelle was taken aback.

'Of course, darling, I've heard on the grapevine that you're on her ladyship's committee now and if you can organise things for Lady Worthington, then that's good enough for me.' Verity took a mouthful of champagne and closed her eyes in delight, 'That tastes good. Now what I've in mind is red.'

'Red?' Annabelle took a small sip from her flute.

'Yes, isn't fortieth a ruby theme? Anyway, I want everyone to wear red or at least have a red item, although you can't have the men in red tuxedos – that would be ridiculous. We could have a red velvet cake, red candles, napkins, that sort of thing. The invitations could have red gems on them… could we get red chandeliers do you suppose?'

Annabelle's mind was in a whirl. 'Where are you planning on having the party?'

'I don't know whether to have a marquee in our garden or simply go to Ashdale Hall. What do you think?' Verity took another large mouthful and topped up her glass. She looked at Annabelle's almost full one and tutted. 'Darling, do try and keep up – don't make me drink this all myself.'

'Actually…' began Annabelle.

'Oh my God!' Verity suddenly clapped her hand over her mouth and sat down at the table. 'You're pregnant, aren't you?'

'No. I—'

'I've to say, Belle darling, I do think you should think about having a baby soon, your biological clock is ticking you know.'

'Well—'

'Why don't you just stop taking or doing whatever you're... um... taking or doing and just let nature take its course?' Verity waved her hand in the air, almost knocking over the champagne bottle.

'I'm not taking or doing anything.' Annabelle moved the bottle away from Verity, whose glass was now half-empty again.

'Oh, well maybe you're not doing it often enough. You need to buy some sexy underwear – that always works with Harry. Not that Harry is backward in coming forward if you know what I mean, but if I "dress up",' Verity did air quotes with her fingers, 'he gets all fired up and we both actually enjoy it.'

Annabelle closed her mouth which had fallen open at this confession.

Verity leaned forward: 'I know a fab place in Leeds which sells amazing stuff... bound to get Simon going,' she added fervently. Annabelle watched as Verity sloshed more champagne into her glass, shaking her head at Annabelle's still nearly full one.

'Actually, Verity, Simon doesn't like that sort of thing.' Annabelle knew she sounded rather prim.

'Nonsense, of course, he does. All men do.'

Annabelle lowered her gaze. 'No, he doesn't. I tried it last night and he was horrified.' She looked back up at Verity suddenly deciding to defend her man. 'He said he didn't want me to be a Leeds tart – that's not what he wants for the eventual mother to his children.'

The grin disappeared from Verity's face. 'Simon said that? Good grief! I always had him down as a man who would enjoy a tart! Oh well, you'll just have to do it more often to get pregnant.'

She drank some more champagne as Annabelle wondered what plans Verity had made for getting home.

'Simon doesn't like to do it often, he's working so hard…'

'Doesn't like to do it often? Are you serious, Annabelle? Most men want it two or three times a week! Even when they have man-flu, they still get the urge.'

Annabelle took a sharp intake of breath.

Verity frowned at her. 'How often *do* you and Simon make love?' she asked seriously.

Annabelle flushed at the intrusive question, not really sure she wanted to answer it.

'Well…' she began.

'Oh God, Annabelle, you don't limit it or deny him his conjugal rights, do you?' Verity waved her glass in the air.

Annabelle lifted her chin. 'We make love as often as he wants and I don't deny him anything,' she said defensively, 'and it's at least once a month…'

'Once a month! Annabelle, men have needs that require attention more than once a month.' Verity put her glass down on the breakfast bar and looked at her friend.

'Well, as I said, Simon is very…' Annabelle broke off as Verity suddenly stood up, walked to the window and looked out over Annabelle's garden.

Annabelle waited and watched as Verity seemed to come to a decision.

'Annabelle, there's something I need to tell you…' Annabelle's heart sank, this did not sound good. 'Look, darling, I've been sworn to secrecy but honestly, I think that the sooner you know, the sooner you can sort it out. I've discovered, only recently, that Simon might be having an affair.'

'An affair?' Annabelle whispered, her worst nightmare realised. Verity walked a little unsteadily back to the table and sat down. She took hold of Annabelle's hands and spoke gently. 'There's a young girl, Bella, who is also in the panto – Simon has been seeing her for quite some time. Apparently, she believes that you and Simon are estranged and about to divorce.' Annabelle caught her breath, as Verity carried on: 'She works in a salon in Ashdale and it was through a chance conversation with the salon manager that I discovered this.'

Annabelle was stunned, she couldn't speak; her mind was in a whirl. Simon was seeing someone else. Annabelle grabbed her glass of champagne and took a huge mouthful, but after swallowing it she coughed and her eyes watered.

Verity sat back in alarm. 'Are you all right?'

Annabelle nodded and then shook her head. 'She… Bella… thinks we're *divorcing*?' Annabelle murmured. 'Why?'

'Well, presumably because Simon told her that. Look, darling, it's probably nothing… just a little dalliance… men will do this. Harry has had a couple of… dalliances, but we're still together.'

'Dalliance?' Annabelle repeated softly.

Verity nodded vigorously. 'The main thing to remember is that *you've* the ring on your finger, hmmm?' Annabelle looked at her wedding ring; they'd made vows, agreed to love and to cherish.

'But—' Annabelle began.

'There's nothing to worry about, I'm sure. You should speak to Simon about this, reassure him that everything is all right. He knows that I know, although I haven't spoken to him directly, but I do know he's keen to keep it quiet until after the panto.' Verity spoke practically as a woman with experience, whilst Annabelle nodded and took some deep breaths.

'I don't know what to say to him.' She felt as though she had been winded and all the stuffing knocked out of her.

'Just ask him for the truth.' Verity waved her hand vaguely. 'There are always two sides to every story and we've not heard his side. For all we know, this could be a complete fabrication on the girl's part, you know… wishful thinking.'

Annabelle looked at Verity. 'You don't really believe that, do you?'

'I don't know darling, I don't know what to believe. I can only repeat what I was told.' Verity's phone suddenly came to life, 'Oh, it's Harry... Hi babe... yes, I'm still with Belle... five minutes then... ok, bye.'

'We're going out for lunch, he's picking me up here so I'll leave my car for now – is that ok?' Annabelle nodded mechanically and began to move the flutes and champagne bottle off the table. Verity stood, unsure of what to do, then she suddenly needed to check her make-up and re-apply her lipstick.

'I'm sure Simon isn't going to ask you for a divorce or anything drastic, he's too much to lose—' she said as she twisted her lipstick case.

'*He's too much to lose?*' Annabelle interrupted her, turning from the sink.

'Yes... no... what I meant was he doesn't want to lose *you*. Look Belle, men find it difficult to refuse attention from young girls who thrust themselves at them – you only have to look at footballers to realise that. Trust me, you only have to forgive him and then you both move on.' Verity put her lipstick and mirror back in her bag.

Annabelle stared at her in disbelief. 'Forgive him and move on?'

'Yes, don't make a big deal out of this, men don't like dramas. Just ask him about Bella, wait for him to look all sorrowful and then you can tell him how hurt you are, but that you forgive him this once. Works every time. I usually get a fabulous piece of jewellery out of Harry.'

There was a blast of a car horn from outside.

'Oh, speak of the devil...' Verity picked up her handbag. 'Talk to me tomorrow morning darling, and let me know what Simon says. If everything's ok, then Harry and I'll pick you up tomorrow night at six forty-five.'

'Verity, don't say anything to Harry or anyone else. Let me speak to Simon first. I don't want this getting out if it's not true,' Annabelle said urgently.

Verity stood by the kitchen door. 'Of course, just let me know what he says, and until then, my lips are sealed.'

Annabelle nodded and watched her friend leave before sitting down and allowing the tears to fall.

Councillor Hugo Marshall

Hugo paused outside the offices of Babcock, Coombes & Wilks; he was a little early for the appointment, but he wanted a pre-meeting chat with Albert Wilks to impress upon him that he wished to retire immediately. Hugo also wanted to know how long it would take to complete a transfer of the business to Tom, for example. He needed Albert to confirm that this would be a smooth operation and, if possible, give him some idea of the value of the agency. He also wanted to give Albert a heads-up on this information, so that it would appear that he had been thinking about it for some time and that it wasn't a sudden decision.

He pressed the button on the intercom and it crackled as a dismembered voice asked him to come in. There was a click as the door unlocked and Hugo strode purposefully over the threshold. A perky young blonde woman sat behind the reception desk and smiled winningly at Hugo. She had long, pink sparkly fingernails and Hugo wondered how on earth she managed to type with them.

'Good afternoon,' she said politely.

'Good afternoon,' replied Hugo. He looked around for the reassuring face of the usual receptionist. 'Is Miss Brown not here? I do hope that she isn't indisposed.'

The blonde stared at Hugo uncertainly. 'Umm … Maureen's not in and I don't know if she's been disclosed,' she replied slowly, clearly not understanding what Hugo had said. 'But I do know that she's not well,' she said a little more confidently and looked at Hugo with heavily mascaraed eyes, 'so, the agency sent me, my name is Saffron. Could I have your name please?'

Realising her confusion, Hugo spoke a little more slowly than he normally would, just to help with clarity: 'I see, well my name is Marshall and I've an appointment with Mr Wilks, I'm afraid I'm a little early so I do hope he'll not be inconvenienced.'

Saffron chewed her lip and thought for a moment, her eyes not leaving Hugo's face as she wrestled for an answer. 'I don't think he's unconvinced,' she said carefully, baffled once again, then glanced down at a piece of paper on her desk and added cheerfully, 'but the other chap is already here, so I'll just let them know you've arrived.'

Hugo frowned. Charles was here first? Saffron picked up the phone and pressed a couple of buttons. 'Albert? Hugo is here for you, shall I send him through?'

Hugo's eyebrows shot up at the use of Christian names. Miss Brown would never have used those. Standards were clearly slipping.

Saffron replaced the receiver. 'Go on through, they're waiting for you.'

Hugo nodded curtly and walked determinedly down the corridor. He shrugged his overcoat off and draped it over his arm before he pushed the door open to see Charles sitting in one of two chairs in front of Albert Wilks's desk.

Albert Wilks stood up immediately, and Hugo noticed how little he had changed over the years. He looked exactly the same as he had around thirty years ago – straight out of a black-and-white film from the 1940s. Albert was a slightly built man with a short-back-and-sides haircut but with a thin section left long and combed over a bald head. He wore black round-rimmed glasses which looked like original NHS issue and had a small, neat moustache. He completed the look with a three-piece black pinstripe suit, an immaculate white shirt and a black tie.

'Ah, Councillor Marshall, good afternoon.' Albert extended his hand which Hugo shook, replying curtly:

'Afternoon.'

As he sat down, Hugo turned to Charles, 'You're here early,' he said, ungraciously.

'Just as you are,' responded Charles coolly.

Albert looked uncertainly from Charles to Hugo and cleared his throat. 'Now, I understand that you both wish to discuss the possibility of dissolving the partnership and selling the estate agency business,' he began and shuffled some papers on his desk.

'Yes!' Charles and Hugo replied in unison, Albert smiled, sat back and steepled his fingers. 'Right, well in that case—'

'But not yet. We just want an idea of how we would go about it, should we decide to do so,' interrupted Charles.

'What do you mean "not yet"? I want to sell now!' protested Hugo. Albert's smile vanished, he sat forward anxiously in his chair.

'We are not rushing into things, Hugo. I've taken advice and now isn't the time to sell,' Charles replied firmly.

'Advice? Advice from whom?' Hugo turned in his chair and faced Charles angrily.

'Someone who may want to buy,' Charles said vaguely and smiled benignly at Albert Wilks, who looked alarmed at the obvious discord between the two men.

'What the hell are you talking about, Charles?'

'Well, if you already have a buyer, perhaps—' began Albert.

'I know someone who is possibly interested in buying the agency,' Charles said smoothly, 'but not yet.'

'Not yet? I'm not going to wait around at your buyer's convenience before I can retire,' snorted Hugo, going a little pink in the face. 'Who is this interested party anyway?'

'Maybe we could begin by discussing your retirement plan, Hugo?' Albert tried again.

'Who is it?' Hugo demanded.

'Calm down Hugo, as a matter of fact, it's Carlton Banks. He's discussed the possibility of buying the agency with his son-in-law, Simon Saxby-Jones. I don't know if you know him, but he'll take over from Carlton in the not too distant future, so Carlton sought his advice.' Hugo's mouth dropped open as he stared at Charles, completely lost for words.

Albert took this opportunity to speak: 'They're house builders I believe, so it makes sense for them to buy an estate agency.' He smiled his best client smile at the two men, but the smile evaporated as Hugo stood up.

'You discussed my personal business with Carlton Banks, who in turn told Simon Saxby-Jones? What the hell were you thinking?' Hugo's glasses had slid a little way down his nose and he shoved them back up, 'I told you that young Tom would be interested – he already works for us and knows the business. If he buys the agency, I can retire immediately.' Hugo, standing at five feet nine inches, appeared to tower over the still seated Charles. He spoke with such fury that Albert also stood up, holding his hands out front, palms facing forward, in an effort to defuse the situation.

'Hugo, Charles…' he began.

Charles looked Hugo steadily in the eye, pushed back his chair and hauled his bulk upright, his six feet two inches height and extra-large girth suddenly dominating the room.

'What's going on? Why do you want to retire now?' shouted Charles.

'There's something else I want to do and…' Hugo paused then made his mind up, 'and I'm sick of carrying you. You do nothing for the agency. Over the last couple of years you've ignored the business yet you still take your cut out of it – well I want to do the same!'

'Gentlemen! Gentlemen!' Albert rushed around the desk and put a hand on either man's chest.

'Do nothing?' bellowed Charles 'it was my damn business in the first place, I let *you* in.'

'I *bought* my way in, you were happy to take my money,' retorted Hugo glaring at Charles.

'Only because you're my brother-in-law! God knows why Celia married you!' There was an awkward pause as Hugo removed Albert's hand from his chest and took a step back,

'True colours coming out now, Charles,' he said quietly and seriously. 'Well let me tell you something, I'm not carrying on anymore. I'm retiring with immediate effect.' His eyes swivelled around to Albert, who stood nervously at one side, 'Albert, will you let me know how I can disengage myself from this partnership, as soon as possible please?' Albert nodded and took his hand off Charles's chest, grateful that the shouting had stopped.

'Hugo, come on let's sort this out amicably, you can't just walk away,' Charles held his hand out in a gesture of peace.

'Sorry Charles, you walked away months ago, and now I'm just following your example.' Hugo smiled sardonically as Charles crossed his arms defiantly.

'Well, I'm not going to agree to any sale or dissolution,' he announced.

Hugo shrugged. 'Suit yourself, but you'll have to go back to work then. One of us will have to be there.'

'That's not going to happen,' snapped Charles, uncrossing his arms.

'So, agree to sell then.'

'Not yet!'

'It's because of what bloody Simon Saxby-Jones said, isn't it?' Hugo pointed his finger at Charles.

'Well, he's a businessman!' Charles had broken out into a sweat with all the exertion and he pulled his collar away from his neck. Albert hastily stepped in between the two angry men again, but as a slightly built man of five feet seven inches, he felt at a distinct disadvantage and just as quickly, took a step back again.

'*We* are businessmen, *we* can make our own decisions,' Hugo roared, flinging his arms out.

'I'm sorry Hugo, but Simon said to wait until May or thereabouts when we would get a better price,' Charles took out his handkerchief and wiped his damp forehead.

'He asked you to wait, so he could pay you more in May? That doesn't sound like good business to me,' mocked Hugo, pushing his hands into his trouser pockets and cocking his head defiantly.

Albert nodded. 'I agree. If the return is ultimately higher, then…' he added brightly. As both men looked at him, he took another step backwards.

'Ok…' began Charles benevolently, 'I'll tell you what we can do… I'll agree to sell in May to either Aztec or Tom, whoever gives us the best price – how about that?' He held his hand out for a second time for Hugo to agree, but Hugo shook his head,

'No, it's the principle here. If you had not heard what Saxby-Jones had to say, you would have agreed to sell to Tom, and we would have all been happy. Saxby-Jones has just put the brakes on this – for his personal gain, you can bet on it.' Hugo knew of course exactly why Simon had recommended stalling the sale of the agency, but he couldn't say why.

Charles angrily withdrew his hand. 'I too, can be stubborn, so we are at a stalemate and any further discussion today is pointless! But mark my words, you had better not abandon the agency or run it into the ground before we come to a satisfactory agreement.' Charles took a step towards the door, but Hugo got there first,

'And you'll stop me doing either of those things, how?' he hissed.

'I won't, but your greed will. Now, out of my way!' Charles elbowed Hugo away from the door and walked out of the office.

Albert scuttled back around his side of the desk again. 'So, err, shall we just leave things as they are? For the moment at least?' he asked gently.

Hugo had watched Charles lumber down the corridor and waited until he heard the outer door open and slam shut. 'Do whatever you like, I really don't care,' sighed Hugo as he put on his coat and left the office. As he passed the reception desk he heard Albert on the intercom to Saffron:

'Could I have a weak tea please? And hold my calls for the next thirty minutes.'

Vinnie Buckley

Vinnie was once again deep in thought. He was in a bar in Saint Maarten, right opposite the beach, where he had sought respite from the sun and was attempting to catch up on his emails. Fortunately, the bar offered free Wi-Fi to its patrons.

Last night's black-tie dinner had not ended well. Although Vivienne had dressed more or less appropriately, she had drunk far too much and finished the evening on stage with the singer and the band, demonstrating her enviable twerking technique to the shocked diners. Vinnie realised that whilst Vivienne loved the attention and recognition, she had no idea that it was the wrong sort of attention – the elbow nudging, whispering and sniggering type of attention.

Vinnie now admitted to himself, that he had made a grave mistake in marrying her. Vivienne was strictly good-time girlfriend material, someone who was great to fall into bed with, full of sexy fun. She knew how to make a man feel a million dollars and Vinnie had been hooked. Coming home each night to be greeted by an amazing-looking woman, albeit the looks and body were mostly not natural, he was in his element. He basked in the glory of the admiring glances of other men and their envy at his stunning arm candy, but, and it had become an important 'but' – spending twenty-four hours a day with her, realising the lack of intelligent conversation and social skills, had brought home to Vinnie the stark reality of Vivienne as his wife.

Vinnie sighed heavily. He was looking forward to going home next Tuesday evening and returning to work, a thought that had never crossed his mind on previous holidays. He would be free to chat and schmooze again, without looking over his shoulder to check on what Vivienne was doing or saying; and being constantly on tenterhooks was stressing him out. The big question which persistently hovered in his mind was what the hell was he going to do about it? The current answer was he didn't bloody well know. He just wanted an attractive wife, someone he could converse with, and discuss topical news with. She should have a sense of humour, a good dress sense, not be overly extravagant, not be needy or whining, have self-confidence with new people, and be able to conduct herself in the correct social manner. Why couldn't he find a wife like that? His attention was caught by a waitress, a local girl with a voluptuous body wrapped in a skin-tight bright blue dress. She flashed him a dazzling smile which lit up her face, her white teeth contrasting with her dark skin, 'Do you need somethin' to eat, sir?' Her voice was deep and husky, her eyes large and brown. Vinnie was mesmerised for a moment and then pulled himself together.

'No, no thank you,' he smiled back at her. *Now she's a stunner!* He watched her walk away, the cheeks of her rounded bottom quivering with each step.

His phone beeped as an email arrived and he reluctantly switched his gaze from the waitress to the screen on his phone. The email from work told him that a meeting had been arranged for him with a potential new client for the following week. The client was a development company and they were looking to market a new housing development. The meeting included dinner on Thursday evening where Vinnie could get to know what the client was specifically looking for. He would then put together a proposal on Friday morning and present it at the client's offices on Friday afternoon. The client was Aztec Developments in Harrogate, although the Thursday evening dinner would be at Ashdale Hall and a room had been reserved for him locally at the Coach & Horses pub.

Vinnie did a double-take, Ashdale! That was where Lydia had gone to live! Maybe he could find time to meet up with her and have a catch-up. The more Vinnie thought about meeting Lydia, the more he liked the idea. He, therefore, decided to send her a friendly text, just keep in contact over the next few days. He tapped out his message and pressed Send, then sat back and smiled.

The barman, Leroy, according to his name badge, noticed that his customer's glass was empty and, mindful of utilising every possible opportunity to improve his tips, prepared another rum and coke.

'Hey man,' he drawled, 'I see your glass is empty an' I guess you wan' another drink, eh?'

Vinnie glanced at his glass and it was indeed empty.

'Well, I got you another one comin' righ' up.' The empty glass was whisked away and replaced by a full glass, the ice clinking as Leroy set it down.

'Thanks,' muttered Vinnie. He didn't really want another drink, but there wasn't much else to do. While Vivienne was laid on a sunbed on the beach, Vinnie decided to carry on enjoying his own space.

'Now that – I can really appreciate,' Leroy practically purred. Vinnie looked up to see Leroy staring at the beach: 'That's one hot lil' chick.'

Vinnie followed Leroy's line of vision and his eyes opened wide when he realised who Leroy was looking at. Vivienne had come out of the sea and returned to her sunbed. She stood, legs planted a little apart wearing one of the minuscule triangle bikinis, which today, happened to be a nude colour, and from where Vinnie sat, Vivienne looked naked. Before she laid down, she squeezed the water out of her long hair tossing it over her shoulders. As she did so, her breasts jiggled enticingly, and then in one swift movement Vivienne pulled the string behind her and the two triangles covering her nipples fell away.

'Whoa...' Leroy growled, 'I would sure like to get hot 'n' sweaty wit' her. You know what I'm sayin' bro'?'

Vinnie felt sick and pushed his rum and coke away. He threw a handful of dollars onto the counter-top and walked out of the bar. It was one thing for Vivienne to be noticed when she was out with him and he could be envied, but for his wife's assets to be flaunted in such a wanton way for all and sundry to lust after, well it just wasn't on anymore.

10

Lydia Buckley

Act One had finished and Lydia eventually made her way to the bar towards the end of the interval. She could see Elsa chatting away to an older man, and as she drew closer she picked up on the conversation:

'Well, as I said to Brian, this panto is for all folk regardless of age and I'm right glad you came, Edward. Isn't that right Barb?' Elsa spoke over her shoulder to her friend who was busy washing up. 'And if you're of a mind, how about you come to the Coach with us for a nightcap when it's finished? Is that all right with you Barb? We'd love to have your company, Edward. You ought to get out more, we hardly see you... do we Barb?'

'Well, that's very kind of you I'm sure, but—'

'No buts, Edward – I'll not have you feeling left out. Me and Brian will wait for you. You'll save 'im a seat as well, won't you Barb? We've to save seats, see, 'cos it gets busy after a do. Everyone goes for a nightcap. Hello Lydia love, what can I get you?' Elsa drew breath and looked in Lydia's direction. The beleaguered man also turned to see who his saviour was,

'Just a coffee please, Elsa,' replied Lydia.

'Well, hello...' She recognised the voice in an instant; the man with the hat she had bumped into twice last Saturday.

Lydia turned to him. 'We meet again.' she smiled.

'How are you?' he asked politely, extending his hand.

Lydia took it as she replied, 'I'm very well thank you, and yourself?'

'I'm tickety-boo,' he replied, his blue eyes twinkling mischievously. He looked every inch the country squire in a tweed suit with a silk cravat at his throat – very dapper thought Lydia.

'Here you are, Lydia, love.' Elsa pushed a mug of coffee across the counter-top, 'I didn't realise you two knew each other.' Elsa nodded at her two customers.

Lydia picked up her drink. 'Oh, we don't, really,' she quipped and smiled benignly at Elsa's confused expression before she and 'Mr Phillips' moved to one side as a few customers suddenly approached the bar for final refills.

'Do you know, I think we should formally introduce ourselves, especially if we are going to keep on bumping into each other,' the man suggested.

Lydia laughed in agreement. 'My name is Lydia Buckley,' she told him.

'And I'm Edward DeVere Jones, at your service,' he slightly inclined his head as he spoke. 'I should really thank you of course.'

'Thank me? Why?'

'For rescuing me from dear Elsa.' Edward glanced over his shoulder at Elsa busily serving her customers.

Lydia grinned. 'Do you know Elsa well then?'

'Well enough to know that, although her heart is in the right place, she doesn't often take no for an answer. I moved from Sussex to Ashdale just before Christmas and Elsa was the first person to knock on my door, the very next day. She had a home-made sponge cake with her and invited herself in for a cup of tea, not to mention a spot of interrogation. I had to invent a lunch engagement to get her to leave.' Edward took a sip from his glass of red wine.

Lydia giggled. 'So, what made you come to the panto? Was it Elsa's influence again?'

'No, it was all my own idea. I say, I hope you don't think I haven't got a sense of humour?' Edward looked a little hurt.

'Oh God, no! I mean, I'm so sorry… I …' Lydia was horrified at the thought that she may have caused offence.

However, Edward's eyes crinkled as he chuckled. 'It's fine my dear, I'm just teasing you. I'm sure you didn't mean to imply that persons of a certain age wouldn't enjoy an old-fashioned panto, hmmm?' He raised his eyebrows and took another sip of red wine. 'It's not bad this, but I probably wouldn't buy a bottle of it – my personal preference is a Chilean Merlot.'

'That's my favourite red too!' exclaimed Lydia.

'Perhaps we may share a bottle one day, I would like that. In the meantime, this will just have to jolly well do.'

'I hope you're enjoying the panto, the audience usually tends to be families – that's why I was surprised to see you here,' Lydia explained.

'I quite understand, but between you and me there are two reasons why I'm here. The first is that, in my sometimes misspent youth, I used to tread the boards myself. Just in various amateur dramatic productions, including panto, so I'm always interested to see what the local talent is like.'

'Really? I bet panto hasn't changed over the years. What type of roles did you play?' Lydia warmed to this eloquent and amusing man.

'Oh, the baddie, darling, always the baddie. Although I always played my character with a certain charm and a just a touch of evil, Ha, ha, ha.' Edward laughed devilishly and pulled his version of an evil face, 'Not unlike your Abanazza in this show actually.'

'And your other reason for coming to the panto? You mentioned you had two reasons.'

'Ah well, that's more personal.'

'Oh, I'm sorry, I didn't mean to pry.' Lydia felt she had overstepped the mark.

'No, no, it's quite all right.' Edward paused as he made up his mind. 'Do you know my dear? I've enjoy talking to you so I'm going to let you into a little secret.' Edward bent closer to Lydia, 'But you must keep it a secret, at least for now.'

Lydia nodded. 'Of course I will.'

'Well, the other reason I'm here is to see my son whom I haven't seen for over twenty years… and he doesn't know I'm here.' Edward stared at the floor as though he were suddenly embarrassed.

'Good lord, that'll be a surprise for him.' Lydia drank some of her coffee which had now cooled enough.

'It will be a shock. We had a falling out over an incident whilst he was at university and we haven't spoken since.'

'Heavens! And he's no idea you were thinking of meeting again?'

'None whatsoever.' Edward shook his head. 'I've retired and I'm a widower now. I woke up one morning and decided that it was time to make amends – to reconcile, so I sold my house and moved up here. I've been settling in and mulling over the best way to "bump into" him, so here I am. I'm going to wait outside until he finishes this evening, say hello, and then just go from there. What do you think?' Edward finished his wine as he waited for Lydia's answer.

Lydia thought carefully before she replied, 'I think that will be ok, provided you speak to him alone.'

Edward nodded in agreement. 'Yes, I agree – will he be alone do you think?'

Lydia shrugged. 'I don't know, you haven't said who he is.'

'How silly of me, the chap who plays Abanazza – Simon Saxby-Jones, as he now styles himself. He's my son!'

Lydia gasped,.'*You're* Simon's father?'

'Oh, you know him?'

'I'm a member of the Ashdale Players – I'm the prompt so I do know Simon, but not too well as I only joined at Christmas.'

Edward leaned forward. 'Can you tell me anything about him? Is he married? Does he have children? What does he do for work? Where does he live?'

Lydia gasped.

Edward apologised, 'Oh, I've put you on the spot, so sorry, it's just that now I've told you my little secret and you know Simon, I'm just anxious to know more about him.' He looked mortified.

Lydia smiled gently. 'Simon is an architect, he lives in Harrogate and…' she stopped suddenly as she realised, she didn't know what to say about Annabelle. And then several thoughts collided in her head:

Hang on a minute! Hasn't Simon's father just had a heart attack?

If Edward is friendly with Elsa, how come he hasn't heard of Bella?

Edward was waiting for her to carry on speaking, but when no words were forthcoming, he sighed resignedly. 'It's complicated, isn't it? It's always complicated, always was and probably always will be. Simon uses people, they're just stepping-stones to get himself further up the ladder. "It's not what you know, it's who you know" – that's what he used to say. In the past, he's trampled on people's emotions, broken hearts, been unable to commit to a relationship, and pushed aside anyone who stood in his way, abandoning colleagues by the wayside. He's driven to succeed, but his desire to be the best has consumed and hardened him, I fear.' Edward looked sadly at Lydia, 'He hasn't changed, has he?'

Lydia swallowed. 'Um… well…' she stuttered, struggling to find the right words,

'You don't have to say anything, I quite understand. However, I want him to know that I'm here for him once again, so please say you'll keep my secret. Don't tell him you've spoken to me or even that I'm here,' he pleaded.

'I wouldn't dream of breaking your confidence,' she reassured him. 'You must speak with him first and break the ice, even if it's not tonight.'

'Ladies and gentlemen, please take your seats for Act Two!' The announcement came over the speakers.

'I must go,' Lydia told Edward. 'I wish you the best of luck and hope that everything works out all right. My lips are sealed.'

Edward smiled gratefully and Lydia moved away to resume her role as prompt but then suddenly turned back again:

'I'll tell Elsa that you couldn't go for a drink with them,' she winked at Edward.

'Thank you, my dear,' he said, and Lydia made her way back to her prompter's seat. As she sat down, she checked the time on her phone and was surprised to see a text from Vinnie:

Hi Babe, cruised to St Maarten now & just thinking that you would enjoy this. Have you found a place to buy? Let me know how you get on xx.

Cruising? Vinnie had never offered to take *her* cruising and what was all this chatty stuff about? Lydia shrugged and put her phone away, and as the house lights dimmed, she opened her script and waited for the opening lines.

After the curtain had closed on Act Two, Lydia made her way through the excitable cast to the kitchen where she found Elsa putting wine bottles away.

'Elsa, I just wanted to mention that Edward asked me to say thank you for the invitation to join you in the pub tonight but unfortunately he's unable to accept – his words.'

Elsa stood upright. 'Now that's a shame, did he say why?' She pulled a sad face. 'I told him earlier that he should get out more... well, you heard me didn't you?' Lydia nodded and backed away towards the door. 'I was just saying to Barb how I was looking forward to chatting to Edward... find out a bit more about him, you know. He keeps himself to himself does Edward... but I hope that's not because he don't feel welcome, I'd hate for him to think that.'

'No, I don't think it's that, it's…' Lydia thought quickly. 'He thought he was coming down with a cold and decided he would go straight home, and talking of home… Oh!' Lydia was suddenly bumped from behind as the kitchen door opened and Barb came in carrying a tray full of glasses and something brightly coloured under her arm. The tray wobbled and the glasses all slid to one side, 'Whoops, nearly!' Barb righted the tray in time and the glasses were safe.

'Lydia here has just said that Edward isn't feeling up to a nightcap and he's gone home … coming down with a cold. I'll call round to his place in the morning and see if he needs anything. Being a man he probably has no paracetamol, hot lemon or tissues. Are you joining us at the Coach, Lydia?' Elsa spoke as she turned on the taps and squirted washing up liquid into a bowl in the sink.

Lydia shook her head. 'My boyfriend has just come back from a week-long conference in Birmingham and is waiting for me at home, so I'll probably have a nightcap with him.'

Elsa chuckled. 'A nightcap and the rest, eh, Lydia?' she smirked saucily and Lydia blushed. 'Just teasing. You get off home then and see your man. Give me those glasses Barb and I'll quickly wash them. You go on to the Coach and save me and Brian a seat, I won't be long.'

Barb didn't need telling twice, and she lifted her coat and bag off the hook on the back of the kitchen door and took Lydia by the arm. 'Come on, we can walk out together.' She nodded her head towards the door. 'Shall I drop the latch on the way out, Elsa?'

'Yes please, I think all the audience has gone, and anyone else can use the back door. Don't forget to be here by one thirty for the matinée tomorrow.'

As Elsa began to wash the tray of glasses, Barb and Lydia took the opportunity to go.

Elsa Armitage

When Elsa was satisfied that everything was clean and ready for the next day, she also unhooked her coat and bag, and walked from the kitchen into the main hall. Kevin, Graham and Nick were discussing the evening's technical performance near the stage, and Nick lifted his hand by way of saying goodbye. As Elsa approached the main door, she suddenly heard someone outside hammering on it. When she pulled it open, she stood back in surprise as a dark-skinned woman barrelled past her.

'I gotta come back in,' the woman puffed, 'I need to find a unicorn!' She glanced around the hall before turning back to Elsa. 'Have you seen a unicorn?' Her acid-green Lycra top strained over large breasts which quivered as she spoke.

Elsa was rarely speechless, but right at this moment, she was lost for words and just shook her head dumbly.

The woman tutted and began to walk down the neat rows of chairs pulling them about as she looked underneath and around them. Elsa pulled herself together and followed the woman rearranging the chairs back into neat rows as she went.

'What does it look like?' Elsa asked.

The woman stopped searching, stood upright and planted her hands on her generous hips. 'It's a unicorn, you know – a horse with a horn?' A little bit of irony crept into her voice and her black ringlets shook as she spoke. 'It's, like, multicoloured.' And then to clarify things a little more she added, 'That means lots of different colours.'

The pleasant smile left Elsa's face. Of course she knew what multicoloured meant, 'I know what—' she began.

'My Shanice left it here an' she ain't gonna sleep without it. I telled her not to bring it, but would she listen? No. That's the problem with kids, they think they know better and jus' don't listen. I mean, normally she's a good girl an' takes note of what her mama tells her, but the unicorn had to come an' now she's left it behind. We were almost halfway home when she jus' stopped walkin' and started screamin'. My heart stopped for a moment there. Jus' what in the world is wrong wit' you? I says to her… then she tells me that she left her unicorn behind.' More chairs were pushed aside and Elsa valiantly put them back in order, 'Er… I'm locking up now. I've to go home,' Elsa explained as it became obvious that the unicorn was nowhere to be seen.

'It must be here somewhere, I mean how do you lose a unicorn?' The woman began walking down another row. 'I'm sure we were sittin' jus' here… or was it the next row?'

'Have you lost something?' Nick ambled over to where Elsa stood, watching the woman searching under chairs.

'No, I jus' thought I would come back an' see how you was doin'!' the woman snapped sarcastically, arching an eyebrow.

'O-kay,' Nick said warily.

'My Shanice's unicorn… I mean it can't jus' get up and walk outta here, can it? You know what I'm sayin'?'

'Is it brightly coloured?' Nick asked helpfully.

'I think 'multicoloured' is the correct description,' Elsa answered with a modicum of smugness.

The woman's eyes narrowed as she deliberated on whether Elsa was mocking her.

'Are you disrespectin' me? Cos if you are, I might not be too happy 'bout that,' she pursed her lips and took a step towards Elsa. Nick quickly took a step forward and placed himself between the two women.

'I think I saw Barb pick a brightly coloured object up when she was collecting the glasses. I believe she took it into the kitchen,' he said to Elsa taking her by the arm and gently steering her away.

'I'll go and check.' Elsa hurried into the kitchen suddenly remembering Barb having something 'multicoloured' tucked under her arm. Nick smiled winningly at the woman.

'I'm sure it was the unicorn and it would be in the kitchen for safe-keeping. We've the matinée tomorrow and if it had been left in here, it might have found a new home.'

'That wouldn't have been good. My Mikey – that's my husband, said to come back here tomorrow to look for it, but I know that my Shanice won't sleep tonight without it an' he's not the one who will have to sit with her. I don't know what I would have told her if someone else had taken it.' The woman pulled down her acid-green top, which had ridden up over her ample hips as she had searched for the unicorn.

'Did you all enjoy the panto?' Nick asked chattily, 'it would be nice to tell the cast something an actual audience member had said.'

The woman's face lit up, her vibrant red lips parted in a big smile. 'Oh, we all really enjoyed it. My Shanice thought the princess was beautiful an' my Mikey was real glad he wasn't sat on the end of the row, 'cos he might've ended up wit' that Widow Twanky sat on his knee. He might not have been real comfortable wit' that, you know wha' I'm sayin'?'

Nick laughed. 'Hmm, I know what you mean – that Widow Twanky is none too light.'

At that moment, Elsa appeared carrying a multicoloured stuffed animal,

Is this what you were looking for?' she asked the woman.

'It is, oh thank you so much, my Shanice will be real glad she got her unicorn back an' we can all get some sleep tonight now. Right, well now I can't stand here talkin' as I gotta get home, so I'll jus' say goodnight.' The woman took the unicorn and tucked it under her arm.

'I'll come out with you and lock up,' said Elsa. She turned to Nick. 'Will you and the boys go out through the back door?'

'No problem. Good night,' replied Nick.

Elsa nodded her head at Graham and Keith who had watched the whole unicorn episode with ill-concealed mirth and then let herself and the woman out of the hall. As she turned the key in the lock, she thought she heard the men laughing but, then again, she could have been mistaken. Elsa turned towards Brian, who was waiting for her and noticed that the woman with the unicorn was squinting at the small group of people standing near the back door of the hall, as though she was trying to make out someone in the group. Then she shook her head dismissively and walked away.

'Come on love, I've been waiting for ages, what've you been doing?' Brian was stamping his feet.

'Looking for a unicorn,' Elsa told him.

Brian scratched his head. 'What?' he exclaimed.

'Nothing, love. Let's get going.' Elsa slipped her arm around Brian's elbow companionably.

Brian shrugged his shoulders, obviously glad to be headed to the pub at last.

Bella Sturdy

After Elsa had left and locked the door, Nick, Graham and Keith decided to call it a night and leave with the rest of the cast, so they walked through the hall to the Green Room where everyone appeared make-up and costume free. Most of the group were talking of going to the pub and as they piled out into the car park a few of some of the cast members' friends were waiting to walk with them.

Bella had hung back with Simon, she had something to tell him and she fervently hoped he would be pleased. She now grasped his hand.

'I need to talk to you,' she whispered urgently.

'Are you two love-birds coming to the pub for a drink?' Desmond asked as he locked the door.

'No, I'll probably have a small one at Bella's,' Simon replied.

'Righty-oh, we'll see you both tomorrow at half past one then. Goodnight.' Desmond hurried to catch up with the crowd who were already walking up the street and Bella noticed someone else, who had been waiting, also tagged along behind.

She waited until everyone was out of earshot, apart from the old guy in the trilby who stood at the bus stop, and he was engrossed on his phone.

She took hold of Simon's hand. 'You do love me, Simon, don't you?' She scanned his face anxiously.

Simon held her at arm's length and smiled. 'Of course I do, Bella sweetheart, you know I do.' He pulled her to him.

Bella took a deep breath. 'I'm pregnant,' she said softly.

Simon froze. 'What? Pregnant?' He stepped back, a look of horror on his face.

Bella's smile faded.

'Are you sure?' he queried forcefully.

Bella gulped and nodded her head.

'Bloody hell,' he said finally.

Bella was trembling – this wasn't the reaction she had expected. In her mind, Simon would have been delighted, would have kissed her and told her that now he would push for his divorce. Instead, he was just staring into the air above her head and saying nothing. He was thinking, she could see that, but his face was stony and gave nothing away. Bella shivered and rubbed her arms; the sudden movement seemed to remind Simon that she was still there.

'Have you told anyone else?' he asked.

Bella shook her head.

'Not even your parents?'

'Definitely not my parents!'

'Good, then let's keep this to ourselves for a while until I can sort things out. I want to be able to face your father with some positive answers – not a lot of "I don't knows". He isn't going to be happy. Come on, I'll drop you off at home.'

'I thought you might be pleased…' Bella began sulkily.

'Pleased! What in God's name made you think I would be pleased?' Simon shouted.

The man at the bus stop looked in their direction, and then quickly turned away, not wanting to appear to be listening.

Bella stopped walking. 'Well I certainly didn't expect you to be horrible about it,' she pouted.

Simon took a deep breath and closed his eyes as he appeared to struggle with his emotions. 'I'm not being horrible,' he said through gritted teeth. 'I'm just shocked. It's so unexpected, unplanned and, if I'm honest, a little bit inconvenient.'

Bella's eyes filled with tears. Was Simon going to abandon her? They stared at each other for a moment, then Simon took hold of her hands.

'Bella darling,' he began patiently, 'I'm not free to marry you and won't be for some months, probably not until after the baby is born. This isn't what I wanted for you.'

Bella flung herself at him and wrapped her arms around his body. Simon stroked her hair and she relaxed into him.

'I didn't mean this to happen,' she told him. 'I know your situation, but what are we going to do?'

'There's not a lot we can do about *your* situation, but I'll talk to my wife and, as she has someone else in her life too, we'll see if we can make some legal advances that suit us both, all right?' he replied soothingly.

'Ok,' Bella replied.

'But you must do as I ask and keep this between us for now. I don't want my wife to get wind of it and use it as an excuse to halt or delay proceedings, do you understand?'

Bella nodded happily. At last! He would be free soon.

As she pulled away, she noticed Simon exchanging a glance with the man at the bus stop. The man abruptly turned away.

'Do you know him?' she asked.

Simon let out a ragged sign before replying: 'Never seen him before.'

Lydia Buckley

After leaving the hall, Lydia went straight to Greg's, where he greeted her with a big hug and a long, lingering kiss. A little while later, they settled at the breakfast bar with a mug of hot chocolate each and a notepad and pen.

'Are you sure you want to write all this down? It's not really the scandal of the century,' Lydia commented.

'It has the makings of a good story and my investigative nose tells me there's more to come. Anyway, if I don't use it, there's no harm done.' Greg picked up his pen. 'Now, let's start at the beginning.'

Lydia began with what Zoe had told her about Verity's visit to the salon and how they discovered that Simon was married to Annabelle while dating Bella, and that neither woman knew the truth. She told him how Simon had told Bella he was taking her to the ball, but at the last minute made up a story about his father's heart attack and that he had gone to the ball with his wife, which had obviously been his intention all along.

Greg put his pen down. 'You see, that's the bit I don't understand. Why would you invite your girlfriend to the ball if you knew all along that you were going with your wife? I just can't see the point.' Greg took a drink of hot chocolate.

'It's not the first time Simon has done that to Bella, apparently, so she was very disappointed but not overly surprised.'

Greg shook his head in disbelief. 'He sure complicates life,' he added and picked up his pen. 'Go on, what next?'

'Well, as you know, both Elsa and I saw him at the ball, but Elsa saw him with Zoe which led her to assume they'd gone together, but they hadn't. Simon was surprised to see Zoe at the ball and wanted to talk to her so that's why they went off to somewhere quiet.'

'I thought Elsa said they were kissing?' Greg paused and frowned.

'Let me demonstrate what *actually* happened,' suggested Lydia standing up.

'Oh, I like the sound of this.'

'Behave,' Lydia remonstrated. 'Stay sitting down so I can be taller than you and I'll show you what Simon did and said.' Lydia put her both hands on Greg's shoulders and said, 'You do trust me,

Zoe don't you?' Then she bent her head so their cheeks touched. 'Because if you don't, I'll ruin you and your business.'

She stood up and looked at Greg's surprised face,

'Bloody hell! Did he say that? And can he? Ruin her business, I mean?'

'Yes, he said those exact words, and he probably *can* ruin her business. Aztec Developments are her landlord and the lease will be up for review next month, and he says he'll not recommend its renewal. Zoe also lives in the flat above the salon so she would be homeless as well.'

Greg's mouth had fallen open. 'He *is* a nasty piece of work, and this is because she threatened to tell Bella the truth about his wife?'

'I believe so and that's why Zoe said nothing on Sunday afternoon. However, Nick – he's the assistant stage manager – heard Zoe and Simon arguing on Monday at rehearsal. Zoe told Simon that unless he came clean to Bella this coming Sunday, *she* would tell her on Monday morning. So, Nick is also aware that something is going on.'

Greg wrote a few more lines and then said, 'So, if I've got this right, only you, Zoe and Nick know that Simon is leading a double life, and both Bella and Annabelle are blissfully in the dark.'

'That's about it. The other thing to note is that Simon's father has turned up.'

'Turned up? What do you mean?'

'I bumped into an older chap a couple of times last Saturday and I saw him again tonight at the panto. He's a charming old boy and we struck up a conversation during which he told me that he's moved to Ashdale to reconcile with Simon as they'd not spoken for over twenty years. So Simon has been lying to Bella about his father as well, using him as an excuse not to see her on various occasions.'

Greg made some more notes. 'Do you happen to know his father's name?' he asked.

'Edward DeVere Jones and he wasn't very complimentary about Simon either.' Lydia told Greg what Edward had said.

After making more notes, Greg eventually sat back. 'Simon is certainly weaving a web of lies and deceit, but why?' he pondered.

'I'm sure I'll find out next week if Zoe tells Bella what she knows.'

'Do you think she will?'

'I do actually. I think she'll call Simon's bluff. You said that Carlton Banks won't be too happy if he finds out that Simon has been cheating on his daughter, so Simon may find that he isn't in a position to hurt Zoe in the way that he's threatened to.' Lydia stood up and carried their mugs to the sink, 'Come on let's go to bed, I'm shattered.'

Greg yawned and stretched,

'Me too and we can have a lie-in tomorrow morning.' They left their thoughts on the Simon/Annabelle/Bella triangle behind and contentedly made their way to bed.

Annabelle Saxby-Jones

In Harrogate, Annabelle had waited until Simon was settled on the sofa, bracing herself for the unpleasant conversation to come. This had brought back all the memories of Robert and that awful morning when she had received the envelope containing those dreadful photographs. She could not believe that this was happening to her *again.*

Annabelle had thought of many ways to broach the subject, but now the time had come her nerves were all over the place and she couldn't remember what she had rehearsed. She took a deep breath and tried to speak calmly. 'Verity told me today that you're having an affair with a young girl from Ashdale called Bella.' There, she had said it!

Simon did a double-take. 'What?' he gasped.

'It came out in conversation. She thought—'

'Came out in conversation? What sort of conversation were you having?' he snapped.

Annabelle was startled for a moment, wrong-footed, as there was no way she wanted to tell him what she and Verity had been talking about.

'Well?' he demanded.

Annabelle frowned.

Hang on a minute, I'm not the one at fault here!

'That's irrelevant, the point is…' she began, but Simon cut her off again,

'Irrelevant? I'm accused of having an affair and you call it irrelevant? I want to know exactly what Verity said, and where she got it from.' Simon stood up and pointed his finger at her.

Annabelle sat on the sofa looking at her furious husband. She was shocked. She had expected Simon to be contrite and to beg for forgiveness, not to be cross with *her*.

'Verity went to the salon where this Bella works and she found out from the salon manager – I think her name is Zoe, that you're cheating on me with Bella.' Annabelle spoke quietly and firmly, her eyes never leaving Simon's face.

Simon turned away and paced up and down.

Annabelle watched him until she could bear it no longer, 'Have you nothing to say to me?' she asked.

Simon stopped pacing and stood in front of her. 'I was hoping that I wouldn't have to have this conversation with you as I knew it would upset you…' he began, then held up his finger as Annabelle opened her mouth to speak. 'Please, just listen. For some time now, I've become aware that Zoe – yes, the salon manager, has been attracted to me. She's also in the Ashdale Players albeit just for make-up backstage; but recently she's made it clear that she would like to start a clandestine relationship with me.'

Simon sat down next to Annabelle on the sofa and took hold of her hands. 'I want to make it absolutely clear that I love you and do not want an affair of any kind. I thought I had explained this quite clearly and gently to Zoe, but she took umbrage and became angry, refusing to accept that I had rejected her.' Simon sighed dramatically and lowered his eyes, 'I believe that she saw an opportunity to cause mischief between you and me when she realised that Verity was your friend.'

Annabelle was stunned into silence. She stared at Simon as her brain processed what he had just told her. *This whole thing was fabricated? Zoe had lied to Verity?*

'But why would she make up something like that? *Is* there a girl called Bella? Did you know what Zoe has told Verity?'

'There is a girl called Bella and she's in the panto. She's a sweet farmer's daughter somewhere in her early twenties, but she's hardly 'other woman' material,' answered Simon.

'But—'

'Zoe told me earlier this week what she had said to Verity. She laughed in my face and said that if I tried to deny it, she would tell people that she was *also* having an affair with me, as though I was some sort of serial womaniser.' Simon stood up and walked away towards the sitting-room window. 'That's the other reason why I was so upset last night when you dressed in that red outfit, I felt as though you were mocking me, even though you couldn't possibly have known it.'

'But—'

'Belle, there isn't anything for you to worry about. The fact you don't believe me when I say I'm not having an affair is exactly what Zoe is hoping for.' Simon returned to the sofa and sat down.

Annabelle saw that his eyes blinked furiously as though keeping tears at bay.

'Don't you see? If you throw me out, Zoe will have won. There's a saying 'Hell hath no fury like a woman scorned' – that's Zoe to a "T". Please Annabelle, don't give up on us because of one woman's wrath.'

Annabelle saw the anguish in her husband's face, the unshed tears in his eyes, and felt a strong fire flare within her heart,

'Oh Simon, I've been so miserable today, I thought you were going to leave *me*. Of course, I won't throw you out.'

Simon pulled her into his chest, wrapping his arms around her, 'I *love* you,' she mumbled into his shirt.

'My darling Belle, I'm so relieved that you believe me. We can be stronger now, more than ever.' Simon kissed the top of Annabelle's head. 'Promise me, that you won't believe any more lies or gossip.'

'Promise,' came the muffled reply.

'Come on, let's go to bed. I believe you mentioned making babies at breakfast this morning?'

Annabelle pulled away from him, her heart soaring with joy. 'You mean—?' she whispered hopefully.

Simon took her hand and pulled her to her feet. 'There's no harm in trying,' he teased suggestively as he led her to the stairs.

11

Annabelle Saxby-Jones

Annabelle woke up and stretched languidly. She smiled contentedly as she recalled how last night Simon had gently made love to her and told her wonderful things. She giggled as she realised that she was still naked – normally she never slept without her pyjamas. She got out of bed and slipped into the discarded sleepwear and matching robe, found her slippers and headed downstairs to join Simon for breakfast. She knew he was still in the house because as she crossed the hall, she could hear him talking in his office,

'Good morning Hugo, you do realise it's Saturday… Oh? What's the panic?… Another letter eh? You're a popular man, Hugo… Well, I'm rather committed today… Ok, well the only time I can suggest is five o'clock this evening… You'll have to come to the Jubilee Hall to meet me after the matinée… No. Everyone goes to the Forget-Me-Not Café for tea so it'll be just us… Don't come to the main entrance, come to the back door, it's through the car park. You'll need a code to get it and its five, five, six, eight, have you got that?… Right then, I'll see you later.'

Simon disconnected and opened his office door as Annabelle walked past. 'Morning sleepyhead,' he smiled at her and pulled her close for a kiss. Once the kitchen, Annabelle prepared their coffee and croissants and chattered happily about maybe doing some shopping in town and wondered if Simon wanted to come along.

Simon shook his head. 'I'm sorry Belle,' he said, 'I've a meeting this morning.'

'But it's Saturday!' she exclaimed.

'I know, but Bruce is going back to Spain this afternoon and it's the only time I can catch him. We've some business to discuss – he's in the property game as well, you know,' Simon explained as he buttered his croissant.

'Bruce?'

'Yes, Bruce Harvey, Fiona Cavendish's husband – they came to the ball last weekend.'

'Oh yes, I remember. Are you thinking of building in Spain, then?' Annabelle asked.

'No, I'm actually thinking of buying a villa for us, for holidays and long weekends away. What do you think?' Simon looked at her over the rim of his mug of coffee.

'Oh Simon,' Annabelle gasped, 'that would be fantastic. Could we go over to Spain and have a look or will you buy from brochures?'

'I think a little holiday in Mar Menor to shop for a villa would do us both good – give us some quality time. I should also mention that I'm planning to use the villa as a business asset – to entertain clients, so there will be times when I go there without you.' Simon stood and picked up his phone as he prepared to leave.

Annabelle nodded her head. 'Of course, darling. Will you be back today for lunch?' She took their breakfast pots over to the sink.

'No, I'm going into the office now to collect some papers and then I'm driving over to Bruce and Fiona's house, I'll have lunch with them and then come straight back for the matinée.'

'Quite a busy day then. Well I'll see you tonight at the panto, so good luck.' Annabelle waited until she heard Simon's car drive away before she picked up her phone and scrolled through her contacts to find Verity's number.

'Verity, hi – you ask me to call you, is now a good time? Great, well I just wanted to say that Simon and I have sorted everything out and we're fine... yes, it's all a complete fabrication. You know that salon manager, Zoe?... well, she made it all up, guessing you would tell me, and hoping I would then accuse Simon of cheating and throw him out... Why? So that she could be there to pick up the pieces and have him all to herself. Apparently, she wanted to have an affair with him and he rejected her... Of course I believe Simon, he's my husband... Yes, well, he's not Harry! Anyway, Simon and I are fine, which is the important thing, so can you and Harry still pick me up as arranged, at six forty-five please?... Great, see you then. Bye.'

It wasn't until she had disconnected that Annabelle realised she had forgotten to mention the villa in Mar Menor. Never mind they would find out soon enough. Annabelle hummed to herself as she climbed the stairs to take a shower and get dressed. Funny how one minute everything seemed to be awful and the next, everything was wonderful – just because people didn't tell the truth!

Councillor Hugo Marshall

Hugo was decidedly grumpy as he stomped into the agency that morning. Felicity glanced up as he closed the door with more force than was necessary, causing the recently mended blind to flap against it noisily.

'Morning,' he grunted.

'Good morning, Councillor Marshall,' Felicity said with clipped tones as he strode passed her into his office and closed this door also a little firmly. In his office, Hugo flung his briefcase down petulantly and paced the floor. *Damn Charles!*

Not content with the bit of a spat at the accountant's yesterday, Charles had straight away rung Celia and told her what had gone on. That was really out of order!

Celia had bent his ear all evening about what people might think when all he wanted to do was retire. Charles had retired, Beatrice was talking about retiring as a magistrate, that's what people do eventually. The more Hugo thought about it, the more he convinced himself that it had nothing to do with Planet Properties' latest project – he just damned well wanted to retire.

He thought back to Monday and his conversation with Bruce Harvey following the meeting at Freddie's office. Bruce had talked in more detail about his company, Spanish Sun, and how Hugo could be a part of it by becoming a UK agent. It had been a very positive and interesting conversation, but then Bruce had mentioned that he also wanted someone to work with him in his Spanish office in Mar Menor.

When Hugo returned to his office after the disastrous meeting yesterday, he had Googled Mar Menor and Spanish Sun and was impressed by what he saw.

Now, as he paced back and forth, he realised that he was seriously considering calling Bruce and offering his services to the Spanish office. Could he really do that though? Just pack his bags and go; give up the opportunity of becoming mayor? If things went pear-shaped here, he might just have to. It might not be a bad idea to pursue this opportunity, as a sort of Plan B. Hugo like the idea of Plan B, at least Simon had nothing to do with it; the blasted man had so far, blocked his plans to leave both Planet Properties and Lewis Marshall, but he couldn't stop him from going to Spain. Hugo made his mind up to speak to Bruce and sat down at his desk. But before he could do anything else, there was a knock at the door and Felicity entered,

'The post has arrived Councillor Marshall,' she said curtly, putting a pile of envelopes on his desk.

He glanced at the pile and froze as he saw a bright-pink envelope sitting on the top. He looked up at Felicity who raised a disapproving eyebrow before she turned and left his office.

Hugo stared at the pink envelope, another reason to go to Spain. He ripped it open and read the letter within:

Not going according to plan?

It was as usual, created with words cut from other publications and glued onto pink paper, but Hugo felt that this was no random member of the public – *someone* knew what going on, how else would they know that, actually things were *not* going according to plan? He snatched up his mobile and scrolled for Simon's number; it was time for tough-talking.

'Simon, I need to see to you today… I know it's Saturday, but this can't wait… I've received another of those damned pink letters… I really must insist that we meet today… I don't care if you're committed, find some time to see me, anywhere, anytime… I'm desperate and no, everything isn't all right… Five o'clock, yes that's fine, where? Jubilee Hall? But it will be full of your fellow actors… well, as long as they've all gone. Shall I just come to the main entrance?… Right, back door – five, five, six, eight. See you then.'

Hugo immediately dialled Bruce Harvey's number:

'Bruce, good morning… I wonder if I might have a word about Mar Menor, have you got a moment?'

Fifteen minutes later, Hugo ended his call with Bruce, sat back in his chair and sighed with relief. The conversation had gone well. Bruce had been receptive and had made positive noises about Hugo's suggestion of joining him in Spain. Of course, there were a lot of details to work out and nothing was definite, but it was a step forward and gave Hugo a good feeling. If he left the business and moved to Spain, he wouldn't be able to support either Lewis Marshall or Planet Properties and they would have no option but to dissolve the partnerships. *Damn well teach them a thing or two.*

As for Celia, well she could choose to follow her husband as a good wife should, or stay in Ashdale with her lazy brother and boring sister-in-law for company. Hugo was surprised to find that he didn't really care which option she chose.

Lydia Buckley

Lydia had the house to herself as both Kate and Ben were at work. Olivia was helping Kate at the café preparing food for the Players post-matinée tea. She was in her bedroom working on her next novel, when her phone burst into life. The caller-id told her that it was Zoe.

'Lydia! Oh God!' Zoe sounded distraught.

'Whatever is the matter?' Lydia asked with concern.

'Bloody Simon Saxby-Jones, that's what the matter is.'

'Why? What's he done now?'

Zoe took a deep breath in an effort to calm herself,

'Listen to this. I've just spoken to Verity, and apparently yesterday she told Annabelle that Simon is having an affair with Bella. Annabelle spoke to Simon about it last night and she says he…' Zoe was soon out of breath. Lydia heard her breathing heavily with emotion and said nothing, waiting for her to calm herself.

'…He told Annabelle that I had made the story about Bella up because *I* wanted him for *myself* and thought that Annabelle would divorce him if she knew!'

'*He said what?*' Lydia was astounded.

'He said that I had wanted an affair with him, but that he had rejected me, and so this was my way of getting back at him, or something like that… I'm *so* bloody angry!'

There was a silence as Lydia digested the news. 'Have you spoken to Simon?'

'No, he isn't answering his phone, I guess he's avoiding me… Well, he won't be able to avoid me this afternoon!' Zoe snapped.

'Zoe, I thought we had agreed to wait until after the panto before saying anything,' Lydia reminded her.

'We did and I'm not going to say anything to Bella, but I'll have a word with Simon in his "private dressing room". He isn't getting away with this.'

'Whatever happens, this isn't going to end well for anyone, so please be careful what you say,' warned Lydia.

'I hear what you say, but I'm not taking the blame for his shoddy behaviour.' Zoe sounded a little calmer now. 'I'm sorry for ranting, but I had to get this off my chest and you're the only person I could rant to.'

'Zoe, it's fine and I do understand, but what I don't understand is why he's doing all this in the first place.'

'I can only think it's something to do with Bella's father. Jonathan Sturdy is quite well off and his business, Harefield Park, is about to expand into the farm next door which Jonathan has recently bought. Look, I've to go, my next client is here. I'll see you this afternoon… and thanks again.'

Lydia chewed her lip for a moment, then she called Greg. She repeated what Zoe had told her about Simon and asked what he thought about Jonathan Sturdy and Harefield Park.

'Hmm,' Greg, was obviously turning things over in his mind. 'You know I did some research for Robbie Parker? Well, it involves planning permissions which, on the face of it, appear above board, but there may have been some dodgy goings-on regarding the sale of certain properties. Let me explain: Property A is a house, couple of barns and some land. The owners want to convert the barns and sell them with some land for a pony paddock or two, so they have the plans drawn for a couple of executive-type houses. The plans are passed and they sell the houses and land to a small developer. The developer has the plans re-drawn to include a small housing estate on the land, and these are submitted to the council. When the new plans are given the go-ahead, the small developer sells the whole thing to a bigger developer and makes a lot more money. The original owners are left in the middle of a housing estate instead of the couple of executive houses they planned.'

'Is that even legal?'

'The process regarding the planning permission is legal, but the question is, how can the small developer guarantee that they will be the buyer in the first place? Interested parties have to submit sealed bids.'

'So, they would have to make sure they submit the highest bid.'

'Yes,' replied Greg, 'but that's risky as you would have to put in a ridiculously high offer to guarantee being way above the other bids and that isn't good business sense.'

'So, what are you saying?'

'Robbie has been approached by three landowners who, quite separately, found themselves in the exact circumstances I've just described to you. They all had the same architect, estate agent, and sealed bids from the same companies. The properties were all bought by Planet Properties who are a small developer and who re-drew the plans,' explained Greg.

'That does sound a bit too coincidental, have you tracked down Planet Properties?'

'Not yet, the only contact address is an accountant's office in Harrogate, and the architect for Planet Properties is a Nicholas Edwards and I can't find any trace of him.'

'So, do you think this might have anything to do with Jonathan Sturdy?'

'I don't know, but I'm going to have a look and see if Harefield Park or the farm next door have submitted any plans recently, it's just a thought.'

'Ok. Let me know if you find anything out. In the meantime, I'll look forward to seeing you all after the panto.'

Lydia pondered on their conversation before deciding to make herself a cup of coffee and get back to her writing.

Councillor Hugo Marshall

Hugo had just returned from a successful viewing with a couple of prospective purchasers, and expected them to put in an offer on the large property by the end of the day. He leaned back in his chair, closed his eyes and allowed his mind to return to Spain; the more he thought about living in warmer climes, the more he liked the idea. If Charles continued to be difficult, Hugo supposed that they could leave Tom to run the agency – at least as a short-term solution. Hugo wondered what permits and other paperwork he would need to put his plan into action. He sat up and purposefully and pulled his laptop closer, deciding to Google *permits for moving to Spain* and set the wheels in motion. He wanted to be ready to go at short notice.

The telephone rang and Hugo was surprised to hear Bruce's voice.

'Bruce, you know, following our little chat this morning—'

'Hugo, I'm going to come straight to the point. I don't think you have been entirely honest with me and I am a little disappointed, to be frank.'

'What?' Hugo spluttered.

'I understand from a potential client of mine, that you have recently found yourself compromised and that there are certain circumstances which you are trying to avoid. It seems this situation has led you to make the rash decision to sell your agency under the guise of retirement. They know this because your current partner in the agency, your brother-in-law I believe, has expressed concern at the speed with which you wish to proceed.'

'What—' Hugo spluttered again, not quite believing what he was hearing.

'This person's company was prepared to consider purchasing your agency in May, but I understand you have declined as you need an immediate sale.'

'But I—'

'To put it bluntly, Hugo," Bruce continued cutting Hugo off mid-breath, "I do not wish to become embroiled in your shady shenanigans. So, upon reflection, I don't think it would be beneficial to Spanish Sun to continue our association.'

'This "potential client" is Simon Saxby-Jones, isn't it?' sneered Hugo.

'I couldn't possibly say, but I wish you the best of luck and hope you are able to extract yourself successfully from the difficulties you're experiencing. Goodbye Hugo.'

Hugo replaced the handset and sat, staring at his blotter for a good few minutes, his heart hammering and his hands shaking. He took several deep breaths, and as soon as he felt able, asked Felicity to bring him a black coffee with two sugars. When Felicity had placed the steaming cup on his desk, and, closing the door firmly behind her, had returned to her desk, Hugo opened his drawer and took out a hip flask. He poured a measure into his coffee and then, with only a two-second hesitation, swigged directly from the flask, before concealing it back in his drawer. What to do now? How was he to escape from Simon's clutches?

Come on, Hugo – think!

Bella Sturdy

As the cast launched into the finale, Bella noticed Lydia silently leave her chair behind the prompt screen. She had told the cast, and cleared it with Desmond, that she would leave at that point to go and help her sister at the Forget-Me-Not Café.

After the curtains had closed, the cast, with the usual heady mix of post-show euphoria and adrenaline hurried back to the dressing rooms to change and remove make-up. It was four thirty and it took at least ten minutes of loud chatter and banter amid organised chaos before everyone was ready to leave for the five-minute walk to the Market Place, where they were expected at the café for the matinée tea. Bella took her time getting changed, she knew that there would be a queue at the café – and Simon did not like to queue. As she pulled on her boots, she heard her name being called. 'Bella darling? Bella, are you still here?'

Bella stepped into the corridor as Desmond minced his way towards her.

'Bella, I just wanted to congratulate you on a superb performance. Your timing was on point and your delivery was fab-u-lous!' Desmond pulled her towards him and air-kissed each side of her cheek, 'You've upped your game and improved with each show. Darling, I am so impressed… and I'm definitely going to cast you in a stronger role for the next panto. Now, I must get off to the café. Are you and Simon joining us?'

Bella was stunned for a moment. 'Wow, thank you, Desmond… that means a lot to me, it really does. Yes, we'll meet you there.'

Desmond blew her a kiss as he flounced away. Bella couldn't stop grinning.

A stronger role next time!

'Well done, I thought you were brilliant too,' Maggie said from behind her.

'Oh, thanks, Maggie. I can't believe Desmond said that! It means such a lot coming from him.'

Then Bella remembered: *I'm pregnant. I'll have a baby this time next year. I probably won't even be in the panto.*

'Are you all right, Bella?'

'What? Oh… yes, fine. It's the shock… you know … what Desmond just said … stronger role and all that … God!' Bella bluffed.

'Ok, see you at the café then.' Maggie paused for a moment and gave her a concerned look.

'I'm fine – honest. See you there.'

As Bella watched Maggie walk quickly away down the corridor, another voice caught her attention:

'Bella, well done this afternoon, brilliant performance,' Zoe said as she came out of the Green Room. Bella stiffened,

'Thanks, Zoe,' she answered crisply and turned back into the dressing room. She heard Zoe sigh and listened to her footsteps as she walked away. Bella wasn't sure how she felt about Zoe. Maggie had said nothing was going on between the salon owner and

Simon, but Bella couldn't shake off the feeling that they shared a secret of some sort and it worried her. She decided that when she saw Simon tomorrow, when they were alone, she would have a chat with him and tell him her worries, especially now that she was… *pregnant.*

Bella picked up her coat and handbag and, as everyone else had gone, she wandered down the corridor to the Parish Clerk's office or "Simon's Dressing Room" as the Players referred to it.

As she approached the closed door, she could hear Zoe's angry voice:

'Why are you telling so many lies, Simon?'

'What I do is none of your business!'

'It is *my* business now you have dragged *me* into it!'

'You should have kept your mouth shut to Verity!'

'It's not *my* fault that your wife's best friend came into my salon. It is not *my* fault that your wife and your girlfriend have similar names and it is certainly not *my* fault that Verity has told your wife about your girlfriend.'

'I've dealt with that!'

'Dealt with it! You told your wife that I wanted an affair with you and that when you rejected me, I made up a story about you dating Bella! How the hell is that *dealing with it*?'

'Will you just calm down, it's all sorted now. Annabelle believes me.'

'More fool her. But what about Bella? What are you going to tell *her*?'

'For now, absolutely nothing, and neither will you.'

'Nothing? *Nothing?* I work with Bella, who also thinks I'm having an affair with you. If you think I am going to carry on with this… this… deceit – well, you can think again because I'm not.'

'Oh, I think you will. Have you forgotten that I won't allow the renewal of the lease on your precious salon if you breathe a word of this to Bella? I'll let Bella down when I am good and ready and not before, it's just that things are a little complicated at the moment.'

Bella stared at the closed door.

Simon had lied… to her… to his wife… he'd threatened Zoe's business… and was going to let her down… *Gently?*

Suddenly fury overtook her and she flung open the door to the office. Simon was dressed in his 'civvies' in front of a desk on which a mirror with bulbs around it had been propped up. He looked relaxed with one knee over the other and had turned slightly to face Zoe, who had her back to the door. They both started in surprise at the sudden intrusion.

'What's going on? What are you both talking about?' Bella demanded.

Simon was quickly on his feet and holding his arms out towards her. 'Sweetheart, this is nothing to concern you, it's just a disagreement about the lease on the salon – isn't that right, Zoe?' Simon reached Bella and put his arms around her, looking at Zoe for confirmation, but before Zoe could say anything, Bella pushed Simon away.

'You said you would refuse to renew the salon lease if Zoe told me something. What's the big secret?' she demanded. Simon looked a little shaken at being shoved to one side, but he recovered and smiled sympathetically.

'I had hoped to spare you this, but if you want to know, then I'll tell you,' he said gently. 'Zoe wanted to break up *our* relationship and I have tried to stop her, this was the last resort.' He looked beseechingly at Bella, his eyes pleading with her to understand his dilemma.

'Enough!' hollered Zoe, her eyes flashing with rage. 'I refuse to be a part of this web of deceit and lies any longer.' She turned to Bella. 'This man is cheating on you with his *wife*, whom he has no intention of divorcing – and never has had.'

Simon rolled his eyes. 'Bella,' he said soothingly, 'are you going to listen to this pathetic woman, or believe *me* when I tell you that I love you?'

He smiled and Bella was reminded, for some random reason, of Shere Khan, the tiger of *Jungle Book* fame. Bella also realised that Simon had no idea just how much she had heard of their argument from the other side of the door.

She turned to Zoe. 'Tell me everything, Zoe,' she said quietly.

So Zoe told her about the initial meeting with Verity, how she had seen Simon at the Valentine Ball, and how their meeting which had been observed by Elsa, and about the decision to keep quiet until after the panto.

'I told Simon, that if he didn't confess to you tomorrow, I'd tell you the truth on Monday.'

'But this is nonsense, it doesn't prove anything! Bella, you've known all along that Annabelle and I still live in the same house – I've told you before… we're separated.' Simon waved his hand dismissively. 'I've heard enough; will you please leave us Zoe? I want to speak to Bella alone.'

Bella looked uncertainly from Simon, to Zoe, who shook her head sadly.

'You're still not admitting the truth, Simon,' Zoe said. Then turning to Bella she continued, 'Lydia, our prompt is, as you know, a lash technician. Annabelle Saxby-Jones was a client of hers last Wednesday. Lydia told me that Annabelle chatted happily about her marriage – separation and divorce were never mentioned. She also said that she and Simon were hoping to start a family.'

Bella caught her breath, and Simon frowned.

'Start a family? Don't be ridiculous, I have no intention of starting a family. Why the hell would I want a screaming brat?' Then he seemed to register, belatedly, what Bella had told him last night. He reached out for her and added a trifle lamely, '… with Annabelle, I mean.'

But it was too late.

Bella stared at Simon and backed away towards the open door, her eyes filled with tears. 'I heard you say that you were going to let me down gently. You have no intention of looking after me *or our baby*.'

Zoe gasped, and Bella continued as the tears spilt over. 'Yes, that's right Zoe, I'm pregnant with Simon's child. I told him last night and he said he would sort things out. I thought that meant he would get on with the divorce so he could marry me, but I see now that that it's not going to happen.' Bella broke down and sobbed, 'I'm going home and I'm not coming back!'

Simon stepped forward and caught Bella's arm as she turned to go. 'Bella, wait…'

Bella shook his hand off her arm. 'Let go of me and leave me alone!' she shouted. Bella turned and ran. She raced down the short corridor, wrenched open the back door and out into the darkness of the late afternoon, leaving the door to slam shut behind her.

Nick Bradley

Nick, Graham and Kevin had decided that they wouldn't go to the café, but instead stay behind. Kevin was anxious about leaving his expensive equipment, and anyway, they could get fish and chips and have some quiet downtime, maybe with a can of beer. Graham and Nick set up the scenery for Act One, then Nick collected the props in his crate and headed once more to the prop room. As he stepped out of the hall into the annexe part of the building, he stopped in his tracks as he heard Bella shout that she was going home and not coming back. He saw her run out of Simon's dressing room, down the hall and out of the back door which slammed behind her. He frowned as he entered the prop room; that had sounded quite a serious lovers' tiff. He hoped Bella would come back for this evening's performance.

However, as he refilled his crate with the props for Act One, he heard more raised voices – Zoe and Simon. This time, Nick didn't hesitate to listen, given that he had heard Simon get nasty with Zoe previously.

'Did you have to tell her everything?' Simon sneered angrily.

'Of course I did! Do you expect me to continue to lie for you and cover your tracks?' Zoe fired back, 'Why did you start a relationship with Bella in the first place?'

'Because I wanted to get to know her father. I just didn't think it would take this long or get this complicated, and if you had just kept your mouth shut, everything would have worked out. My business arrangement with Jonathan Sturdy would have been completed by May at the latest and then I would have let Bella go.'

'You used Bella as a pawn *in a business arrangement?* Zoe's voice did not disguise her shock.

'She would have got over it and I would have moved on. I'm poised to take over Aztec Developments within the next twelve months and then I really will be in complete control,' Simon said pompously.

'I suppose you manoeuvred yourself into that position too, or was that just good luck?' Zoe flung at him.

'Actually, women do find me attractive, Zoe, you must admit that…' Simon laughed mockingly, 'although I do confess that I had to get rid of Annabelle's fiancé first, but then what woman would remain engaged to a man who cheats, especially when there are photographs as proof.' Simon did air quotes as he said "proof".

Zoe frowned.

'When you say, "get rid of", you surely don't mean…'

'Murder?' Simon roared with laughter. 'Zoe dearest, even I wouldn't go that far. No, I just arranged for some Leeds tart to drape herself all over him and he was, I believe the word is, "papped". After Annabelle received some anonymous photographs, it was easy to be at her side, pick up the pieces, be supportive and sympathetic and then propose to her. She was practically begging me for it.'

'You used her too?' Zoe gasped in disbelief at Simon's audacity.

'You mean I should have turned down a young woman who was clearly besotted with me and has a rich daddy? Not many men would do that!' Simon laughed sardonically.

In the prop-room doorway, Nick's mouth fell open.

What an arrogant…

Words failed him. Poor Bella, and as for his wife, what would she think if she heard all this?

'Why are you telling me all this? Don't you think that I might tell Annabelle?' Zoe asked.

'Annabelle won't believe you. Simple as that. She already thinks you're a rejected would-be lover who is determined to break up my marriage with more lies and spite,' Simon told her smugly.

'You've no morals at all,' Zoe told Simon with disgust, 'you're playing with people's lives, their feelings – have you no conscience?'

Simon laughed again. 'Absolutely none, Zoe darling – so what are you going to do about it?'

'Well, I'm not going to listen to any more...'

Suddenly the door to the hall opened and Graham stood there holding a white packet from which arose a delicious smell of fish and chips. He looked quizzically at Nick and without speaking nodded towards the hall where Kevin sat with the promised cans of beer. Nick nodded and quietly closed the prop-room door to follow Graham, deciding to keep what he had overheard to himself.

Vinnie Buckley

Vinnie strolled around the ship on the Promenade Deck, it was an 'at sea' day as they cruised towards their next port of call, Dominica. He was a little miffed that he had not had a return text from Lydia but then again, perhaps he would pick up messages when they got closer to land. He stopped and leant over the railing. He was loving the Caribbean – the sea was a stunning turquoise; the islands were so proud of their individual cultures, and the people were so welcoming, he would definitely come back. He wasn't sure which island he would come back to, and they still had a couple more to visit, but one thing he was sure of – he wouldn't be bringing Vivienne.

She was refusing to speak to him now, all because of yesterday. After he had left the bar on St Maarten and joined her back on the beach, Vivienne had been lying on her front after her swim in the sea. Apart from a string of beige fabric around her waist and between her bottom cheeks, she was naked, the discarded bikini top lay on his sunbed next to her. Vinnie had picked up the triangular pieces and thought carefully before suggesting that she might like to be a little more conservative.

Vivienne had propped herself up, squinted at him and said, 'Conservative? When have I ever been conservative? You know I don't follow politics.'

She had lain down again and Vinnie had realised that they were not on the same page at all. The argument had come later when they were back in their cabin, Vinnie had tried again to express his unhappiness at the way she flaunted her body, and this time she had clearly understood what he was saying.

There followed much shouting during which Vivienne made it clear, that what had attracted him to her in the first place, wasn't going to be hidden under polo neck jumpers and baggy tracksuit bottoms.

They'd more or less avoided each other today and Vinnie had found solace in the solitude. He stood up, stretched and wandered inside the ship, then spotting a bar on the far side, decided a drink would be in order. His watch told him that it was five o'clock and he had a good hour at least before he had to face Vivienne again. There was only one other customer at the bar, a man reading a newspaper with a cold lager in front of him.

'Yes sir?' asked the barman. Vinnie eyed the lager. He had been thinking of a gin and tonic, but suddenly the lager looked thirst-quenching,

'I'll have a lager please,' he replied as he perched on a stool, leaving a respectful empty stool between him and the man with the newspaper. Vinnie hadn't read a newspaper in years, all his information came from his phone or laptop, but of course, on board a ship there was virtually no Wi-Fi to speak of. He wondered if the newspaper was recent and leaned forward, squinting his eyes to pinpoint the date on the front page. As he leaned further forward, the newspaper was suddenly lowered and Vinnie found himself staring into a pair of brown eyes.

He jerked upright, embarrassed. 'Sorry, I just wondered how old the paper was,' he explained.

The man grinned. 'No problem. I bought this yesterday and it's Wednesday's paper, they're usually two days behind. I get a paper as it's more relaxing to read than scanning my tablet.'

Vinnie nodded in agreement, 'I wish I'd thought of that.'

'My wife has gone to the spa for a treatment of some sort,' the man said chattily, 'so I thought I would find a quiet spot myself. I found this bar the other day and I like to come here each day around this time. It gives Susannah the cabin to herself to do whatever she wants to do and give us both a little time to ourselves.'

'That's a great idea,' Vinnie said. 'Being with one's other half twenty-four seven can be a little… testing.'

The man chuckled and then stuck out his hand. 'My name is Richard and I'm an escapee husband.'

Vinnie accepted the proffered hand and shook it. 'My name is Vinnie and likewise.'

The men laughed at their own joke and clinked their lager glasses in comradeship.

'Where are you from?' Richard asked.

'Oxford, how about you?'

'Harrogate in North Yorkshire,' was the reply.

'Good heavens! I've a meeting up there next Thursday with a company called Aztec Developments,' said Vinnie, 'do you know of them?'

'Yes, I've heard of them, but apart from the fact that they're builders, I know very little else. I'm a solicitor and I deal with divorce law generally, so they wouldn't really come across my radar.'

Vinnie nodded thoughtfully and took a sip of lager. *Divorce Law eh? That might come in useful.*

12

Councillor Hugo Marshall

Hugo sat in his car, drumming his fingers on the steering wheel. He stared through the windscreen at the back door of the Jubilee Hall. It was almost five o'clock; he was ready for his meeting with Simon and he had the latest pink envelope in his jacket pocket, which he believed would prove that the sender wasn't a random member of the public. In his mind, Hugo had prepared his speech, the very words he was going to say to that snake, that back-stabber. If Simon Saxby-Jones thought that he could intimidate this particular upstanding Councillor, the mayor-elect no less, then he had another thing coming. Hugo had never felt so much rage, so much animosity towards another human being before. Three times this week Simon had thwarted his plans, *three.* It was monstrous, outrageous, and Hugo had had enough; Simon had gone too far.

His heart thudded and he was too warm; his hand shook as he pulled the car keys out of the ignition. The back door to the hall opened and as the light from the hallway spilt out into the car park, he watched a woman in a light-coloured raincoat step out. The door slammed shut behind her as she pushed her hands inside the pockets of her coat and marched across the car park towards King Street.

Hugo waited and then thought about changing his mind. He might make matters worse, God knows what Simon could do to his reputation, but if he did nothing… He looked at his watch, it was five past five. Time to decide whether to go ahead with this meeting, bearing in mind what he hoped to gain. He was nervous and took a deep breath before pulling himself out of the car. He straightened his coat and walked determinedly towards the back door. He pressed the numbers on the keypad, heard a click, and then turning the handle he stepped inside, closing the door behind him.

Jonathan Sturdy

Jonathan sat at his desk Googling *Ashdale estate agents* on his laptop. He had checked out Lewis Marshall noting that it had received favourable reviews. He had also discovered that one of the partners, Hugo Marshall, was a local councillor who was tipped to become the next mayor, so surely that gave the business some credibility. But Jonathan still didn't feel comfortable with what Simon had suggested; he preferred to find his own agent. He sighed and sat back – perhaps he was making hard work of this, maybe it would be simpler to just hand the project over to Lewis Marshall and have two million pounds in the bank by the end of April. But something niggled him at the back of his mind and he couldn't shake it off. Jonathan had always trusted his instincts. Anyway, it was Saturday – he glanced at his laptop, five o'clock, almost drinks time. His attention was taken by the headlights of an unexpected car pulling into the driveway. The movement of the car triggered the outside lights and he was surprised to see Bella's car. He closed his laptop and walked towards the kitchen as he heard Bella open the door.

'Pops? Pops!' Bella hurled herself at her father and buried her face into his sweatshirt. She was sobbing.

'Bella, whatever is the matter?' Jonathan said urgently.

'It's Simon …' there were more racking sobs, and Claire appeared.

'Darling, what's going on? Bella? Sweetheart, what's happened?' She wiped her hands on the tea towel she was carrying, anxiously looking at Jonathan.

'Bella, please… you're worrying us. Has something happened to Simon?' Jonathan urged his daughter to explain.

Bella pulled herself away from her father and took some deep breaths. 'Nothing…' she managed to say.

Jonathan frowned and shook his head in bewilderment. 'But you said…' he began.

'It's what he's done!' Bella blurted out. 'He's been lying to me, and now he's dumped me… and I'm pregnant.' Bella burst into tears again.

Jonathan and Claire were speechless for a moment, and then Claire spoke first:

'Darling, are you sure about this?'

'About what? The lies? Yes, he isn't leaving his wife, they're happily married. Being dumped? Yes, because I heard him say so, and being pregnant? Yes, to that too!' Bella shouted. She was angry now and stamped her foot.

Jonathan sat Bella down, then quietly and calmly, through gritted teeth, asked her to explain what had happened. As Bella told them about her conversation with Simon on Friday evening through to the latest revelations thirty minutes ago, Jonathan's anger grew. When Bella tearfully said that she couldn't face going back for the final performance, Jonathan told her that it was only right, and that Desmond should be informed of her decision not to return. He asked where everyone would be – especially Simon.

'I left Simon at the hall, but he's probably at the café by now, you know the Forget-Me-Not Café in the Market Place. Desmond will be there as well, please can you go and tell him I'm so sorry, but I really can't perform again tonight.'

'I'll tell him that you've been taken poorly which is why you came home. The fewer people who know about this, the better, for now. If he's not at the café, how do I get into the hall? Will it be locked?' Jonathan struggled to maintain a calmness in his voice, as he didn't want to alert Bella to the strength of his anger in case she had some misguided idea to hold back on where he could find Simon.

'You can only get in through the back door with a code. Pops, please don't do anything silly,' Bella sniffed as her eyes watered again.

'I just want to talk to him and give him an opportunity to explain. I think that's only fair – remember we are doing business together. What's the code for the back door?' Jonathan deliberately didn't look at Claire, who wisely said nothing, but he knew she was upset by this revelation about her whiter-than-white, smooth-talking, assumed son-in-law to be.

'It's five, five, six, eight – but we're not normally supposed to tell anyone,' replied Bella.

'This isn't really a normal situation, but don't worry I'll be discreet,' Jonathan smiled gently at his daughter.

'Darling, come on, let's go and wash your face. I've some lovely skin cream from Rathbones, it will be soothing and hopefully take away those red blotches, they're so unbecoming,' Claire coaxed. 'We'll have a little talk about things and when Pops gets back he can tell us what Simon has to say. I'm sure it's all just a misunderstanding.'

'It's more than a misunderstanding, Mummy, I doubt we shall see Simon again.'

Jonathan's smile evaporated the minute he was out of Bella's sight, he snatched up his car keys and a jacket and strode out of the house. *I knew there was something underhand about you Saxby-Jones, well you've gone too bloody far now.*

As Jonathan drove to Ashdale, it started to rain, heavily. At one point, the rain was so bad that he was forced to slow down, but eventually, he pulled into the Market Place.

At the Forget-Me-Not Café, Lydia had helped her sister and niece to serve food and drinks to the Players. She had just given a plate of shepherd's pie to Maggie who had told her that Nick, Graham and Kevin were making their own arrangements and that she believed that it included beer. 'Zoe, Bella and Simon were the only others left at the hall, so I expect they'll be here any minute,' Maggie added as she turned away to take a seat with some of the cast.

Lydia was clearing away some of the empty stainless-steel food containers when she heard the familiar tinkle of the bell over the café door, and turned to see Zoe enter the café.

'Hi, what can I get you?' Lydia asked.

'I'll have the chicken, please and a coffee. I need to speak to you urgently, can you sit with me?' Zoe spoke in a low voice as she shrugged off her raincoat.

Lydia frowned. 'What's wrong, Zoe?'

'Come and sit down and I'll explain.'

When Lydia and Zoe were seated at their table with food and drink, Zoe told her what had happened back at the hall after everyone had left.

'*Pregnant?*' whispered Lydia. 'Well that'll upset everything in more ways than one.'

'But that's not all of it – he's admitted he only married Annabelle for her father's company, he also said that *he* engineered the break-up of her engagement.' Zoe repeated Simon's tale of the contrived photographs.

'Annabelle mentioned it to me, but – *Simon did that*?' Lydia was taken aback as she learned the full extent of Simon's disregard for people in his pursuit of power. 'But what happens now? Do you think Bella will come back tonight?'

'I really don't know, she was so upset. Do you think I should tell Desmond?' Zoe pushed a piece of chicken around on her plate.

'No, not yet, she may still return. Where's Simon? Is he coming here?'

'I walked off and left him there – I couldn't bear to stay a moment longer.' Zoe sighed. 'Simon will definitely throw me out and destroy my business now. It's everything I have and he'll take it from me.' Her eyes filled with tears and Lydia put her hand over Zoe's.

'Don't give up, something will happen to make it right. He'll go too far and somebody will find out. He'll get his comeuppance one day.'

Lydia was thinking about Greg, the notes he had made, and the potential story that might expose Simon. The problem was that it would also drag Annabelle, Bella and Zoe into the limelight and Lydia didn't think that would be a good idea.

Suddenly, the café door burst open and a wet and wild-eyed man stepped over the threshold out of the heavy rain that could be heard hammering onto the pavement. His eyes scanned the café obviously looking for someone.

Zoe stood up. 'Jonathan,' she called. The man came over to their table, 'Is everything all right?' Zoe asked him. The man was struggling to control his anger,

'Where's Simon?' he growled.

'I'm not sure, maybe still at the hall? He certainly hasn't come here,' Zoe replied looking with consternation at Jonathan's furious face. 'Please Jonathan, sit down for a moment. Where's Bella?'

Jonathan looked at Lydia and hesitated. Zoe understood his hesitation at once.

'It's fine, Lydia knows what's happened, but…' Zoe put her hand on Jonathan's arm as he frowned, 'she's the only other person.'

'Bella's at home and she isn't coming back tonight, she's too upset. She wanted me to tell… Desmond, is it? That she was poorly. She… we… don't want anyone to know about her condition until this business is sorted. As for me, I need to speak to that… that…' Words failed Jonathan and his fists clenched in rage.

'Jonathan, please sit down, you're attracting attention,' warned Zoe. Jonathan glanced around the café to see a few people staring at him, so he sat down next to Zoe and the hum of conversation in the café resumed.

'This is Lydia, our prompt. She realised that Simon wasn't telling the truth when she saw him at the ball last Saturday,' Zoe explained. Then she turned to Lydia, 'Lydia, this is Jonathan Sturdy, Bella's father.'

Jonathan gave Lydia a cursory nod of his head in acknowledgement, but Lydia studied the man in front of her. His thinning blond hair was plastered to his head and water dripped off his leather jacket. It wasn't the ideal circumstance for introductions but at least they all understood the situation.

'I just want to know where that man is. Bella has told me everything and I need to talk to him face to face.' Jonathan spoke quietly but there was a menace in his voice.

'I don't think that's a good idea right now…' began Zoe.

Jonathan stood up. 'Can you let this Desmond character know about Bella please? I'm going to the hall.' Jonathan said no more, but simply turned and strode out of the café. Lydia and Zoe looked at each other,

'Should we follow him do you think and make sure there's no trouble?'

Zoe shook her head. 'I don't think we need to, Jonathan can't get in as the front door is locked and he needs a code for the back door, and anyway Nick, Graham and Kevin are there. We'd better tell Desmond. I've no idea how he's going to get around not having Bella to play Shar Sue.'

They both stood up and made their way to Desmond's table to deliver their bad news. Desmond looked in horror as Zoe told him that Bella had been taken poorly, that she was at home and wouldn't be returning for the evening performance.

'Oh my God!! What will we do?' the back of his hand went dramatically to his forehead.

The rest of the cast muttered between themselves and looked at each other helplessly.

Suddenly Desmond had some inspiration. 'Lydia darling, you'll have to do it!' he announced.

Lydia stared at him in amazement. 'Me?' she gasped.

'You know all Bella's moves, cues, entrances – you're the only person who can save the show,'

'But I don't know all her lines or the songs,' Lydia protested.

'Take the script on stage. Please Lydia,' Desmond begged as the cast nodded their heads and joined in the persuasion.

'I don't have a costume either. Bella's won't fit me,' Lydia added

'Actually, there's a spare one,' Maggie piped up. 'If you remember, Tracey left the show after Christmas, so you could use that one. If Lydia and I leave now, we can be back at the hall by six and I'll have time do a quick fitting.'

Lydia looked around at all the hopeful faces waiting for her answer,

'Right, ok I'll do it but…' she was cut off as everyone cheered.

'Lydia, thank you,' gushed Desmond, 'we can make an announcement before curtain up, so the audience knows why you've a script. You can avoid the songs with dance routines, I believe Bella was only in two of them and you should be ok with the finale song.'

'I don't mind taking over as prompt,' Zoe suggested, 'then Lydia can concentrate on her role.'

Desmond positively beamed. 'Thank you, lovely people, this is real team-work. Maggie and Lydia, you both get off to the hall for the fitting, the rest of us can have a quick chat to see if there's anything we need to change to make it easier for you. We'll follow you to the hall shortly.' Desmond blew kisses as Lydia and Maggie donned their coats and left the café.

The rain had thankfully stopped, but there were huge puddles everywhere and at one point, they jumped back as a car drove quickly past them, fountaining water onto the pavement.

They arrived at the back door to the hall and let themselves into a dark hallway. Maggie snapped on the light and Lydia popped her head into the main hall where Nick, Graham and Kevin sat nursing cans of beer.

'You're back early,' called Kevin, 'it's only six o'clock.'

'Slight change of plan, Bella has been taken poorly so I'm playing her part. Maggie is sorting out a costume for me so we'll be in the Green Room, the others won't be long.'

Kevin gave a thumbs up by way of response and returned to his beer.

Maggie found a costume for Lydia and thankfully it didn't need much alteration, just taking in down the side seams.

By the time the rest of the Players returned to the hall, Maggie's sewing machine was going at full pelt. Desmond had decided not to change anything, which would probably keep things simpler and help Lydia be in the right place if she struggled. He suggested that they run through the finale song, and, as there was no sign of Simon, Nick volunteered to stand in.

By half past six, the cast felt they were as ready as they could be and began to prepare themselves for the final performance. Zoe offered to do the make-up for Shar Sue and Lydia gratefully accepted.

'Are you feeling nervous?' Zoe asked as she applied a pale foundation.

'I'm not sure what I feel, to be honest, I think I'm still in shock,' replied Lydia.

'You'll be fine, you know the part. It's the last show, we always have fun with it. The audience is mainly our own friends and family, and to be honest, they just drink a lot and laugh at everything. They'll be very glad you've stepped in and will be very supportive,' Zoe told her. 'Now close your eyes please.'

Ten minutes later when Lydia looked in the mirror, she was taken aback at the successful transformation. 'Wow! That's amazing, you're so talented, Zoe,' she enthused.

'Thank you,' replied Zoe. It's pretty good, even though I say so myself.'

'Right, I've got a wig and a costume for you.' Maggie bustled in, and in no time, Lydia became Shar Sue.

Desmond was almost overcome with delight when he saw her. 'Lydia, you look amazing, I don't know how to thank you.'

'Well, let's hope I can pull this off – it's just crazy,' Lydia laughed.

'Let's go and see Simon, he must be nearly ready by now and he's the only person who doesn't know you've taken Bella's role.' Desmond theatrically took Lydia's arm.

He knocked on Simon's dressing room door and shouted: 'Simon darling, are you decent? I've something to show you.'

There was no response. Desmond frowned and looked at Lydia who shrugged in bewilderment. 'Simon, are you there?' Desmond knocked again. There was still no reply. 'Oh, please don't say *he's* missing now,' said Desmond with some impatience. He turned the handle and the door swung open. As they stepped over the threshold, Desmond flicked on the light.

Annabelle Saxby-Jones

Harry had dropped Annabelle and Verity off at the Jubilee Hall to join the queue for the show. Harry didn't queue, so he drove back to the Market Place to park the car and have a swift beer in the Coach & Horses, promising to be back in time for curtain up. Verity and Annabelle chatted about the plans for Verity's fortieth birthday party as they waited. 'I've decided to hold the party at Ashdale Hall,' announced Verity, 'because as much as I would love a marquee in our garden, I would have to provide extra facilities and there's the problem of parking, not to mention the clearing up the next day. Ashdale Hall would take care of all of that.'

'I think that's a wise move,' agreed Annabelle, 'if it rains as heavily as it did earlier on, your lawn would soon be a mud bath.'

'You know, I hadn't thought of that. This is why I need your expertise, Belle. Together we'll plan an awesome party.'

'Have you spoken to Karen Hunter yet? She's the Events Manager at Ashdale Hall.'

'I have, and when I told her about the red theme, she said I could probably use some of the red décor from the Valentine Ball if I wanted. I thought you and I could go over and have a look at some point.'

'Yes, I would like that and—' Annabelle broke off suddenly as they became aware of a siren and blue lights approaching the hall. The queue of people became silent as the police car pulled up in the car park by the rear entrance.

Verity clutched Annabelle's arm. 'Oh God! What's going on?' she said in alarm.

Annabelle shook her head, then gasped as an ambulance and a second police car arrived. The people waiting in the queue began to mutter as they tried to guess what had caused such activity. A little way in front of Annabelle and Verity, two men left the queue and ran around to the back of the hall.

The mutterings grew louder: 'Hey, where do they think they're going?' someone shouted.

'Maybe, they've gone to find out what's going on,' replied another.

Everyone was craning their necks to try and see around to the back of the hall, and some had shuffled closer to the edge of the building to peer around the corner. A police van arrived carrying more officers who soon moved the crowd back, but remained tight-lipped about what was going on.

'Text Simon and ask him what's happened,' Verity urged, 'everyone else is texting people they know in the play.' She nodded her head in the direction of the mass of people, quite a few of whom were typing furiously. Annabelle got her phone out of her handbag and quickly sent a message to Simon. As she waited for a reply, one of the men who had run around to the back a few minutes before appeared at the corner of the hall and held his arms up for silence; the crowd obliged.

'Ladies and gentlemen,' he announced, 'I'm afraid that there has been an incident and the panto is cancelled.' There were gasps and groans from the queue. 'Your ticket money will be refunded. If you paid by cash, please wait here and someone will be with you shortly to take your details. If you bought the tickets online, you're free to leave and a transfer will be made to your bank account as soon as possible.'

The crowd began to talk and as the volume increased, a voice cut through all the chatter as the man had now been joined by his companion.

'My name is Detective Chief Inspector Appleton, I can confirm that there has been a serious incident but I'm not at liberty to give any more details at present. I understand that some of you have friends and family that were due to appear in the panto, but at the moment the Ashdale Players are helping us with our inquiries. They'll be released as soon as possible. Please, go home and wait for them there. Thank you.'

The crowd began to move amid a cacophony of chatter, and Annabelle looked at Verity in bewilderment. 'Shall we go to the Coach and meet Harry? I can text Simon to meet us there.'

Verity nodded and reached for her phone. 'I expect that's the best plan,' she agreed as she waited for Harry to pick up. They both turned to follow the hundred or so people who were beginning to drift away, when Annabelle felt a hand on her arm.

'Excuse me, Mrs Saxby-Jones?'

Annabelle turned to see DCI Appleton at her side. She took a sharp intake of breath. 'Yes?' she replied anxiously.

'Could you come with me, please? I need to have a word.' DCI Appleton spoke calmly but firmly.

'Oh! Is everything all right?' Annabelle asked before realising that, no, everything was probably not all right.

'Just come this way please,' repeated DCI Appleton and indicated with his arm that Annabelle should follow him to the front entrance of the hall. Annabelle turned frightened eyes to

Verity who had frozen on the spot, her mouth open, her phone clamped to her cheek.

Verity pulled herself together and spoke quickly into the phone.

'Mrs Saxby-Jones, this way.' DCI Appleton's voice was firmer now and he put his hand under Annabelle's elbow to steer her from the crowd.

Annabelle turned to face him. 'Can my friend come too?' she asked in a small voice.

'Very well,' he agreed. But when they both looked back, Verity had disappeared into the crowd. DCI Appleton led Annabelle into the empty hall and invited her to sit down. He sat down next to her and indicated a woman standing in the row behind them.

'This is Detective Sergeant Oakley. I'm afraid we've got some bad news for you. Your husband, Simon Saxby-Jones has been found dead. He has been murdered.'

Annabelle stared at DCI Appleton for a good few seconds before looking away towards the stage as the news sank in. Then she turned back to the policeman and whispered, '*Murdered?*'

'I'm afraid so, Mrs Saxby-Jones.'

'When? Where? How?' her voice sounded dry and hoarse and she coughed.

'Would you like some tea?' DCI Appleton asked gently, Annabelle shook her head.

'A coffee please, I don't like tea, Simon does... did,' she croaked and then the tears came. DCI Appleton reached behind him and plucked a handful of tissues out of a strategically placed box. He said no more and allowed her to cry until DS Oakley returned with a mug of coffee, which he placed carefully on the chair in front of her. When Annabelle appeared a little calmer and the sobs had reduced to sniffles, DCI Appleton spoke again:

'Your husband was discovered a little while ago, here, in the Parish Clerk's office. Apparently he used it as his dressing room – he has been stabbed.'

'Stabbed? But why?'

'That's what we intend to find out, Mrs Saxby-Jones. Now, I'm afraid I'm going to have to ask you some questions, just so we can start our investigation, ok?' Annabelle nodded and DCI Appleton continued, 'When did you last see your husband?'

'This morning at breakfast. He left to go to a meeting with Bruce Harvey and Fiona Cavendish at their home – he was lunching with them then coming straight here for the matin*é*e performance.' Annabelle answered all their questions as best as she could but, as she had not seen Simon since the morning, there was very little information she could provide about his movements during the day.

As she sipped the sweet coffee she had been given she suddenly remembered something. 'Wait a minute, Simon arranged to meet someone here, at the hall, at five o'clock. It was Councillor Hugo Marshall.'

'Do you know why?'

'I overheard Simon talking to him on the phone this morning. Simon was surprised that Councillor Marshall insisted on seeing him today and the break between the matin*é*e and evening performance was the only time he had available.'

The Chief Inspector nodded. 'Thank you, Mrs Saxby-Jones, I'll arrange for one of our cars to take you home now. You live in Harrogate, I believe?' Although her head had filled with a dense fog, Annabelle knew that the last place she wanted to be was the house she shared with Simon.

'Yes, I do, but I can't face going back there on my own. My father lives here in Ashdale, so could I go there please?'

'Of course, that's no problem,' he replied.

Whilst DS Oakley organised a car, Annabelle called her father: 'Daddy? Something terrible has happened… Simon has been murdered… yes, murdered… here at the Jubilee Hall. He was stabbed… um, a little while ago, they said… Can I come home?… No, it's fine, the police will bring me… I'll see you soon.'

'Mrs Saxby-Jones, the car is ready for you.' DS Oakley helped Annabelle to her feet and steadied her when she wobbled.

As the police car pulled up outside the front door of The Manor, Annabelle saw her father's welcome silhouette in the doorway. The minute the car door was opened for her, she ran towards Carlton Banks and flung herself into his arms.

'Oh Daddy…' she cried and burst into a fresh flood of tears.

Lydia Buckley

Greg pushed a shot of brandy across the breakfast bar.

'I don't like neat brandy,' Lydia said, pushing it away, but Greg sighed and pushed it back. 'Drink it, it's good for shock.'

'So is sweet tea and I don't like that either,' she replied.

'If I make coffee, will you have the brandy in that?' he asked patiently.

Lydia nodded. She had stopped shaking now, following the shock of finding Simon's body. When Desmond switched the light on they'd seen Simon slumped over on the desk in front of the mirror, his shirt covered in blood. Desmond had fainted and now had a concussion from hitting his head on the floor when he fell. Lydia had stumbled into the hall and thankfully bumped into Nick who had been marvellously supportive and organised. Nick had checked for a pulse and, not finding one, they'd called the police.

Lydia had given her statement, but, as she had left the hall just before four thirty and not returned until six o'clock, she was unable to give the police much information. The details of the argument between Zoe, Simon and Bella, she assumed would be covered by their own statements, because as far as Lydia was concerned, it was only what Zoe had told her and therefore just hearsay.

Greg had been in the queue of would-be panto goers with his brother-in-law Will, DCI Appleton, when they'd seen the arrival of the police cars. Will and Greg had immediately run around to the back door of the hall to assist. Greg had promised Will that he wouldn't release any information without official consent, provided he was allowed to make sure that Lydia was safe. Having ascertained that Lydia was unharmed, Greg had returned to the crowd to make the initial announcement.

When at last, Lydia had been allowed to leave, they'd returned to Greg's apartment to mull everything over.

'Right, now we've the coffee and my notes from last night, tell me everything – it will help to clear your mind.' Greg poured some brandy into Lydia's mug and to keep her company poured a healthy measure into his own. When they were settled, Lydia told him about the argument between Zoe and Simon which Bella had overheard before she burst through the door and ultimately revealed her pregnancy.

'You're absolutely sworn to secrecy on that detail, by the way. Bella, her parents, Zoe, you and I are the only ones who know and Jonathan asked us to keep quiet about it – ok?' Lydia looked at Greg with a raised eyebrow until he nodded his agreement. Then she took a drink of her enhanced, shock-reducing coffee. 'Actually, this is quite nice,' she told him. Greg gave her an I-knew-it-would-be look as he rapidly updated his notes.

'So,' he announced after a few minutes, 'Bella now knows that Simon is hoodwinking her into believing that he'll divorce his wife and she's run off home to her parents.' Lydia nodded. 'Ok, what next?'

'Simon told Zoe that he deliberately wrecked Annabelle's engagement by staging the suggestive photographs – you remember I told you about those when we spoke on Wednesday? Anyway, Simon only wanted to marry Annabelle to be in with a chance of getting his hands on Aztec Developments – in a nutshell.'

'This guy is some piece of work, talk about ruthless!' Greg shook his head in disbelief.

'That's pretty much what Edward told me yesterday evening. Simon just tramples on people in his desire to succeed.'

'Bella is in an awful situation now. Thank goodness she's got her parents to look after her.'

'Jonathan was pretty angry when he arrived at the café looking for Simon. You don't suppose *he* killed Simon, do you?' Lydia suddenly asked.

'Let's make a timeline of what happened to see who could have done it – bearing in mind that the hall was locked – who had the opportunity, and motive,' suggested Greg as he turned to a clean sheet of paper. 'Let me see if I've got all this right. So, when you left at four thirty, everyone was still there, and it's approximately a five-minute walk from the hall to the café?'

'Yes,' agreed Lydia, 'Most of the cast arrived around four forty-five and we had more or less just finished serving them all when Maggie arrived about five minutes later.'

'Maggie arrived at four-fifty,' Greg muttered as he wrote. 'Who was still at the hall at that point?' he added.

'Maggie told me that Simon, Zoe and Bella were still there along with Kevin, Graham and Nick.'

'Ok,' said Greg as he made his timeline. 'Right, what next?'

'Bella must have left the hall around four-fifty as Zoe arrived at the café a little after five o'clock and she and Simon had continued to argue. Zoe told me what had happened and then Jonathan arrived at about five-thirty.'

'What time did you and Maggie return to the hall?'

'We got back there at six, everyone else returned at about six-fifteen, and we discovered Simon just before seven o'clock.'

Greg wrote everything down and sat back. 'So, Simon was killed sometime between Bella leaving at around four-fifty and you returning with Maggie at six. Who does that point to?' he asked.

'Zoe!' gasped Lydia, 'It can't be, she wouldn't do that.'

'She certainly had a motive and the opportunity, but unless she carried a weapon, there's no method.'

'But what about Nick, Graham and Kevin? They stayed behind in the hall,' reasoned Lydia.

'Well, we don't know of any motive, but one of them may have had an opportunity if they didn't stay together the whole of the time. Perhaps one of them made a hot drink, took a knife from the kitchen…' suggested Greg.

'Was it a knife that was used?'

'I don't know actually, the weapon wasn't left behind. We'll have to wait for forensics for the detail.'

Lydia was silent as she thought about the possibility of Zoe being a murderer. She liked Zoe, and although Simon had put Zoe in a dreadful situation, was she capable of murder?

'Could Jonathan have done it? He was pretty angry.'

'Could he have let himself into the hall?' Greg asked. 'I thought you had a code to get in.'

'We do, but what if Bella told him what it was? He could have brought a knife or something from home. Jonathan would then have had motive, means and opportunity,' explained Lydia.

'So, we've at least two suspects, Zoe and Jonathan for definite with possibly Nick, Graham or Kevin thrown in for good measure,' concluded Greg.

'You haven't mentioned Annabelle.'

'Why should I mention Annabelle? You mean as a suspect? Why would you include her?' Greg frowned.

'Because they always suspect the spouse, at least they do on television *and* she was upset because Simon was supposedly having an affair,' Lydia twirled a curl around her finger.

'You watch far too much *Midsomer Murders* on television. Anyway, I thought you said Simon blagged his way out of that with the story of Zoe being a wanton woman?'

'True, but maybe she didn't believe him,' Lydia said thoughtfully.

Greg pondered for a moment and then said, 'What about Bella? She might have come back with Jonathan, and he dropped her off at the hall to murder Simon whilst he went to the café.'

'No way! Bella is totally incapable of murder and Jonathan wanted to confront Simon himself. This is hopeless, we haven't eliminated anybody at all,' Lydia was disappointed. 'I thought it would be easier, given we have the time of death.'

'We shall just have to leave the detecting to Will, I'm afraid. However, on another note, I did some research today on Jonathan Sturdy's place at Harefield Park *and* the farm next door, and guess what? Jonathan has had plans submitted recently and his architect was Simon Saxby-Jones. Robbie thinks I should go and talk to Jonathan,' Greg said with enthusiasm.

'Talking of Robbie, I saw him today. It was after I left the hall and I was on my way to the café. He parked on the Market Place and headed off towards the Coach & Horses,' remarked Lydia.

'Obviously meeting someone for a drink. Come on, let's go on to bed, it's been quite a day.' Greg put his arm around Lydia as they headed to the bedroom.

13

Annabelle Saxby-Jones

Annabelle opened her eyes and realised she was at The Manor and not her house in Harrogate. She closed them again quickly, but it was too late – her brain was awake and reminding her of the events of last night. Simon had gone away. He often went away on business and usually Annabelle would go to stay with her father, except on this occasion, Simon wouldn't be returning.

Annabelle turned over onto her back and stared at the ceiling; it was painted white and there were one or two cracks, but apart from that it was a pretty normal ceiling. She turned her head to the right – her built-in wardrobes were white with one central mirrored door; she looked to her left – there was the door to her en suite, white again, and guess what? Her dressing table and chest of drawers were white as well. Why was there so much white? She sat up suddenly and caught her breath – thank God her duvet cover was damson! Her carpet was also a dark red, the wall behind her bed rose pink, and the curtains matched the duvet.

Annabelle snuggled back under the duvet, this was *her* room. She felt safe here and she could stay as long as she wanted. If she stayed in bed, she could tell herself that Simon was just away and would be away for probably a long time, maybe he had gone to Mar Menor to buy their villa. She thought back over the few days and how her conversation with Tasheka had set certain events in motion. If she had not gone to Lush Lashes in Leeds, she supposed things might have turned out differently. She thought about Kitty and Coco being paid to have flirty fun with married men. If she had known more about those types of girls, then she may have been more inclined to believe Robert.

Robert. She wondered if he was married by now. Maybe he had children. She had noticed that he had written a review for the pantomime in the *Harrogate Herald* so he must live locally. What would her life have been like if she had married him? She had truly loved Robert and, until those photographs had arrived, believed he truly loved her. However, the betrayal had been too much and had almost destroyed her faith in men, but then Simon had shown her that she *could* trust and love again; he had swept her off her feet and declared his undying love for her. He'd taken her to Rome and proposed in front of the Trevi Fountain, it had all been so romantic.

She had made a big mistake buying that red silk chiffon set. She mentally chastised herself for behaving in such a wanton way. Of course, men like Simon expected their wives to be… what was the word her grandmother always used? *Genteel.* 'The Thursday Night Disaster', as Annabelle mentally referred to it, had been the topic of conversation with Verity, which had then led to the Bella revelation. Later that evening, when she had been so quick to accuse Simon of an affair, he had explained that it was that salon manager stirring up trouble. So, Annabelle concluded, if she had not gone to Leeds then none of this would have happened. When Simon had finally taken her to bed on Friday night, he had been so romantic and caring, to the point that he had held himself back instead of leaving her feeling dirty and sticky. Just how many men would be that thoughtful?

Her mind travelled back to yesterday morning, was that all it was? It seemed a long time ago now, to her last conversation with Simon about buying a villa for quality time for the two of them. That wasn't going to happen now unless Simon had already made plans to view villas whilst lunching with Bruce Thingummy. Maybe she could still buy a villa in Mar Menor? She and Daddy could go with Daddy's friend Eleanor, she would speak to him about it.

Thinking about finances, Annabelle realised that she hadn't got a clue about what to do next. She knew she did not want to go back to Harrogate, ever – she just wanted to stay here at The Manor. Daddy would probably sort everything out legally and financially and make everything right, but there was a funeral to arrange and Annabelle wasn't at all sure if she could cope with that. Maybe Eleanor would help.

Funeral, that was a horrid word, it sounded like the word 'final', but then Annabelle supposed ironically that it was right that it did. Final, the end, no more, never again *I'll never see you again, Simon.* She whispered the words to herself. Then it happened, her eyes filled with tears, her heart broke and she sobbed with the realisation that she was now a widow.

She was scared and unsure of her future now that Simon was dead.

Zoe Birch

Zoe, sitting in her kitchen, didn't know how she felt – her emotions were all over the place. She thought back to when she had first met Simon, how she was immediately attracted to him and she had believed it was reciprocated. Everybody liked Simon, all the Players had talked about him being a breath of fresh air, a new leading man and an impressive amateur actor. After one of the rehearsals for the previous panto, *Babes in the Wood,* they'd stayed behind at the Coach after everyone else had gone, and she remembered readily agreeing to Simon's suggestion that they should see each other for dinner one evening. But that date had never materialised. Instead, he had taken Bella out, somewhere in Leeds. The hurt, rejection and embarrassment that Zoe suffered had chewed her up inside, but on the surface, she had maintained a smiley face and expressed her happiness for Bella as the weeks had gone by.

Even after *Babes* had finished, she still had to listen to Bella chattering away about how gorgeous Simon was, how attentive Simon was, how her parents thought he was just wonderful and then how he was helping Jonathan with a project. But in Zoe's mind, something just did not add up. The relationship between Simon and Bella was one-sided and although Zoe had expressed her concerns to Maggie, they'd fallen on deaf ears. Maggie just thought she was jealous. Was she jealous though? Goddammit, yes she was! Yes! Yes! *Yes!* Simon should have been hers. She would have known eventually that he wasn't intending to divorce his wife but it wouldn't have mattered. As a woman of the world, she would have assured Simon that his being married wasn't a problem and that she could have kept his secret. The benefits of a clandestine affair would have been enjoyed in the privacy of her flat. But no, he had to have young, innocent Bella, and for a long time Zoe couldn't work out why. She had toyed with the idea that it was the twenty-year age gap and the naivety that Simon desired, that ridiculous fantasy that men had about having a virgin, but Simon did not strike her as being that stupid. Nevertheless, the situation had not helped with Zoe's self-esteem.

Eventually, as Bella chattered about how her father had bought the farm next door and the plans for expansion of the family business, it became clear that Simon was becoming involved in it. She had met Jonathan on a few occasions, when he would sometimes pop into the salon to pick Bella up, and she had liked him, but was surprised that, he too, appeared to have also fallen for Simon's charm. She had also met Claire, Bella's mother and seen her silly, girlish, cringeworthy behaviour when in Simon's company; stupid woman. It had eventually become clear to Zoe, and apparently, nobody else, that Simon had ingratiated himself into the Sturdy family for a purpose, and it wasn't to marry Bella.

Last Saturday, when Verity had come into the shop and mentioned that she was a friend of Belle's, Zoe had known there and then that this was a golden opportunity to find out the truth. She knew perfectly well that Verity wasn't a friend of Isabella's – for a start Bella had never mentioned her, so all she had to do was just innocently pretend that they were talking about the same person and, Bingo! Simon's deception had been revealed. It was just unfortunate for him that his wife was named Belle and his girlfriend was Bella – not difficult to confuse the two.

Zoe pushed her cold coffee away, stood up and went to her kitchen window. She gazed out over the Market Place. In the sudden rush of euphoria she had felt at getting back at Simon, knowing that she had been right all along to mistrust him, she had not taken into account that he would threaten to put her livelihood and home in jeopardy.

Simon was witty, handsome, intelligent and charming, a character as smooth as the first layer of an onion, but peel away that first layer and you found an uncaring, selfish, and unscrupulous bully; take away another layer and you realised he was a threatening, malevolent and devious liar who destroyed other people in his desire to be successful and powerful. During that final argument, Simon had revealed his true colours – even his wife had not escaped his manipulative schemes. At that moment, Zoe had hated him for everything he had done to her, to Bella, and even to his wife. *Simon Saxby-Jones – you bloody rat!* She had shouted at him in rage. However, this morning, as she watched people go about their business, and as news travelled about the events of yesterday evening, Zoe realised that she just felt relieved.

Her home and her business were safe now that Simon was dead.

Isabella Sturdy

Bella leant over the gate and watched her horse contentedly pulling at the grass. Every so often, he lifted his head to look at her, maybe wondering why she wasn't calling him over.

Bella had cried so much she had no tears left. The police had come to their house last night to interview her and her father about Simon's murder. Now there was no chance of the reconciliation her mother had suggested, and quite honestly Bella wasn't sure if, even had it been an option, it would have been what she had wanted.

Simon had made it perfectly clear that he would have let her down gently sometime in May – why May, she had no idea. She thought about what Zoe had shouted at him and how he had laughed at her. His threat to close her salon if she spoke out and told the truth. Someone called Verity was involved as well. There was a lot that Bella didn't understand, but she knew that Zoe had been at odds with her for many months. All through this last week, everyone had thought that Zoe was having a secret affair with Simon when, in truth, she was just keeping a secret.

Bella's horse trotted over, his curiosity getting the better of him. His soft mouth nuzzled her hand expectantly and Bella reached into her pocket for a mint – she usually had a supply in this particular jacket. She stroked his face.

'What am I going to do?' she asked him. 'I've got a decision to make, Spritzer,' she told the horse. 'I can terminate this pregnancy…' the horse snorted and shook his head as Bella's eyes opened in surprise, '… or not,' she added tentatively. Spritzer just stared at her with brown eyes and licked her hand before nudging it. He just wanted another mint, and when no mint was forthcoming, he ambled away. Bella stuck her hands in her pockets and turned away from the gate.

Part of her wanted to keep the baby, it was hers – well hers and Simon's, but she now knew that it had not been conceived in love, and the realisation that Simon had just been using her was devastating.

Could she love and look after this child or would resentment take over at some point? Her mother had been horrified at the thought of Bella having the baby, and had spoken about it with distaste. It was she who had made the suggestion of "dealing with the problem." Her father had been more practical and told Bella that there was no rush, and that she should not make any decision in a hurry. She was in shock and needed time to carefully consider all the implications. But whatever the outcome, he would always support her. He had also said that he had felt misgivings about Simon for a little while now and if he could have got into the hall last night, he would have made sure that Simon knew how he felt.

But Bella was worried; she had given her father the code to get into the hall and although he thought he had disguised it well, Bella had known he was furious when he left their house last night. He had told the police that when he left the café to go to the hall, he was unable to remember the code to get in and had furiously banged on the door hoping that Simon would hear and come to see who was at the door. Nobody had heard him, and that he had returned home and not seen Simon at all. Bella wanted so desperately to believe her father, but she had seen the anger and the clenched fists.

She had no idea how she would make her next big decision now that Simon was dead.

Nick Bradley

Nick, pacing up and down in his flat above the bakery, had craved some fresh air. He decided to go for a walk to the church, but of course it was Sunday and there were a lot of people heading in that direction on their way to attend the eleven o'clock service. He changed direction and walked to the canal; with his hands stuffed in his pockets and his head bent down, he had the look of a man who wished to be ignored.

When Lydia had run into the hall last night and cannoned into him, he had just followed her back into The Annexe. Then, after stepping over Desmond who was lying prostrate on the floor, he had seen Simon's body sprawled on the desk. He was face down and had obviously been stabbed in the back. He noted that there was no visible weapon and had been careful to just reach out and check for a pulse without touching or disturbing anything else. He had retreated to the hallway and shook his head at Lydia, indicating that there were no signs of life, and then he had called the police.

This morning, Nick felt anger and frustration. He hadn't known Simon very long, but he didn't like the way Simon had spoken to Zoe last Tuesday. Of course, he'd been aware that something was going on between them – all of the Players had witnessed the upset at last Sunday's rehearsal, but he could not have imagined the enormity of it until he had overheard the bitter argument between Simon and Zoe yesterday evening. He had been genuinely shocked at the revelation that Simon had plotted the break-up of his wife's previous engagement, just so that he could marry her to get his hands on her father's company. Not only that, but he had used Bella to get to know her father for some business dealings, and as for poor Zoe – she had clearly got caught in the crossfire.

It all brought back memories of the bitterness his mother had felt when she'd been abandoned by Simon all those years ago. Falling in love at university, he knew how easy that was when students spent so much of their time together. Although he knew his mother hadn't wanted to get pregnant, she had never made him feel unwanted – quite the opposite in fact. She had never married and put all her energies in bringing him up. She had told him what she knew about his father, that he was a handsome and intelligent man but cold-hearted, refusing to answer her letters or even acknowledge the existence of a son. Nick thought back to the pretty forty-something who had attended his graduation with so much pride and the gentle way she had talked about the handful of letters she had received over a period of years from a man whom, she explained, was Nick's grandfather. She had told him that his grandfather, Simon's father, hadn't wanted to interfere with Nick's upbringing but he had kept in touch sporadically, knowing that Simon had no interest at all. After Nick's mother had died last year – the cancer only giving them three months warning – Nick had written to his grandfather, but sadly, had received no response. Nick had, however, successfully managed to track down his absent father, even though he had hyphenated his name to Saxby-Jones, but he had been so very disappointed in who he had found.

His mind returned to the present and the situation surrounding the Ashdale Players. He had witnessed how Simon had been on the verge of crushing the lives of genuinely lovely and welcoming people and he was in no doubt, that there were others outside of this particular group who had been nothing more than disposables in his quest for power.

How could somebody be so cold and ruthless? Nick was disgusted and ashamed, but at the same time regretful.

The meeting with his father would never happen now that Simon was dead.

Robbie Parker

Robbie rinsed his plate and loaded it into the dishwasher. He sighed, then making a decision, put on his coat and walked out onto the rooftop terrace of his apartment in the Dockland development in Leeds. What he'd done last night was stupid, *stupid!* He realised that now – now that he had come to his senses. He had thought that he had got over Annabelle and that returning to Ashdale would have been fine, nostalgic – but fine.

Well, it hadn't been fine when he had found out from Lydia that Simon had managed to marry Annabelle six months after their broken engagement. He was upset at first, but had then become suspicious. It all seemed a bit too convenient; the staged anonymous photographs that Annabelle had received; the constant chattering in her ear about infidelity and leopards not changing spots, etcetera, until she had begun to believe it and broke off the engagement. This, from someone who according to Greg, appeared to be a serial philanderer.

When Greg had phoned him yesterday afternoon and told him the story of Simon and the tangled web of deceit he had created with Annabelle and an unsuspecting girlfriend, not to mention dragging another woman in to cover it up, Robbie had begun to think. It was the thinking that had prompted his rash decision to go to Ashdale and confront the arrogant, double-barrelled, pretentious adulterer. He had called in at the Coach for a swift measure of whisky which had, he realised upon reflection, fired him up even more He had then walked down to the hall, and unfortunately, the heavens had opened and he'd been wet through by the time he got there. The front door was locked so he had wandered around to the back, where he had seen a chap leaving, and that's when Robbie had seen an opportunity.

This morning in the cold light of the day, he thought about Annabelle and how she must be feeling – devastated he supposed. He guessed she would have read his review of the pantomime in the newspaper, so she would know he had been in Ashdale. In which case, it would be very fitting for him to send a card of condolence – he would send it to her father's house and hope that he would forward it on. That decided, Robbie immediately returned to the apartment and picked up his phone and wallet before heading out to the city centre. He sincerely hoped that she would be able to see at last the true character of her husband.

Maybe she would be able to find happiness now that Simon was dead.

Councillor Hugo Marshall

Hugo sat at his desk at Lewis Marshall. He had gone to the office to escape from Celia – it was the only place which offered the solitude he craved.

When the police arrived at their house this morning Hugo had been alarmed. How in the world had they found out about his meeting with Simon? Of course, they wouldn't tell him, but it had been awkward, especially as Celia had watched him like a hawk. He'd had to think quickly and then waffled something about a business deal to be worked out in the future regarding his impending retirement. In his statement, he had said that he had changed his mind about the meeting and left without seeing Simon, so it had never taken place. However, Hugo could tell by the look on the officer's face that they didn't believe him. The upshot was that Hugo had no alibi and was near the top of their suspect list.

When the police had gone, he had got both barrels from Celia. She ranted about what the neighbours would think about the visit from the police – *on a Sunday* of all times, that this could jeopardise the mayoralty, her position in the town and her position on various committees. What would the Worthingtons at Ashdale Hall make of it? And so she went on and on. Hugo heard it all, but hadn't really listened and, in the end, whilst Celia was mid-rant, he had put on his coat, picked up his keys and left the house.

Now, of course, he realised that he would have to go back at some point – but not just yet, he needed time to think. He would have to speak to Freddie first thing in the morning as Hugo had no idea about the implications Simon's death for Planet Properties. He sat back in his chair and closed his eyes. How had his life spiralled out of control in this way? Bloody Simon Saxby-Jones, that's how – that man had manipulated him and tried to ruin him.

But one thing was certain, the latest risky project wouldn't go ahead now that Simon was dead.

Vinnie Buckley

Vinnie was anxious. Earlier, at around five, he happened to meet his new friend Richard at the bar on the Promenade Deck, who had been full of news from Harrogate. There had been a murder in a small village called Ashdale, Richard had told him with excitement.

Ex or no-ex, Vinnie still cared about Lydia – she was the mother of his son for God's sake. He had sent a text straight away to see if she was ok and she *still* hadn't replied. He glanced at his watch – half past seven so it would be half past three in the afternoon at home. She *must* have read his text by now. All he wanted was to know that she was ok, that's all.

Perhaps he should text Matt, surely Matt would have been in contact with his mother. Vinnie reached for his mobile and as fast as his fingers would go, he sent a hurried text to his son. He had just pressed Send when the sliding doors of the balcony opened and Vivienne popped her head out.

'I'm ready babe, wha' d'ya think?' she stepped out onto the balcony and Vinnie nearly passed out. Vivienne was dressed in a Greek-goddess type costume, which looked as though it was a piece of fabric that had been wrapped around her. The dress had a draped neckline which, as she twirled around, swung sideways revealing the smooth roundness of her breasts underneath. The outlines of her nipples were visible under the thin fabric and it had a very short but full skirt which flared out as she spun.

'You're *not* going out like that!' he told her when he found his voice.

'I most certainly am!' Vivienne retorted, 'It's White Night so everyone has to wear white. *You're* the one who is dressed all wrong,' she pointed at his navy linen suit.

'Vivienne, it's not the white I'm talking about, it's the dress itself. It's indecent and you're *not* wearing it,' Vinnie said quite firmly.

Vivienne put her hands on her hips. 'And just who do you think you are? Telling me what I can and cannot wear,' she shouted.

'Please don't shout out here Vivienne, we've got neighbours.'

'I don't give a damn about the effing neighbours. I'm not going to be told what to wear as though I'm some stupid kid.' Vivienne flounced away from the sliding doors, sat down on the bed and began to put on her ridiculously high-heeled shoes.

Vinnie stood up followed her into their cabin, closing the doors behind him. 'Vivienne, that dress isn't suitable for this event, and I'm not going to dinner with you wearing it.' Vinnie tossed his phone onto the bed, leaned against the cabin wall and crossed his arms determinedly.

'Fine, I'll go on my own!' Vivienne spat back at him, her eyes full of rage.

At that moment, Vinnie's phone chirped with an incoming message and Vivienne, who was closest, saw who it was from. 'What's *she* texting you about? Have you been in contact with her?'

Vinnie picked up his phone and glanced at the reply:

It's all right, everything's ok.

'Of course she's all right, why the hell wouldn't she be all right? I'm sick of her still being in our lives, I thought that once we got married, she would be gone, but oh no! You still text her all the time. Just forget her, will you?' Vivienne yelled.

'There's been a murder in Ashdale, where she lives, I was just making sure she was ok.'

'*She* hasn't been murdered has she? So… she's ok. Now, can we just forget her and enjoy this bloody holiday?'

Vinnie forced a smile,

'I would very much like to enjoy this holiday Vivienne, so if you would like to change out of that dress and put something nice on, we can go to dinner,' he said calmly.

'I'm *not* going to change and *that's final!*' snapped Vivienne, 'so if you're not going to take me to dinner, I'll go on my own.' And with that, Vivienne snatched up her clutch bag and marched out of the door.

Vinnie shrugged his shoulders, picked up his cabin key card and left the cabin. He knew Vivienne would head for the Pool Deck where the Barbeque and White Party was being held, so he decided to eat at the Italian restaurant with just himself for company.

He thought he should email the office tomorrow for confirmation whether his meeting in Ashdale was still on now that Simon was dead.

14

Councillor Hugo Marshall

Monday dawned bright, clear and very cold. Hugo opened the door to the agency and gratefully stepped into the warmth.

'Good morning, Councillor Marshall.'

Felicity greeted him without lifting her eyes from the computer screen. She looked the same as she did every morning, neat and composed. For one bizarre moment, Hugo wondered what she would look like without the black-rimmed glasses and her hair loose about her shoulders. What underwear lay beneath the prim blouse and sensible skirt? He mentally shook his head and mumbled a vague response.

Felicity glanced at her employer and watched as he removed his leather gloves. 'Nice day, isn't it?' she asked brightly.

Hugo nodded his head and disappeared into his office, closing the door a little firmer than he intended. He glanced at his expensive gold watch, five to nine he noted. He removed his cashmere overcoat and scarf, carefully hanging them up. He paced up and down in front of his desk. Last night had not been a good night's sleep by any stretch of the imagination. He had tossed and turned, haunted by thoughts of prison until Celia had finally lost patience and banished him to one of their spare rooms *again*. Hugo checked the time again, eight fifty-seven. It was unlikely that Freddie would be at his desk before nine. Hugo put his head in his hands and sighed.

There was a discreet tap on the office door and Felicity pushed it open. 'I've brought you a cup of coffee, Councillor Marshall,' she said and deposited a cup and saucer on the desk.

Hugo smiled appreciatively,

'Thank you, Felicity.'

'Nasty business about Mr Saxby-Jones.'

'Indeed it is.'

'Murder, in Ashdale of all places, who would have thought it? Let's hope the police catch the perpetrator quickly.'

Hugo nodded but could not quite look Felicity in the eye. Felicity, obviously realising that he was somewhat distracted, left the office and returned to her desk.

Hugo looked at his watch for the third time; at last, nine o'clock. He picked up the telephone handset on his desk, but then changed his mind and reached for his mobile.

'Freddie – a bit of a bugger, this situation, eh?'

'Top o' the mornin' to yer, Councillor Marshall. Aye – we got a bit o' t'inkin' to do now.'

'Thinking? How do you mean, Freddie?'

'Ah well now, the t'ing is Councillor Marshall, sir, we need to decide whether we want to carry on wit' Planet Properties or not, because if—'

'Carry on? Oh no. No, no, no. We can't carry on without Simon,' Hugo declared emphatically holding his breath for Freddie's reply.

'I see, well now that makes t'ings a lot simpler, so it does. I'll have to put the wheels in motion to dissolve the partnership and the business will have to be valued.'

'Will *you* be able to do that?' Hugo stood up and resumed his pacing in front of the desk.

'Oh no, it'll have to be someone else to do that, someone independent, like.'

Hugo took a sharp intake of breath. 'I was hoping we could just do it all quietly, Freddie,' he almost whispered as though someone might overhear.

'Well, we don't have to announce it from the rooftops, Councillor Marshall, but we do have to tell the taxman that one of our partners has died,' replied Freddie cheerfully.

'And after that?' Hugo stopped at his desk and tapped a pencil distractedly on his blotter.

'Well then, once we've liquidated all the assets and paid all the liabilities, the surplus will be divided between you, me and Mr Saxby-Jones's estate. We are then at liberty go our separate ways, but if you want any help sorting out your personal tax affairs, then I'm only too happy to oblige, Councillor Marshall.'

Hugo cleared his throat,

'Yes, well thank you, Freddie, I'll bear that in mind. So, Planet can be kept quiet then – no one will know about it apart from the taxman,' he said, trying to sound as matter of fact as possible.

'Well, there's Simon's solicitor, but he'll only be interested in the final profit in order to execute the will. I expect his wife will get everything and I don't suppose she'll be bothered about where the money has come from.'

'Can my agency handle the sales of the Planet Properties?'

'I don't see why not as all the accounts are above board, Councillor Marshall; it's just how you and Mr Saxby-Jones conducted the business that was, shall we say, a little tricky.'

Hugo winced. 'Now look here—'

'But of course, we don't want to be falling out about the goings-on now, do we? I'll be straight wit' you and you'll be straight wit' me, and everyt'ing will be just fine. Now, I'll email a list of the properties, according to our books, and we'll just stay in touch when we need to. Will that be all for now, Councillor Marshall?'

Hugo cleared his throat. 'Yes, yes I think so Freddie.'

'In that case, I'll be saying good day to you.'

Christ! What a mess. Hugo rubbed his eyes. He was tired and, if he was honest, he was bloody scared. It was no joke being one of the prime suspects in a murder case. He sat down behind his desk and pulled the cup of coffee closer but before he could take a drink he became aware of a loud voice in the outer office.

Charles had not been near the agency in months, possibly two years, so when his office door was thrown open, Hugo was taken aback to see the large bulk of his brother-in-law standing there.

'What the bloody hell is going on, Hugo?' Charles bellowed. 'Celia is most upset about the police coming around to the house on a Sunday, asking questions, taking statements. Good God man, what have you done?' Charles slammed the door shut behind him and stared at Hugo with bulging eyes.

'What the hell do you think you're doing? Bursting in here like this?' Hugo retaliated.

'I'm still a partner in this agency, Hugo, have you forgotten that I started the damned business? I only agreed to let you in to please Celia.'

'You made that very plain on Friday afternoon, Charles.'

'Never mind all that! Have you lost your mind? One minute you suddenly announce you want to sell the agency, then I take the advice of a trusted friend not to sell at the present time and the next minute he's dead!'

'Trusted friend? Hah! That's not what I would call Simon Saxby-Jones.'

'Goddammit Hugo, the man is dead!'

'I hope you're not insinuating that I had anything to do with his death.' Hugo said rather pompously.

'I don't need to insinuate anything. Celia told me that the police already suspect you, because you were there! What did you need to see Simon about on Saturday evening that couldn't wait until today?' Charles had been pacing back and forth, but now he came to a stop in front of Hugo's desk. Placing two pudgy hands on it he leaned forward, staring at Hugo.

Hugo pushed his chair backwards and tried not to be intimidated. 'It's actually none of your business – it was a private matter.'

'Poppycock!' Charles roared thumping the desk and sending Hugo's stationery holder flying, his pens and pencils scattering over the floor.

Hugo stood up and for the first time in his life, his courage did not desert him: 'When I spoke to you last Tuesday about selling the agency, I did *not* expect you to discuss our business with Carlton Banks who, in turn, discussed it with Simon Saxby-Jones. I believed that *we* would discuss it rationally with *our* accountant and then come to a mutual decision. I admit I was taken aback when you told me that Aztec Developments would make us an offer in a few months' time.'

'Damn good businessman is Carlton Banks,' remarked Charles.

'Of that, I've no doubt, but the decision to sell to Aztec wasn't yours to make.' Hugo felt calm now and very strong-minded.

'Of course it was… is …'

'No, we're a partnership and should make decisions together. You assumed that I would just go along with you. However, when I said I wanted to sell, I meant immediately, not when it suited Saxby-Jones. You've not done a day's work in this agency for two years or thereabouts, yet you still take fifty per cent of the profits – as is your right of course – but who do you think does the work? Me! With Tom!' Hugo's voice got louder as he spoke.

'Just a minute—' interrupted Charles.

'No, hear me out! You're right! I was furious with Simon Saxby-Jones for suggesting a delay in selling the agency. Why the hell should I wait at his convenience?' Hugo continued belligerently.

'You'd have nothing if it weren't for me! You married my sister, I gave you a partnership in *my* business, *I've* introduced you to well-connected and important people, supported you in the local elections, and you think you can sell *my* agency when it's convenient to you? You're delusional. You've upset my sister *and* you may have jeopardised my chances of renaming the Ashdale Handicap to the Lewis Marshall Mile now that you're dragging our good name through the mud!' Hugo had never seen Charles so angry, so red in the face, and his bravado evaporated.

'I phoned Simon and he suggested I go along to see him between the shows,' Hugo explained somewhat lamely.

'You just couldn't leave it, could you?' Charles sneered.

'I didn't damn well know he was going to get murdered, did I?' Hugo snapped defensively. 'As it happens, I decided not to exacerbate matters further and changed my mind. I didn't actually see Simon.'

'Well, of course, you *would* bloody well say that now, wouldn't you?' Charles shouted.

'Now look here—'

Charles took a deep breath and drew himself up to his full six feet and one inch.

'I've only two things to tell you, Hugo: Firstly, I'll arrange an appointment with the accountant and begin the process of dissolving our partnership. I'm deeply disappointed with this situation and can see no benefit in continuing. Secondly, Celia has decided to come and stay with Beatrice and me until all this is over. She does not want to be tarnished with your wrongdoings.'

'But I've not—' began Hugo.

'There's nothing more to say for the moment, Hugo.'

Lydia Buckley

After breakfast, Lydia decided to spend some time on her new novel; it was coming along nicely and she thought that immersing herself in her narrative would help with the flashbacks of the awful discovery of Simon's body. She settled down in front of her laptop and began typing, but half an hour later she realised that she had only written a couple of pages and her mind still kept returning to the events of Saturday evening. With a sigh she closed down the document and shut the lid on the laptop. It was no good, she still felt shocked and restless. Poor Annabelle, she thought, having just found out that her husband might have been cheating on her was bad enough, but then to discover he had been murdered. Lydia suddenly made her mind up – she would take a card and flowers to Annabelle in person, and offer her condolences.

Thirty minutes later Lydia was driving up the tree-lined driveway to The Manor. She was quite taken aback at the size of the beautiful Yorkshire-stone house. She parked carefully next to a small white hatchback and stepped out onto a gravelled forecourt. The large oak door, complete with leaded glass and polished brass lion-headed knocker was answered fairly quickly by a small rounded woman with a kindly face.

'Hello, my name is Lydia Buckley and I would like to give these to Annabelle along with my condolences if possible, although I quite understand if she isn't up to seeing anyone.'

'Hello love, come in out of the cold,' the woman smiled and opened the large door further. Lydia gratefully stepped inside. 'Give me two minutes and I'll just pop along and see how she's feeling this morning.'

The woman disappeared down a hallway and Lydia took in her surroundings. A spectacular carved oak staircase rose up from the parquet-floored entrance hall. There was a smell of polish, and fresh flowers were arranged neatly in a large vase on top of a semi-circular table. The double-height ceiling had beautiful ornate plasterwork and from its centre hung a large chandelier. Lydia turned towards the sound of returning footsteps and saw Annabelle hurrying towards her with a big smile on her face.

'Lydia! How lovely to see you, have you time to stay for a coffee?' There was almost a desperate tone to Annabelle's voice.

'Yes, of course.' Lydia held out the flowers and card. 'I'm so sorry for your loss, Annabelle.'

The smile on Annabelle's face faltered for a couple of seconds but then she brightened again. 'Come on through to the kitchen – we can have coffee and some of Mrs Simms's gorgeous cake.'

'I wonder if I could just pop into town to pick up some fresh produce, now that you've some company, Miss Annabelle.'

'Of course, Mrs Simms, don't rush. I'll be quite all right with Lydia,' Annabelle chirped. Mrs Simms looked meaningfully at Lydia and raised an eyebrow.

'I'm sure I'll still be here when you get back, I'm in no hurry,' Lydia told her reassuringly.

Mrs Simms nodded appreciatively. 'Well I shouldn't be too long anyway,' she said as she fastened a headscarf over her grey curls and pulled on a coat.

Lydia turned and followed Annabelle to the kitchen. The kitchen was a huge farmhouse type with quarry tiles on the floor and an Aga against one wall, and there was also a quantity of very fine cabinetry. An old scrubbed-wooded table stood in the centre and Annabelle laid out cake and a knife whilst the kettle boiled.

'Sit down, it won't be long.' She busied herself with coffee and a cafetière, mugs, milk and sugar before finally sinking into a chair. Annabelle looked understandably pale and tired, her chin-length hair was lank and unwashed.

Lydia had watched her carefully during her preparations and decided that Annabelle was putting on a brave face and really not feeling as chirpy as she sounded.

She put her hand on the young woman's arm. 'How are you really, Annabelle?' she said softly.

Annabelle swallowed and took a deep breath. 'I… don't

know. Sometimes I feel really sad but sometimes I just feel numb.' Annabelle glanced up and tears filled her eyes. 'I'm so glad you came to see me, I've not heard from anyone else.'

'What? But surely your friend Verity has been in touch? Weren't you with her on Saturday night?'

Annabelle looked downcast. 'Yes, I did go to the panto with her and Harry but since then, no, not a word. I did tell you that she and Harry were Simon's friends and not mine, didn't I?'

'Well yes, but I would have thought they would have at least sent a message or asked how you were.'

'No.' Annabelle shook her head. 'As soon as the police asked me to go with them on Saturday night, I assume she went to meet Harry at the Coach & Horses.'

Lydia decided to say nothing more about Verity's lack of consideration for the moment.

'Anyway, I'm so pleased you're here,' continued Annabelle 'I wished I'd asked for your number last Wednesday as I desperately wanted to talk to you on Friday.'

'Friday?' asked Lydia, not wanting to reveal what she already knew. Annabelle told Lydia about the conversation with Verity on Friday morning and about Simon's supposed affair.

'After she left, I was absolutely devastated. I just wanted someone to talk to and you were so nice to me when you did my lashes even though we don't really know each other.'

'Oh Annabelle, I wish I could have been there for you.'

'And then the strangest thing was that I looked at the local paper and there he was.'

'Who?' Lydia was puzzled at this.

'Robert. He wrote the review for the panto and there was his name right in front of me,'

'Robbie Parker? He was your ex-fiancé?' Lydia was surprised at this revelation.

'Yes, do you know him?'

Lydia suddenly remembered that Annabelle didn't know of

her connection to the panto and thought it was wise to keep it that way for now.

'He's a work colleague of my boyfriend, I heard his name mentioned.'

It's not a lie, just not all the truth.

Annabelle shrugged, 'Small world. Anyway, that night when Simon came home, I asked him about what Verity had said.' She repeated what Simon had told her about Zoe being the scorned woman and although Lydia had heard this story from Zoe, she made sure she looked suitably shocked,

'Really? You believed Simon though?'

'I was hesitant at first, but he convinced me that he loved me and agreed we could start a family, but now…' Annabelle's eyes filled with tears and she picked a clean tissue from a box on the table.

Suddenly she sat up: 'Oh my God!' she exclaimed, 'you don't think this Zoe has… has… *killed* Simon, do you? She was there on Saturday night.'

'But why would she do that?' asked Lydia.

'Jealousy! If she couldn't have him, nobody could. You do hear of these things.' Annabelle looked at Lydia expectantly.

'W–e–ll,' Lydia began carefully, 'jealousy can be a motive, but I wouldn't like to jump to any conclusions in this case.'

'It might have been Councillor Marshall then,' Annabelle suggested.

'Councillor Marshall? Who killed Simon? Why on earth would he do that?' This was news to Lydia and she needed more information.

'Well, he rang Simon on Saturday morning and although I only overheard one side of the conversation, it was obvious that Councillor Marshall was upset with Simon about something. I know that because Simon was trying to placate him. Councillor Marshall desperately wanted to see Simon, and eventually Simon agreed to a meeting and suggested that Councillor Marshall came to the Jubilee Hall at five o'clock, but to come round to the back entrance, then he gave him a code for the door. I wonder if it was anything to with astronomy; they have talked about that sort of thing before.' Annabelle frowned briefly and then took a bite of her lemon cake. 'This is really delicious, you know, Daddy is very lucky to have Mrs Simms, her cooking and baking skills are amazing – what do you think of the cake?'

Lydia was trying to process the last chunk of information,

'Did Councillor Marshall have his meeting with Simon?' she asked.

'I don't know. I assume so, but what if he lost his temper and killed Simon?'

'But why would he? And what's all this talk about astronomy?'

'God knows! They have previously discussed stuff about planets or whatever. Councillor Marshall wanted to do something and Simon disagreed. Maybe Councillor Marshall killed Simon so he could do whatever it was.'

'Have you told the police all of this?'

'Yes, it was all in my statement.'

'Oh Annabelle, you've had quite a trauma over the last few days.' Lydia felt genuinely sorry for her. 'Have you any idea what you're going to do?' she asked eventually.

'I'm going to stay here. I can't go back to the house in Harrogate, not at all,' Annabelle said decisively.

'I'm so sorry. Look, is there anything I can do to help?'

'Well actually…'

'Please, I mean it – what can I do?'

'I'm going to ask Tasheka to sort out Simon's stuff – she's my weekly help. I wondered if you could go with her and perhaps bring some of my things back here.' Annabelle raised her head and looked hopefully at Lydia.

'Yes, of course. When does she go to your house?'

'Wednesdays, from around nine o'clock until twelve noon. I'll ring her and let her know. Why don't you come here on Wednesday morning and I can give you a key? Actually, if you meet Tasheka here, you could both go in her car, and then you could drive mine back here, would that be all right?' Annabelle smiled weakly.

They agreed that that was a good plan and Lydia stood up to go.

Annabelle walked her to the front door and Lydia gave her a hug. Let me give you my number, even if you just want to talk, call me,' she said.

'Thank you for being so kind. We hardly know each other, but talking to you is a great help,' Annabelle was tearful again. 'I'll see you on Wednesday morning.'

Lydia nodded as she put on her coat and said goodbye. As she left The Manor, Lydia didn't feel like going back to do more work on her novel straight away, so she decided to treat herself to lunch at her sister's café before doing some shopping at MegaMart.

Nick Bradley

Nick stepped out of MegaMart and into the cold, fresh air. He strolled around the Market Place wanting inspiration for lunch and came to the Forget-Me-Not Café. This was the place where everyone had gone for the matinée tea and would do very nicely, he thought. Nick opened the door and a delicious scent of home-cooking filled his nostrils. His stomach rumbled appreciatively as he headed to the counter.

'Hello, Nick,' said a familiar voice, Nick turned his head and saw Lydia sat at a table.

'Hi,' Nick smiled, 'How are you?'

'Still a bit shaken and shocked, how about you?'

'Just the same. Are you having lunch here?' he asked, looking at the empty place in front of her.

'I've just ordered, would you like to join me?' Lydia indicated the other empty chair.

'Yes, I'd like that, I could do with some good company.' Nick ordered his lunch and then sat opposite Lydia. He sat and played with a paper napkin wondering how to start the conversation to say what was on his mind.

'I … um …' he began, 'you know that I told you how I heard Zoe and Simon arguing earlier last week?' Lydia nodded and opened her mouth to say something, but Nick rushed on. 'Well I heard them arguing again on Saturday evening after everyone had left to come here to the café – and it wasn't good.'

Lydia leaned forward. 'I know about the argument, but I would like to hear your take on it, she said quietly. Nick sighed in relief, at least she knew about it, it would make it easier to talk now. He explained how he had come into The Annexe just as Bella had left, so he had not heard what had gone on before that, but he had heard the rest of it.

'I've no idea what time Zoe left or what happened after that and I'm worried that Zoe … err… well…' Nick couldn't say that he thought Zoe might have killed Simon because it sounded ridiculous. He liked Zoe.

Lydia pondered for a moment and then she said, 'Another consideration is that someone else could have entered the hall by the back door and…' Lydia broke off as Kate brought their lunches over. They thanked her and then Lydia continued, '…hid somewhere before… well, you know.'

'Really? How could this other person have got in?' Nick asked.

'Well, there are two ways that I can think of: firstly they may have been given the code by someone, or secondly, Simon may have let them in.'

'You think? But we're not supposed to give the code to anyone,' he pointed out.

'Yes, but that doesn't mean that we all stuck to the rules.' Lydia sat back at looked at him

'True.' Nick thought for a moment and screwed up his eyes as he remembered something else. 'After we'd finished our fish and chips I went to go to the toilet. While I was in there, I thought I heard banging on the outside of the back door. I did go and have a look, but there was no one there. However, I did see a car pulling out of the car park, it was a Range Rover, a dark coloured one.'

'What time was that?'

'Around five-thirty, I think.'

'Have you told the police that?' Lydia asked him.

Nick shook his head. 'No, I didn't think it was important at the time, as whoever it was didn't come inside so I guessed they had nothing to do with the murder.'

'Nick, I think you should mention it, it may corroborate something someone else has said,'

'Oh hell, I hadn't thought of that, damn it. I'll make a call this afternoon.'

They both ate in amiable silence for a few minutes until Nick realised that Lydia had something on *her* mind,

'What is it?' he asked after a few minutes, 'I can tell you want to say something.'

Lydia sighed and put her fork down. 'I'm going to ask you something – and I've good reason, although you might think I'm sticking my nose in. I'm not, well I might be, but it's with the right intentions. Of course, you may decide not to speak to me about it but I do hope…'

Nick laughed. 'For God's sake Lydia, just come out with it, what are you talking about?' Nick looked at Lydia, but she didn't laugh or smile. He immediately realised that whatever it was, it was serious. 'What is it? What do you want to know?'

'Simon was your father, wasn't he?'

Nick carefully put his knife and fork down, and took a breath. He said nothing for a few minutes.

How had Lydia worked that out? He thought back and remembered the conversation with Simon during a rehearsal when they'd talked about the university, but how had Lydia come to this conclusion? Did it matter that she knew the truth? The man was dead now.

Nick looked at Lydia. Slowly, he nodded his head.

'Yes. He was my father. He left my mother and never wrote, visited, or had any contact at all – he broke her heart. I only recently tracked him down, but I didn't really like what I found, which was pretty much how my mother had described him. I had thought, that perhaps her memory was clouded by bitterness or that he may have changed – mellowed a bit. Unfortunately not, he was nasty and, to be honest, I'm… was ashamed to call him my father.' Nick had not spoken like this to anyone and he found it a relief to be able to speak freely, and now he just wanted to carry on and let it all out.

'I had hoped that there might have been a moment when I could have had a private word with him but, as the week went on, I wasn't sure I wanted to get to know him at all. A man who had a wife and a girlfriend, a man who would threaten another woman's livelihood, a man who would lie and cheat his way to get what he wanted was no one to be proud of. Am I sad that he's dead? Not really. I mean I wouldn't have wished him harm or anything, but he wasn't a nice person and he very clearly pushed someone over the edge.' Nick suddenly remembered that Lydia had asked him the question for a reason: 'Why did you want to know, anyway?' He spoke gently so as not to give the impression that he was angry or upset, which he wasn't.

'Do you know anything about Simon's family – his parents, for example?' she asked by way of an answer.

'My mother had letters from Simon's father, they were sent sporadically over a period of several years and although she didn't tell me about them, she kept them. I found them after she passed away last year.'

'Oh Nick, I'm sorry to hear of your mother's passing,' Lydia broke in, 'please don't carry on if it's too painful.'

'No, it's fine. She died of cancer. We only knew she was ill for three months and in the end she passed away in her sleep. It was very peaceful.' Nick clamped his lips together as his emotions threatened to get the better of him. When the moment passed, he continued, 'I found the letters when I was going through her things, so I wrote to… my grandfather, I suppose he is… anyway I didn't receive a reply so I don't know what happened to him, maybe he had died as well.'

'That's a real shame. Would you have liked to get to know him? I mean, were the letters nice?' probed Lydia.

Nick smiled. 'Yeah, they were, he sounded fun. The letters were really witty and written in an old-fashioned sort of style, you know, phrases like "I say" or "jolly good" and "dashed exciting". Yes, I would have liked an opportunity to meet him. Maybe I'll look into it and see if he did pass away.'

Lydia nodded. 'I suppose you could do that… sometime. Oh! Sorry to change the subject so abruptly, but before I forget, Desmond asked if he could have your mobile number to add to his contact details. We all usually get together for a bit of a night out in the summer and we can't get in touch with you.'

'Yeah, of course, no problem,' Nick reeled off his number and then suddenly looked at his watch. 'Bloody hell! Look at the time, I've got to get back to work.' He jumped up and picked up his jacket. 'You know Lydia, it has been so good to talk to you, thank you. Gotta dash!'

Nick rushed out of the café and ran across the Market Place to the supermarket. He arrived at the offices and, out of breath, plonked himself into his chair. As he settled back into his work, he reflected on the conversation with Lydia. He had meant what he said – it had been so good to talk to her.

Elsa Armitage

Brian pushed the trolley around the supermarket while Elsa directed operations.

'So, I was thinking we could pop into Let's Go Travel when we've finished in here… can you put a punnet of those mushrooms in please, Brian? Barb has agreed that she'll at least look at some brochures… and some tomatoes… I told her that there was no flying involved… no, not those tomatoes, the other ones, the smaller ones… yes, those there. We could drive down to Southampton, leave the car and simply board the ship… can you choose some big potatoes, for jackets… once on the ship, it's all-inclusive, all our meals and drinks… how many? About six, please… I think we would all really enjoy it. Do you fancy a pizza for tonight? I know cruising is more expensive, but you do get a lot for your money. Oh hello, Lydia, love.' Elsa stopped in her tracks as she saw Lydia at the deli counter. Brian wandered on with the trolley.

'Hello Elsa, how are you?' she replied.

'Well, I'm better than I was, love… I was right out of sorts yesterday. I said to Brian – we've never had anything like this in Ashdale before… fair gave me a turn, I can tell you. To think there we were, having our matinée tea, and all the time… I've not slept a wink since… not while there's a murderer on the loose.'

'Oh, I don't think you need worry, Elsa,'

'Not worry? I said to Brian, you never know what's going to happen next, we could all be killed in our beds. I told him to push a chair under the door handle. That'll stop them, I said.'

'I think Simon was specifically targeted, I'm sure you're quite safe, Elsa.'

Elsa digested this piece of information before she furtively looked from left to right and waved her hand for Lydia to come closer. 'He *was* at that ball you know. It was him with that Zoe… now I'm not one to tell tales but…' Elsa looked around her again, '…I'm sure he was carrying on with Zoe and I reckon it was her who done him in.' Elsa nodded her head knowingly. 'When I gave my statement – can you believe that? Me, giving the police a statement – I never would've believed it. Anyway, when I'd done, they thanked me for my osber… oberva…' Elsa struggled to remember the word, it had to do with seeing something.

'Observations?' suggested Lydia.

'Yes, them. Anyway… I was thanked, and that was it, but Zoe – I heard them tell her that they would be in touch and she wasn't to go anywhere.' Elsa nodded her head sagely and raised her eyebrows to emphasise her point. 'I know what that means… she's a suspect!' she added with relish, Elsa loved her television crime dramas.

'It doesn't mean that Zoe is guilty, Elsa. I hope that rumour isn't circulating, because gossip like that could ruin her business.'

'Well, we all know that she came late to the café *and* that she and Simon had some sort of secret goings-on,' Elsa justified her comments, looking a little miffed.

'We don't know everything though. Anyway…' Lydia changed the subject, 'I'm glad I've seen you as I wondered if you could give me Edward's address?'

'I'm not sure I can do that, you know, with all this confidence malarkey. We're not supposed to give out private information.' Elsa sniffed, still a little put out.

'Please Elsa, I promise I'm not going to harm him, I just need to talk to him. You won't be breaking any confidentiality laws,' Lydia pleaded. Elsa thought for a moment and remembered that Lydia and Edward had had a very cosy chat that night at the panto. Edward had been very cagey about what they'd been talking about even though Elsa had tried her hardest to worm it out of him – without being obvious though, she was sure.

'He lives in the same residential park as us, number eighty-seven. Our park is on the far side of here, between MegaMart and the canal; the entrance is down past the church. Oh I've lost Brian now! Where can he have got to? By the way, I do hope it's not Zoe, 'cos she's a nice person… Oh look, there he is! I'd best go Lydia, love. Take care, bye.' and Elsa moved off, keeping Brian firmly in her sight.

I'd best keep an eye out for when Lydia comes calling on Edward.

Elsa wasn't a devout member of the Neighbourhood Watch for nothing.

When Elsa and Brian had finally got home and unpacked their shopping, Elsa made a pot of tea. They settled in their favourite chairs, Brian with his newspaper and Elsa with her travel brochures.

'Brian, these cruises are amazing… just look at this …' Elsa leaned over and shoved her brochure in front of Brian's paper so he had no choice but to look at it. It was a picture of a cabin with a double bed, en suite and sliding doors onto a balcony.

'Looks a bit like our hotel in Bournemouth,' he remarked, going back to his paper as Elsa shifted back to her chair.

'It's nothing like Bournemouth – we don't have a balcony in Bournemouth.' Elsa rested the brochure on her lap and stared out of the lounge window at number eighty-seven. 'You know, Brian, I've been thinking…' she mused.

Brian looked up from his newspaper and waited patiently. 'Yes… and?' he said after a few moment's silence.

'When we were in MegaMart and I was talking to Lydia… you know that lady what was the prompt… well, she asked me for Edward's address.'

'And did you give it to her?' Brian's eyes had strayed back to his paper.

'I did, but I was thinking that I might have to pop over to Edward and tell him, just so that he knows she might be coming to see him some time.'

'I don't think you need do that, it's not like he needs a warning or anything,' Brian replied.

'No, but it's only manners to let him know that I've given his address to someone. He might not have wanted me to.' Elsa closed her brochure.

'If he didn't want you to, it's a bit late now though, 'cos you already have,' Brian pointed out.

Elsa huffed. 'Well I still think I should tell him.'

Brian took a drink of his tea and carried on reading his paper.

15

Lydia Buckley

Lydia took her coffee to her desk and opened the laptop to take a look at the Lewis Marshall website to see if any properties that were available to let took her fancy. There were several possibilities, so she reached out to pick up her mobile, but as her hand closed around the phone it burst into life as a call came in. Lydia was surprised to see that it was Tom.

'Hello, I was just about to call you,' she said as she answered.

'Great minds think alike then. We've some new properties available and I wondered if you had some time to visit them with me. Are you free this morning by any chance?'

'That would be lovely, what time shall I meet you?'

'Well actually, I could pick you up in say, ten minutes?'

'Perfect, I'll be waiting.' Lydia shut down her laptop, picked up her list and slipped into a pair of trainers.

Ten minutes later, Tom pulled up outside. 'Hi, how are you doing?'

'Still getting over the trauma of the weekend, to be honest. It's just so shocking.'

'Poor you, finding Simon's body like that. I can't imagine how you feel.'

'I'm struggling to come to terms with the fact that Simon has gone and that it may be someone I know who did it!'

'Why do you think that?'

'Well, whoever it was, must have known the code to get in, so I guess it might have been a member of the Ashdale Players or someone known to one of them.'

'Interesting you should say that. Let me tell you what went on at work yesterday morning.' As Tom drove, he related the argument between Charles and Hugo. 'So Simon gave Hugo the entry code in order to have his meeting. Felicity and I couldn't help hearing everything – they were practically shouting at each other.'

Lydia closed her mouth which had fallen open. 'So, he may have been the last person to see Simon alive – that means that he …' Lydia trailed off at the implication.

'Hugo maintains that he didn't actually see Simon – says he chose not to go ahead with the meeting.'

'Well, he would say that,' Lydia pointed out.

'That's what Charles said. But then, I can't see Hugo killing Simon.'

'No, but you say that Simon had prevented Hugo from selling the agency and retiring. Why?' asked Lydia.

'I think it was something to do with the timing of it. Aztec wanted to buy the agency in May, but Hugo didn't want to wait until then, he wants to retire now – immediately.' Tom pulled up outside a small parade of shops near an industrial estate on the outskirts of Harrogate. 'Anyway, the upshot of the argument with Charles is that they have agreed to end their business partnership and Hugo has asked if I would like first refusal of the agency.' Tom looked at Lydia and grinned.

'Wow, what an opportunity. What does Amy think?'

'She agrees that we should try to raise funds to buy the business, so I've an appointment with the bank later this week.'

Tom pulled the keys out of the ignition. 'Now, back to the job in hand. This retail unit is for sale,' he said indicating a One-Stop shop. 'The business isn't for sale, just the premises and it includes the flat upstairs. This would give you two rental incomes for the one property purchase.'

Lydia looked at the property, it was a medium-sized not particularly attractive unit and the flat looked shabby. Lydia knew it wasn't for her.

'You're not keen, are you?'

Lydia shook her head. 'No, it looks as though it may need some renovation and I'm not keen on the area, it's a bit… um … well, I'm just not keen,' she finished lamely.

'This would be a practical option, but I do understand what you mean about sprucing it up. Let's go through this list I have before we go any further. I'll tell you a little bit about each one,' suggested Tom.

'Why don't we get a takeaway coffee from here and just sit in the car?'

Five minutes later, when they were both settled back in the car with their hot drinks, Tom opened his folder. 'These properties have just become available. Hugo gave me the list this morning, it's the property portfolio of an acquaintance of his. The company is being dissolved and they want to sell everything.' Tom handed Lydia a list of properties on headed paper.

'Planet Properties?'

'Have you heard of them?' Tom said in surprise.

'Yes, but I can't think where. Are they a local company?' Lydia hated telling fibs to Tom, but she knew that she couldn't talk about Greg's investigation to anyone – not even his brother.

'The only contact we have is an accountant's office on the industrial estate in front of us, F. Flannigan Associates,' replied Tom.

'Oh well, it doesn't matter. What's on the list?'

Tom took Lydia to four or five properties, some retail and some residential. Lydia promised to consider them carefully, discuss it with Greg and speak to Tom later in the week.

After Tom dropped Lydia back at home and she immediately rang Greg.

'Hi, how are you?' It wasn't a very good connection as Greg was driving. He'd been away in Scotland on another assignment and was due home this afternoon.

'I'm ok,' he shouted. 'Robbie has invited us to his apartment in Leeds for dinner this evening to talk about this Planet article. He said to tell you that you're most welcome, but that he'll understand if you decide Planet isn't your thing…' the connection drifted away and then Greg spoke again,'… so if you want to come, I'll pick you up at seven, ok?'

'Yes…' replied Lydia and then the phone went dead. She shrugged, her news about Planet Properties could wait until this evening.

In the meantime, she retrieved Greg's notes on the murder, which she had brought from his apartment, and regretfully added Nick's name to the list of suspects. She was pretty sure that he hadn't killed Simon, but he had admitted that he didn't like his father, so revenge could be a motive. He had left the hall to go to the Gents so that was the opportunity and presumably he could have taken a knife from the kitchen – assuming the weapon *was* a knife – which would provide the means.

The next name to add to the list of suspects was Hugo. Lydia now knew that Simon had given the door code to Hugo, and Hugo had admitted that he went to the hall, albeit he reckoned that he had not seen Simon. Hugo had the means if he had taken a knife with him, the motive if he was indeed desperate to sell the agency, and the opportunity. Lydia sighed, the list was getting longer and they were unable to definitely cross anyone off.

The other person that she added to the list was Robbie. He was in Ashdale on Saturday evening and could have gone down to the hall. Admittedly he didn't know the door code, but he could have been let in by someone else. She decided that she would mention that she had seen him in Ashdale during dinner tonight, just to see his reaction. After all, there could be a perfectly innocent reason. She looked again at the list: Zoe, Jonathan, Nick, Hugo and Robbie. Which one of them had been pushed too far?

After her lunch, Lydia took out a condolence card she had bought for Edward whilst she was in MegaMart the day before and gave some thought as to what to write in it. She didn't know him very well and didn't want to overdo the sentiment, so in the end she settled for:

Please accept my sincere condolences.

Lydia followed Elsa's directions and drove past the church where she found the Canalside Residential Park for the over-fifties. At the entrance was a sign which designated the site as a Neighbourhood Watch area where cold-callers and doorstep-sellers were prohibited. She pulled into a large site which presumably had once been a field. Now it was full of park-home bungalows laid out in neat rows. Each had their own plot which the owners had either lawned, decked or paved. Today, however, it was cold and windy and there was very little sign of life as Lydia drove slowly, observing the speed limit of ten miles per hour. She gazed at each of the little dwellings; some had names and others had a number, the sequence of which wasn't always logical. At last, she reached a park home bearing a plaque with 87 on it, so she parked her car and switched off the engine.

As Lydia glanced round, she thought she saw the curtains twitch at number eighty-four. Neighbourhood Watch is active then, she thought to herself as she got out of the car and locked it. She heard her name being called and turned around.

'Hi Elsa,' Lydia said in response.

'I just thought I would let you know that Edward *is* in... well, I've not seen him go out.' Elsa stood outside her door with a cardigan draped over her shoulders.

'Ok, thank you,' Lydia called in response as she walked around her car.

'If you were going to talk to Edward about the murder,' Elsa continued, 'did you want me to come over as well, just so I can give you my osberva... er, tell you what I saw?'

Lydia stopped, waited until Elsa had finished speaking and then turned to face her.

'I'm not going to talk to Edward about the murder, it's another matter entirely, but thank you, Elsa,' she replied, smiling graciously.

'In that case, can I offer you a cuppa over here, when you've finished over there?' Elsa asked hopefully.

'I'm not sure how long I'm going to be Elsa, perhaps another time? Now don't stand out in this wind, you'll get cold.' Lydia raised her hand in a farewell gesture and hurried up the drive to Edward's door.

Edward had already opened the door having heard Lydia's voice. 'I say, it's a bit chilly, come on in.'

'I hope you don't mind me calling in unexpectedly, but I didn't have your phone number and I wanted to see you,' Lydia explained as she stepped over the threshold.

Edward closed the door behind her. 'I should mention that it's not unexpected. I believe you saw Elsa in MegaMart yesterday. She popped across to let me know that you would probably pay me a visit, and I must say that it's jolly good to see you. May I offer you some refreshment? I expect it's a little early for a glass of red, but I do have some Earl Grey tea which you can have with either a slice of lemon or milk.' As he spoke, he filled the kettle and switched it on.

'The Earl Grey with lemon sounds lovely, thank you.'

'Please take a seat and I'll be with you in a jiffy.' Edward bustled about and Lydia looked at the generous sized lounge with elegant but comfortable furniture. It somehow didn't surprise her to notice an art deco theme in the geometric shaped mirror, wall prints and ornaments.

In no time at all, Edward produced a tray with cups, saucers, a teapot and a plate of shortbread biscuits. He poured the tea into the cups which already contained the lemon slices.

'Now, I expect the events of last Saturday have something to do with your visit, especially as you're the only person who knows...' Edward's voice cracked with emotion. He broke off and suddenly looked away, 'How embarrassing, I do beg your pardon,' he apologised when he had recovered.

'Edward, there's no need to apologise. I've brought a card and wanted to say I'm truly sorry for your loss.' Lydia handed him the white envelope. She then made a great show of unnecessarily stirring her tea and selecting a piece of shortbread whilst he read the card.

At last he looked up. 'It's a damn shame I didn't get to speak to him on Friday night. I was waiting at the bus stop and he came out with his girlfriend, or was it his wife? Anyway, all the rest of the cast were there and the right moment just didn't arise,' he said sorrowfully. 'I can't imagine what that young lady must be feeling, she was only a young girl and... well, I heard her tell him something and I've been thinking of her since then.' Edward took a sip of his tea.

'Would you mind telling me exactly what you saw and heard, Edward? It's very important.'

'Is it? In that case, of course.' Edward put down his teacup and leaned back in his chair. 'There were about half a dozen other folk waiting by the door at the back and I didn't want him to see me with everyone else about, so I stood at the bus stop. They all came out chattering and laughing and someone mentioned going to the pub, but Simon said no, he was going back to... I didn't quite catch the young lady's name, it sounded like Ella.'

'Bella,' corrected Lydia.

'Bella, that's right. The man who locked the door told them not to be late the next day and he set off to catch up with the rest of his group who had walked on ahead. His girlfriend was waiting for him and she tagged along at the back…'

'Girlfriend!' interrupted Lydia, 'Desmond doesn't have a girlfriend, he's … um, well, he doesn't have a girlfriend,' Lydia wasn't sure whether or not Edward would understand.

'Gay?' suggested Edward, 'I'm not shocked Lydia, I've had several very dear friends in the past who were gay. But there was a lady who had waited and followed this Desmond character, I just assumed she was his girlfriend.'

'Do you remember what she looked like?'

'Well as a matter of fact I do, she looked a damn fine woman, rather classy. She had blonde hair to here,' he indicated his chin, 'and wore a striking coat, it was a dark colour – I can't really say whether it was black or navy blue, but it had lighter colour cuffs. I noticed her in particular because she stood at the back of everyone else, and when the cast and crew all piled out of the door, she took a step back into a shadow, as though she didn't want to be seen. I thought it was rather odd, actually.'

'It's a strange thing to do if you've come to meet someone,' agreed Lydia.

'After the others had left… Bella, is it? She said something to Simon and he said "Pregnant?" quite loudly. I pretended not to hear. They spoke quietly for a few minutes and Simon then exclaimed, "Pleased! What in God's name made you think I would be pleased?" I glanced around at that and saw that Simon looked angry, then I looked away again. I didn't want them to know that I'd overheard and I certainly didn't want Simon to recognise me at that moment. After a while, they got into his car and drove away. I got the distinct impression that Simon wasn't overjoyed at Bella's news.'

Edward looked expectantly at Lydia who digested all of the information and then thought about how she would tell Edward all that had happened and who was who.

'I need to tell you what was going on and I'm afraid it won't show Simon in a good light, so I apologise in advance if I say some things that you find upsetting,' Lydia began.

'Does all this have a bearing on why Simon was killed?' Edward asked in trepidation.

'I believe so, but until his killer is found, we won't know for sure.' Lydia then told Edward, as gently as she could, how Simon had broken up Annabelle's engagement in order to marry her himself, in order to ingratiate himself into her father's company.

Edward looked stunned. 'Good Lord!' he uttered, then, after a moment, 'That's dashed underhand of him and yet, I'm not surprised. So, who was the girl called Bella, then?'

'This is where it gets complicated,' continued Lydia and she explained how Simon had begun an affair with Bella because of her father's business project.

Edward's face was devoid of expression as he took in what Lydia had said, and then he frowned. 'So, Bella is expecting Simon's baby, but you say he wasn't going to leave Annabelle for her? What a dreadful situation! But what has that to do with Simon's murder? Surely you don't think one of those ladies killed him?'

Lydia explained the rest of the story and how Hugo, Jonathan, Zoe and Robbie were also potential suspects. When she had finished, Edward stood up, walked to a shelf and picked up a photograph which he gave to Lydia.

'This is Simon and his mother, my late wife Veronica. Her maiden name was Saxby, which Simon has now hyphenated with Jones. Simon must have been around four years old at the time, he looks like an angel, doesn't he? Who would have thought that such a sweet little boy would grow up into a self-centred man whose drive for ambition, power and control would be his ultimate downfall?' he said sadly.

'Edward, I'm so sorry to have had to tell you this, but I felt it was the right thing to do and there's something else...'

Edward sat down and closed his eyes in despair. 'What more could there be?' he groaned.

'I'm hoping that what I have to say is positive. You remember you told me that you and Simon had a disagreement whilst he was at university?'

Edward opened his eyes and looked at Lydia suspiciously. 'Go on,' he croaked.

'Was the reason to do with a pregnancy?'

Edward sighed. 'Yes, Simon fathered a child but refused to acknowledge it. I wrote to the child's mother, Tamzin, on several occasions to follow the child's progress, but my last letter went unanswered and I don't know where she is now,' he said wistfully. 'The child! Ha! He'll be in his twenties now – definitely not a child.'

'Edward,' Lydia began carefully, 'he lives here in Ashdale.'

Edward's eyes opened in amazement. 'Good Lord! Here? How on earth do you know that?'

Lydia told him about her conversation with Nick and how he came to be in Ashdale.

'Do you think he would meet up with me?' asked Edward trying hard not to show too much excitement.

'I'm sure he would. Shall I arrange something, say a meeting at the Forget-Me-Not Café?'

Edward's eyes shone with happiness.

'Oh! I say Lydia, would you? Take my mobile number. I'm going away for a few days and won't be back until Friday, so Saturday would be good. Let me know what time he can manage, if he agrees.'

Mobile numbers thus exchanged, Lydia stood up to leave. 'I hope that out of this sorrow comes a new beginning for you and Nick,' she said.

'I cannot thank you enough. I've a lot of thinking to do now.' Edward clasped Lydia's hand in sincere appreciation and kissed her on both cheeks.

As Lydia drove home, she was quite emotional and when she had parked the car, she had to blow her nose and pull herself together.

Jonathan Sturdy

Jonathan stared out of his office window wondering if he had done the right thing by agreeing to see this reporter chap. It hadn't surprised him to hear that someone had picked up on dodgy goings-on and that it had a connection to Simon Saxby-Jones. Also, Jonathan had felt that he should be acquainted with all the facts before deciding whether or not to go ahead with handing over the sale of the Thornberry property to Lewis Marshall. All he had to do was listen to what this chap, Greg, had to say. After all, Jonathan had done nothing wrong but – and this was a big but – Jonathan did not want to be involved in any big revelation by a newspaper. A metallic blue Volvo pulled in through the gateway. Jonathan looked up and watched as it parked next to his own Range Rover. He sighed. *Well here we go.*

Jonathan opened the front door and smiled warmly at the man who stood there – they were about the same age and quickly weighed each other up.

'Come in, pleased to meet you, I'm Jonathan Sturdy,' Jonathan stuck his hand out and was impressed by the firm handshake he received.

'Greg Craven, thank you for seeing me.'

'We could go to my office if you want to be formal, although I can confirm that the kitchen is warmer and more homely, plus that's where the coffee or tea can be found.' Jonathan raised his eyebrows.

Greg smiled his eyes crinkling at the outer corners. 'Informal and homely is fine with me and I would appreciate a coffee. I've just travelled back from Scotland,' he replied as Jonathan led the way into the kitchen.

'My wife isn't at home and my daughter is out with her horse, so it's just the two of us. Before we begin, can you clarify your intention with this article? I would rather not be included in some sensational breaking-news story.' Jonathan set down two mugs of coffee.

'It wouldn't be anything as dramatic as that and would probably not even make the nationals but I quite understand your concern, so let me reassure you that at this stage I'm undertaking research, only to ascertain if there is indeed a story worth writing. If there is, I would probably not involve you as, I understand, you've not sold your property as yet,' explained Greg.

Jonathan felt himself relax. 'That's quite correct, our plans have only just been approved.'

'Yes, I've seen them online, and they're impressive. May I ask what you've been advised to do, and by whom?' Greg placed his notebook on the table and took out a pen, 'I'm not going to record our conversation, but I'll take notes, if that's all right with you?'

Jonathan nodded and told Greg what Simon had suggested about the Thornberry farmhouse. 'To be fair to Simon, what he said makes business sense but…' Jonathan broke off, not wanting to elaborate on his reasons for mistrusting his architect.

'But…?' prompted Greg.

'Let's just say that I like to be in control of what happens to my land and it all sounded too easy to just hand it over to an estate agent. I just felt… well, manipulated, that's all,' Jonathan said in the end, which was most of the truth. 'May I ask where all this is leading?'

Greg explained using the same scenario he had used when explaining it to Lydia.

'Good grief! So, I could have ended up with quite a large number of houses in that field instead of pony paddocks?'

'That's right and you would have not been able to stop it. The only fraudulent part would have been the bids. We suspect that Planet Properties would know what the other bids were in advance so they could put in the highest or best bid. The other alternative is that the other bids would be fake and much lower so that you would naturally choose Planet.'

'What sort of money are we talking? I can tell you that Simon mentioned two million for the barns and field as it is,' Jonathan said candidly.

'Well I'm no expert but my research suggests that a field of that size could quite easily accommodate around eighty to a hundred houses, in which case a major developer would pay in the region of maybe nine or ten million pounds for it,' Greg replied.

'Bloody hell!' gasped Jonathan, 'Really?'

Greg nodded.

'Ten million pounds? For that field?' Jonathan was stunned.

'With the planning permission for that number of houses, yes,' confirmed Greg.

'So, if Planet Properties bought Thornberry as it is from me for two million, altered the plans and sold it on, they would have made around eight million pounds profit!' Jonathan could not believe the figures.

'At least that amount, possibly more.'

'Could I have sued someone?'

'I'm no lawyer, but I understand that the agent would probably have been at fault. However, a judge may decide that, even if the bids had been conducted correctly and the purchaser had not been Planet, the eventual purchaser may have done exactly same thing, so you would still have had the housing estate on your field. If that were the decision, then you would have no case for recompense.' Greg took a welcome drink of his coffee.

Jonathan was shell-shocked. 'I'll have to bear all this in mind before I decide what to do next,' he said thoughtfully, 'and it may delay my plans to extend my business. What made you contact me?'

'Your planning application is similar to other developments that fit the scenario. And unfortunately, they *have* ended up with more houses than they originally planned for,' he said.

Jonathan hesitated only for a couple of seconds before he spoke: 'This has something to do with Simon Saxby-Jones, hasn't it?'

Greg said nothing.

Jonathan pushed his chair back suddenly and stood up. He walked to the other end of the kitchen, then turned around. 'You know about his death, don't you?' he said with some trepidation.

'Yes, my girlfriend discovered his body,' Greg said quietly.

Jonathan was surprised. 'Lydia?'

Greg nodded. 'Yes, unfortunately. It was a nasty experience for her.'

'Then you know about the situation with my daughter, Bella.'

It was more of a statement than a question, so Greg said nothing.

'I'll admit, I was furious when she came home after the matinée and told me everything that had been said, especially when she said that she was…' Jonathan stopped mid-sentence as he realised what he had been about to say,

'That's quite all right, I understand how you must have felt, and personally, I would have done the same. Lydia said you had turned up at the café and then gone to the hall, she was worried that you were so angry.'

Jonathan sat back at the table and put his head in his hands. 'The irony is that if I had got into the hall, I would have thumped him – probably more than once, and I'm not a violent man, but he's lied to, cheated on and was intent on abandoning my daughter.'

Jonathan looked up at Greg. 'Bella had given me the door code to get into the hall, but in my rage, I had forgotten it by the time I got there. I just banged on the door, hoping perhaps that Simon would hear and open it. But I realised that there was no one there because when I looked through the letterbox, the lights in the hallway were off and there was no sign of life – err, no pun intended,' Jonathan grimaced at his own choice of words. 'Anyway, no one came to the door and it was throwing it down by then, so I decided to just go home and sort it out the next day.'

Greg let the silence drift on before speaking.

'I appreciate your honesty, Mr Sturdy and rest assured, that it has nothing to do with this planning business, although without disrespect to your daughter, Simon Saxby-Jones may have seen a benefit in befriending her.' Greg has chosen his words carefully and held his breath for the reply.

Jonathan lifted his head. 'Of that, I'm most certain,' he said.

'My suggestion, for what it's worth, would be to remove the pony paddock from the sale and keep it yourself as protection from any further unwanted development opportunities,' Greg advised as he stood up. 'Thank you for your time today, Mr Sturdy. I'll be in touch if the story develops and I need any further input from you.'

Jonathan nodded. 'May I also rely on your discretion?' he asked.

'Yes, you can. It's a distressing business and I've no wish to exacerbate it.'

The two men shook hands in mutual understanding and Greg drove away.

Jonathan reached for his phone. He needed to speak to his son, Josh, and update him on what Greg had just said.

Lydia Buckley

As Greg drove to Leeds, Lydia asked him about his meeting with Jonathan and he told her what Jonathan had said.

'He looked a bit embarrassed when he said that he'd looked through the letter box into the dark corridor and there was no sign of life, it probably wasn't the best thing to say and I hope he didn't say that to the police.'

'Not the best turn of phrase I agree but what did you think of him generally?'

'Actually, I quite liked him. He came across as honest. Yes, he was angry because not only had Simon shamefully deceived his daughter but there was also an intention to double-cross him. I know he can't be ruled out but…' Greg shrugged. 'Anyway, as for the other business with the planning permission, I'll tell you more later when we discuss it with Robbie.'

Lydia was completely blown away by Robbie's stunning penthouse apartment overlooking the dock. The lounge area had floor to ceiling windows opening onto a wraparound roof terrace with panoramic views over Leeds. He proudly showed her the state-of-the-art kitchen with its granite worktops and integrated appliances from which emanated the wonderful aroma of the coq au vin he had prepared for their dinner.

'I'm so envious, Robbie,' Lydia exclaimed, 'this is absolutely gorgeous. The views are incredible and the terrace will be fabulous on summer evenings. That's one thing that Greg's apartment lacks, a terrace for dining and sitting out.'

Greg shrugged. 'That hasn't bothered me at all, but seeing this … well, I have to agree with Lydia, it is rather magnificent.'

Robbie, clearly chuffed that they were impressed with his home, offered them drinks and nibbles whilst he made final preparations on dinner. Eventually, they sat down and raised their glasses. 'Cheers Robbie, thank you for inviting us to share this with you,' Greg said amiably.

'It's my pleasure, let's hope we can do this again in the summer, so you can enjoy my terrace.' Robbie grinned.

'Hear, hear!' added Lydia and they clinked their glasses together. As they tucked into Robbie's excellent food, he became serious. 'I don't suppose you know how Annabelle Saxby-Jones is, do you?' he asked, looking at Lydia.

'Well, as a matter of fact, I do,' Lydia replied putting down her fork. 'I went to see her yesterday with a card and some flowers. She's moved back to her father's house in Ashdale and she's still in shock.'

'I imagine she is. What a terrible business.' Robbie shook his head.

'She's quite lonely I think, and the friends she has seem to be Simon's friends and they haven't been in touch at all yet. She was very pleased to see me and… well, confided in me.' Lydia looked pointedly at Robbie, who took a drink from his wine glass. 'She told me about you.'

'Did she? What made her do that?'

'She had seen your name in the paper when she read the review, and, well it brought back memories.'

'I see,' Robbie said shortly.

'What's she like? She seems very nice, but clingy, and a bit naïve maybe?'

Robbie placed his knife and fork on the empty plate and pushed it away. He stared into his wine glass and twizzled the stem between his thumb and forefinger as he spoke.

'Annabelle and I had a very happy and peaceful relationship. There was no fireworks and dramatics; she wasn't high maintenance – you know all Botox and hair extensions, she was who she was. Annabelle is kind, sweet and intelligent – very intelligent. You could be fooled into believing she's naïve, but she isn't.' Robbie looked up at Greg and Lydia. 'Her mother died when she was young. I doubt she remembers her much and, Carlton, her father, was very cut up at losing his wife. He employed Mrs Simms as a live-in housekeeper and she more or less raised Annabelle.'

'How did you meet her, Robbie?' Greg asked.

'At one of Carlton's launch parties for a new housing development in Leeds. She sometimes went along to support her father and we got chatting – she was great company. Annabelle wasn't ambitious for herself, but she was someone you could rely on, you know. She took an interest in everything I did, I looked forward to seeing her and I was pretty much gutted when she called our engagement off,' Robbie replied pensively, 'and then Simon Saxby-Jones appeared on the scene …' Robbie frowned and took a drink from his glass.

Lydia glanced at Greg with a let's-change-the-subject look and Greg immediately picked up Robbie's plate. 'That dinner was superb. I have to say, I'm looking forward to dining on your terrace. How are you at barbeques?' Greg stood up with the plates and carried them to the kitchen.

'Absolutely brilliant, how about you?' Robbie replied as he cleared the rest of the table. The two men talked about their barbequing prowess as Robbie made coffee and soon they returned to the table with the coffee and mints.

Lydia and Greg pulled out their notebooks and when they were comfortable, Robbie made a start. 'Let's begin with the initial enquiry. I received communications from the owners of properties that were originally Woodside Farm, Pennypot Farm and Greystone Farm. They got together and realised that they'd all had a similar experience whereby their property with planning permission for two or three executive homes had been bought by Planet Properties via Lewis Marshall. In each case, Planet had submitted amended plans, drawn by an architect called Nicholas Edwards, and subsequently built, not two or three houses, but up to ten.'

Greg nodded in agreement. 'We know that the office of Planet Properties is listed at an address for an accountant in Harrogate by the name of F. Flannigan Associates. So, although we can tie Lewis Marshall and Planet together, we can't implicate Simon Saxby-Jones at this stage, can we?'

'Actually, I've a couple of things to add which may help,' announced Lydia. Greg and Robbie looked at her in surprise. 'When I was talking to Annabelle yesterday, she mentioned that she overheard Simon talking to Hugo and they said something about planets and she thought they were talking about astronomy. Well, it was possibly Planet Properties they were discussing – as I don't believe Simon and Hugo are particularly interested in astronomy.'

'Hmm, that sounds interesting, but you said a couple of things, what else?'

'Simon has a son called Nicholas and his father is called Edward.'

'It's not conclusive, but it's very coincidental,' admitted Robbie.

'I went to see Jonathan Sturdy this afternoon.' Greg relayed his talk with Jonathan and told them about the money Planet Properties were likely to make.

'At least eight million profit? Well, at least he probably won't sell to Planet Properties,' Robbie commented.

'He wouldn't be able to anyway, they're folding.'

Robbie and Greg stared at Lydia in amazement. 'How the heck do you know that?' asked Greg.

'I looked at some properties this morning with Tom, and they were from the Planet portfolio – he told me.'

Robbie stroked his chin. 'What if Planet Properties was a partnership?' he said thoughtfully. 'That would ensure a modicum of privacy as they wouldn't need to register at Companies House. However, it also means that upon the death of a partner, the partnership itself is dissolved, the assets and liabilities worked out and the surplus is divided between the partners for their own individual tax returns.'

'So, if Simon Saxby-Jones was a partner in Planet, that would explain the sale of the portfolio!' declared Lydia. The three of them looked at each other as bits of the jigsaw fell into place.

'I wonder how the other partners feel about losing out on a share of the eight million profit?' pondered Greg.

'Well, if I were Hugo Marshall, a borough councillor who was about to become mayor, I would be worried about a project like this in my locality – I might think about retiring!' Lydia considered. 'In fact, that might explain why Hugo is so adamant about leaving Lewis Marshall. Tom told me that Charles and Hugo had a huge argument yesterday morning because Hugo wants to sell up, but Charles had been advised by Simon to wait a few months.'

'Simon? What's he got to do with it?' asked Robbie.

'Well, if Hugo sells Lewis Marshall now, who will market Thornberry Farm?' Lydia asked.

'So, you think that Hugo probably doesn't want to go ahead with this project and Simon has somehow blocked his intended escape route?' summarised Robbie.

'It's a promising theory. We just need some proof. I think I'll pay Lewis Marshall a visit tomorrow, see if I can call Hugo's bluff – put the wind up him a bit,' said Greg with a malicious grin.

'By the way, Hugo and Charles have now agreed to dissolve their partnership, Tom has been offered the first refusal on the agency,' added Lydia.

'Good grief, is there anything you don't know?' laughed Greg. 'But seriously, I may be able to use that piece of information to get to speak to Hugo – watch this space!'

'By the way Robbie,' Lydia turned to her host, 'I just wanted to thank you for such a glowing review of the panto, I hope you enjoyed Act Two just as much as the first half?'

'It was my pleasure,' grinned Robbie, 'I'd forgotten how good it is to laugh out loud. It was a great evening.'

'Have you been back to Ashdale since last Wednesday?' she asked innocently.

Robbie hesitated a fraction too long before he replied, 'No, I haven't.'

Out of the corner of her eye, Lydia saw Greg frown and open his mouth to speak. She tapped him on his arm and looked at him meaningfully. 'In that case, we must return the hospitality, shouldn't we Greg?' she said and raised one eyebrow.

'Of course, it would be our pleasure,' he agreed smoothly

Vinnie Buckley

The cruise ship had docked in Barbados and the passengers were all safely checked in at Grantley Adams International Airport for the overnight flight home. Vinnie and Vivienne were barely speaking and if they did to talk to one another it was in a polite and clipped tone, without warmth. Vivienne had gone duty-free shopping and Vinnie sat at a bar, alone, nursing a gin and tonic. He reflected on his last evening aboard the cruise ship and wondered what he would do once they were home.

Following his disagreement with Vivienne, he had arrived at the Italian restaurant on the ship to find he had to wait at the bar for a vacant table. This wasn't a problem as he wasn't in a hurry, but as luck would have it, he wasn't alone for long. He had been waiting for only five minutes when his new friend Richard arrived, along with his wife Susannah. They'd been up to the Pool Deck to check out the Barbeque and White Party but had found it was too rowdy. Susannah had said it was a younger crowd and that one particular lady – dressed like a Grecian goddess in a white costume which left very little to the imagination – was drinking heavily and dancing provocatively. The whole scenario had been quite embarrassing so they decided to have a quiet meal in their favourite restaurant instead. When they asked where his wife was, Vinnie had told them that Vivienne was feeling a little unwell – probably just too much sun – nothing to worry about, but she had decided to rest.

Richard and Susannah insisted that Vinnie join them for dinner, which he accepted and enjoyed. In truth, it was the best evening of the whole holiday. Before saying goodbye to Richard and Susannah, he had taken a note of Richard's contact details saying that he may have an opportunity to look him up when he came north later in the week.

Therein lay Vinnie's dilemma; what to do about Vivienne. Since they'd married, Vivienne had changed, Vinnie was sure about that. He did not remember her being so… brassy and downright embarrassing. Thank God, Richard and Susannah had not known who she was. And there was another thing – he was fully aware now that Vivienne wasn't blessed with an abundance of social graces. She was definitely not the sort of wife that could help entertain his business associates – well, not in any acceptable way, he thought wryly.

He knew that if she had been with him at dinner on Sunday night, she would have been bored *and* made it perfectly plain that she was. At the beginning of their relationship, she had made him feel like a million dollars, especially in bed, but now it felt like all she did was spend, spend, spend. He had benevolently given her a credit card, but she had got through its five thousand pound limit in two months, and he had been forced to reduce the limit.

Goddammit, he just wanted a wife that would complement him, enjoy his company and that of his acquaintances, but unfortunately that wasn't Vivienne, so what was he to do?

16

Lydia Buckley

Lydia parked her silver Nissan Qashqai next to a lime green Ford Focus at The Manor. When she glanced into the Focus, there was a child's booster seat in which a brightly coloured unicorn sat smiling blankly at the back of the driver's seat. Lydia walked up to the front of the house and rapped on the door using the brass lion-headed knocker. Mrs Simms answered the door, and, recognising Lydia from her previous visit, stood back and invited her in.

'Go on through, love – they're in the kitchen,' she said shaking a duster from the front door. 'I'm just doing the sitting room.'

Lydia remembered her way to the kitchen where she found Annabelle talking to a dark-skinned woman wearing skinny black jeans and a bright-orange, oversized shirt.

Annabelle immediately smiled at Lydia. 'Hi, Lydia, this is Tasheka,' she indicated the other woman who had stood up and smiled warmly.

'Hello, do you mind if I call you Lydia seein' as how we are gonna be workin' together this mornin'?' Tasheka greeted Lydia.

'No, not at all,' Lydia replied, a little taken aback.

‘’Cos I don’t see the point in bein’ over formal. Now if you’re ready to go, we’d best make a start. Mrs S-J has told me what she wants an’ I believe you’re bringin’ her car back, so we are goin’ in mine.’ Tasheka nodded at Annabelle and set off for the front door.

‘Thank you for doing this, Lydia,’ Annabelle said.

‘It’s not a problem, I’m glad to be able to help,’ Lydia replied.

‘I jus’ can’t believe this has happened…’ began Tasheka as she accelerated, too quickly, down the driveway. ‘I said to my Mikey, there was I talking away to Mrs S-J in MegaMart an’ all the time Mr S-J is getting hisself murdered.’ She applied the brakes harshly at the gateway, jerking Lydia forward, glanced to her right before screeching out onto the road in front of a white van who blasted his horn in annoyance. Lydia had closed her eyes in anticipation of a collision; as the car hurtled forward, she opened them again.

‘I don’t know why him behind is gettin’ all upset, it’s not my fault he’s drivin’ too fast. Anyway, it gives me the heebie-jeebies jus’ thinkin’ about poor Mr S-J… we was jus’ standin’ there an’ talkin’, but I didn’t keep her long ’cos she was so wet from the rain. I jus’ kept thinkin’ that she needed to get home, ’cos I remembered that she was goin’ to see that panto that night, you know what I’m sayin’?’ Lydia’s left hand gripped the door handle as Tasheka swerved around a cyclist.

‘I don’t rightly know what she’s gonna do now that he’s gone… I mean she don’t work no nothin’. She might sell the house.’

Lydia’s eyes glanced at the speedometer – they were doing sixty miles an hour.

‘Do you think maybe I could ask if she needed any help at that big house? I know that she’s got that Mrs Simms, but she’s getting on now… she must be ready to retire.’

Ahead of them, a car pulled out of a side road and Lydia automatically jammed her foot hard against the foot well in a futile attempt to slow the car down. She closed her eyes again as Tasheka braked and the car slowed.

Tasheka then blasted her horn in frustration. 'Now that's no way to drive a vehicle – he just pulled right out in front of me!' She glanced at Lydia who became conscious of her rigid position in the seat and the white knuckles on her left hand. '…and scarin' my passenger. I've a good mind to pull him over… do you think I should pull him over?'

'No!' Lydia practically shouted, 'No, we've a lot to do, let's just keep going,' she added a little more calmly. The elderly couple in the car in front were in no hurry to get to Harrogate and there wasn't an opportunity to overtake them, so Tasheka had to be content with driving at forty miles an hour, for which Lydia was extremely grateful.

Tasheka chatted happily the rest of the way into Harrogate and by the time she pulled through the tall, brick gateposts of 12 Suffolk Chase, Lydia knew a lot about Tasheka's family. They had arrived at a large detached mock-Tudor style house with a lawned garden to the front, edged with neat borders. Tasheka continued down a block-paved driveway around the side of the house and past a detached garage. She parked on a gravelled area next to a red Mercedes Cabriolet and stopped the engine.

They got out of Tasheka's car and looked at the Mercedes.

'That's Mrs S-J's car that you'll drive back to her, the keys should be in the house.' Tasheka nodded at the red sports car.

'Wow, that's a lovely car,' expressed Lydia, noting the personalised number plate *ASJ1*. 'It's very distinctive.'

'Well, I parked near it at MegaMart so I knew she was in there even before I saw her. I told my Mikey that I wanted a car like that, but he wasn't for gettin' one… better off with the Focus in my line of work, he tells me… so I was thinkin' about getting' a personal plate, you know? An' I came up with a real good one… listen to this… TID 13D. That's my initials, Tasheka Irena Dixon but when you put thirteen dee after it and put that on a plate it spells "tidied", which is good with my business, you know what I'm sayin'?'

Lydia nodded and opened her mouth to suggest they went inside before it started to rain, but before she could utter a word, Tasheka carried on speaking. 'Anyway, we can't stand here chattin', we got work to do. Now, we'll need these.' Tasheka opened the boot of her car and removed some black bin liners. 'We'll use these for Mr S-J's things an' I thought that his shoes, shirts, jackets an' trousers could go to that charity shop on Church Lane. All his underwear, socks and pyjamas could go to The Elms Nursing Home, 'cos they're always short of men's stuff. Wha' d'ya think?'

Lydia simply nodded her agreement and followed Tasheka to the back door of the house.

'I just have keys for this door. Now this here's the porch and just through that door is the kitchen diner,' she explained as though she were giving a conducted tour. 'As you can see, they have these granite worktops… now I'm not too keen on those, on account of it might be too easy to break glassware, if you get my meaning.'

Lydia wondered how many pieces of glassware had suffered because of the granite worktops.

Tasheka continued with her description of the kitchen diner: 'However, I do like this island… I said to my Mikey that I might like one of those, but he said our kitchen wasn't big enough an' I told him that we could take the wall down an' have open plan… but he wasn't too keen on remodelling the whole ground floor an' said that it might cost a whole lot of money … but I says that it's an investment… you gotta have an investment. If you've an investment, then you feel might comfortable an' I like to feel comfortable, you know what I'm saying'?'

Lydia understood perfectly what Tasheka was saying, but also had some sympathy for her Mikey.

They walked through the well-appointed kitchen diner and into the large polished marble-tiled hallway. 'This here's the hallway,' said Tasheka, somewhat unnecessarily, and waving her arm towards a half-open door, 'that's the sitting room.'

Lydia glanced through the door and saw oak flooring and a predominantly white room. Tasheka led the way up carpeted stairs and opened the door directly ahead into the master bedroom. Lydia gasped.

'Lovely, isn't it?' said Tasheka proudly. Lydia took in the pale grey carpet, mirrored dressing table and bedside cabinets and the magnificent antique French-style bed made from silver-painted carved wood and finished with a black crushed velvet fabric buttoned headboard.

Tasheka indicated two doors on their right. 'That one there's the en suite and this here's the walk-in wardrobe. Mrs S-J has three main sections, casual, smart and formal, an' she's asked for her things from casual and smart, on account of she don't anticipate goin' anywhere over formal for a while. Although she's goin' out to dinner with her father tomorrow an' she's asked for one particular outfit. Now I'll jus' go and get her suitcases from one of the other rooms an' we can get started.'

Lydia wandered over to the huge bay window which looked out over the front garden and to the quiet, tree-lined road beyond. The house was luxurious and beautiful, but it felt like a show house and not a real home. Lydia could see why Annabelle hadn't wanted to stay at there, because, although The Manor was a larger property, it had a heart, a warm feeling and a welcoming atmosphere.

'We can get lots in these two cases.' Tasheka hoisted two large, but fortunately lightweight, suitcases onto the bed.

'We can get lots of clothes in, but we must remember that we've to haul them out to the car,' Lydia pointed out, but Tasheka was already in the walk-in wardrobe. Lydia sighed and followed her.

One wall was taken up with three huge floor to ceiling wardrobes, Tasheka slid one of the doors open to reveal a quantity of casual clothing, jeans, shirts, sweat tops, jumpers and she began to pull out a pile. 'Here you are,' she said shoving it at Lydia.

They worked quickly, filling both suitcases with the assorted clothing until the cases would hold no more. They filled two bin bags with shoes and handbags and a third with Annabelle's underwear.

Tasheka picked up a red silk chiffon chemise and G-string set with a matching robe, 'This looks like something my friend sells in her shop. I mentioned to Mrs S-J that she ought to go there and see Orlena – that's my friend – an' she would suggest something to rev Mr S-J's engine, if you know what I'm sayin'.' Tasheka knowingly winked her lash-extensioned eye, 'cos I told her that she needed to be more like a ho – and that isn't a garden rake – in the bedroom, well it looks like she took my advice.' Tasheka nodded proudly at the thought that her words of wisdom had been acted upon.

Lydia looked at the sheer red lingerie which looked so out of place among the sensible white, nude and black bra and brief sets they'd pushed into the bin bags.

'I'm not sure she'll need it now, though,' said Lydia doubtfully as Tasheka shoved the delicate red pieces into the bag.

'Not right now, but Mrs S-J won't be a widow for long. She'll find somebody else to take care of her an' then she'll need this.'

Lydia decided not to comment on that remark. After all, Tasheka knew Annabelle better than she did.

Tasheka found a smaller carry-on type bag and loaded that with Annabelle's toiletries and jewellery. Lydia surveyed the mound of luggage and baggage with trepidation, dreading the effort of getting it all downstairs and into the Mercedes.

Tasheka finally brought out a one-shouldered caramel-coloured jumpsuit with a navy chiffon overlay still on its hanger, along with a tailored coat with camel-coloured turn-back cuffs. 'This coat is what she wants to wear tomorrow. It's one of Mrs S-J's favourites. She was wearing this when I saw her at the hall last Friday night, that's how I knew it was her,' Tasheka laid the garments on a chair.

'Friday night? I thought Annabelle went to the panto on Saturday evening?'

'Oh, she wasn't at the panto to see it. Y'see me and my Mikey took our Shanice to see the panto an' my Shanice really enjoyed it. She thought the princess was really pretty… but after we left, we was halfway home when my Shanice remembered that she had left her unicorn, so I went back to get it… and there was this older person who didn't even know what a unicorn was. Anyway, I found the unicorn and as I was leaving, I saw Mrs S-J waiting outside the back door for Mr S-J. I knew it was her 'cos she was wearing this coat… an' I thought that was real nice of her to go and meet him after the show. You know, I wouldna' seen her at all if I hadn't gone back for that unicorn.'

Lydia was taken aback for a moment – Annabelle had been waiting for Simon outside the back door to the hall on Friday night? Then she remembered what Edward had told her about the classy lady in the dark coat with turn-back cuffs. What had Annabelle seen and heard?

At last, Tasheka was satisfied and they dragged everything down the stairs and out to the Mercedes, the keys of which they'd located in the kitchen. When everything was in the car, they returned to the master bedroom to make a start on sorting out Simon's clothes. Eventually, they'd filled Tasheka's car with bin bags and had done as much as they could in one morning.

Tasheka set the alarm and handed the house keys to Lydia for her to give back to Annabelle. 'Well, it was real nice working with you today and now you're friends with Mrs S-J, I s'pose I'll see you again, but I'm hopin' it will be in better circumstances, if you get my meaning?'

'Likewise, Tasheka. Shall I ask Annabelle if she wants us to sort out any more things next Wednesday?'

'Well I am available, but I've been thinking, an' I'm gonna speak to her in regards to my earlier thought about helpin' Mrs Simms at The Manor, on account of that's one big house for one lady, an' of course I've my Wednesday mornings free now,' announced Tasheka.

Lydia nodded. 'Ok, well I'll see you again no doubt. Bye for now.' She got into the driver's seat of the Mercedes and waved, then winced as Tasheka accelerated away, creating a fountain of gravel behind her. Lydia made some adjustments to the rear-view mirror and seat, started the engine and gently moved off.

Hugo Marshall

Hugo was feeling a little calmer as he anticipated a less complicated life in a few months' time once Freddie had sorted out Planet Properties, and hopefully, Tom had bought the agency. He allowed himself a few moments to consider what he wanted to do with his impending retirement. He still quite fancied the idea of Spain and wondered if he might approach Bruce Harvey again now that Simon was out of the way, well... passed away. He could appeal to Bruce's sense of fair play – to give him chance to put his side of the case as it were, tell him that Simon was deliberately trying to stop the sale of the agency and that the things that Simon had said were not true. Most of that was accurate and, in any case, the agency *was* for sale – he and Charles had both agreed to retire and it was likely they already had a buyer. The more Hugo thought about it, the more he liked the idea. Once Bruce was in full possession of the facts, he would see that Simon was just being vindictive.

Hugo reached for his phone. However, before he could make the call, there was a tap on his door and Felicity entered the office, closing the door behind her. 'Councillor Marshall, there's a gentleman to see you. I told him that he should have made an appointment, but he says you'll probably see him.' Felicity had a very disapproving look on her face.

Hugo frowned.

'Did this man give you a name, Felicity?' he asked.

'A Mr Frederick Flannigan.'

'What?' Hugo spluttered.

'Do you know him, Councillor Marshall?' Felicity queried.

Hugo collected himself. 'I think I've heard his name,' he said in what he hoped was a nonchalant tone. 'Show him in, I've a few spare moments,' he smiled benignly.

Felicity pursed her lips, nodded her head curtly, and opened the door,

'Councillor Marshall will see you now,' she said efficiently and stood aside as Freddie ambled into Hugo's office.

'What the hell are you doing here?' exploded Hugo as Felicity closed the door.

Freddie took a sharp intake of breath at Hugo's harsh words. 'I take it you're not pleased to see me, Councillor Marshall?' he said with a mischievous grin.

'Goddammit Freddie, I thought we agreed that you wouldn't come here,' snapped Hugo.

'I don't see why I shouldn't, Councillor Marshall, after all, we're business partners and you've seen *my* office, have you not?'

'Now look here…' began Hugo.

'Come, come, Councillor Marshall, we don't want to be getting all upset now, do we? Not if we are going to finalise our business matters amicably, and I'm sure you'll want to do that.' Freddie sat down in the chair opposite Hugo and unbuttoned his coat. 'Although it's a great shame we won't be able to make all that lovely money we was talkin' about…'

'Keep your voice down, Freddie, for God's sake,' Hugo said nervously.

'You look a little flushed Councillor Marshall, so you do. Maybe it's because it's a lot warmer in here than in my office, don't you t'ink?' Freddie's eyes twinkled. He was clearly enjoying Hugo's discomfort.

Hugo's eyes narrowed with suspicion. 'All right Freddie, what *do* you want?'

'I don't want anyt'ing Councillor Marshall. I've some papers for you to sign and I was comin' this way to see a… well, a client of mine, so I thought I would pop in personally, so I did,' Freddie took a sheaf of papers from his inside coat pocket, 'I'll leave them with you to look at and sign and then, shall I pop back an' collect them later?'

'No!' said Hugo at once, 'No, I'll bring them to you.'

'As you wish Councillor Marshall,' replied Freddie pleasantly, 'Oh! I was wondering, have you had any more of those pink letters since last week?'

Hugo frowned. *What the blazes…?*

'No, I haven't. Now, is that all? I've a lot of work to do so…' Hugo indicated the door.

'Ah well, I'll be bidding you goodbye then.' Freddie stood up and looked around the office. 'It's a nice place you got here, Councillor Marshall, very nice.'

Hugo marched to the door and held it open. 'Thank you for coming by, Mr Flannigan, I'll be in touch with you in due course,' he said a little over loudly.

'I'm sure you will, Councillor Marshall.' Freddie doffed his hat respectfully at Felicity who stared stony-faced as he left the agency.

As soon as the door closed behind Freddie, Felicity followed Hugo back into his office.

'There's another gentleman to see you, Councillor Marshall, a Mr Greg Craven. He says he's some information on a company called Planet Properties which may be of interest to you.'

Hugo had not had the chance to sit down before Felicity spoke, but now he felt his knees give way and he was thankful that his chair was just behind him.

'Are you all right, Councillor Marshall?' asked Felicity with concern at Hugo's sudden ashen face.

'Yes, I'm fine… just a little warm. Perhaps you would show Mr Craven in.' Hugo knew from previous conversations that this was Tom's brother, but what information could he have regarding Planet Properties? The portfolio had only become available yesterday and there wasn't anything suspicious about that. Hugo stood up when Greg entered the office and put out his hand. He received a firm handshake in return.

'Good morning Mr Craven,' Hugo smiled and indicated for Greg to take a seat, 'how can I be of assistance?' Hugo sat back in his own chair and tried to relax.

'First, I wish to make it quite clear that my brother, Tom has nothing to do with what I'm about to say. He doesn't even know I'm here.' Greg spoke firmly and Hugo had a growing feeling of trepidation as he waited for Greg to continue. 'I believe that the gentleman who just left is Mr Freddie Flannigan?' Greg asked.

'That's the name he gave me, so yes,' Hugo replied cautiously.

'You're acquainted with him though, are you not?' probed Greg.

Hugo frowned. 'Might I ask the reason for your visit, Mr Craven?'

'Very well, I'll get straight to the point. As you may know, I'm a journalist and I've been approached to investigate the purchases of some small developments. The developments in question are Woodside Farm, Pennypot Farm and Greystone Farm, all of which were bought by a company called Planet Properties. I've done some research and I now know that Lewis Marshall has connections with Planet, as does Mr Flannigan, and the late Mr Simon Saxby-Jones,' stated Greg.

'Woodside, Pennypot and Greystone?'

I knew this would come back to haunt us! Hugo swallowed nervously. 'We are the acting agents for Planet Properties, yes,' he replied, 'but I fail to see what business that is of yours, Mr Craven.'

'Planet Properties have been successful in their bids to purchase properties with planning permission to develop agricultural barns, and in order to be the selected bidder, they had to submit the highest price. In each case, the bid from Planet was just a tad better than their nearest bona fide rival, and the other bids were ridiculously low – from other developers whom I've been unable to trace, and which I believe to be fake. Once Planet Properties bought these barns, in each case, they amended the plans to increase the number of houses, obtained the necessary planning consent and sold the development for a considerable profit.'

Hugo's could feel a sense of panic growing. Where was this going?

'I see, well there's nothing wrong with making a profit. That's what we are all in business for, Mr Craven,' Hugo blustered.

'I quite agree, Councillor Marshall, however, a judge may take a very dim view of an agency which deceives its clients – especially in the way it conducts its business concerning sealed bids.'

'Well, I don't think... I mean... It's not... Look here, what exactly are you trying to say?' Hugo floundered as he tried to think about what to say – something that wouldn't incriminate himself.

'Firstly, that you advised your seller to choose Planet Properties, who had been given an unfair advantage in the sealed bid process. Secondly, that you've not been entirely honest with your seller, as they did not know of the ultimate intention to build more houses on the land. And thirdly, that they were unaware that they could have sold the property for more money if they had known about the possibility of more housing.'

Hugo listened to Greg with growing horror, this is what he had been dreading, but had Simon and Freddie listened? No! What made matters worse was precisely the fact that it was the agency who had acted inappropriately – no, not the agency, but him, Hugo. Hugo tried to keep his face expressionless, but that effort had caused the knuckles gripping the chair arms to go white. He forced himself to relax.

Greg waited patiently for a response as Hugo pulled himself together.

Finally Hugo was able to speak calmly: 'Well, of course, I can't comment on how our sealed bid process was conducted on the properties in question, or on the activities of Planet Properties—'

'You see,' continued Greg, 'as an estate agent whose fee is a percentage of the sales price, it would have been in your interest to have sold these properties for the best price. The fact that you did not advise your client of the possibility of an improved sale, but allowed Planet Properties to ultimately benefit the most, suggests that you've a connection with Planet Properties. This, of course, is a conflict of interest and I would go so far as to suggest that you're not acting in accordance with the Code of Practice as outlined by the Property Ombudsman.'

Hugo was speechless, but Greg had not finished: 'I'm also led to believe that the next property to be purchased by Planet Properties would be the farmhouse and barns at Thornberry Farm including a large field. The field is permissible for redevelopment and could sustain a build of around eighty houses netting Planet Properties a profit of several million pounds.'

Hugo felt completely out of his depth. How on earth had all this come to light? Were pink letters being sent to other people? He realised that Greg was waiting for a response.

'I can assure you that... er...' Hugo was at a loss as to what his assurance was without admitting anything, but Greg simply smiled knowingly.

'... that Planet Properties won't be involved in any future developments?' he suggested.

Hugo grasped the lifeline gratefully: 'Yes, the business is ceasing to trade—'

'I would imagine that's because of the untimely death of one of its partners? A certain Simon Saxby-Jones?' Greg broke in mildly.

Hugo turned red, ignored the interruption and carried on speaking: '... and is selling their own property portfolio, so—'

'... so, you're able to reassure me that this agency will be impartial when dealing with sealed bids in the future and that no developers will be given, shall we say, inside information?' Greg helped Hugo finish his sentence.

'I'm not sure that "inside information" is how I—' began Hugo, but then he caught Greg's raised eyebrow. 'I see... quite,' he finished lamely.

'This would make an interesting story for my newspaper, although I believe Woodside, Pennypot and Greystone are all in the Leeds district, so perhaps…'

'Newspaper? Oh, I don't think that's necessary, Woodside Court was built at least a couple of years ago, it's not of interest now.' Hugo tried to brush aside his fears.

'Oh, so you do know that Woodside Farm became a development called Woodside Court then?' Greg asked simply.

Hugo knew at once that he had put his foot in it and clamped his mouth shut.

'I believe I can speak frankly to you, *Councillor* Marshall,' Greg continued and leant forward over the desk, 'neither of us wants this issue with the sealed bids to come to light. You, because you're currently the mayor-elect and me, because my brother would like to buy this agency and I would prefer that it wasn't tarnished. So, I'm prepared to put the results of this investigation on the back burner, whilst you carry on with running the business until such time as Tom, or someone else, takes over. If there are any more underhand activities, then I'll not hesitate but to write my story. Do we understand one another?' Greg stared at Hugo.

'I think we've a mutual understanding about this matter, Mr Craven and I take it this is just between ourselves?' Hugo said eventually.

'Tom has no idea and I see no reason to enlighten him. As you say, Planet Properties are ceasing to trade so I anticipate that it will be the end of this matter.' Greg stood up. 'Thank you for your time Councillor Marshall,' he said as he walked to the door.

Hugo practically ran around the desk to open it for him. 'It was interesting to hear what you had to say and of course, we should be delighted to sell your property should you decide to sell,' he said loudly for the benefit of Felicity, who of course could hear everything now the door was open.

Hugo and Greg shook hands and then Greg nodded politely at Felicity and left the agency.

Hugo sighed. 'Coffee please, Felicity,' he said wearily as he returned to his desk.

God, what a morning!

Annabelle Saxby-Jones

Annabelle found she was feeling less numb now it was beginning to sink in that Simon wasn't coming back. She was upset of course – Simon had been her husband and they'd shared many happy memories, but the fact that he had not agreed to start a family was a great sadness. Annabelle would have loved to have had a baby – a little person who would depend on her for its very life. A little person to love and cherish and who would show the same feelings back. That would never happen now.

Being home with Daddy had helped – it was almost as if she had never been away and once Lydia brought her things, she could settle in properly. Daddy's lady friend Eleanor had been so sweet, helping Daddy to deal with the business of the death certificate and gently discussing funeral arrangements. Daddy was going to speak to Simon's solicitor today about the will and there was a life-insurance policy to deal with.

Annabelle had struggled to cope initially and was immensely grateful to Mrs Simms, who had let her just take her time and had allowed her the space she needed to grieve. She was just glad to back at The Manor – she felt she belonged here. The house in Harrogate had always been Simon's, it had never felt hers or theirs. Daddy had said that this would probably be her house now and they could have a little chat and decide on whether to keep the house and possibly rent it out or sell it and invest the proceeds. She would take her father's advice, but she knew she would have to think about what she wanted to do next.

Mrs Simms had brought the post into the kitchen and there was a card from Sir James and Lady Victoria Worthington expressing their sympathy. The card also enclosed a hand-written note from Lady Victoria saying that of course they missed her at the committee meeting and would be delighted to welcome her back when she felt ready. Annabelle thought about that and decided that she would like to resume her garden-party project as soon as possible, but of course, her laptop was still at the Harrogate house and she had not specifically asked Lydia to bring it with her. Maybe she could fetch it herself, but as soon as that thought crossed her mind, she knew that she could not go back to that house any time soon. Perhaps Lydia could collect it the next time she was in Harrogate. Annabelle thought she would ask Lydia when she came by later today.

Thinking about working on her garden-party project led Annabelle to consider her father's suggestion of a job at his office. When she had told him about her committee role and how she was enjoying it, he had offered her a job in the marketing department at Aztec. She could learn more about advertising, sales techniques, copywriting, and perhaps make contacts which could also prove beneficial to the Worthingtons. She told her father that she would give it some serious consideration. To gently introduce her to the business world, her father had invited her to join him and a marketing executive chap for dinner tomorrow evening. Daddy had invited Eleanor as well to balance their table and provide some feminine company and alternative conversation topics. They were going to dine at Ashdale Hall, and Annabelle had asked Tasheka to pack a specific outfit which would look quite dressy but not over formal.

One of the other sympathy cards was from Robert. Annabelle had been both surprised and delighted. Then, without spending too much time thinking about it, she phoned the newspaper office and had eventually been put through to him. It was lovely to hear his voice again and after Robert had expressed his sincere condolences, he had asked how she was, and before she knew it, they were chatting away. Twenty minutes later, Annabelle found herself agreeing to have lunch with him on Saturday. After the phone conversation, Annabelle felt her spirits had lifted – a lunch with an old friend was exactly what she needed, and she trusted Robert to be sensitive to her raw emotions.

A little after twelve o'clock, she heard Mrs Simms talking to Lydia and jumped up from the kitchen table to help bring her things into the house. Lydia helped Annabelle take everything upstairs to her bedroom and stayed a while to help to empty the suitcases and bags. The jumpsuit Annabelle wanted to wear for the Thursday night dinner was still on a hanger so it wouldn't crease, and Lydia laid the navy coat on the bed.

'Do you think the jumpsuit will be ok for a dinner at Ashdale Hall?' Annabelle asked as she hung the garment carefully in the wardrobe. 'It's just a business dinner with Daddy, but I do want him to be proud of me.'

'I think it's perfect, very smart and classy, but not over the top. Presumably you've a bag and shoes to match?' replied Lydia.

'Yes, navy ones and then I've that coat. You know, this is a favourite coat, it always looks smart for a variety of occasions.' Annabelle picked up the coat and held it up for Lydia's approval.

'Tasheka mentioned that and err… she also said she had seen you wearing it at the hall last Friday night?'

Annabelle took a sharp intake of breath and looked at Lydia guiltily. 'Tasheka saw me at the hall?' she gasped.

Lydia nodded. 'Did you see Simon?'

Annabelle sat down on the bed and shook her head sadly. 'No,' she said quietly and sighed. After a few moments she continued: 'After Verity told me that Simon was having an affair, I was chewed up and could think about nothing else all day. I hated him. I loved him. I believed Verity. I thought it couldn't be true. I didn't know what to think or what to do, whether to ring him. Even going to the salon crossed my mind. In the end, I decided I would go and meet him after the performance and see for myself. When I arrived, there were other people waiting outside and I… well, I just lost my nerve.' Annabelle felt her eyes welling up. 'I'm just not good at confrontations, especially in front of strangers, so I just went home and waited for him there.'

'Oh, Annabelle…' Lydia said sympathetically.

'That's why I wished I'd had your number. I had no one to talk things through with and I just felt so wretched.' A tear rolled down Annabelle's face.

'I wish I could have been there for you. I do know what it feels like to find out your husband has a girlfriend.' Lydia sat down next to Annabelle and put her hand on her arm.

'You do?' Annabelle blinked tearfully.

'Yes, my husband left me for a younger woman. I felt hurt and betrayed, but I got through it and here I am. Your circumstances are tragic, but you'll be all right, Annabelle, trust me. You've people here who love you – your father and Eleanor, and Mrs Simms is also clearly fond of you,' Lydia reassured her.

Annabelle nodded and took a deep breath. 'Thank you for listening to me, you're a true friend.' Annabelle smiled bravely and brightened as she had an idea: 'I wonder, do you have time to stay for lunch? I would like to tell you about the garden party I'm organising for Lady Worthington.'

Lydia smiled. 'Lunch would be lovely, thank you and I really would like to hear about your garden party,' she replied.

As Annabelle and Lydia enjoyed a light lunch of salad with home-made quiche and garlic bread, Annabelle chatted animatedly about her plans for Lady Worthington's garden party. She told her about the fairground rides, donkey rides, children's races, fancy dress, Punch and Judy and the typical handicraft stalls she intended to book.

'It will be the best garden party ever!' Annabelle announced and she could see that Lydia was impressed.

'Have you done this sort of thing before, then?' Lydia asked as she put down her knife and fork on an empty plate.

'Only the odd jumble sale and coffee morning, but once I got started on this project, my ideas just flowed – I'm so excited. But that's where I need your help once again,' Annabelle looked at Lydia expectantly.

'What would you like me to do?'

'I wonder if you could call at the Harrogate house once more and collect my laptop, with its bag and the cable, please? I'm so sorry, I forgot to mention it this morning.'

'Do you need me to go back today?'

'Oh no,' Annabelle shook her head, 'I wouldn't ask you to do that, but I wondered if you were going to work at Lush Lashes any time soon?'

'Actually, I'm there on Friday afternoon so I could call in, pick up everything and drop it off here with you on Friday evening, would that be ok?'

'That would great, I can't thank you enough. I'm sure I left it all on the table in the kitchen where I was last working on it.'

'Have you ladies had enough to eat?' Mrs Simms picked up the empty plates and glasses.

'That was delicious, thank you, Mrs Simms,' replied Lydia as she stood up. 'I really must go now, Annabelle.'

'It's been a pleasure to chat to you and I can't thank you enough for helping me so much.' Annabelle looked at her new friend and impulsively flung her arms around Lydia and hugged her. 'It means so much so have someone who likes me for being me,' she mumbled, as voice shook with emotion and she felt tears welling up.

Lydia hugged Annabelle back then released her and looked her straight in the eyes.

'You're a lovely woman, Annabelle and I'm only too happy to help you.'

Annabelle nodded, unable to speak, so Lydia picked up her bag and jacket and headed for the front door.

Annabelle watched her go.

If only she had met Lydia earlier.

As Greg prepared their evening meal, Lydia called Nick on his mobile and told him about her visit to Edward. At first, Nick was stunned and didn't know what to say, Lydia suggested that he take some time to think things over as Edward would be away until Friday. She said Edward had suggested that Saturday would be a good day, so Nick promised that he would let her know before then. As a bit of an afterthought, Nick also confirmed that he had spoken to the police and amended his statement.

When Greg had served up his chicken casserole and roast potatoes, he told Lydia about his visit to Lewis Marshall and that Hugo had not denied the allegation that Greg had put to him.

'You know, I've been thinking about all that and I wondered why Hugo was desperate to sell the agency so quickly *and* before Planet had bought Jonathan Sturdy's buildings,' pondered Lydia.

'Desperate?'

'Mmmm, I'm just going over what Tom told me. During the argument between Charles and Hugo on Monday morning, he overheard Charles say that Simon had recommended that they didn't sell the agency until May. I wondered why May was so important, but then you told me that Jonathan Sturdy talked about the bids and how he would have the money in his bank by the end of April,' Lydia explained thoughtfully.

'So, Simon needed Hugo to be in control of the agency to ensure that Planet was the preferred bidder,' concluded Greg.

'Exactly!' agreed Lydia, 'but, I reckon that Hugo got cold feet. If this dodgy bid business had got out, it would have been Hugo's neck on the line, not Simon's or Freddie's. Thornberry is very close to home, whereas the other developments were in another district altogether.'

'Hugo's reputation would have been irreparably damaged not to mention his mayoral plans,'

'But now that Simon is dead, all Hugo's worries have gone away. Planet is closing and he's selling the agency. Unfortunately, that also gives Hugo a motive *and* he was at the hall at the time of the murder,'

'I would have said that puts Hugo right at the top of the list, along with your friend, Zoe. God! Surely it can't be one of those two who committed murder?' Greg pushed his empty plate away.

'People who are desperate, take desperate measures, Greg, who knows how desperate either Zoe or Hugo really were?'

'True, and on another note entirely, I've been thinking about a holiday…' Greg said as he topped up their wine glasses.

'Greg! How the heck do you go from murder to holiday in more or less the same breath?' Lydia admonished him.

'Quite easily. I'm simply dying to go away with you,' he grinned sheepishly at Lydia.

'You're quite disgraceful, do you know that? Ok, enough about murder. Where did you have in mind?'

17

Isabella Sturdy

Bella opened her eyes and glanced at the clock, it was seven thirty. She heard the wind gusting outside and pulled the duvet around her shoulders. She would have to get up very shortly as she had agreed to go back to work today. Zoe had been to visit her last night. They'd had a heart-to-heart conversation and now they both understood the full situation. Although Zoe knew about Bella's pregnancy, she had agreed to keep it to herself for now especially as Bella had yet to make up her mind what to do about it.

Bella went over the conversation again – how Zoe and Verity had discovered that Belle and Bella were two different women in Simon's life and how Simon had given Zoe no option, but to keep quiet once she had discovered the truth. Bella's emotions had been on a roller coaster ever since last Friday – which felt like a lifetime ago. The anticipated joy at telling Simon the baby news, her feelings of uncertainty after his initial reaction of annoyance, and the guilt she had felt at keeping the pregnancy a secret from her parents, had all been whirling around in her head. But none of that could prepare her for the hurt and anger that had washed over her after overhearing *that* argument and, finally, the shock of the dreadful news of Simon's death.

It had taken days for her to stop crying, shaking, and banging doors in frustration, until the talk with Zoe last night had finally calmed her, and the realisation of Simon's true character had emerged. She got out of bed and headed to the bathroom, and, after a shower, she felt fresh, clean, and, if not chipper – ready to face the other staff at the salon. Zoe had said that the staff wouldn't ask her any difficult questions and would welcome her back.

As Bella stepped through into the staffroom at the back of the salon, she received a round of applause from her colleagues, all with smiling faces. Zoe allowed her a few minutes to thank them all before encouraging them away to prepare for the day ahead.

Thursday was market day in Ashdale, and, as usual, the Market Place was buzzing with stalls and shoppers, and fortunately, although it was cold, the weather was dry. As the morning wore on, Bella was pleased she had decided to come back to work. She felt a little more like her old self, but between answering the phone and dealing with clients, there were odd moments when the memories would return and she felt emotional.

A little before ten o'clock, the door opened and Lydia stepped inside the salon.

'Hi,' Bella greeted her warmly. She liked Lydia and knew from Zoe that Lydia had found Simon's body and was also aware of all that had happened.

'Hello Bella, how lovely to see you back here. How are you?' Lydia held her arms out and Bella came from behind her desk to receive the hug.

'I'm doing ok. Coming back here was a good idea. I'm ready to begin to move forwards,' Bella replied as she returned to her chair.

'I'm so pleased to hear that. Now, I wonder if there's a chance I could have a very brief word with Zoe,' Lydia asked.

Bella consulted the diary. 'She's with a client at the moment and should be finished in about five minutes.'

'Can I just wait here? It's literally a quick question.'

'Of course you can, oh – excuse me,' the telephone rang and Bella answered the call. It was a brief call from a client just checking her appointment time and when Bella had replaced the receiver, she decided to say what was on her mind.

'Lydia? Zoe mentioned that you know Annabelle Saxby-Jones, I believe you did her lashes?' Bella had been pondering about Simon's wife over the last few days and how she must be feeling.

'Yes, I did her lashes, although I don't know her well,' Lydia said carefully.

Bella picked up on the caution in Lydia's voice and hastily reassured her: 'I don't mean to be nosey, it's just that I've been so upset over Simon and it occurred to me that she must be quite traumatised too… and she must hate me.' Bella looked sorrowfully at Lydia who smiled gently.

'She's been very shocked but, like you, she's slowly coming to terms with what happened. You should also probably know that she's moved back here to Ashdale and for the foreseeable future, she'll be living at her father's house, you know the one? The Manor?'

Bella gasped. 'Oh no! I might bump into her. What does she look like?'

'Don't worry Bella,' Lydia said soothingly. 'I'm sure she doesn't blame you. She still thinks that Zoe made the whole thing up, but I'm sure that in time she'll accept the truth.'

Bella chewed her lip nervously. 'If I keep the… If I go ahead with…' Bella glanced quickly around the salon and then down at her stomach before turning her eyes back to Lydia, 'well, you know …'

Lydia smiled. 'Yes, I know, go on.'

'How will she feel? I mean, should I consider her feelings when making my decision about whether to keep it or not?' Bella had wondered how she would cope with a baby at all, let alone deal with any hatred from Annabelle Ashby-Jones, but now Annabelle was living in Ashdale, well it just complicated things even more.

Lydia leaned over the reception desk to reply quietly. 'This has nothing to do with Annabelle. You must make your decision based on how *you* feel, how you'll manage. And remember, you'll have this responsibility for the rest of your life. I expect that you'll remain at home initially and have help from your parents, but that may not be the case forever – circumstances change. Don't let anyone else put pressure on you or make you feel guilty. You make your decision on what is right for *you*, ok?'

Bella nodded. 'Thank you, thank you so much, Lydia. That's the first piece of sensible advice I've had. Mummy is concerned about what people will think and Pops just keeps his thoughts to himself and says he will support my decision. I didn't like to bother Zoe as she's so worried about the murder investigation. It's all a bit of a mess really,' she replied.

'If you need someone to go anywhere with you or to talk to, please call me. Don't ever feel you're alone. Give me your phone and I'll add my number,' Lydia suggested.

Bella nearly burst into tears as she fumbled in her pocket for her mobile. She passed it to Lydia and then looked up as the door opened again.

'Good morning, Mrs Armitage,' welcomed Bella.

'Good morning, girls.' replied Elsa, 'how are we today? Do you know, I was just saying to Barb… whilst we was just having a look at that nice new stall, you know the one with the handbags and purses? He's got a lovely bag that would just do nice for our holidays, we're thinking of cruising this year. Anyway, I was just saying to Barb that we hadn't seen young Bella since, well… since last Saturday… and that I do hope that she's all right. As I said to Brian, it was a right carry on was that and Bella will be right upset…'

As Elsa paused for a breath, Lydia took advantage by interrupting: 'We're both doing fine, thank you, Elsa. We were both shaken and shocked by the events of last Saturday, but we are settling down a bit now.'

At that moment, Zoe approached the reception desk with her client, and Elsa and Lydia stood to the side to allow them to pass.

Bella looked up at Zoe and her client. 'Everything all right, Mrs Baxter?' she inquired.

'I feel like a new woman, may I make another appointment please?'

'Of course. Zoe, before you go, Lydia would like a quick word, please. Now Mrs Baxter, when would be convenient?' Bella made the new appointment and took payment for the treatment Mrs Baxter had just enjoyed. When Mrs Baxter had left, Bella tuned in to the conversation between Zoe, Elsa and Lydia.

'Have you got an appointment, Elsa?' Zoe asked.

'Not yet, I've just popped in to make one whilst Barb is in the bakery, and then I'm taking her to Let's Go Travel. We're going to look at cruises,' Elsa replied nodding her head emphatically. Bella called across to Elsa,

'I can look at the diary for you now, Mrs Armitage.'

'Oh, thank you Bella, love.' As they discussed available hair appointments, Bella could see that Lydia was discussing something with Zoe.

The door to the salon opened again and Bella was astonished to see DCI Appleton and DS Oakley enter. The officers nodded an acknowledgement to Bella and looked at Zoe expectantly.

Zoe finished speaking to Lydia and walked towards the police officers. 'Good morning, how can I help you?' she asked.

'Ms Birch, I need to ask you to accompany us to the station please. We need to ask you a few more questions,' DCI Appleton answered.

'Now?' queried Zoe.

'I'm afraid so,'

'Can you tell me if this will take long? I've clients booked in today.'

DCI Appleton raised his eyebrows. 'I would suggest that they're rescheduled,' he advised.

Zoe nodded. 'Can I just get my coat and bag?'

'Of course. DS Oakley will come with you.'

Zoe turned and walked towards the staffroom with DS Oakley behind her.

Bella watched her go, then turned and looked at Lydia for support.

Lydia walked over to the reception desk. 'Don't worry, it's just routine, the questions probably can't wait, and here isn't the right place to ask them anyway,' she soothed.

Bella glanced at DCI Appleton for confirmation of that, but he kept his face expressionless, and then she noticed Elsa. 'Right Mrs Armitage, I think we've got you booked in now. Is there anything else I can help you with?' Bella asked firmly.

Elsa was staring after Zoe and DS Oakley, but on hearing her name she abruptly turned around. 'What? No, that's fine, thank you,' she replied and turned to keep watch for Zoe.

Lydia took Elsa's arm. 'Well, if you're all finished here, I'll walk out with you. We don't want to embarrass Zoe by staring, do we?' Lydia said meaningfully and encouraged Elsa to walk with her.

No sooner had they left the salon than Zoe returned with DS Oakley. She stopped by the Bella's desk. 'Bella…' she began.

'Don't worry, I'll sort everything out, leave it to me,' Bella told her and with that, Zoe was escorted out of the door.

As the door closed behind them, Maggie hurried over to Bella. 'Bella! What's going on? Was that the police taking Zoe?'

Bella nodded. 'Oh, Maggie!' she cried.

'Dear God! Have they arrested her?' Maggie demanded.

'No, they said just for questioning. What are we going to do?'

'There isn't anything we *can* do. What did Zoe say before she left?'

'Just to reschedule her appointments,' Bella replied. Then she grasped Maggie's arm: 'You don't think Zoe *did* do it, do you?' she looked at Maggie beseechingly.

'*I* don't think she did, but it's what the police think that matters. Look, come on, see what you can reschedule, we've to keep her business going – whatever happens.'

Councillor Hugo Marshall

Across the Market Place, Hugo was nervously awaiting the arrival of Jonathan Sturdy. He wasn't sure how much Simon had told Jonathan about selling the Thornberry buildings through Lewis Marshall. However, he had decided that from now on, everything would be completely above board after his conversation with Greg Craven.

Felicity tapped on the door. 'Mr Sturdy to see you, Councillor Marshall,' she said before ushering in a slim-built man, probably in his fifties, with thinning grey hair.

Hugo offered his hand: 'Mr Sturdy, pleased to meet you, I'm Hugo Marshall.' Hugo's hand was gripped firmly, almost firmly enough to cause Hugo to wince, but he turned the wince into a smile instead. 'Please sit down. Coffee? Tea?'

'Nothing for me, thank you. I'm afraid I can't stay long, I've another appointment but I'd like to have a preliminary chat,' Jonathan replied.

Hugo glanced at Felicity, who shrugged and withdrew.

'I'm going to come straight to the point. The plans drawn by Simon Saxby-Jones to convert the farm buildings at Thornberry Farm are exactly as I want them to be built. However, at the moment there's a field included in this plot, described as a pony paddock, and I should tell you that this field won't now be included in the sale.' Jonathan wasn't in any way abrupt, but Hugo picked up immediately that this man had made a decision and wasn't about to be swayed in any way.

'I think that's wise,' Hugo commented, 'you can rent it out for ponies, etc. but you still own it and that way it would remain grassland.'

'Good, I think we understand each other.' Jonathan looked hard at Hugo, who made a great effort to smile benignly.

'I understand that the way this works is that a sales pack is created, which is then sent to interested developers. They subsequently submit bids which remain confidential to *everyone*, until a prearranged date,' Jonathan continued.

The slight emphasis on the word 'everyone' alerted Hugo to the fact that Jonathan may be aware of the previous dealings with Planet Properties.

'That's correct, although I should mention that one of our developers, Planet Properties is going through the process of dissolution and therefore won't be involved. However, there are still several other very good smaller developers that would definitely take an interest.'

Jonathan's eyes narrowed. 'I take it that the dissolution of Planet Properties has something to do with the demise of Mr Saxby-Jones?'

'I'm afraid I couldn't possibly…' Hugo blustered.

'Oh, save it!' said Jonathan dismissively, waving a hand in the air, 'I can tell you quite frankly, that I didn't like the man, nor did I trust him.'

'Likewise, Mr Sturdy. Likewise.'

The two men looked at one another and at that moment, they understood that each of them had been deeply affected by Simon Saxby-Jones in some way and that there was a mutual unspoken understanding.

Hugo then explained the marketing, bid process, final payment and the agency's commission, and fifteen minutes later, Jonathan stood up.

'Thank you, Councillor Marshall, I understand the way it works much more clearly now and I thank you for your honesty,' he said genuinely.

Hugo positively beamed with delight. He pumped Jonathan's hand enthusiastically as he walked him to the door. 'It's been a pleasure to meet you, Mr Sturdy. I hope Lewis Marshall can help you sell your property. I look forward to hearing from you.'

Hugo opened the door and walked with Jonathan into reception, but his smiled faded as soon as he saw DCI Appleton and DS Oakley waiting there.

Jonathan also looked uncertain until the Chief Inspector spoke. 'Councillor Marshall, I need to ask you to accompany us to the station please, we need to ask you a few more questions.'

Hugo felt the blood drain from his face and swallowed nervously. 'Right now?' he croaked.

'Yes, please,' replied DCI Appleton. Hugo looked nervously at Jonathan who simply nodded,

'I'll be in touch,' he said quietly, and glancing at the police officers he left the agency.

Hugo turned to Felicity. 'I… um… you'll tell Tom where I've gone?'

Lydia Buckley

After Lydia had eventually said goodbye to Elsa, she made her way through the busy market and, as she waited to cross the road, she was astounded to see a police squad car drive past with Hugo Marshall in the back next to a uniformed police officer. *Good grief! Hugo as well?*

Lydia wondered if some new evidence had come to light and the police were preparing to make an arrest.

She went straight home – she had planned to do some writing and have lunch, however she took out the notes that she and Greg had written and added a comment about Zoe and Hugo being taken to the police station. There were other questions that had sprung to mind following her recent conversations with various people and she made a note of these as well.

Robbie's name caught her eye and she decided to call him and ask why he had denied being back in Ashdale.

Robbie picked up straight away: 'Hi, how are you?' he asked cheerily.

'I'm good thanks. Robbie. Actually, I need to ask you something,' Lydia replied.

‘Oh? This sounds ominous. What’s the matter?’ he asked with a modicum of humour.

‘When we had dinner at yours on Tuesday, you said that you had not returned to Ashdale, but I saw you there on Saturday night just after four thirty.’ Lydia held her breath.

There was silence for a good few seconds before Robbie spoke. ‘Right, I see… well, actually…’ he faltered.

‘Robbie? Did you go to the Jubilee Hall?’ Lydia asked bluntly.

Robbie sighed. ‘Yes. Yes, I did.’

‘Oh God, Robbie—’ Lydia couldn’t finish her sentence.

‘No! No, I didn’t kill him, but I did see a man leaving who might have,’ Robbie blurted out.

‘What? Have you told the police?’

‘They haven’t asked me, to be honest,’ Robbie replied, a little sheepishly.

‘What were you doing there?’ Lydia wanted to know.

‘To be honest, it’s all a bit embarrassing. After I had been to Ashdale to review the panto and saw Saxby-Jones, I got to thinking about what you said about him marrying Annabelle so soon after calling our engagement off. I got it in my head that he was the one who set me up. I know, I know, it sounds ridiculous, but it made sense to me at the time.’

‘Oh Robbie,’ Lydia said softly.

‘Anyway, I had this mad idea to go and confront him face to face, so I drove to Ashdale and parked on the Market Place. I went to the Coach & Horses for a drink first, to go through what I was going to say to him, and then I walked to the hall. The main entrance was locked, so I went around to the back and as I approached the door, it opened and a man came out.’

‘Do you know who it was? What did he look like?’

‘I don’t know who he was, but he was tubby, like a barrel and he wore circular glasses.’

Lydia took a sharp intake of breath. ‘Do *you* know who that might have been?’ Robbie asked.

'It sounds a bit like Hugo Marshall,' Lydia replied. 'Go on, what did you do next?'

'Well, when he opened the door, I thought it would be an opportunity to get in but the light from inside lit up quite a bit of the car park and I didn't want to be seen, so I flattened myself against the wall of the building in the shadows, like you see them do on the TV.' Robbie sniggered, but there was no response from Lydia, 'I watched him get into his car and drive off.'

'What type of car was it?' Lydia demanded.

'A silver Mercedes. Anyway, after he had gone, I went up to the door and saw the digital lock and realised that I couldn't get in. I stood there feeling furious and frustrated, then it started to rain, heavily, and I was getting drenched. I suddenly felt a right prawn cocktail, realised that this was a stupid idea, and so I just went back to the Market Place, got into my car and drove home.'

'How did Hugo Marshall look?'

He just looked...' Robbie paused to think of the right word, 'resigned, brow-beaten, defeated – that kind of thing.'

'Hmmm,' Lydia thought out loud, 'You may have to give a statement, Robbie. The police took Hugo Marshall in for questioning this morning. What time was it when you saw Hugo come out of the hall?'

'I left the Coach & Horses at five past five, I remember that because I put my phone on to silent and noticed the time. It's what? A five-minute walk so, I guess ten past five or thereabouts. You think I should contact the police then?'

'Yes Robbie, I do,' Lydia told him. 'Ring Harrogate police station and ask for DCI Appleton, he's in charge of the case.'

'Ok, I will. By the way, there's something else you should know.'

'Gracious! What else have you been up to?'

'Annabelle phoned me yesterday, we got talking and I'm taking her for lunch on Saturday,' Robbie blurted out.

'Oh! Robbie, are you doing the right thing? Getting involved again, I mean?'

'I don't know about "getting involved", but we had a long chat yesterday and she confirmed my suspicions that it *was* Simon who'd arranged for those photographs that ultimately broke us up,' Robbie explained.

'She did?'

'Yes, and we both felt that we needed to talk things through, explain and hopefully understand what happened and how we felt at that time.'

'Look, I hope you both have a lovely lunch and manage to clear the air, but remember Robbie, she's very vulnerable at the moment,' Lydia warned him.

'I know, I'll be sympathetic and tread carefully, but it will be nice to see her again,' he replied.

After they'd said goodbye, Lydia frowned and glanced at her notes again. She added some comments about what she had just learned from Robbie, then opened her laptop to begin writing.

Vinnie Buckley

Vinnie turned left and right as he admired his reflection in the mirror – for a man in the second half of his forties, he cut quite a dash. He still sported a full head of blondish hair and, thanks to his recent cruise, his skin was golden brown. He had booked a room at the Coach & Horses for a couple of nights and he was looking forward to this evening's dinner with Carlton Banks. He had decided on a dark-navy lightweight suit, a cream shirt and a navy silk tie which incorporated a fine cream stripe. The taxi was booked to pick him up at seven-fifteen and it was now ten past, so he collected his wallet and overcoat and made his way downstairs to the bar.

The taxi came to a stop outside the portico entrance of Ashdale Hall and Vinnie whistled appreciatively.

'It's a grand place this, sir – are you eating here?' the taxi driver asked.

'Yes, I've got a business dinner,' replied Vinnie as he pulled out a note from his wallet.

'May I give you my card, sir? In case you need a taxi back to the Coach.' The driver offered a business card to Vinnie. Vinnie took the card and handed over a ten pound note.

'Mikey Dixon,' he read, 'so you're local then?'

'Yes sir, I live in Ashdale. Here's your change, sir.' Mikey offered some coins to Vinnie who shook his head.

'No, that's all right, I don't need the change. I don't know what time I'll be ready to leave later on.'

'No problem sir, you just give me a call when you're ready. It'll take me ten minutes to get here,' Mikey replied.

Vinnie got out of the car and headed into Ashdale Hall, where he was immediately struck by the opulence and grandeur of the place. Carlton had suggested that they meet in *The Balmoral Bar*. Vinnie spotted the sign and turned right. It was a large light and airy room which had once been a drawing-room. Ornate plasterwork served as a cornice around the ceiling, the floor to ceiling windows were draped with gold-coloured velvet curtains, and paintings of previous Worthingtons hung on cream walls. Vinnie ordered a gin and tonic from the bar and sat on a barstool to await Carlton's arrival. He didn't have to wait long, and he was surprised to see that Carlton was accompanied by two ladies. Vinnie noted that although Carlton wasn't heavily overweight, he carried a few extra pounds. His hair was silvery grey but his eyebrows and moustache were more of a charcoal colour, and his dark eyes scanned the room before settling their gaze on Vinnie, rather like a hunter spotting its prey.

Vinnie stood up to welcome the trio: 'Good evening Mr Banks, I'm Vinnie Buckley.' He put out his hand, which was grasped in a firm handshake.

'Good evening Vinnie, please call me Carlton. This is my very good friend Eleanor Matthews and this is my daughter, Annabelle Saxby-Jones.' Carlton spoke with a deep voice in a business-like manner.

Vinnie shook hands with Eleanor Matthews, a tall, thin elegant woman that, although she was dressed immaculately, because of her hooked nose, reminded Vinnie of a witch. He was careful not to grasp her thin, bony hand too tightly as it felt fragile and he was almost afraid he would crush it. He then turned to Annabelle Saxby-Jones, and just in time, he remembered that this must be the widow and, according to the landlady of the Coach & Horses, it was all a bit of a scandal.

'Annabelle, I'm very pleased to meet you and may I first offer my sincere condolences on your recent loss.' Vinnie took her hand gently and was surprised at the firmness of her grip as she shook hands.

A pair of cool grey eyes looked at him. 'Thank you, Vinnie, that's most appreciated.' Her voice was soft and wavered slightly with emotion.

Vinnie was mesmerised. Annabelle wasn't a stunner, but she had an aristocratic air and held his gaze confidently. She didn't giggle or behave coyly as most of the women he met did and she was the first to look away. There was no gasp of admiration at his handsome features and, for a moment, Vinnie felt slighted.

Carlton cleared his throat and ordered drinks, then they sat on two of the beautifully upholstered bronze velvet sofas and made small talk about the attractions that North Yorkshire had to offer. When eventually they were seated at their table in *The Osborne Suite,* the food and wine ordered, talk turned to the business in hand.

'Vinnie, as you know Aztec Developments will be starting work on a large housing development and we hope that it will be one of many. We are looking for an advertising agency to promote our business, and as you know we approached your employer, Major Marketing, hence your visit here,' Carlton began.

'I'm looking forward to our discussion this evening and my presentation tomorrow at your offices. I do hope our business talk does not bore the ladies, however,' Vinnie replied smoothly.

'On the contrary, following Annabelle's recent bereavement, she's decided to come on board with me at Aztec. I've offered her a position in our small marketing department and she already has an idea, which I quite like. I wonder if you could give me your opinion.' Carlton looked proudly at his daughter as he spoke and Vinnie knew that whatever Annabelle said, he would have to make positive noises.

Annabelle smiled with a modicum of embarrassment at her father's words. 'Daddy, really,' she chided, 'don't put Vinnie on the spot before I've even spoken.' She turned her grey eyes to Vinnie. 'It's only a little idea that I mentioned to Daddy.'

'Please, tell me and I'll give you an honest answer,' Vinnie desperately hoped that the little idea was something he could work with.

Fortunately, as Annabelle summarised her idea about using an outline of the *Templo Mayor* in Mexico City as the letter 'A' in Aztec, Vinnie saw the potential.

'You see, *Templo Mayor* is an Aztec temple, and the Aztecs were renowned for their amazing architecture and I thought it could be incorporated into a new logo,' she explained.

'I think that's quite inspired,' he told her honestly, 'and I would like to give it much more thought.'

Carlton beamed at his daughter. 'I told you it was a good idea.'

Their first course was served and, as the meal progressed, Vinnie and Annabelle chatted non-stop about how they could promote the housebuilding division of Aztec Developments. Their conversation wandered on to other topics and Annabelle told him about her plans to up-scale the summer garden party to be held here at Ashdale Hall, and how Lady Worthington had put her in charge of the project.

Annabelle had become quite animated and Vinnie noticed that Carlton was delighted that his daughter seemed eager to overcome her recent distress. Vinnie himself was very taken with Annabelle – she was intelligent, looked glamorous in an understated way and had all the social graces necessary in the cut-throat world of business. As she turned to speak to her father, Vinnie found himself thinking how different his cruise would have been with someone like Annabelle as his wife instead of the brassy Vivienne. Vivienne was great in bed, but that was all she was good at. A man like Vinnie needed a wife to be proud of, a wife that could hold her own, a wife like Annabelle … The fact that she had a wealthy father had absolutely nothing to do with it, he told himself.

By half past ten, they'd all finished eating and drinking and Carlton made a move to leave. As he shook Vinnie's hand, he slapped him on the arm. 'I've really enjoyed this evening, Vinnie, and I look forward to seeing you at our office in Harrogate tomorrow afternoon, especially since Annabelle has given you the seed of an idea,' he said convivially.

'Likewise, Carlton,' replied Vinnie. 'It was a pleasure to meet you also, Eleanor.' Vinnie carefully placed his hands on the woman's arms and very gently kissed each hollow cheek, it wasn't a particularly pleasant experience. He turned to Annabelle who stood with a slightly mischievous look on her upturned face, she had clearly guessed Vinnie's reason for kissing Eleanor's cheeks in the first place.

'Will I see you at the office tomorrow?' he asked her.

'Maybe, I'm not sure of my plans yet for tomorrow,' she replied coyly and then lowered her gaze.

After they'd gone, Vinnie pulled out the card given to him by the taxi driver and as he waited, he thought about the evening. Annabelle was different, she had not fallen at his feet immediately, but, Vinnie thought, she had given him positive vibes, especially when he had kissed her cheeks politely on saying goodbye. However, he had to deal with Vivienne first and that, he had no doubt, wasn't going to be easy.

18

Councillor Hugo Marshall

Hugo sat at his desk with a large mug of coffee and thought about the week he'd just had. After Simon's murder, he had become a prime suspect in a murder case; Celia had left him; Planet Properties was finished, and Lewis Marshall was for sale. None of which he would have predicted a fortnight ago.

Two weeks ago he had been bobbing along more or less quite happily, apart from the pink envelopes. Ah yes, the pink envelopes. Peculiar how Freddie had mentioned them – Hugo nodded to himself. *I always suspected he was behind those!*

He wondered if, now that Planet was no longer trading, he would receive any more of the letters. Probably not!

It was a shame about the three million pounds though – that would have been a nice little nest egg; still, he would have money from the sale of Lewis Marshall. He glanced at the note left on his desk last night by Tom – he had raised the funds and would like to go ahead with the legalities. Tom would do well with the agency.

The only thing that hadn't been mentioned was the building which was home to the Lewis Marshall agency. Hugo and Charles had not included it in the sale price of the business, assuming that they would rent it to Tom, but Hugo thought now that a clean break would be preferable. Relations between them were strained and Celia was somewhere in the middle, so Hugo resolved to speak to Tom about the premises.

Hugo also reflected on his meeting with Tom's brother, Greg, which had certainly caused Hugo's stress levels to rocket. It was precisely the fear that somebody might find out about the unorthodox bids, which had been gnawing away at Hugo for some time. It was all very well for Simon and Freddie to mock and dismiss his concerns, but they'd not been the ones who would have been in the firing line. Hugo was relieved that not only was it the end of the road for Planet Properties, but that it was Tom's brother who had connected all the dots. Hugo felt reassured in the belief that Greg would keep his word and not write a naming and shaming article.

Jonathan Sturdy had been a rather nice chap – he could quite easily have taken umbrage at the revelation that Planet had been going to cheat him out of around nine million pounds, but he still seemed to be considering using the agency to market his property. If he chose Lewis Marshall, Hugo might suggest he wait until Tom took over. It would be a great start for him, and would be seen as an endorsement for the agency.

Hugo's thoughts then turned to his conversation yesterday afternoon with Bruce Harvey, who had returned from Spain. Bruce had heard of the death of Simon and after both men had expressed sympathy, Hugo could not resist passing on the gossip relayed to him by Felicity about Simon's extra-marital affair. Simon Saxby-Jones, the sanctimonious son-in-law of Carlton Banks, wasn't so saintly after all. A wife *and* a girlfriend who happened to be the daughter of Jonathan Sturdy, no less. Bruce was surprised to learn of Simon's duplicity, and Hugo had pressed home the point that Simon was also malicious in that he had deliberately sullied Hugo's character to Bruce to prevent their further association. He also told Bruce that Simon had attempted to prevent the sale of the agency, which was now going ahead. Hugo did not mention the fact that he was a murder suspect, nor did he give any indication of the discord between himself and Charles. By the end of the conversation, Hugo had accepted an invitation to go to Spain on a viewing visit.

The letter on his desk just required his signature, Hugo picked up his pen and reread the content before signing his name to confirm his intent. His decision to stand down as a borough councillor wasn't one he had taken lightly and, of course, it meant that he wouldn't become mayor in May. However, given the events of the last two weeks, he felt that the last thing he should do was to put himself in the spotlight and become fair game for the inevitable nudges and finger-pointing. There was also the possibility that rumours surrounding Planet Properties might emerge in the future, not from Greg but other people. From people like Freddie – Hugo did not quite trust Freddie to keep his mouth shut, and then there was Simon's solicitor who was a complete unknown, and of course, Jonathan Sturdy also knew what had gone on. That wasn't the sort of reputation he wanted nor was it the legacy he would have chosen for his mayoralty.

Following yesterday's very uncomfortable 'helping the police with their enquiries' session, Hugo wasn't confident that his alibi was substantial enough to prevent an arrest. The police were able to pinpoint Hugo's visit to the Jubilee Hall on that fateful night as he had seen Zoe Birch leaving around five o'clock, and apparently Hugo had been spotted leaving at ten past five or thereabouts. No one, however, could corroborate Hugo's claim that he had not kept his appointment with Simon and therefore had not seen him at all.

Annabelle Saxby-Jones

Annabelle sat at the scrubbed kitchen table. It had been quite a morning. Lydia had called for the key to the Harrogate house again, promising to collect her laptop and drop it off late this afternoon.

Mrs Simms had been full of the latest gossip, direct from Sheila Houseman at the bakery who had heard it from Doreen Rider, the landlady at the Coach & Horses who had seen it with her own eyes. The police had called at the beauty salon and taken away the owner for questioning. Mrs Houseman had thought that Zoe Birch had been arrested, but Elsa Armitage, who had actually been in the salon at the time, had confirmed that it was only questioning. Then Mrs Simms had told her that the police had also taken away Councillor Marshall. It seemed to Annabelle then, that either Zoe Birch or Councillor Hugo Marshall would eventually be arrested. Although Mrs Simms had said that Mrs Taylor from the charity shop had a niece, Trisha who worked at the police station, and Trisha had said that other suspects had been questioned too.

Annabelle sighed. She had forgotten how gossip travelled in the small market town. No doubt she would hear soon that even Tasheka was under suspicion! Mrs Simms had then sat her down and told her the rest of the gossip from the bakery. Elsa Armitage had spoken about Simon's girlfriend Bella, how they'd all been hoodwinked into believing that he was about to divorce his wife. How Elsa had nearly let the cat out of the bag at a rehearsal when she claimed to have seen Simon at the Valentine ball, but that he had denied even being there. Annabelle had listened as Mrs Simms explained that her reason for telling Annabelle this was that when she felt able to go into town, she needed to be aware of the truth. She was at great pains to point out that Annabelle wasn't being blamed for any of this and that she was a victim of Simon's infidelity and deceit.

Mrs Simms had then put the kettle on and made Annabelle a nice cup of tea and cut her a slice of lemon cake, whilst she then got on with 'doing the bedrooms'. As her coffee cooled, Annabelle wondered about Bella – she must be upset too. Would she want to attend the funeral? Bella might appreciate an opportunity to say goodbye as Simon was laid to rest. Eleanor would know the right thing to do, Annabelle decided.

Annabelle was thinking all this through when her father had phoned. He was furious. He had just been in contact with Simon's solicitor, who had been a little short with him. The upshot being, that all Annabelle was to get from her late husband was his personal items. The remainder of his estate which included his life insurance, house and any other proceeds and assets from his business dealings were to go to his son! Simon had never mentioned a son at all. The solicitor had been reluctant to say any more other than that as soon as he had located the son, he would be in touch again regarding funeral arrangements. Carlton had blustered about contesting the will and Annabelle had patiently listened to her father venting about Simon.

But now, she just felt discarded like a pair of old comfy trainers that had finally fallen apart. Simon had used her only for his own benefit – love had nothing to do with it – she could see that. He hadn't cared about her feelings or her needs – he hadn't even provided for her future. He had used Bella too; lied to her without any thought or regard to how she might cope when eventually he had let her go, and Annabelle was sure that he would have done that. Annabelle had come to realise that she had an opportunity to start afresh and she was going to take this chance with both hands.

Last night at dinner, she had been thrilled by the attention that Vinnie paid to her. He had listened, really listened when she talked about her ideas for branding Aztec's new housing division. He had made her feel that she had a talent and that she could contribute something useful to her father's company. Daddy had clearly been impressed too.

She liked Vinnie, he had a sense of humour and he had a way of telling stories about his business dealings that had them all in stitches. She thought he had liked her too. He was ambitious but not power-hungry; he worked hard because he enjoyed his work;

he liked people and Annabelle felt that she could learn a lot from him. She hoped that Daddy would agree that Aztec should become one of Vinnie's new clients. However, she had declined to attend this afternoon's presentation as she did not wish to appear too eager to see Vinnie again. Let him chase her, she thought smugly.

Tomorrow, of course, she had lunch with Robert to look forward to, and who knows, maybe they could rekindle their past romance. As she took a bite of the piece of lemon cake, she decided that she would like that. How exciting her prospects suddenly appeared, a new job with Daddy, volunteering for Lady Worthington, and possibly *two* men in her life.

Jonathan Sturdy

Jonathan stretched and stood up, he needed a coffee and a break. He headed into the kitchen and put the kettle on. He was on his own as Claire had gone into Harrogate and Bella was at work. He went over his conversation with Greg Craven again – they'd spoken yesterday afternoon following Jonathan's meeting with Hugo and compared notes. They agreed that Hugo was probably not the instigator of the rocky path of fake bids, but Jonathan still had concerns about putting Thornberry with Lewis Marshall. Greg had explained that his brother Tom would be buying the business, that he would be a sole-trader and that he could vouch for his integrity if Jonathan would at least consider waiting until Tom was in charge before making a final decision about which agency to choose.

Jonathan felt an obligation to Greg as he had warned him about Planet Properties. In fact, Jonathan decided he would like to meet Tom and have a chat with him, probably next week. He would prefer to give his business to a local company. Jonathan could see a bright future for his business – Harefield Park with the extra facilities that the Thornberry land would provide.

He took his hot coffee and wandered over to the kitchen window, where he could see Bella's horse contentedly munching grass. What would Bella decide to do?

If it was up to Claire, Bella would be whisked off to the nearest hospital for a termination. Jonathan recalled their heated discussion on the subject and he had been a little shocked at Claire's insistence that it was the right thing to do. Claire's problem was that she was a bit of a snob, she worried what people might think. It worried him that Claire had initially believed that Bella had got pregnant on purpose to trap Simon. Fortunately, she hadn't expressed that opinion to Bella and he had warned her to not even think about doing that. Claire had even referred to Simon as a victim during their argument, as though their daughter was some kind of siren who had lured him to his doom. Well, he had soon put her straight on that point, stressing that Simon was a liar and a cheat and if Claire had not been so blinded by the man's charms, she could have seen it for herself.

They rarely disagreed, mainly because Jonathan was an easy-going man who just buried himself in his business, but this whole episode regarding Simon's murder had brought out another side to him. Although he had given his statement the day after the murder, he had been a primary suspect because he had gone to the Jubilee Hall looking for Simon around the time of his death. Claire had been upset when he had returned from the police station on Wednesday after they'd taken him in for further questioning. He also knew from Bella that Zoe had been collected from the salon and taken to the station in a squad car, so they must be getting closer to an arrest by now he thought.

As far as Bella was concerned, Jonathan would support his daughter whatever her decision. She would have a home with them until such time as she chose to leave, and if she kept the baby they would have a grandchild to love and cherish. However, if she decided not to continue with the pregnancy then she would have to come to terms with that decision and start to live her life again. Either way, Claire would have to accept Bella's decision and Jonathan was sure she would – he suspected she was just severely shocked at Simon's behaviour and felt a little embarrassed at her own.

On the whole, Jonathan was thankful that Bella had found out about Simon's intentions before the pregnancy was too far on, so at least she had some time in which to make her decision.

Isabella Sturdy

Bella left the salon and tucked her hands into her coat pockets – it was her lunch hour and she wanted to go somewhere quiet to think. As she glanced around the Market Place, she realised it was too cold to sit on a bench and it wasn't very quiet. Then she saw the church spire, and although Bella wasn't religious at all, she was drawn to the place.

She entered through an arched doorway and was immediately enveloped in a feeling of tranquillity. She wandered down the centre aisle and slid into a front pew, placed her handbag on the floor and exhaled. At last, silence. She closed her eyes and allowed the calmness to wash over her and then she began to think. Her mind travelled back over her relationship with Simon. Now Zoe had spoken to her candidly, she could see how sneaky he had been. All those excuses about a sick and ailing father – lies, the time spent down south in Cornwall with a sister – lies. The whole relationship had been a scam to ingratiate himself with her father to ultimately cheat Pops out of millions of pounds. How could she have been so stupid? She should have known that someone like Simon wouldn't want a long-term relationship with a girl like her. However, it was no use crying over spilt milk, as her grandmother used to say.

If she continued with the pregnancy she would probably stay at home, certainly in the beginning. She knew that she could rely on her father for support unless—. She knew her father had not killed Simon, but the police were not convinced of that and Pops was still a 'person of interest'. No doubt her mother would come round eventually.

How would she cope with bottles or breast-feeding, nappies, sleepless nights, teething? Did she want to have all of that to deal with? Even if she managed with the parenting, there were still people who would point and stare, gossiping about the child whose father had been murdered. What would she tell the child as it grew up? There was also the question of Annabelle Saxby-Jones; Bella had yet to meet her, but she was sure that they would bump into each other at some point. How would they both feel about that? Having another man's child might also hinder her chances of meeting someone she could share her life with.

If, on the other hand, she took her mother's advice and terminated the pregnancy, all this would just go away. Her life would carry on as normal and no one would be any wiser, although she would have to carry that guilt with her for the rest of her days. However, she would be free to meet someone else and hopefully have children one day – maybe she did not need to have one now.

As the enormity of her decision weighed heavily on her mind, and the pros and cons swirled around her brain, she thought about what Lydia had said and resolved to talk it over with her. Lydia was practical and she was also one of the very few people who knew the situation. Bella felt as though she was at a T-junction but somehow knew that whichever direction she chose, she would be strong and take responsibility for her own life and her own decision.

Nick Bradley

Nick left his office and wandered down to the shop floor where he bought a sandwich and a packet of crisps, then took out his mobile phone. It had taken him all week to decide whether or not to meet his grandfather and eventually he had come to the conclusion that he should. Whatever Nick had felt about Simon, at least the old man had made an effort to keep in contact. Nick also understood that his grandfather would be grieving the loss of his son, and whatever else had gone on, Nick felt at the very least, he should show some respect to the older man.

He sent Lydia a brief text to confirm his willingness to meet his grandfather. After that, he wandered outside into the Market Place and sat on a bench to eat his lunch. Nick was worried. Following Lydia's advice, he had phoned the police and told them he wished to add to his statement. He had been asked to go to the station, which he had done but when he told them about hearing banging on the back door of the hall at around five-thirty and seeing a Range Rover driving away, they'd implied that he was making it up to cover up for something.

They had even been suggested that he had taken a knife from the kitchen and killed Simon himself, seeing as how he had the opportunity. Well, let them try and prove it, he thought to himself.

The problem was, he hadn't admitted to being Simon's son and he was concerned that if the police found out, it might make matters worse, but then again, he wasn't about to volunteer the information as that could be used as a motive in some way. Nick didn't know how these things worked.

In the meantime, he would look forward to meeting Edward Jones and finding out more about his paternal family. The letters Edward had written to his mother were humorous and kind-hearted, this was his grandfather and probably the only family he had.

It was a great shame that the opportunity to approach Simon had not arisen, but there was no guarantee that Simon would have welcomed him with open arms in any case. Nick had also considered not revealing who he was to Simon, as he wasn't the sort of man Nick would have proud to call his father. Simon might even have tried to block any association between Edward and Nick, or even rebuffed the pair of them. At least now they had a chance to build a relationship.

Robbie Parker

Robbie was feeling rather chuffed with himself. When he had first taken the phone call from Annabelle last Wednesday, he had been hesitant about talking to her again. He had been deeply hurt by her refusal to believe him those few years ago, and by her falling into

Simon's arms so quickly. However, as they talked and Annabelle told him that she now knew that Simon had arranged the photos and specifically encouraged her to break her engagement, he had relaxed. Their conversation flowed and Robbie decided he wanted to see her again, so he tentatively asked if she would like that and was a little surprised at how quickly she agreed.

There was a lovely little Italian restaurant on the north side of Leeds that would be ideal for a lunch date. The food was good and it was likely to be busy enough that there would be an ambient atmosphere rather than a romantic one. Robbie had no idea what he or Annabelle would feel about seeing each other. Chatting on the phone was one thing, but sitting opposite each other, well…

The only niggle at the moment was this business of Simon's murder. It was damned annoying that Lydia had seen him in Ashdale last Saturday evening. He'd thought they would have all been busy with the panto. She knew he had lied to her on Tuesday evening when he denied returning to the town, so he had no option but to be honest and admit it when she had phoned him yesterday. When he called the police they'd asked him to go to the station, and he thought he might now be a suspect. The police had told him that he should have come forward when they appealed for information and the fact that he hadn't led them to believe he had something to hide. The fact that he had a history with Annabelle and revenge on his mind, had given him both motive and opportunity, and they also suggested that he could have taken a knife with him, giving means.

Yeah right, let them try and prove it!

The bravado was only on the surface though, because deep down he was worried – he had been at the hall around the time that Simon was murdered and the police had made it clear that he was a 'person of interest'.

For now, though, he was looking forward to seeing Annabelle, and, if he was honest, rekindling their relationship. Robbie wanted someone to share his life with and, as Annabelle had once been that special someone, he hoped that she might become that person again.

Zoe Birch

Zoe sat in the inner sanctum of her office and reflected on the past couple of weeks – a roller coaster of emotions, secrets, arguments, ending dramatically with a murder. Then there was the aftershock when secrets had been revealed. Thank goodness she and Bella had now put their relationship back on track. Bella had also told her about the devious scheme Simon was involved with, which potentially would have cheated her father out of a few million pounds. Zoe wasn't clear on all the details, but knew that had been the reason for Simon's interest in Bella.

Zoe wondered what Bella would do about her pregnancy. It was a momentous decision and Zoe had made it clear that she would help in any way she could. Whatever the outcome, Bella would always wonder if it had been the right thing to do, it was exactly the same situation that had Zoe had found herself in some twenty years ago, and she still thought about how different her life would have been if she had decided differently.

The other person on Zoe's mind was Annabelle Saxby-Jones. Zoe felt that, for some reason, she should express her condolences to Annabelle. The poor woman had been thrust into widowhood under terrible circumstances, of which Zoe had been a part. She decided she would buy a card and write a separate letter to enclose within it and put it through Annabelle's letterbox this evening.

Zoe had also taken stock of her own feelings and, although she wasn't *glad* that Simon was dead, the thought of being jobless and homeless had terrified her. She had decided that it was time to take matters into her own hands, and had approached her landlord, Aztec Developments enquiring about purchasing the property in which she lived and worked. They were considering the possibility and looking into a reasonable price. Zoe had then approached her bank about borrowing money to buy it, and only this morning, confirmation about a loan had arrived.

It was a massive relief, although Zoe wasn't able to go any further forward with the purchase at the moment because of the murder investigation. She shuddered when she recalled her visit to the police station yesterday – more questions culminating in a suggestion that she had committed the murder. It wasn't a formal charge, but they'd tried to force her to admit that, in her fury, she had taken a knife and stabbed Simon. They'd gone on and on and Zoe almost wished she *had* stabbed the blasted man, then she could admit it and they would leave her alone. But, she had stuck to her story that he was alive and well when she had left the hall and gone to the café.

Vinnie Buckley

Vinnie was sitting in Betty's Tea Room in Harrogate, apparently it was famous, and to be fair, he had enjoyed his coffee with a 'fat rascal', a sort of plump and fruity scone. He had also decided to take a box of *Cheeky Little Rascals* and a bag of *Bettys Café Blend Coffee* back home with him. So far, it had been a very positive day – he had worked extremely hard on his proposal this morning, incorporating quite a lot of Annabelle's ideas, which he had liked. Then he'd presented it this afternoon at the Aztec offices. He had been disappointed that Annabelle had not been there, but on the other hand, he had been able to concentrate solely on the presentation – which had been received very well indeed.

After leaving Aztec's offices, Vinnie had wandered into Harrogate's town centre and purely by chance, he had come across a firm of solicitors, Holdsworth & Crossley. The chap he had met on holiday was called Richard Holdsworth, so Vinnie had popped into reception and discovered that this was indeed the same Holdsworth. Richard had come down to the reception area to welcome Vinnie and have a quick chat, but then, unfortunately, his next client had then arrived, so Vinnie had left – but it had set him off thinking.

If, and it was a big if, he decided to let Vivienne go and *if* Aztec became his client, they would be a major client taking up a lot of his time, and he could consider moving up north – somewhere like Harrogate. The town was well placed in the centre of the country, it had good links with motorways, trains and even an international airport only twenty minutes' drive away. It was a prestigious town, with numerous bars and restaurants and yet close to the countryside. He would be closer to Lydia, which would make it easier for their son Matt, to visit them both, and of course, he would be able to get to know Annabelle better – *purely for business purposes*, he told himself. However, should things develop romantically, then he wouldn't be unhappy about that.

Annabelle was still grieving and Vinnie would have to take things slowly, but this could be an opportunity to work his way up the social ladder. After all, Annabelle was on very friendly terms with the local gentry, Sir James and Lady Victoria Worthington. The Worthingtons, he had discovered, owned Ashdale Hall, the impressive pile where they'd had dinner. Now if Vinnie could include them as clients as well…

Vinnie finished his coffee and 'fat rascal' and checked his phone. He had sent a text to Lydia in the hope that she was free to meet him for dinner, but there was still no reply. He noticed that there was a text from Vivienne which he decided to ignore. He paid for his refreshments, bought his goodies to take home and stepped out of the café into the pouring rain. He hurried to his car and oncc inside, wondered what he should do this evening as, in the absence of any response from Lydia, he was at a loose end. Perhaps he should just go back to the Coach & Horses and think more about his plan to move to Harrogate because that, he decided, was what he would really like to do. The landlady of the Coach & Horses, Mrs Rider, would be only too happy to fill him in on the recent goings-on regarding the murder and Vinnie felt he ought to be fully in the picture if he was going to get to know Annabelle better.

Lydia Buckley

Lydia pulled in at the back of 12 Suffolk Chase and stared through the windscreen – the rain was lashing down. She made sure that she had the house key handy along with the alarm code before she jumped out of the car and ran towards the door. She cursed as she ran through a large puddle, soaking her feet and the bottom of her trousers. When the alarm was safely switched off, she removed her shoes and padded into the kitchen.

She saw the laptop and its cable immediately and found the bag on one of the chairs. Lydia unzipped the bag and tutted as a celebrity gossip magazine fell out onto the floor. She bent down, picked it up and flicked through it, surprised to see that several words had been cut out from various pages. Then she stuffed it back into one of the internal pockets of the bag, noticing as she did so, a small quantity of bright-pink notepaper and envelopes. She pulled out one of the envelopes and realised that it looked and felt identical to the one she had handed to Hugo Marshall on her first visit to the agency. *Oh, Annabelle, what have you been up to?*

Lydia zipped the laptop and cable safely into the bag, set the alarm and ran back to her car. She checked her phone before driving off and was pleased to see that she had received a text from Edward. He was clearly delighted that Nick had agreed to meet him and suggested eleven o'clock at the café. He also asked if Lydia would be there to introduce them just to break the ice. Lydia called Nick immediately and sensed that although he was pleased to meet his grandfather at last, he was also a little nervous.

'Edward is a bit nervous, so he's asked me to come along and introduce you both, I hope you don't mind.'

'No, I'm pleased that you can do that as neither of us knows what each other looks like, for a start. It would be damned awkward if I approached the wrong man,' Nick replied with amusement.

Lydia chuckled. 'I look forward to seeing you tomorrow then,' she said.

'Provided I haven't been arrested,' Nick replied cynically.

Lydia tried to reassure Nick that he would be fine, and told him that others had been brought in for questioning as well. There was something that Lydia needed to ask Nick about – the lights in the corridor at the Jubilee Hall. Then they chatted a little more and by the time they said goodbye, Lydia hoped that she had been able to set Nick's mind at rest.

As Lydia drove up the drive to The Manor, the rain had eased slightly so she quickly jumped out of the car, ran for cover under the porch and knocked on the door.

Mrs Simms appeared and ushered her in. 'Ooh, Lydia love, you're wet through. Come on into the kitchen and I'll make you a hot drink,' she fussed.

'No, it's ok, I'm on my way home. I just want to drop this off for Annabelle, she's expecting it.' Lydia held out the laptop bag. There was the sound of light footsteps and Annabelle appeared in the entrance hall as Mrs Simms headed back to the kitchen.

'Lydia! God, you're wet through.'

'It's been bucketing down and I splashed through a puddle which has made it worse,' Lydia replied ruefully, staring at her wet trousers.

'Well, I won't keep you long in that case. I was just the same last Saturday. Anyway, I've things to tell you: the first is that I'm seeing Robert tomorrow for lunch and I wondered if you and I could meet up tomorrow afternoon in that café on the Market Place? I'll want to tell you about my lunch date and I've some other news to share. Please say you will?' Annabelle looked so beseechingly at Lydia, that she felt obliged to agree.

'Yes, but I can't be there until four o'clock, will that be ok with you?'

Annabelle flung her arms around Lydia and nearly knocked her off her feet,

'Oh yes!' she exclaimed, 'I'm so looking forward to tomorrow. I've masses to tell you,' Annabelle's eyes were bright and she looked radiant.

Lydia said goodbye and stepped out into the porch, and as the rain had got heavy again, she ran for her car. Once settled in the driver's seat, she glanced at the still open door of the house. Annabelle waved before closing it.

Well Robbie, you've certainly perked Mrs S-J up.

That evening, Greg and Lydia had agreed to meet Tom and Amy for dinner at Fratellis', an Italian restaurant in Ashdale. Once they were seated at their table, food and wine ordered, Lydia could tell that they were both bursting with excitement.

'Ok bro, go on tell us the news,' Greg said.

'Well, there's good news and slightly not-so-good news,' began Tom. 'The good news is that I can raise the necessary funds to buy the agency.'

'The not-so-good news,' broke in Amy, 'is that we'll have to sell our lovely house to be able to buy the office and that pokey flat upstairs.' She looked glumly at Tom.

'That's great about the agency, but why do you need to buy the building?' asked Greg.

'At first, Charles and Hugo had agreed to sell the agency and retain the office and flat for additional income, but their relationship has completely broken down, so Hugo has decided to cut all ties and sell everything,' explained Tom.

'Do you *have* to sell your house?' Lydia enquired.

'It's the only way to afford to buy the property,' replied Tom.

'The girls are a bit shocked,' Amy said, referring to their daughters, 'but fortunately Cathryn will be going to university in September so only Caroline will be at home most of the time.'

'It'll be fine, once we've done it up a bit,' Tom said positively.

'But the idea of living in a flat...' Amy pulled a face.

'I live in a flat,' Greg pointed out.

'Yes, but yours is a *nice* flat,' Amy replied petulantly.

'And this will be a nice flat when you've put your stamp on it.' Tom slipped into estate agent mode.

'I suppose so,' responded Amy without enthusiasm.

'What about a name for your agency? Have you thought about that?' asked Greg brightly.

'I've only come up with Craven's at the moment. Amy has suggested Craven Properties, so any suggestions would be most appreciated.'

They discussed various ideas as their food and wine arrived, and then the talk turned to the murder.

'Have you heard anything from Will about the investigation, Greg? Surely the fact that our brother-in-law is the DCI has an advantage for you?'

'He only gives me information that I can officially report which, in a nutshell, is (a) that the knife used was probably a kitchen knife with a serrated edge, similar to a bread knife; (b) the death occurred between four thirty and five-thirty, which we knew already, and (c) they have a number of 'persons of interest' as you're aware, Tom,' replied Greg.

'God yes, poor Hugo,' agreed Tom. 'When he returned from the police station yesterday, he was a bit shell-shocked. But what I don't understand is why he had to go and see Simon Saxby-Jones on Saturday evening at all. I would have thought that any business could have waited until Monday.'

Greg and Lydia did not enlighten him.

'Well, whatever his business was with Simon, it has put him fairly in the frame for murder,' Amy observed, 'and I understand the police took Zoe Birch from WOW! Rumour has it that she was having an affair with Simon as well,' she added salaciously.

'I can tell you that Zoe was most definitely *not* having an affair with Simon,' Lydia told them firmly. 'He implied she wanted an affair to cover up his actual affair with someone else.'

'Really?' gasped Amy. 'Do tell us more.'

Lydia did not want to gossip, but thanks to Elsa Armitage and other members of the Ashdale Players, the word was already out about the love triangle between Simon, Annabelle and Bella.

'Simon was having an affair with Bella who works at the salon, but Bella was under the impression that Simon was estranged from his wife.' Lydia gave a shortened version of events.

'It's a bit like a soap opera, who would have thought a murder would happen in Ashdale,' Amy remarked.

'Have you thought about holidays this year or will that be on hold now?' Greg asked suddenly. The conversation took a different turn as they discussed what their plans might be.

Much later, Lydia lay next to Greg as he slept, listening to his shallow breathing. Her mind wandered over the events of the last two weeks. There was something she had learned that was important, but for the life of her, she could not remember what it was. She turned over and snuggled under the duvet – it would come to her eventually.

19

Lydia Buckley

Lydia was clearing up after a late breakfast, and Greg had popped out on some errand or other, muttering about seeing her later in the day. Lydia told him that she had two appointments that afternoon in Harrogate at Lush Lashes and that she was meeting Annabelle at the café at four o'clock. As she washed and dried the breakfast pots, she tried to remember what it was that kept nagging at her. When she was finished tidying up, she pulled out the murder notes and read through them again.

Gradually, the pieces came together and the answer stared her in the face.

'Oh my God!' she said out loud.

She checked her notes again and still came up with the same answer. She scribbled a name on the notes and circled it several times, then checked the time – ten forty-five. She had to meet Edward and Nick in fifteen minutes and she simply could not be late.

As she drove into town, she called DCI Appleton on his mobile. When he didn't answer she left a message to say she thought she knew who Simon's killer was but that she was going to work so her mobile would be on silent and that she would call him later.

Lydia parked her car and hurried to the café. Fortunately neither had arrived, so she sat at an empty table and waited. Nick arrived first and he nervously greeted Lydia, then sat down next to her. He was dressed simply in a white shirt, jeans and a black leather jacket.

'Hi, are you ok?' Lydia asked him, he simply nodded and smiled wanly, then jerked his head towards the café door as it opened. Edward entered, paused, and walked over to their table. Nick and Lydia stood up immediately.

As Lydia made the introductions, she was struck by the similarity between the men in the shape of their noses and chins.

Edward smiled and held out his hand which Nick took. 'I can't tell you how pleased I am to have this opportunity to meet you, Nick,' Edward said with a catch in his voice.

Nick cleared his throat. 'I'm a bit overwhelmed to be honest. I didn't expect this, but I'm looking forward to getting to know you.'

Lydia bought them both a drink and after a few minutes decided to leave them to get to know each other. She left the café and made her way to Lewis Marshall.

Lydia knew that Tom was out this morning appraising properties from the Planet portfolio and that therefore it was an ideal time to speak to Hugo if he was available.

'Good morning, it's not a bad day weather-wise, is it?' she said as she entered the agency.

Felicity glanced up. 'No, it's quite pleasant for February. How may I help you?'

'I wonder if I might speak to Councillor Marshall, if he's free please.'

'I'm not sure he's available. Is it something I can help with?'

Why was Felicity always so… well, frosty? 'I'm afraid not, it's a personal matter,' she replied, equally curtly.

Felicity looked over her spectacles at Lydia. 'Just a moment,' she muttered and knocked on the office door behind her and disappeared inside.

A few moments later, she reappeared. 'Councillor Marshall can give you a few moments. Would you come this way, please?'

Lydia moved behind Felicity's desk and into Hugo's office.

'Good morning, Ms… Buckley? I believe?' Hugo stood up and extended his hand, 'How can I be of assistance?'

Lydia took his hand and shook it,

'There are a couple of matters I wish to discuss and I've taken this opportunity to come now whilst Tom isn't here,' she began.

'Oh? Is there a problem with Mr Craven?' Hugo frowned.

'On the contrary, I wish to help him. You may not know, but I'm seeing Tom's elder brother Greg.' At the mention of Greg's name Hugo stiffened but Lydia made no comment and continued, 'Last night, we had dinner with Tom and Amy, and Tom told us the good news that he was able to buy this agency. He also mentioned that he and Amy would have to sell their house in order to buy this building.'

Hugo visibly relaxed,

'Yes, well that's unfortunate, but it's not essential that Tom buys it himself. The property could well be purchased by another party who is quite happy for Tom to rent the offices. Now, if that's all?' Hugo briefly smiled and began to shuffle papers on his desk clearly indicating that he felt Lydia's time was up.

'I'm interested in buying the property and I would like to see the flat upstairs… if I may.'

Hugo stopped shuffling and looked at her with interest. 'Oh, well I see. In that case, I would be only too happy to show it to you. Do have time now?' He rummaged in a drawer in his desk and withdrew some keys on a keyring.

‘Thank you.’ Lydia stood up and waited for Hugo to open his office door.

‘Just showing Ms Buckley the flat, Felicity,’ he said briskly and ushered Lydia into the office kitchen. He led her through a door and into a hallway, ahead of them was a staircase.

‘It’s completely self-contained, with a private entrance down that hallway,’ he told her pointing to an outside door. ‘Separate meters, council tax, etcetera, although it will need a bit of renovation,’ he said as he climbed the stairs.

Lydia made no comment as she looked around the flat. It had a decent-sized kitchen, although it would need a complete refit; a huge lounge with French doors led out onto a flat-roofed terrace. Upstairs were two double bedrooms, a smaller single bedroom and a bathroom which would also need to be replaced.

‘It has potential,’ she said to Hugo.

‘It does. It could be a lovely apartment. We just never got around to renovating it when the last tenant moved out. The terrace is south-facing and very private – with a few potted plants and outdoor furniture—’

‘Councillor Marshall,’ Lydia broke in, ‘two weeks ago when I first came into the agency, you may remember that I handed you your mail. It had fallen onto the floor and included in the bundle was a bright-pink envelope.’

‘What of it?’ Hugo snapped.

‘I understand that you may have received other pink envelopes and I just wanted to ask if they were, shall we say, unwelcome.’

Hugo’s mouth opened and closed like a fish, his double chin wobbled and he was slightly breathless.

Lydia waited as Hugo struggled to find words and took pity on him. ‘I know about Planet Properties and its business. I’m not here to cause trouble, but I can tell you that you won’t receive any more of these letters.’

Hugo, who had gone pink in the face at the mention of Planet, was now visibly embarrassed. He pushed his glasses further up his nose and cleared his throat. 'Yes, well thank you for letting me know. Can I ask who sent them, and how you know?'

'I don't think that's something you need to know and the less said, the better?' Lydia suggested.

Hugo nodded. 'I quite agree. Well, if we've finished here, shall we return to my office?'

Lydia smiled at Hugo. 'I think we should. I've a good feeling about this place – you may have a buyer.'

Hugo's eyes lit up. 'Very well, shall we crunch some numbers and think about a suitable rent to charge Mr Craven?'

When Lydia left the agency a little while later, she had shaken hands with Hugo as they'd agreed on a price. Hugo had said he would tell Tom he had a buyer for the premises, but he agreed not to tell him who it was – to mumble something about them wishing to be anonymous until the contracts were exchanged. As she walked back to her car, Lydia realised she needed to get a move on if she was to get to Harrogate in time for her appointments at Lush Lashes.

At a quarter to four later that afternoon, Lydia checked her phone and was delighted to see that she had received texts from both Edward and Nick. There was also a missed called from DCI Appleton, but before she was able to respond to anything, her phone died. She was cross with herself as she rarely let her phone get low on battery. However, there wasn't anything she could do and she had to return to Ashdale to meet up with Annabelle.

At last, with a welcome, large cappuccino coffee, she was sitting opposite Annabelle who was clearly bursting with news.

'Ok Annabelle, how was lunch with Robbie?'

Annabelle's eyes sparkled and she spoke excitedly: 'It was just wonderful. He explained everything and I told him that I was sure he had been set up by Simon, and then we talked about what we had both been doing. We just slipped back into the way we had been before and then I realised that this man, Robert, had loved me for *who* I am, not *what* I am. It doesn't matter to him that I'm Carlton Banks's daughter, it makes no difference to his career at all. He made me feel so special, Lydia, and I told him about my plans for the garden party, which he thought were brilliant.' Annabelle's face had a bit of colour and she was so animated. A far cry from the grieving widow of only a few days ago.

'I'm pleased you enjoyed your lunch date, it seems it has done you the world of good,' Lydia said sincerely.

'I did have some not-so-great news yesterday though, I was going to tell you when you dropped the laptop off.' Annabelle's face clouded over,

'Oh dear, nothing too awful, I hope?'

'It's to do with Simon's will. He's left everything to his son!'

'His son?' gasped Lydia,

'Yes, we've no idea who or where this son is, all we do know is that he's an adult. Daddy is so angry, he's thinking of contesting the will.'

'I don't know what to say, Annabelle, I'm shocked.' Lydia was truly surprised. 'When you say you don't know where the son is, presumably the solicitor does?'

'I don't think so because Daddy says Mr Crossley will be in touch when he has located him.'

'Sorry, who's Mr Crossley?'

'Oh, he's Simon's solicitor. Daddy found his number in Simon's papers in his office. I think he's a partner of a firm in Harrogate,'

'Do you have anything at all from Simon?'

Annabelle pushed her empty coffee cup away. 'Only his personal jewellery – signet ring, cufflinks, those kinds of things.' She spoke resignedly, but not unhappily.

'That doesn't seem right,' Lydia said sympathetically.

Annabelle shrugged. 'No, it's not very nice to be passed over, but I don't see what I can do about it.'

'Annabelle, there's something I would like to ask you about,' Lydia began carefully. 'When I put your laptop in its bag yesterday, I noticed a magazine with various words cut out, with some pink notepaper and envelopes. Has this got anything to do with Councillor Marshall?'

'Why Councillor Marshall?' Annabelle asked suspiciously.

'Because I was in the agency when he received a pink envelope in his mail, and he looked horrified to receive it,' Lydia replied.

Annabelle played with her coffee spoon as she thought about her answer.

'I didn't mean any harm,' she said at last, 'I was just bored. I sometimes overheard Simon talking in his office – I liked to listen to him talking so I would sit on the stairs. Usually it was just boring business stuff, but his conversations with Hugo Marshall were quite interesting, I thought Simon was quite clever in the way he could just manipulate Councillor Marshall. Then I got this marvellous idea about teasing Councillor Marshall, so I began to send the letters with vague references to things not being transparent and what if certain things became public knowledge, stuff like that.' Annabelle put the spoon down and shrugged. 'Anyway, it doesn't matter now, I shan't be sending any more letters.'

'I'm glad to hear that, Annabelle, it wasn't a nice thing to do,' Lydia told her sternly.

'Anyway, let me tell you about last night now…' Annabelle's face it up once again.

'Last night? Oh, your business dinner – it went well then?' Lydia was taken aback at the sudden change in Annabelle, but she clearly had something thrilling to say. At that moment, however, the café door opened and Vinnie strolled in.

He spied Lydia immediately. 'Ah, there you are, I've been looking for you, sweetheart,' he announced. Then he stopped as he caught sight of Annabelle.

Both women looked up in surprise.

'Sweetheart?' Annabelle repeated and looked at Lydia quizzically.

'I'm her husband, actually,' Vinnie said sheepishly.

'Husband?' Annabelle repeated, looking from Vinnie to Lydia, 'but I thought you were dating someone else?' she frowned curiously.

'I am,' confirmed Lydia, finding her voice at last.

'You are?' Vinnie asked, the smile disappearing from his face.

'Actually he's…' began Lydia, but she broke off as the café door opened once again and a woman with blonde hair wearing a leopard print fur jacket marched inside. Her breasts bounced with each angry step as they strained under a red V-necked sweater tucked into a black mini-skirt, complete with thigh-high black boots.

'I knew it!' the woman screeched, 'I knew you had come to see her!' she pointed a red talon-tipped finger at Lydia.

'Vivienne!' gasped Lydia, 'what the hell are you doing here?'

'Checking up on him!' The finger swung in Vinnie's direction. 'You just can't get over her, can you? You ought to be more careful who you send text messages to. I got one which was clearly meant for her,' Vivienne jerked her thumb in Lydia's direction.

Vinnie scrabbled in his pocket for his mobile. 'You did?' he gasped.

'Yeah, last night's dinner invitation,' Vivienne crossed her arms.

'Last night's what…?' questioned Lydia, staring at Vinnie.

'You should remember, you left *her* for *me*!' Vivienne retorted.

Annabelle blinked in astonishment. 'Your husband left you, for *this* woman?' she asked Lydia in surprise.

Vivienne rounded on her. 'And what exactly do you mean by that?' she snapped, putting her hands on her hips aggressively.

Annabelle jerked in alarm and shuffled as far back in her chair as she could. 'I just meant you're very different from Lydia – the complete opposite, in fact.'

'Of course I am, that's why he left her,' Vivienne spat. 'Then we got married because I was pregnant,' she added smugly.

Lydia was about to say something, but the words never made it past her lips as Annabelle suddenly pushed her chair back and stood up. She leant on the table and glared at Vivienne: 'Oh, *pregnant* were you? How convenient!' she sneered. 'Is that how you trapped him? Hmm? Just like my husband and his girlfriend – pregnant, my ass!'

Lydia gasped and clapped her hand over her mouth and looked at Vinnie who was equally horrified and speechless.

'Just what the hell are you implying?' Vivienne yelled.

'I'm not implying anything, merely stating the obvious,' Annabelle shot back. 'That women like you and Bella, get yourselves pregnant on purpose, to steal somebody else's husband!'

Vivienne took a step forward. 'So, your old man had a bit on the side as well, did he?' she smirked. 'Well, I'm not surprised – you look as frigid as her!' Vivienne jerked her thumb at Lydia, who had now also stood up,

'Ladies, stop…' Lydia implored.

Annabelle's eyes dropped from Vivienne's face to the gaping V-neck of the sweater and the ample cleavage now displayed.

'Lady? I don't think so!' she said haughtily.

Vivienne screamed and launched herself at Annabelle. Vinnie grasped Vivienne's arms and pulled her back as Lydia instinctively did the same with Annabelle.

'For God's sake Viv…' he hissed.

Vivienne rounded on him, snatching her arms out of his grip,

'Get off me!' she shouted, 'and don't call me Viv! I've had just about enough of being told what to do.'

'Vivienne…' began Vinnie soothingly.

'I'll say and do what I bloody well please!' Vivienne shouted in response.

'Vivienne, please stop,' said Lydia holding her hands up, palms forward.

Vivienne spun round to face Lydia. 'And you can go to hell!' she yelled, 'Your constant texting has ruined our holiday – ok? Happy now?'

'VIVIENNE!' roared Vinnie, 'Enough!'

Vivienne was shocked into silence. She stared at Vinnie and then folded her arms across her chest petulantly.

Annabelle had watched this little spat with interest, a smirk on her face, but now she turned her attention to Vinnie. 'Well, I *am* surprised, Vinnie,' she purred. 'Last night at dinner you didn't mention you had such… err… a *colourful* wife.' she looked Vivienne up and down distastefully, and then her voice hardened. 'In fact, you didn't mention a wife at all.'

'Annabelle, please don't say any more, just leave it,' Lydia advised, deciding that they'd created enough of a scene already for the other two customers

But Annabelle wasn't finished. 'You're just like Simon,' she told Vinnie, 'you believe women are here only for your pleasure or betterment, and when they have served their purpose, you simply move on to the next one,'

'I don't think that's a fair assessment at all,' Vinnie objected.

'Really?' challenged Annabelle. 'Simon was so duplicitous, so devious that he ultimately married the boss's daughter, he then got himself a nice little blonde girlfriend whose father had land he wanted, so don't tell me—'

'But I'm not like that!' Vinnie protested.

'So, the fact that my father has a successful company had nothing to do with the way you flirted with me last night?'

Vivienne uncrossed her arms and narrowed her eyes.

'That wasn't flirting,' he explained carefully, smiling hesitantly at his wife, 'I was just being chatty, I'm hoping to sign Aztec up as a client.'

'It was *you*, wasn't it?' Lydia said suddenly, looking at Annabelle, 'You killed Simon!'

Two older ladies had finished their drinks and were openly

stared at the scene unfolding in front of them. Kate and Olivia stood behind the counter listening in astonished silence, hesitant to clear the table.

Lydia's words brought gasps of horror.

'What? You think *I* killed Simon?' Annabelle looked at her friend incredulously.

'I don't *think* you did, I *know* you did!' Lydia replied.

Vivienne opened her mouth to speak, but Vinnie nudged her so she closed it again.

The café door opened and DCI Appleton, and DS Helen Oakley walked in, with Greg close behind them.

'Your girlfriend, here, has just accused me of murder,' announced Annabelle, looking at Greg.

'And do you deny it?' asked the Chief Inspector blandly.

'Of course, I do!' Annabelle snapped. 'Why would I kill my husband? I loved him.'

'Yes, you *did*,' Lydia agreed, 'but then you realised that he didn't love you. He had sabotaged your engagement to Robbie and pursued you, married you just to become your father's right-hand man. He cheated on you with young Bella so his underhand company could buy her father's land for less than its true value. He lied to you about his affair and when you confronted him, portrayed Zoe as a scorned woman. He also denied you the one thing you truly desired, a child.'

Annabelle stared at Lydia in shock. 'But I didn't know all this until after he was killed,' she replied.

'That's not true, is it Annabelle? You saw Simon with Bella on Friday night after the show, so you knew then that he was having an affair and that it wasn't with Zoe. Simon made matters worse by trying to convince you that the affair was invented by Zoe, but you knew by then, that he was lying.'

'I explained why I was at the hall on Friday night and I told you I didn't see Simon – that I left before everyone came out.'

'That's not true either, there's a witness who saw you leave at the same time as Desmond. Desmond locked up, so you must have seen Simon with Bella as they stood outside the door.'

'Well, all right so I *may* have seen her with Simon on Friday night, but so what?' Annabelle was decidedly agitated now.

'That's when you planned to murder him,' Lydia told her.

Vivienne gasped and took a step back towards Vinnie, who put himself in front of her protectively.

Annabelle giggled. '*Murder* him? I was at MegaMart when Simon was murdered, you know that,' she aimed her answer at the police officers.

'No, your *car* was there. Tasheka saw it and parked near it at around five o'clock. *You* parked earlier, probably about half past four. You walked to the hall and let yourself in, just before everyone left to go to the café.'

'I couldn't have got in, apparently there's a door code,' Annabelle said smugly.

'Yes, but you knew the door code – you overheard Simon give it to Hugo Marshall that morning.'

'You've no proof that I was there,' Annabelle blustered.

'You've repeated things that you could only have known by listening to the argument between Zoe and Simon that evening, so you had to have overheard them shouting, which means you were there.'

Annabelle stared at Lydia. 'You're bluffing. You're making this up to protect Zoe. I know you're friends with her...' she shouted and raised her arm to strike Lydia.

Vinnie stepped forward and grabbed her, pulling her away from the table. DCI Appleton nodded at DS Oakley who pulled out her handcuffs and snapped around Annabelle's wrists, before arresting her on suspicion of murder. Two uniformed officers entered the café and Annabelle screamed and thrashed about. The officers held onto her and then suddenly she seemed to deflate and was still.

She lifted her chin. 'I think you'll find that I've done a favour for everyone involved with that man, Hugo, Bella, Zoe, Robert and even his son – they'll all be better off without him,' she declared before being led outside to a waiting police car.

'Can you come to the station as well Lydia, please? I think you've more to tell us about how you came to this conclusion, and I'd like you to make a statement.' DCI Appleton smiled at Lydia, who nodded her head,

'I'll follow you there,' she replied.

The police officers left the café, and Kate and Olivia were galvanised into action. The two other customers left in a flurry of excitement, no doubt to pass on what they'd witnessed to anyone who would listen.

Greg put a protective arm around Lydia. 'You ok?' he asked.

Lydia smiled. 'Yes, fine. Look I'd better get off to the station.'

'Do you want me to come with you?' he asked tentatively.

'No, I shouldn't be long and I'll come back to yours when I'm finished,' Lydia replied.

Greg squeezed her shoulder before letting his arm drop and walked to the door. As he passed Vinnie, he nodded a brief acknowledgement and then he was gone.

Vivienne looked pointedly at Vinnie with a raised eyebrow,

'Well?' she challenged.

Vinnie shrugged. 'We'd best make tracks home then, I suppose,' he murmured.

'Oh no, now we're here, you can take me out for dinner and find us somewhere to stay – and I don't mean in that dingy little pub across the street.' Vivienne turned to look at Lydia, lifted her chin and continued to speak, 'I've had my fill of this place. I want to go to Harrogate, somewhere a bit upmarket. I want somewhere nice to lay my head,' she smiled superciliously.

Lydia shook her head, picked up her coat and handbag and walked to the café door,

'Bye Vinnie,' she called, stepped outside and closed the door behind her.

When Lydia returned to Greg's apartment later that evening, he had prepared a shepherd's pie and had a bottle of red wine open. He served up their meal, poured the wine and then asked Lydia to explain how she had come to the conclusion that Simon had been murdered by his wife.

'Annabelle has now confessed to killing Simon, by the way. So firstly, I knew something was odd when I found out that she told Robbie that Simon was behind the staged photographs. Simon only revealed that to Zoe during their argument, so Annabelle had to have been at the hall at that point.

'Secondly, Tasheka mentioned that when she spoke to Annabelle in MegaMart last Saturday, Annabelle was wet through. However, it didn't start to rain until around a quarter past five so she must have got wet on her way back from the hall to the supermarket.

'Thirdly, the lights. Robbie said that when he saw Hugo leaving, the lights from the hallway spilled out into the car park, but Jonathan said that when he looked through the letterbox, the hallway was in darkness. Nick also confirmed that the lights were off when he looked out as he saw Jonathan's car leaving, so that's corroborated. So someone else must have been in the hall and turned the lights off on their way out.

'Finally, just this afternoon in the café, Annabelle yelled at Vivienne about her and Bella getting pregnant deliberately. Annabelle can only have overheard that at the hall when Bella shouted at Simon.'

Greg had listened to all this in amazement,

'So, you just put all the pieces together, like a jigsaw?' he remarked.

'I suppose you could say that,' replied Lydia, taking a large mouthful of wine.

'What happens now, then?'

'On Monday, I'm going to phone Simon's solicitor in Harrogate and advise them where they can find his son, but I shall leave it to them to contact Nick and to take matters from there.'

‘I feel sorry for Carlton Banks, he must be devastated about Annabelle,’ Greg murmured.

‘Yes, I wonder what he’ll do now,’ Lydia mused. ‘Anyway, I’ve some good news!’ she added brightly.

‘Go on, then,’ encouraged Greg.

‘I’ve agreed to buy the Lewis Marshall premises. I’m going to be Tom’s landlord and live in the flat upstairs,’ she announced.

‘Good grief!’ exclaimed Greg.

‘It requires some renovation, but it’s a great flat size-wise and it has an outdoor terrace so you can practice your barbequing skills before we invite Robbie over.’

Greg laughed and raised his glass,

‘Here’s to you and your new flat,’ he proposed.

Lydia clinked her glass with his. ‘Here’s to us,’ she said.

Matador